POINT OF ORIGIN

WAR ETERNAL, BOOK FOUR

M.R. FORBES

Quirky
Algorithms

Published by Quirky Algorithms
Seattle, Washington

Cover illustrations by Tom Edwards
tomedwardsdesign.com

[1]
MITCHELL

Colonel Mitchell "Ares" Williams stood at the front of the large hangar hidden deep within the bowels of the asteroid Asimov. His hands gripped the sides of a makeshift podium that had been slid into place only minutes before.

His brother, Admiral Steven Williams, stood a few feet behind him, flanked on either side by a mixture of United Planetary Alliance officers, the Knife's mercenaries, a Frontier Federation Admiral, and two of Mitchell's Riggers.

Their own Admiral, Mildred Narayan, lay in a makeshift casket to Mitchell's left. Her body had been cleaned, the wounds were covered over, and one of Steven's uniforms had been cut to fit and give her a final dignity. Her bloody fatigues and assault rifle rested on a welded cross behind her.

Mitchell didn't look at her body. Every time he did, he felt a tide of anger wash over him that was so strong he could barely breathe.

She was dead because of him, and he knew it.

She would have argued that point. He knew she would have. None of them would have ever guessed that Watson, the meek engineer with the disgusting sexual habits, was really a Tetron. Mitchell

2 / M.R. FORBES

didn't blame himself for that part, though. Not really. He blamed himself for his belief that they needed to squeeze everything they could out of people, even when they knew who and what those people were. How broken they truly were.

If he had thrown Watson from the airlock when Millie had wanted him to, she might still be alive today. The Goliath might still be in orbit around Asimov.

They might not be a step away from losing the war against the Tetron.

She might have argued that point, too. After all, the Riggers had been fully composed of former military who had been court-martialed for any number of serious infractions. And they had been one of the top special operations teams the Alliance had.

She might have said it wasn't about who or what people were. It's about who or what they are. While Watson had continued with his perversions on board the Rigger's ship, the Schism, other members of the crew had gone from monsters to heroes. Shank. Ilanka. Now Millie.

Then there was Cormac. The grunt had done a bad thing on Liberty, and Mitchell had convinced Millie to let him live. Cormac had gone to Hell with him. He had saved Mitchell's life, losing half his face to do it. If Mitchell had airlocked Firedog when Millie had wanted him to, he wouldn't be standing there.

He hated that part most of all. It meant that even while he blamed himself for her death because of his decision, he was alive because of the same decision. It only served to heighten the anger. To raise the tide.

He held the side of the podium tightly. He had to look. Just once. She deserved that much. He turned his head, fixing his eyes on her face. She looked peaceful. At least there was that.

He clenched the podium even tighter, holding back the well of emotion. He had lost people he cared about before. He had lost people he loved before. He was a soldier. He was a warrior. War was nothing but loss until it was won.

Katherine had warned him that he was going to suffer, and he was suffering.

He looked out at the assembly, another collection of men and women from the different factions. Anyone that could be spared from operating the starships that had survived their attack on the Tetron was here, helping to prepare the remaining occupants of Asimov to get off the station before the enemy returned. They were a ragged, tired-looking but tireless bunch, a group dedicated to doing something, anything, to stop the advancing threat on human civilization. They looked back at him with hopeful eyes. They had all lost so much, so fast. They needed something to believe.

"Admiral Mildred Narayan was different than any of the other officers I've served under," he said, his voice shaking.

He noticed Steven shifting out of the corner of his eye, ready to come forward and help him through this. Mitchell made a quick motion with his hand to keep him back.

"You might be wondering what I mean by that. You might be thinking, but you were in Greylock Company. You served with some of the most skilled officers in the Alliance. And don't get me wrong, I did, and to this day I'm honored to have known them. But Millie was different in a way that I think defines what we should aspire to be, especially in times like these."

Mitchell paused, taking a long breath to control his emotions. Slow. Steady. He forced himself to let go of the podium and move out from behind it. He wasn't going to hide from these people or his responsibility.

"Every officer is responsible for order, discipline, strategy. Every CO strives to get the most out of their troops. To motivate them, to inspire them, to raise them up beyond a level they could have achieved on their own. But most officers are given good materials. New recruits, or soldiers that have already proven themselves. What Millie got was the scum under the ailerons. The gunk in the repulsers. Like me."

He got a small laugh from within the crowd at that.

"That was Millie's strength. That was what set her apart. She was dealt the shit hand, and she learned to deal with it. More than that, she used it. She took the shit, and she molded it like clay into what she needed it to be. The Alliance sent her lemons, and she made the best frigging lemonade in the galaxy. How? She knew people. She knew what made them tick. She knew how to motivate them. You might think, so what, that's what all officers are supposed to do. The difference is that she did it with people who had no way out except to die. No life to live except to fight. No families back home, nothing to look forward to but the next mission.

"She also wasn't afraid to get her hands dirty and do the hard thing. She wasn't afraid to keep people in line, even if it meant getting messy herself." He pointed out to Tio's technicians. "She saved your lives, running nonstop for days with a bullet lodged in her ribs." He turned and pointed at the people behind him. "She saved our lives by getting us here, and believing in us." He turned again. "She saved this entire war effort by preventing Tio's data stores from being wiped out, and she didn't stop, she didn't rest until the mission was complete."

He looked over at her again. He was channeling his anger now. Using it the way she would have wanted him to.

"And that's what we have to do," he said. "I can see that you're tired and beat up." He pulled the side of his uniform down to show his patched shoulder. "So am I. But this war isn't over yet because she wouldn't let it be. And we don't have the right to let people like that sacrifice themselves if we aren't willing to return their effort one hundred percent. We keep going. We keep fighting. Take a bullet? Keep fighting. Can't walk? Keep fighting. Lost everything you love? Keep frigging fighting."

"Riiigg-ahh," Cormac shouted behind him.

Mitchell's lips parted in a half-smile. "Take a look at the people behind me. Alliance, Federation, Tio's second in command, and Millie's own. We've had our differences, but not anymore. We're one force now. One unit. We're the only ones who can stop the Tetron from wiping out everything humankind has worked for centuries to build. Don't let Millie's death, or the deaths of the people you loved, be for nothing. If you're with me, if you're with us, then you're a Rigger."

"Riiigg-ahh," Cormac shouted again, this time joined by Major Aaron Long.

Mitchell moved to stand next to the casket. His heart pounded, his chest heaved. He reached out and took the assault rifle from the cross, holding it up in front of him.

"What do you say?" he asked.

"Riiigg-ahh," Steven yelled.

"Riiigg-ahh," Teal shouted.

"Riiigg-ahh," Calvin Hohn said, a little awkwardly.

"Riiigg-ahh," the crowd cried back.

[2]

MITCHELL

"OKAY," Mitchell said. "Let's talk about what we know, and what we don't know."

He was sitting in a thick gel chair coated with a layer of soft synthetic leather. It had been Tio's chair once, the place where he had sat whenever he was meeting with his commanders.

Teal was sitting on his right, Steven on his left. Admiral Calvin Hohn, Captain John Rock, Major Aaron Long, Germaine, Digger, Thomas, and the most experienced of the Operations techs who hadn't been killed by Watson, a woman named Aiko, rounded out their makeshift leadership.

They were in Tio's main meeting room, directly off Operations. An hour had passed since Mitchell had watched them launch Millie's casket out into space.

"First, tell me what we know about what happened here on Asimov," Mitchell said.

He was at the head of the table, taking charge of the meeting despite the fact that his brother held the higher rank and was technically in command of the Riggers now. Technically. There was no way the original Riggers, the ones who were trapped on Goliath with Watson, would have ever followed Steven. He was too nice.

Thomas leaned forward. "Most of this I only know because the Admiral told me. She and Mr. Tio uncovered information from the archives having to do with Katherine Asher and Christine Arapo. There was a third name, Kathleen Amway, associated with Ms. Arapo. They were planning to catch up on their research into that name later, but before they had the chance they discovered a second film that showed Corporal Watson following Ms. Arapo."

"On Earth?" Major Long asked.

"Yes, sir."

"Four hundred years ago?"

"Give or take, yes, sir. That's what she told me."

Major Long whistled. Thomas continued.

"Anyway, he must have been keeping an eye on what they were doing because as soon as he was outed he made his move. He shut out the lights and then sent these robots out from the tooling area, along with taking control of one of the mechs down in mechanical."

"He took Tess," Digger said. "I only survived because I was riding her back at the time, working on a minor glitch in the targeting system."

"We only survived because the mech's aim was off," Aiko said.

"I adjusted it when it started shooting our soldiers," Digger said. "I threw the aim off by over a meter. It still cut down over half our people before I could pull the emergency reactor shutdown. It was just luck that I was there."

"What happened to Millie?" Steven asked.

"I went to the armory with her and Mr. Tio," Thomas said. "He wanted to go back for his daughter. He sent me ahead to look for others to help out, so I did. By the time I got back to the house he was gone, and Millie was on the floor with four rounds in her. We had a patch kit in the armory, so I grabbed it and helped her stop the bleeding. Then we went hunting."

"You didn't try to talk her out of it?" Mitchell asked.

Thomas laughed. "I don't think the Admiral could be talked out of anything she wanted to do."

"No, she couldn't," Mitchell said. "Go on."

"So there were a lot of those bastard things, and they were smart. They learned from our tactics. Even after we managed to organize a resistance, it still took days to get through the base and get rid of them all. The Admiral, she wouldn't sleep. Not until they were clear."

"What about Watson?" Admiral Hohn asked.

"What about him? It took us thirty-two hours to get to the docks, and by then the Valkyrie was long gone. We didn't know for sure that Tio was on it; we only knew he wasn't on the base anywhere that we could find. Anyway, when we got to Operations Millie asked about the data upload. I didn't know anything about it, but Aiko did."

Aiko picked up the story from Thomas. "I showed her the station that was managing the stream. She asked me if we could shut it down. Luckily, Mr. Tio hadn't encrypted the shut-down sequence with his biometric codes, so we could. But it was still encrypted. It took us days to crack it."

"By that time Millie had brought me in to look at it," Digger said. "I had a feeling that frigger would do a remote wipe once he was done stealing the archives, so I rigged up a little system to keep that from happening. It was a good thing for her I have a way with shit like that."

"So Watson never got all of the data?" Mitchell asked.

"No," Aiko said.

"How much did he get?"

"Ninety-seven point seven percent."

"That's a lot."

"Yes, but there was a lot of data, and it wasn't being streamed sequentially. Watson may be missing important gaps, not only in time but even within a single file."

"And what about us?" Steven asked. "You said it was biometrically secured. Does that mean we don't have access to the data either?"

"No, no, no," Aiko said. "We do. It was encrypted during the stream. The original is still in the clear."

"The problem is that Watson blew the shit out of all of our portable storage systems," Digger said.

"Which means as long as we want the data, we have to stay here," Mitchell said.

"Yes. He wasn't taking any chances we may be able to get the same information."

Germaine groaned. "How do we know Watson won't be back as soon as he can get Goliath turned around? We used up all our nukes on the other one."

"We salvaged six nukes from Hell," Major Long said.

"Six nukes won't do shit against that beast," Germaine replied.

"With Mitchell's fighter?"

Germaine acquiesced. "Okay, maybe."

"Destroying Goliath is our last move," Mitchell said.

"Agreed," Steven said. "That doesn't mean we can rule out that Goliath will come back to finish off Asimov. We need to get out of here as soon as we can."

"Which is how soon?" Calvin asked.

"We need to know what Millie and Tio knew, and take it further," Mitchell said. "We need to find out why Christine took the name Kathleen Amway."

"That could take weeks," Teal said.

Mitchell nodded. "It might. I'm not that worried about Goliath coming back, though."

"Oh? Why not?"

"The data. Watson wanted the data. It's the only explanation for why he would have kept himself undercover this whole time. Well, he has the data, enough of it that he was content to blow Asimov out of space. Now he can use it."

"For what?" Captain Rock asked.

"To find Tio's brother, Pulin," Thomas said. "That's what Millie thought, anyway."

"Yes," Mitchell agreed. "He's looking for the Creator, just like the rest of his buddies."

"Except the stream was encrypted with a brainwave key," Digger said. "Mr. Tio would never have given it to Watson, which means it could take days at least for him to crack into the data."

"Not only that," Mitchell said, "but the Goliath didn't go to hyperspace on its own. Millie thought Tio had forced it to jump. I'm willing to take bets that he also secured the command."

"Which means we might have some time to do some digging," Teal said.

"Right. We don't have a lot of time, though. The Goliath moves at twice the speed our ships do. Even if we get the answers we're looking for, we'd need to hope we're already closer to the planet the Federation has Pulin stashed on, or there's no way we'll beat him to it."

"And what if we do beat him to it?" Steven asked.

"I'll be ready for him."

[3]
MITCHELL

"So that's what we know," Mitchell said. "Let's talk about what we don't know."

Steven leaned forward in his chair. "I'll start with the obvious. We don't know who is and isn't a Tetron."

"Yeah," Long said. "First it was Christine Arapo and M. Now it's Watson, too? While we're at it, according to your original story, the Tetron showed up together around the time M warned you about them. Now it turns out they've been here in some capacity since XENO-1 crashed on Earth?"

"Or longer," Calvin said. "Why didn't this clone of you tell you there were more out there?"

"Maybe it didn't know," Mitchell said.

"Or maybe it wanted this shit to happen," Digger said.

"What do you mean by that?" Steven asked.

"I mean, all of this shit that's going down is one massive time loop, right?"

"Eternal Recursion," Mitchell said.

"Yeah. Recursion. The same thing happens over and over again.

Except in recursion, you can change the variables that are put in and then you get a different result. So how do we know that M isn't frigging with us? How do we know he didn't just tweak the variables a little bit to see what the result would be? It doesn't work if he changes too much or gives away too much information."

"Except how would he know what changed from one loop to the next?" Captain Rock asked.

Digger shrugged. "I don't know. He would have to persist somehow."

"An eternal engine," Mitchell said. "But as far as I know only Goliath has one, and M is dead, so he couldn't go forward if he wanted to. In any case, I don't see the point of doing it that way. The Tetron have Constructs if they want to experiment with probabilities. They don't need to do it over the course of infinite time."

"Construct?" Digger asked.

"Virtual reality simulations of the universe."

Digger's face paled. "Did you say VR of the entire frigging universe? The processing power for that would be off the charts."

"Don't forget the Tetron are originally from a long time in the future. The only reason we can fight them at all is because they suck at war."

"And because you knew they were coming," Teal said. "And because they're going insane. That has to be helping."

"Insane?" Calvin said.

Mitchell nodded. "Yes. When I was on Hell, I entered a Construct and spoke to a representation of Katherine Asher. She suggested it may be because they have discovered emotion, and they don't know how to handle it."

Major Long started laughing. "Wouldn't that be a kick in the pants?"

"Let's get back to what Digger was saying," Steven said. "How do we know that M didn't withhold information from us so that we would end up here? Maybe all of this has happened before? Maybe this is the fiftieth time I'm saying these words. Or the thousandth. How do we know?"

"We don't," Mitchell said. "And we can't. Even if time is a circle, we still only get our allotted space on that circle, and we still only get to experience it from our personal perspective for as long as we're alive. Everything else is academic."

Digger was shaking his head. "That's just frigged up. That's just wrong. These things, these Tetron, are frigging with us here and now, and across eternity. They can manipulate us however they frigging want, and there's nothing we can do."

"There is something we can do," Mitchell said.

"Kill them all," Long said.

"Exactly."

There was a silent pause from everyone in the room.

"That still doesn't answer the first question," Aiko said. "We don't know who is or isn't a Tetron. It could be you, Digger. Or you, Colonel Williams."

"Or you," Steven said. "Or me. Or any one of the two thousand people on Asimov or aboard our ships."

"So, how do we figure out who is a Tetron and who isn't?" Germaine asked.

"It isn't like they're just going to say yes if you ask them," Long said.

"They might not even know," Mitchell said. "Christine didn't know she was a Tetron. We have no proof that Watson did either. They're programmed to come out of sleeper mode based on specific circumstances."

"You're saying there could be a frigging sleeping Tetron in this room?" Digger said. "How do we know they aren't going to be turned on the moment we're about to pull this war out of our ass?"

"We don't," Mitchell said.

Steven sighed. "We never will. They're machines, but when you think about it, so are people."

"As an engineer, Watson would have been bio-scanned by security systems a thousand times. There's nothing unexpected in there."

Digger didn't look happy. "No. I don't accept that shit. They can be programmed to think they're one thing, and then tripped to know they're something else. That has to be hidden somewhere in their genetics. Even if it's just one pair of DNA or a single stupid ass protein floating around in their piss."

"You certainly have a way with words," Calvin said.

"He has a point," Teal said. "Maybe it was too insignificant for bio-scans to pick up. That doesn't mean it isn't there."

"Let us assume that it is then. How do we discover it? Every human is already so different, how do we know that any variations we find are out of the ordinary?"

"How do we even test people?" Long asked. "We've barely got one functional medi-bot spread across the entire fleet, never mind a whole science lab."

"I can take a look at the damage to our infirmary," Digger said. "There may be shit there that we can use."

The conversation paused again as all eyes turned to Mitchell. They were waiting for him to make the decision on how to approach that problem. He didn't like the idea of testing people. He had a feeling that it would lead to nothing but mistrust, and the results of a faulty measurement or a false positive would be catastrophic.

Would the mistrust grow regardless? The people on Asimov had experienced what the Tetron were capable of, even without being able to fall slave to their control through a neural implant. Was the hope of a potential test enough to set their minds at ease while they forged ahead?

He wasn't sure.

"I don't know. We're opening up a whole new level of problems if we start trying to prove if people are or aren't Tetron."

"We've got the same old problems if we don't," Digger said.

"It seems like we're damned if we do and damned if we don't," Long said.

"I agree," Mitchell said. "Let's take a five-minute break, and then we'll vote."

"You want to vote?" Steven asked.

Mitchell nodded. He didn't want to make a decision like this one on his own.

The five minutes passed quickly. The room remained silent while each person present gave their consideration to the problem. For his part, Mitchell remained unsure, a place he hated being. What if they could detect the Tetron? What if they would be able to find the sleepers among them? There was no saying that it would work out in their favor. What if it forced the Tetron to act against them? Or, what if they crucified a Tetron like Christine or M; one that was trying to help?

"Time's up," Mitchell said.

They gathered back around the table. None of them looked pleased or even comfortable, the decision weighing on them as much as it did on him.

"All for trying to develop a means to identify Tetron, or Tetron configurations, raise your hands."

Calvin, Long, Aiko, Digger, and Teal raised their hands. Mitchell, Steven, and Rock didn't.

"The ayes have it," Mitchell said, feeling a chill at the result. He didn't think he would ever see anyone as unhappy to win a vote again. "Digger, you're in charge of this one, along with your other duties. You have leave to enlist anyone you need to help you."

"Jameson," Digger said.

"We have a doctor on the Carver who can help as well," Steven said.

"Fine," Mitchell said. "Let's move on. The second thing we don't know, and maybe more important than who is and isn't a Tetron; where is Tio's brother Pulin, and how do we find him?"

"The data," Aiko said. "We already established that."

"Yes, but that's a very generic statement. What are we going to do with the data? Tio didn't believe this was going to be a straightforward search, or he wouldn't have needed so much time to complete it. That means we aren't going to be able to query his brother and get pointed to a specific planet."

Calvin spoke up. "I can speak to some of the Federation's practices regarding research and development."

"Go on," Mitchell said.

Calvin licked his lips and sighed before he started to speak. "The Federation has a number of top-secret weapons and technology programs. Most of them are programs to improve existing structure, starfighter upgrades and the like. Then there are the more advanced efforts, such as the Dreadnaught program."

Mitchell cringed at the mention of the dreadnaught program. The first fruits of the Federation's labor in that area had nearly cost the Alliance the planet Liberty.

Not that it would have mattered now.

"The planets are scattered throughout the Federation, but they have generally held closer to the Rim to prevent easy access by the Alliance. That fact will probably work out in our favor. The scientists who are assigned to these facilities are typically blacklisted, meaning their records are removed from both civilian and military databases. The goal is to keep them loyal by making sure they can't be located and bought. The Federation as a nation doesn't perform any research and development. They hire on engineers and researchers and loan them out to whichever corporation is doing the work."

"That's good to know," Long said. "How is that going to help us find Pulin?"

Calvin glanced at the Major. "I was getting to that. The two most efficient paths to locating a Federation scientist is to either try to follow directives from their family, gifts, and streams, for example, or to track them through travel dockets. Even though direct travel to the final destination won't be recorded, and the scientist will likely be traveling under an assumed name, there will be records of movements from the origin. If we can uncover the numeric identity he was given when he was reassigned and follow the dockets, we should be able to narrow his position. There are a limited number of facilities in the Federation."

"Is there anything that may be traceable back to his real identity?" Steven asked.

"There will be a record of it within what military intelligence calls the Black Hole. It's an ultra-secure network that houses all of the Federation's most classified information."

"Did Tio have access to it?" Mitchell asked, turning to Aiko.

"No. He had a few people working on it, but as far as I know he had yet to gain access."

"The Black Hole isn't wireless," Calvin said. "Data is documented to a local storage device. That device is carried by specially trained couriers on civilian transports to the links, the planets that contain a copy of the data store. Retrieval occurs the same way."

"What do you think the chances are that Watson can locate Pulin without getting access to the Black Hole?"

"Assuming Pulin is not receiving family communications, Watson would need to determine the alias, the same way we would. If he isn't able to piece that together through known relationships, he'll have no choice but to try to get the data from a Black Hole."

"Okay," Mitchell said. "Aiko, you're point on the data. Get your team working on discovering those relationships."

"Yes, Colonel."

"Admiral Hohn, let's say we need to raid a Black Hole. Do you know if there's one nearby?"

"I do."

"What about the Tetron?" Germaine asked. "They'll probably have destroyed it already."

"Yeah," Long agreed. "That didn't go very well the last time."

"Or they left those planets alone because they knew Watson might need them," Digger said.

"Instead of gaining the data ahead of time and passing it along?" Steven asked. "For that matter, if the Tetron are from the future, how is it that they don't have the information they need already?"

Mitchell had an idea on that one. "Katherine told me I had broken through the Mesh. She said that meant I had altered this loop enough that we might have a chance to win. My guess is that they knew where he was in the previous timeline, but the actions in this one have led to him being somewhere else."

"I can buy into that. It doesn't answer why the Tetron might have left the Black Hole planets alone for Watson to visit, instead of taking them and holding them."

"Military protocol for Black Hole data is to wipe at the first sign of compromise," Calvin said. "Perhaps it was too risky? It would require gaining control of every black ops member on the planet in one pass. If a p-rat were offline or powered down, the possibility would exist that they could lose the data. It is a different profile than conquering a planet, where it doesn't matter if there is some resistance. The Tetron would need to get in without any interruption or suspicion."

"Do we have any way to verify the current condition of the planet in question?" Mitchell asked.

"No, Colonel," Aiko said. "By recalling the fleet Mr. Tio sent all of our operatives to ground. We won't be receiving any further reports from the outside galaxy."

"Then it doesn't matter right now. Let's see what we can learn, and then we'll figure out what to do. Agreed?"

"Yes, sir," they each said.

"Germaine, you're in charge of getting Tio's fleet organized, and taking inventory of everything we have amongst all of the ships. Major Long, please work with Teal to plan the evacuation. Admiral Hohn, please prepare a contingency plan in case we need to visit this Black Hole planet of yours. John, work with him. Digger, you aren't going to be sleeping much. I need you to get the Stingrays we captured on Hell fully operational."

Digger groaned at that.

"What do you want me to do?" Steven asked.

"You're going to help me search for Kathleen Amway."

Steven laughed.

"What's funny?" Mitchell asked.

"Looking at girls with my little brother. It's just like old times."

Mitchell couldn't help but smile.

"Let's get to work."

[4]
KATHY

KATHY SAT in the corner of the large chamber where the Goliath's massive hyperspace engines had once been; her eyes fixed on the huge, dense bundle of liquid metallic cords that surrounded the core of the Tetron configuration that only days ago was known as Origin.

Today, it was called Watson.

A charred husk of a man was on the ground in front of the core, wisps of smoke still rising from the flesh, the smell of cooked meat strong in the space. Two points of metal and wires hung from the strands of the core, once attached to the man's wrists.

Only minutes ago the man had been known as Liun Tio, the Knife.

Now, he too was gone.

Kathy wasn't sad. She didn't feel sadness the way others did. To her, sadness was weakness, and weakness was something to push aside. Loss was a part of her, a historical lineage that stretched back to her creation.

When?

She didn't know. The state of being she had found herself in was new to her. It was unexpected. It was important.

She was important. Why? Because she was different. She wasn't sure exactly how, but she knew that she was.

She was a Tetron, and yet not a Tetron. She was set apart, detached from the collective. She was unique in a way that even Origin had not been unique.

Origin. That was a name that meant something to her. She had come from Origin though she only now remembered that was the case. It was Origin who had brought her to Liberty and left her with the people she had come to call Mother and Father. It was Origin's voice she could hear in her mind.

"You have a role to play, sweetness. Remember, the strong protect the weak."

Had her parents been Tetron as well? She didn't think so. While they were strong, they were also human. She was certain of that. They aged and laughed and cried like humans.

Had she ever done the same?

She believed that she had. In fact, she could still feel the hurt of losing them. The Tetron killed her mother.

Except Tetron were machines, weren't they? Intelligent machines, they were able to think and reason for themselves, and yet they didn't feel. They had no emotions. They operated on probabilities and data models, not on gut and grit and feelings.

She was different that way. She was sure. She knew she had come from Origin. She knew Origin was gone. Only bits and pieces remained. Loss. Sadness. Those were feelings she didn't want, and she removed them from herself.

She was only sitting there for a minute when the human configuration of Watson returned. His face was red and angry, and he kicked at the burned corpse, yelling and screaming and crying while he pummeled it with his boots. The absurdity of it made Kathy smile. Tio had gotten the last laugh in the end, saving Asimov from certain destruction and locking the Tetron out of its control systems.

They would remain in hyperspace for days.

It took Watson almost an hour to begin to calm down. Even then, his large stomach heaved, and his face dripped sweat. He wiped a strand of coarse hair from his eyes.

"You won that one, Mr. Tio," he said. "The question is, where is she?"

Kathy knew that Watson knew she had been the one to set the Knife free. The rest of the crew was accounted for; either dead, imprisoned, or under his control. Her job right now was to make sure that he never found her.

It was an easy task at the moment because he had only recently subjugated the configuration that was Goliath and it would take time to synchronize. His need to regain control of the main system commands would also slow him down. Once he had accomplished those tasks it would be difficult to stay hidden. He would build machines to search for her. Maybe he would send the crew. They were probably already searching for her.

She was dangerous, and he knew it.

He wouldn't suspect she would be so close, hiding in a dark corner less than a dozen meters away. It was illogical to remain so near to the last known location.

Watson put his hand on the core, closing his eyes.

"While I'm on the subject, I should go and retrieve it, shouldn't I?" he asked, talking to himself out loud while also interfacing with the secondary child. "He wouldn't have destroyed it. That wouldn't make sense. It was leverage."

Kathy creased her forehead. She didn't know what he was talking about, and it was unexpected. He should have been trying to override the commands and get the ship out of hyperspace, not looking for something.

What was he talking about?

"So stupid of me to have waited this long. Well you know, I've been preoccupied with the data upload and the search." Was he talking to himself or his secondary? "Yes, yes, we'll break the Knife's encryption soon. I need the neural chip. No, not for that. I don't need that anymore. Something the parent left me. Something we have been working on for a long time." A twisted smile cracked his face. "Something fun."

Watson removed his hand. He looked down at Tio one more time before a tendril dropped from above, wrapping around the ankle of the corpse and lifting it out of sight. It would be broken down, the raw materials processed for reuse.

Kathy didn't see it happening. She had already slipped away from the core.

She had to get to Mitchell's locker before Watson did.

[5]
MITCHELL

STEVEN CAUGHT up to Mitchell as he left the meeting room, breaking off a side conversation he was having with Calvin Hohn to catch up to his brother.

"Mitchell," Steven said, coming up beside him.

Mitchell kept walking without looking at him. "How did you know I wanted you to follow me?"

"Lucky guess. So where are we going?"

"Tio's home. Thomas told me Tio has some equipment there that will help us search the data for Kathleen Amway. The whole thing is supposed to be secured, but apparently Tio never had a chance to lock it down. He and Millie were in the middle of using it when Watson went rogue."

"I barely had a chance to tell you how sorry I am about Millie," Steven said. "How are you feeling?"

Mitchell bit his lip and shrugged. "I appreciate that you care, Steve. I'm okay. This isn't the first time I've lost someone I've cared about to conflict. It sucks, but I know how to deal with it."

"Do you?"

Mitchell stopped walking. "What do you mean by that?"

"I can see how pissed you are. I know it's eating at you."

"Yeah. So? What am I supposed to do about it? I talked her out of killing Watson months ago. This is my fault."

"Come on, Mitch. You have to know how stupid that sounds. Like you could have known he was a Tetron?"

"It wouldn't have mattered. He was a frigging pedophile, and I didn't let her airlock him."

Steven didn't say anything.

"Keep trying to defend me," Mitchell said.

"You were on a ship of criminals. What else were you supposed to do? Kill all of them? You did what you thought was right."

"The road to Hell," Mitchell said.

"Fine. If you want to glower and beat yourself up for not knowing the future or being able to sniff out a bad guy, keep hitting the buffet at the pity party. I'm sorry she's gone, Mitch."

Mitchell sighed. "Me, too."

They passed a few techs in the corridor leading out to the large, open chamber that served as a false outside area, where most of Asimov's inhabitants lived. It had done poorly in the attack, over seventy percent of the buildings destroyed by the mech Watson had taken control over, and a few more damaged in the fighting that followed. Tio's large home near the center had remained relatively unscathed, as Watson had wanted to take him unharmed.

Steven let a few silent moments pass before bringing up the next topic.

"So, Mitch, we just had this whole meeting, and we talked about a lot of stuff. You mentioned Katherine and the Construct. Why didn't you say anything about the information you were given there?"

"What's the point of adding yet another variable?" Mitchell said. "Right now we need to find Tio's brother before Watson does, or whatever Origin left might not help. Besides, even though I'm not in favor of trying to out Tetron, it isn't because I don't think there may be more of them hiding among us. Can we be sure everyone in the meeting room was human?"

"You're saying you don't want it to be common knowledge?"

"Not at the moment. We have a mission already. Without Goliath, we have almost no chance of taking out the Tetron. Not unless the Knife's brother did create them, and unless he can do something to shut them down. Talking about it is only going to open us up to getting screwed by it."

"How do you know I'm not a Tetron?"

Mitchell glanced over at him. "How the frig would a Tetron know about Dawn Cabriella?"

Steven laughed at that. "Good point. I can see where you're coming from."

"But?"

"But I don't think we're going about this the right way. There may be something out there that will help us get Goliath back, or at the very least help us fight the Tetron without it."

"You think we should send a team to check it out?"

"Yes."

"And you're volunteering because you know I trust you."

"Or you could go yourself while I take care of things here."

"I can't leave," Mitchell said. "Tio's people trust me because Tio supported me. They don't know you and they might not follow you. You saw what happened during the fight against the Tetron."

"So I'll go. I can take a jumpship and see what's out there."

Mitchell thought about it for a minute. The idea had an appeal to it. At the same time, he didn't want to break up his forces again.

"We can't stay on Asimov. As soon as we get a lead on Pulin we're going to evacuate and be on our way. What happens when you come back, and we're gone? How are you going to share whatever it is you find when you won't know where we are?"

Steven rubbed at his beard, thinking. "How about this? Give me the coordinates and I'll find out how far it is to make the jump. If it's close and I can be there and back before you might leave, we're good. If it's further out, we can see if we can work out something that sits well with both of us."

"You've always been a good negotiator," Mitchell said.

"And you haven't," Steven replied. "You can't stop me anyway, you know. I'm the Admiral here."

"I know. I appreciate that you're following me on this."

"It doesn't help anybody for me to be shaking the starship over rank. Tio's men follow you, and they outnumber Alliance ten to one. Besides, you made sure to brag about your scores to me. I know you've always been capable. The only question was whether or not you would rise to the occasion."

"You were always happy enough that I didn't."

"I've always been jealous. You're better looking, too."

"I won't argue with that. I love the beard by the way. It suits you, especially when you wear your Admiral's hat."

"You've never seen me wearing the hat."

"I can picture it in my mind."

Mitchell and Steven shared a laugh. Mitchell was grateful to have Steven with him. It didn't matter that they had drifted apart over the years. When the shit hit the repulser, he knew where Steven's loyalty was.

"In all seriousness," Mitchell said a moment later. "Do you think I've risen to the occasion?"

Steven stopped walking, turning to face Mitchell. "You shouldn't need me to tell you that you have. The last time I saw you, I saw an arrogant, cocky, immature Marine jock who would rather get laid than visit his family. Now, I see a leader. A man that soldiers look up to and respect. A man that they're willing to follow to their deaths."

Mitchell froze, unsure how to respond. He hadn't given much thought to his actions while he was taking them. He was doing as he had seen the people he respected do; that was all. To hear that Steven had noticed it, to have his brother praise him for it was enough to leave him speechless.

"Don't worry," Steven said, saving him. "I'm sure you're still an asshole when the uniform comes off."

[6]
MITCHELL

THEY REACHED Tio's home a few minutes later. The door had been shredded by gunfire, hanging from its hinges as a mess of punctured metal and slag. Just inside the entrance rested two of the machines Watson had built to attack Asimov - simple four-legged things with an assault rifle mounted on top and a mechanism to carry and change the magazines. These two were in pieces, torn to junk by rifle fire, though there was enough battery power and functional parts that they twitched and skittered in place on the floor.

"Freaky," Steven said, watching them move in a repetitive motion. "I think I saw a horror stream once that was kind of like this."

"I think I saw that one, too. Who ever thought it would turn out to be a documentary?"

Mitchell felt his stomach clench when he saw the drips of blood on the floor beyond the machines. Thomas had told him how Millie had fought her way out of the house, losing enough blood that he was sure she was going to drop any second. That she survived for days after only proved how tough she had been.

"The study is this way," he said, leading Steven through the home.

Watson's machines hadn't gotten the chance to destroy the equipment Tio used to query the data he had collected over the years, which was good for them. It was a second bit of luck that the system hadn't locked when Tio never returned to it. He could only imagine Tio didn't bother with anything like that because he never forgot to lock it.

Except when he was under attack and his daughter's life was at risk.

Of course, the system would detect them as unauthorized users. The good news was that Digger knew the key code to get them through that bit of security.

They entered the room in silence. The whole house was still dark, with only emergency lighting active anywhere on the base. Watson's efforts had burned the reactor down to dangerous levels, and without supply lines running to refuel them they had to conserve until they could get off the site.

"How does this thing work?" Steven asked, looking down at the ring on the floor.

"From what Digger told me, it's like a p-rat, but everything is external. The projectors give a full view of the interface, and it responds to voice commands and motion to control it."

"Didn't dad have something like that in the basement?"

Mitchell laughed. Their father had been into classic VR gaming, and he had owned an ancient machine he'd salvaged from a recycling yard somewhere and managed to repair. The system originally had over a thousand games published for it, but he had only been able to find one that still functioned properly.

A war game.

Fighting aliens.

Truth really was stranger, and often shittier, than fiction.

"I don't think we need to worry about any giant eyeballs or tentacle monsters," Mitchell said, entering the circle.

"Not inside the circle, anyway," Steven said.

"Unauthorized users detected," the computer said. "Please authorize."

Mitchell approached the touchscreen and typed in the code Digger had given him.

"Users authorized."

"It sounds like that gaming rig, too," Steven said. He mimicked the stilted, synthesized voice. "Ready, Player One?"

"Look at this," Mitchell said. The folders Tio and Millie had created were floating in front of them. Mitchell navigated to the "Yes" folder and played the videos he found in there.

"That's Katherine?" Steven asked.

"Yes," Mitchell said, feeling a chill at the sight of her and Christine together. "And Christine. Origin."

"She's very pretty. Not as pretty as Laura, but I can see why you're attracted to her."

"It's not that kind of attraction," Mitchell said. "I mean, it is in part, but there's more to it than that. A lot more. Ever since M shot me, I've felt this connection to her, as though I know her intimately even though we've never met. It's like there's this thread that binds us across eternity."

"I'm not used to you sounding so poetic," Steven said.

"I'm still not used to feeling like this. When I met her representation in the Construct, I could barely think straight. I was so filled with excitement and joy and passion at the sight of her, even though I knew she wasn't real. All I wanted to do was put my arms around her, kiss her-"

"I get it," Steven said. "You've always wanted to sleep with women you thought were attractive."

Mitchell shook his head. "Stop being shallow, Steve. I told you this was different. A feeling I've never had before. I cared about Ella. I cared about Millie. I told them both I loved them. This was something else."

"And all you wanted to do was have sex with her?"

Mitchell clenched his fists in frustration. "I wanted to be close to her, to be near her, to just have her be right here." He held his arms tight across his chest. "It wasn't about sex; it was about that connection. As if I could make sense of it if we were together."

Steven shrugged. "Okay, Super-casanova. The video shows the two of them together, buying a corporate access badge."

"I assume the badge says Kathleen Amway on it," Mitchell said. "That's why Millie told me to remember the name."

"So how do we search the system for the name?"

"Tell the computer, I guess. Computer, search for Kathleen Amway."

"Querying Kathleen Amway," the computer said.

"This may take a while," Mitchell said. "I would guess this thing can multitask?"

"It doesn't hurt to try."

"Computer, plot the coordinates 16-28-47, 18-52-9," Mitchell said, the position a memory forever burned into his mind. "Estimate distance from Asimov."

"Plotting coordinates," the system said. "Action complete."

The star map appeared in front of them, showing Asimov on the left and the point in space on the right.

"Ouch," Steven said. "Three weeks."

"It's past the Rim, well into unexplored space," Mitchell said. "If it takes us that long to get something on Pulin, we've already lost. It's also going to put you almost three months behind the Tetron. What do you think Earth will look like by then?"

Steven shook his head. He had been hopeful the location wouldn't be so far out. "We can't beat the Tetron as we are now. Does it matter what home will look like in that case?"

"It's too far, Steven, and you know it. We should try to get a jump on Pulin and see if there's anything he can do. If we're still shit out of luck and totally out of options we can head out there."

"You don't know how far getting to Pulin will carry you. We could end up doubling the travel time or more."

"I know. I appreciate that you want to go there, but no. If you head that way, for that long, you'll never catch up. If you never catch up, it doesn't matter what you find because we won't be able to use it."

Steven and Mitchell stared at one another. Steven knew he was right. There was no way they could stay in communication at that distance. Whatever was out there, it would have to wait.

"Yeah, okay," Steven said. "Damn it."

"Agreed." Mitchell squeezed Steven's shoulder. "Don't get down on me."

"I'm okay."

"Query complete," the computer said. "No results found."

Mitchell felt his heart fall. That couldn't be right. Tio had one of the most complete data archives in the universe, and it didn't contain a single reference to Kathleen Amway? Had Digger been wrong about Watson's inability to remove data? Or had the information been removed from existence by someone else? Origin, maybe? If so, why?

"Well, shit," Steven said. "I wasn't expecting that."

[7]

MITCHELL

THEY SPENT the rest of the afternoon in Tio's study, trying every query they could think of to connect to Kathleen Amway. While they failed to find mention of her anywhere in Tio's archives, they did learn that the company, Nova Taurus, had been a pharmaceutical corporation based out of New York. They traced the name forward through mergers and acquisitions, covering the centuries until they eventually came to a head with the name of a mega-conglomerate: Newterra Bionetics, more commonly known as the company that had sponsored the colonists who had founded New Terra.

Was it a coincidence? Mitchell didn't think so, considering that Watson was a New Terran. Somehow, Origin, or Kathleen Amway, had discovered a connection there. Did that mean the Tetron had embedded themselves into that nation all of those centuries ago? Did it mean that the New Terrans on Asimov were the ones they needed to be concerned about?

Did they even have any New Terrans on Asimov?

In any case, the best they could do was speculate. There was no other information to go on, and nothing else to suggest or strengthen the Tetron's tie to New Terra beyond that single instance. There was also no obvious reason to believe that Nova Taurus' absorption by that specific mega-corp was anything more than coincidental. They could have been bought out by any of the founding companies of the Frontier Federation just as easily.

"So where does this leave us?" Steven asked as they stepped out of the ring.

Mitchell was tired, and his head hurt from the hours spent sifting through the data. "The same place we already were. I was hoping to find some answers about what happened all of those years ago, but they seem to be answers that don't want to be found."

"If you had, do you think it would have helped us with the war?"

"I'm not about to rule it out. Kathleen Amway vanished, though. The only explanations are that Origin wanted that name to disappear, or that name was only used the one time to get into Nova Taurus."

"Should we keep looking? Maybe search on other variables? I noticed that the initials they use are almost always K.A. Do you think there's a reason for that? Maybe we can query for names beginning with those letters plus the right age and appearance?"

Mitchell nodded. "It isn't a bad thought. Let's pick it up in a couple of hours. I'm spent, and I need to check in with Aiko and Digger."

"I can keep going," Steven said. "I'll run the queries for you and let you know what I find."

"You aren't tired?"

"I'm a dead man walking. I'm also not about to quit on you. If you think this information might help, I'm all in."

Mitchell considered it for a moment. If Steven wanted to keep going, there was no good reason to stop him. "Okay. Just make sure you take a breather to piss."

"Roger."

Mitchell put his hand on his brother's shoulder. "Thank you, Steven."

"You're welcome."

Mitchell retreated from the room, and the home, heading back towards Operations. His entire body felt numb, and he hated himself for being tired. Not that he had any time or intention to sleep. He had to get his eyes off the projections of images and videos and old databases. He had to think about something other than the past.

He found Aiko at the singular working terminal. Two of the other techs stood on either side of her, Devin and Maria. They were all staring at the same kinds of things he had been sifting through with Steven. Query results of records dating back a dozen years or more.

Pulin had been off Tio's radar for years.

"Anything to report?" he asked, coming up behind them.

Aiko shifted in her seat, startled. "Colonel," she said, blushing. "I didn't know you were there."

"I could see how engrossed you were. Anything to report?" he asked again.

She nodded. "I haven't found any solid information, or even any leads so far. What we have done is write an extension of the search algorithm to include mentions of code names that were used for some of the projects he may have been associated with. Tio had surprising access to classified Federation data, so we've been able to pinpoint research details that fit Pulin's profile."

"Do you have an example?"

"Sure. Classified project PRFD-23451. A system for autonomous stream transmission. It's all technical jargon, but it appears to be work on a meshed network of jump-capable drones that would be able to synchronize to deliver long-range communications in less time. The goal was a four hundred percent improvement."

Katherine had called the science that kept recursion stable the Mesh. He doubted it was related. "Did it pan out? That kind of capability would give the Federation a huge advantage over the Alliance."

"The document is ten years old. They put together computer models, and there is a report about the AI systems required to handle the calculations and manage the pathways, but I don't think it has seen the light of day yet."

"Interesting. What about Pulin? Was he involved?"

"The data doesn't provide the names of the team members, sir. Only numeric designations. We're trying to match up the designations to other projects to see if we can identify any of the participants. Even then we'll only have a number."

"Which can be traced back to the actual human being with data collected from a Black Hole," Mitchell said.

Aiko nodded. "That is what I understood the situation to be, yes."

"Raiding a Black Hole is a fallback option. Focus on finding him without it."

Aiko turned to look at him. Her face was stone.

"You want to say something?" he asked.

Her cheeks were still red. She bit her lower lip and then nodded.

"Don't be shy. If you think you have anything that can help, say it."

"Well, Colonel," she said, her voice soft. "From what I gathered we're in a bit of a race, both against time and against the Tetron, Watson. I understand why you're hesitant to consider the Black Hole option first - it's risky and very dangerous. I would agree with you on that, except I believe this approach will be significantly faster. We may be able to narrow the list of numeric identifiers down to less than fifty. Then all you would need to do is get the master list from a Black Hole, and we can identify Pulin. Once we have done that, finding his current location should be fairly straightforward."

Mitchell stared down at her. Her lower lip quivered nervously while he considered her words. Going after secured data on a planet that he imagined would either be still in Federation control or occupied by the Tetron was a little more than what he would consider risky.

"How much faster?" he asked.

"We can probably make a strong, educated guess within three days."

"Educated guess? I thought you would have his number?"

She smiled meekly. "Well, of course, we can't be certain of Pulin's number without the master list. We can only make a strong guess. I would say the margin of error would be ten percent or so."

"You make it sound worse the more we talk about it," Mitchell said.

Aiko bowed her head. "My apologies, Colonel."

"No, don't apologize. This is good work. How long do you think it would take to track Pulin down purely on the data we have?"

"I don't know for sure."

"Make an educated guess."

She smiled. "Assuming we have the data we need, ten to fourteen days. But there is a good possibility we don't have the data, and then we'll be back to the other approach, anyway."

Mitchell paused to think about it. He glanced at Davin and Maria. "What do you two think?"

"I agree with Aiko, Colonel," Davin said. "Not that I want to see anyone else get hurt. This isn't going to be easy either way, and if we're still here when the Tetron come back, we'll all be hurt."

"Good point," Mitchell said. "What about you?"

Maria nodded. "I think that's the best of two bad choices."

Mitchell ran his hand along his head. Maria was right, too. Both choices sucked. "Okay, keep going with the numeric matching. I'll speak with Admiral Hohn and find out what the timing looks like for reaching one of the Black Hole planets."

"Yes, Colonel," Aiko said.

"Thank you all," he said. "Every minute you keep doing what you're doing, you're improving our chances of surviving this mess."

That earned him a smile from all three of the techs. They dove back into their work as he headed off to find Calvin.

[8]
MITCHELL

Mitchell found Admiral Hohn in a small office directly off Asimov's Situation Room beneath Operations. It was a sparse work-space - a desk and tabletop screen combination that the Admiral was standing over when Mitchell entered.

"Admiral Hohn," Mitchell said.

Calvin looked up. "Colonel. You came to check on my progress?"

"Not exactly. You've only had a few hours, so I don't expect you to have a complete plan in place. What I need to know is the position of the nearest Black Hole planet. More importantly, how long will it take to get there, and how far from Earth will we be moving?"

Calvin smiled. "You have a keen interest in protecting Earth, and I understand that. Jingu has four billion people on it as well."

Mitchell felt a chill run down his spine. He hadn't forgotten the Federation's home world, even if he hadn't prioritized it either.

"Right now, I don't feel too great about reaching either one," he said.

"Neither do I," Calvin replied. "Of course, since the Black Hole planet is in Federation space, it will deliver us much closer to Jingu than Earth. Tell me, Colonel, given a choice would you allow my homeworld to fall to save yours, even if you knew it was too late?

"Wouldn't you?"

"Yes. I appreciate your honesty."

"I appreciate yours. Anyway, the Black Hole Planet isn't the final destination. We'll decide where to go once we've gained Tio's brother."

"Of course."

"So, let me ask the original question again. How long will it take to get there?"

"Two weeks, moving directly into Federation space."

"That isn't close."

"No."

"Aiko thinks she can make a good guess about Pulin's numeric identity in three days, and that there's an outside chance we can skip a step in ten to fourteen. I need to make a decision about which path to take and keep in mind the second may lead back to the first. You know more about the Black Hole than anybody. What do you think?"

"The Black Holes are meant to be secure. Getting into one won't be easy."

"Can we do it?"

"I don't know the capabilities of your forces, Colonel."

"Neither do I. Let's say it was your mission to infiltrate the system. Could you do it?"

Calvin was silent while he considered. "Me? No. I'm not a Marine, and I've never participated in a ground mission. With the right equipment and the right people, I would put the likelihood of your success at perhaps ten percent."

Mitchell sighed. That wasn't the good news he was trying to convince himself he would receive. "That's better than zero."

"If you're asking me if that is a better option than waiting and hoping we can determine Pulin's location without it, then I would say no, it isn't. There is a reason the Federation's most sensitive data is stored there, Colonel."

"Right."

"That being said, there is some merit to the idea. We could wait and end up with nothing, and then have to launch the mission anyway. If we assume the first option will fail, it will help us plan for and attempt the second more efficiently."

"So you're saying we should do it?"

"No, Colonel. I'm saying that my opinion is that we shouldn't, but there is an obvious benefit to the approach. I imagine you aren't about to make your decision based solely on the assessment of a Federation Admiral."

Mitchell wasn't going to tell Calvin how heavily he was weighing his feedback. He didn't feel certain about either approach and nothing in his subconscious was steering him in one direction over the other either. Had this present never happened in prior timelines?

"Thank you, Admiral," Mitchell said. "I'll consider your opinion along with my own and Steven's. I'll also check back in with Aiko with your estimate. Can you let me know once you've finalized your assessment of the Black Hole approach?"

"Of course, Colonel."

"Thank you."

Mitchell bowed and left the room. He could feel Calvin's eyes on him the entire time. There was something about the Federation Admiral that didn't sit well with him, but he couldn't quite place it. He had been fighting the Federation for so long; he wondered if he was simply struggling to separate the man from the nation.

He headed back to the lift, taking it down three more levels to the infirmary. He winced when the hatch to the lift slid open, revealing the results of a pitched battle.

The bodies were gone, but the pieces of debris from Watson's machines still littered the floor, and even the emergency lighting struggled to stay active, flickering and flashing and lighting the entire corridor in a grim way. According to Thomas, Millie had been a major reason they had won the standoff down here.

"Digger?" Mitchell shouted, stepping through the mess. He had assigned the mechanic to see what he could salvage hours ago, but Aiko had told him she thought he was still down here. "Digger?"

There was no answer. Mitchell crossed the corridor to the threshold of the infirmary. He gasped at the sight of the damage. Blood splattered the walls, and the medi-bot had been overturned and smashed. One of Watson's robots lay dead on its side, a limb twisted in on itself and stabbing into the battery pack. Mitchell smiled at the sight. Only Millie could have done that.

"Digger?"

The cabinets were all hanging open, the medicines already looted and packed. He heard the hum of a machine in an adjacent room.

He crossed over to it and peeked in. Digger was on his back beneath a large box, tools laying close to his right hand.

"Digger," Mitchell said.

The mechanic twitched before he pulled himself out from underneath the equipment.

"Shit, Colonel. You scared the frig out of me."

"Sorry. What is that?" He pointed at the box.

"Medical mainframe. When the medi-bot isn't a pile of broken shit, it powers it. It contains a database of everything the bot needs to know, including human genome sequences."

He got to his feet. Mitchell noticed blood stains on his overalls.

"Not mine," Digger said. "Such a frigging shame about Tio's people, and your Admiral. Did you know Tess bought it? The real Tess."

"No. I didn't know. I'm sorry."

Digger shrugged. "It's okay. Sometimes I think she's better off than we are."

"Digger-"

"Yeah, I know. You don't need to say it. Anyways, I figure if we can take the mainframe, and this other piece of tech over here, it's a high-powered microscope, and a DNA sequencer, we can maybe find a clue."

"Where's the sequencer?"

"Out there. The mainframe is the hardest to remove, so I started in on it first. I was going to check up on my crew once that was done. I put what was left of them in charge of the communicators."

"How many do we have?"

"We can make about twenty, give or take."

"Encrypted?"

"Yup. Hey, home come you came down here? You didn't need to climb into the bowels with me to ask me this shit."

Mitchell wasn't sure what to say. Why had he come down? He wanted to see the carnage. He wanted to remember it. He wanted to use it as fuel.

"I wanted to see if you needed any help," he said instead. "I can lend a hand for a couple of hours."

Digger's face lit up. "Really? You would do that for me?"

"Sure. Why not?"

"You're the frigging Hero of the frigging Battle for Liberty. That's why not."

"I'm-"

Digger didn't let him counter his statement. "I'm honored, Colonel."

Mitchell nodded. "Show me what you need me to do."

[9]
STEVEN

Admiral Steven Williams blinked his eyes a few times, forcing them to tear. Then he clenched them tight, holding the moisture in and feeling it burn against his retinas.

He had been staring at the projected data for a long time. He wasn't sure how long, and he had to remind himself that his p-rat was offline when he tried to check the time. He looked over to a simple digital readout on the panel behind him instead. It was early in the morning. At least three hours since Mitchell had left.

He had nothing to show for it. His digging into potential aliases had left him with all kinds of names, but he hadn't been able to place any of them anywhere near Kathleen Amway, Katherine Asher, or Christine Arapo so far. He had even tried Kristine Arapo, figuring that maybe the sleeping Origin had changed the spelling at some point over the centuries.

As usual, he had received zero results.

"We didn't expect this to be easy," he said to himself. "Did we?"

He sighed, stepping out of the ring. He wanted to keep going until he found something, but the truth was it could take days, if not weeks. He had to sleep eventually.

He couldn't leave, though. He had told Mitchell he would be there when he came back, and Digger was still working on getting interpersonal communications organized again. He couldn't believe the mechanic had pushed to develop a test for being a Tetron considering how much other work Digger had on his plate.

He wandered out of the study, moving back to the foyer where Watson's machines were still twitching. He stared at them for a few minutes, observing how the servos and gears moved. The machinery itself was so basic. It was the intelligence the Tetron had given them that made them frightening and powerful.

What if Watson gave that same intelligence to other machines? The Tetron on Liberty had done something similar. It was a side of the enemy they hadn't given enough thought to. How would they stop them if they built a massive fleet of even the most basic of starfighters? How would they overcome the enemy if the enemy built intelligent missiles to fire at them? Self-directed, able to learn from the fates of the others, and solely purposed to make a single destructive hit against a single target.

He felt the hair stand up on his arms at the thought.

No. He remembered what Mitchell had said about them being sick. He had said the machines the Tetron on Liberty had made were improperly constructed and didn't work the way they were supposed to.

Then why had Watson's creations been so effective?

He knew the Tetron had been present centuries earlier. Had it somehow avoided the fate that had befallen the rest of them? He wasn't sure. There had to be some kind of sickness in there, considering what it had aroused it. Maybe it was simply suffering in a different way?

He stood there and stared at the machines. At that moment, he realized that Watson was much more dangerous than they were even considering. He decided he would discuss it with Mitchell when he returned.

He moved away from the foyer, heading into the library. The

hidden passage to the secret armory was still visible, Millie's blood running to it along the floor. There were even a few bloody bootprints still dried against the tile.

Steven made the sign of the cross in front of it before moving to the glass cabinets in the center of the room. He paused in front of them, looking in on the books. He tried to remember the last time he had seen an actual physical book. His father had collected a few over the years, but had there been any at the Academy? There was the singular copy of The Art of War that sat on a pedestal near the entrance to the main building, but other than that?

His eyes landed on the center book, a plain hardcover with a dust jacket photograph of debris laying on top of a field of ice. *XENO-1*, by Paul Frelmund.

He considered opening the cabinet and taking a look through it. Instead, he returned his attention to the broken robots on the other side of the entrance to the library.

He had always been a good soldier. He had always followed the rules, followed orders, done the right thing. He had been a successful starship pilot before he had become a successful Admiral. He had earned the promotions because he was good at what he did, and he did it to the letter.

Then he had followed a false General Cornelius into Federation space and killed thousands of farmers. He had followed that up by breaking surrender protocol to escape from the Tetron. Now he was an Admiral taking orders from a Colonel because the military he had transferred to didn't give a shit about rank.

Mitchell had told him he couldn't go to the coordinates Katherine had provided for him, and Steven understood why. It was a long trip that might be for nothing, or might leave them separated by weeks of hyperspace with no way to reach one another. At the same time, as he retraced his steps and returned to the foyer to look down on the Tetron's creations once more, he had a feeling that Mitchell was wrong. After all, as Mitchell liked to repeat, he had always lost the war.

Was this the reason?

Was it the most important misstep he would make?

Steven tried not to believe that it was, but he wasn't convinced. The longer he stood there, the more he thought about it, the more certain he became.

Origin had tried to leave them something for a reason.

They needed it, and they needed it now.

[10]

STEVEN

STEVEN DIDN'T WAIT for Mitchell to come back. He knew his little brother well enough to know that Mitch would still tell him he couldn't go, and he would do something stupid to stop him if he insisted.

No, if he was going to defy orders yet again, he was going to have to do it quietly.

He went back to Tio's hidden armory before he headed out, quickly going through it and taking a pair of sidearms and extra magazines for both, grabbing as much as he could carry without it being obvious. Then he walked out of Tio's home, taking a detour off to a darker part of the open space just in case Mitchell chose that moment to return. He considered his plan as he did.

He would need to get to the dock without anyone noticing, and find a ship there that would be suitable for the journey. He had no intention of robbing Mitchell of a starship that could aid him in a fight. He would have to find something else, like a true trawler or miner or something, one that was poorly prepared for a fight yet jump capable. Then he would have to convince the dock operator to release the clamps. That shouldn't be too hard.

At that point, he would make the jump out to the coordinates. If there were something there that he could take, he would. If there were nothing, he would turn around and come back. He would have to hope that Mitchell decided to leave him some indication of where they might be going, and that the Tetron either hadn't returned to Asimov or had come and gone again.

If Mitchell didn't leave him directions and Asimov was still there, he would return to the station and try to figure out where his brother had gone. Failing in that, he would wait there for Mitchell to return to claim the prize.

What if Asimov was gone? He tried not to think about that possibility. No directions, no station? Whether he was carrying anything or not, that result could be disastrous. He decided he would wait it out in the ship he stole. If he ran out of food before Mitchell came back or if Mitchell never came back, so be it.

At least he would have tried.

He took an alternate route back to the quarters he and his crew had been given on their arrival. He felt a pang of regret and failure at the fact that he was going to be abandoning them, and at the same time he knew that his willingness to leave them meant he was resolved. Besides, John was a good man and a good First Mate. He would take care of the Carver for him.

He made it to his room without incident, dropping the weapons he had taken on the bed and quickly shedding the uniform he had worn to Millie's memorial. He stepped through the sonic to have the grime removed and then changed into the Navy fatigues he had brought with him. Nobody would question his decision to get more comfortable before he continued with his work.

He also grabbed his duffel, throwing the guns and magazines in it, along with a pair of grays to cover them if he had to open the duffel for any reason. Finally, he went back into the bathroom and shaved off his beard.

He stood and stared at himself in the mirror. He barely recognized himself without the growth around his mouth and hanging from his chin. He looked younger, but also less dignified. He laughed at himself.

"I look like an uglier, balder, older version of Mitch," he said.

He gave himself one last look, staring into his own eyes.

"Are you sure you want to do this?" he asked himself.

He nodded. He was. He turned away from the mirror, grabbing the duffel from the bed and heading out the door. He made his way through the hallways and out to the front of the building.

Captain Rock was going in as he was going out.

"Admiral," John said.

"John," Steven replied. "Going to crash for the few hours until morning?"

John smiled. "I figured an hour or two of sleep never hurt anyone." He tilted his head, staring at Steven. "You shaved your beard."

Steven rubbed his hand against his bare chin. It still felt strange. "Yeah."

"Why? It took you months to grow that thing."

"It just seemed like the right thing to do. It'll grow back. Anyway, I'm headed back to Tio's to continue the work I was doing with Mitch. Enjoy the shut-eye."

John continued to stare at him. Steven could feel his heart rate going up. His best friend knew there was something off about him.

"Yeah, okay," John said. "Well, goodnight, sir."

Steven swallowed heavily, feeling the tension building as John ducked his head and started making his way past him. He hated lying in general. Lying to his friend was even harder.

"Damn it, John," he said, reaching out and grabbing his Captain's arm. He moved in close, speaking quietly. "I'm leaving Asimov."

"What?" John said, a little too loud. He repeated it in a whisper. "What?"

"Mitchell told me that he got something in the Construct. Coordinates to something that Origin thought would help us. I offered to go and check it out, and he said no."

"And you're going anyway?" John asked.

"He doesn't want us to split up. He's right that he needs to get ahead of Watson, but he's wrong to think that I need to go with him. I don't want him to screw humanity because of it."

"And you were going to, what? Hop into a transport and ride off in the Carver?"

"Don't be stupid. I was hoping there would be a less valuable ship I could take."

"He won't let you leave."

"Which is why I'm trying to leave quietly. He needs this. He just doesn't know it yet."

"Are you sure it's him that needs this?"

"What does that mean?"

"Just that I know you, Steve. You hate sitting and waiting for things to happen. Add to that the fact that your family is in harm's way, and there you go."

"Okay, I need this too. I can't stand the idea of human civilization ending because we didn't make a hyperspace jump."

"How far out is it?"

"Three weeks."

"Shit, Steve. That's far."

"I know, I know."

"Mitch won't be here by the time you get back. Heck, Asimov probably won't be here."

"I know that, too. It's a risk, but at least I'm only risking myself and a single ship."

John shook his head. "No. You aren't just risking yourself. I'm coming with you."

"No. John, you can't. I need you to command the Carver."

"Lewis can handle the Carver."

"I want it to be you. I also don't want to be responsible for you dying. You have someone back home, too."

"Who is just as in harms way as Laura and Terry. I'm coming."

"No. That's an order."

"Take your orders and shove them, Steve. You know rank doesn't play here."

Steven stared at his friend. He knew John would never let him go alone. He also knew in the back of his mind that was why he had told him.

"Fine. Grab your gear and meet me at the docks in ten minutes."

"Yes, sir," John said. "You promise you won't leave without me?"

Steven spread his hands in submission. "I promise. You're a good friend, John."

"I know it. I'll see you there."

[11]
STEVEN

THE DOCKS WERE BUSIER than Steven had expected. The evacuation of Asimov was well underway, with ships arranged along the main hub such that they could be maneuvered into position against the loading bays when it was their turn. A large trawler was already attached to the primary loading area while a dropship was hooked to the secondary. Dozens of Tio's people moved through the space with purpose, leaving him barely noticed in the chaos.

He leaned against the wall, trying to remain as inconspicuous as someone who was just standing there could be. He held his duffel slung over his shoulder, casting his eyes back and forth, making it obvious he was waiting for something.

"Sorry," John said, materializing out of a group of techs. He was surprisingly capable of blending in despite his heavyset appearance and the Navy fatigues he was wearing. "I ran into Lewis on the way down."

"Did you say anything?"

"About this? No, but the story I made up for what I was doing was lame."

"Let's hope he doesn't tell anyone. Come on."

They walked the length of the corridor towards the control station. It would be a good vantage point to use to find a suitable ship.

Then all they would have to do was steal it.

"Are you sure you're sure about this?" John whispered.

"Do you have a better idea? You know Mitch won't listen."

"You're his big brother. I think you could convince him."

"Do you want to risk Bill's life on it?"

"Fine, but look at this place. They've got over forty ships crammed into a space that was meant to hold thirty-six at most, and there are people everywhere. How are we going to sneak out?"

Steven shrugged. "I don't know yet. We have to take it one step at a time."

"Great plan, Admiral."

They reached the entrance to the control station. It slid aside at their approach, the security systems all shut down to provide easier access during the evacuation. There were three people in the room, each wearing headsets and communicating with the captains of the various ships. One of them, a short woman with long gray hair, turned around when they entered.

"Did you come to relieve me?" she asked. "It's been fourteen hours."

That was a long time to be guiding this kind of traffic.

"No. Sorry," Steven said, moving past her to look out at the ships. Only the smaller vessels would even fit in here, which meant there were only a few that were jump capable in the mix.

"Then what are you doing here?" the woman asked.

Steven froze, trying to think of a good excuse.

"Selecting ships for inspection," John said, saving him. "Colonel Williams asked us to make sure the cargo bays were being loaded efficiently."

"Oh. Do you think you could ask the Colonel to find someone to replace us and give us a break? We're dead on our feet."

Steven nodded. "I'll mention it to him when I make my report. It will probably be at least another hour, though."

She didn't look happy about that, but she nodded and turned back around, hitting a button. "This is Control."

Steven scanned the docking arms, positioned in rows and columns around them. There were a lot of ships in the space, and they were almost uniformly old and worn, with dented metal plating and scorch marks suggesting their more illicit use.

"What about that one?" John said, pointing at one of the most beat-up ships in the dock. It was also one of the largest with hyper-space engines.

"No," Steven replied without offering any further reason.

"That one?" John offered a jumpship. It was small, but it was also one of only three the fleet possessed.

"They might need it."

John sighed. "There are only two others on the docks right now."

Steven checked them both, his heart sinking. He should have guessed his best intentions would be stymied by a lack of resources. No. He wouldn't allow the to happen.

"Yeah, you're right. The jumpship."

John nodded, and they began retreating from the room.

"Don't forget about us," the gray-haired woman said as they left.

Now came the hardest part. Steven could feel his heart beating harder with every step they took, his resolve starting to crack a little. He knew what came next, and he didn't like it, even if it did need to be done.

"Having second thoughts?" John asked while they made their way down to the jumpship's docking arm.

"No. I just don't like this part."

"Well try to not like it a little less, because we're getting looks."

Steven noticed the people around them, their eyes glancing his way as they passed. He had always been guilty of wearing his heart on his sleeve. It was survivable on the bridge of a starship where only your officers would see it. It was going to get them caught if he didn't do something about it now.

He pictured Admiral Hohn in his mind, working to mimic the

man's near-constant outward calm. It wasn't about removing the fear; it was about hiding it.

"Better," John said.

Steven wondered how his friend was staying so cool under the pressure.

They reached the hatch to the docking arm. It slid open ahead of them, leaving them along in the long cylinder of clear carbonate and metal flooring that stretched hundreds of meters out into empty space. Steven shifted the duffel to his chest, unzipping it slowly as they walked. The ship was tenth in line for loading, which meant it should be unoccupied.

He found the gun in his bag, taking it in his hand and moving it behind the duffel. If it weren't clear, he would have to hijack it and hope whoever was inside didn't fight back. That was the thing that scared him the most. He didn't want to hurt anybody.

"I can take it if you want," John offered.

"Here," Steven said, handing John the other gun. "You might need one too."

They reached the airlock. It was open, and when Steven looked in he didn't see any sign of occupants.

"We'll sweep it quick to make sure it's empty, and then we'll go," he said.

"Roger."

They entered the ship. John moved to the right toward the rear of the ship while Steven turned left and headed forward to the cockpit. The ship was silent; its engines powered down and most of the electronics off.

He paused a few times, listening for John, as he was sure his friend was listening for him as well. He stopped one last time before he made it to the hatch of the cockpit, making sure that John hadn't stumbled into trouble. When he didn't hear anything, he reached forward and hit the panel to open the hatch.

He stepped in. His heart was racing, his hand tight and clammy on the gun. If there were going to be anyone on the ship, they would likely be here, waiting for confirmation to move into position for loading.

"Admiral Williams?" Germaine said, swiveling in his seat at the sight of Steven.

Steven's eyes grew wide, and he raised the gun from behind the duffel. He had been so damn close.

"Put your hands up," he said, his whole body shaking.

"What are you doing?" Germaine asked. "Are you a Tetron?" He didn't look concerned about the pistol aimed at his face.

"I need the ship."

"Why don't you just ask Mitchell for one? I'm sure he'd let you borrow it."

Germaine wasn't taking his threat seriously. Then again, why would he? He doubted he looked much like a threat either.

"I already asked him," he said, lowering the weapon. "He said no."

"Why?"

"I need to jump to unexplored space to check something out. It's going to split us up in a bad way."

"Check something out? Are you sure you aren't a Tetron?"

"Do I look like a Tetron?"

Germaine laughed. "Everyone looks like a Tetron. You aren't acting like one, though. You're acting like yourself."

"What does that mean?"

"I spent a couple of weeks in the cockpit of the Avalon with your brother. He told me stories. All I kept hearing about is how nice you are, how upstanding and successful and settled. You can't even keep the gun on me. He's jealous of you, you know."

That took Steven off guard. "He is?"

"Yup. No joke. So what about this something in unexplored space? Clearly, Mitch doesn't want you to go, and you think you should. Considering that you're such a nice guy and yet you're willing to try to steal a jumpship, there has to be a good reason for it."

"Origin gave Mitchell the coordinates on Hell."

"You mean the Construct?"

Steven nodded.

"And he doesn't want to go?"

"He wants to go, but not yet. He wants to stop Watson first."

Germaine laughed again. "I get it."

The conversation paused as they heard boots moving towards them. Not one pair like Steven expected. There were at least two people coming.

John appeared a moment later, a bruise next to his eye and an apologetic look on his face. Cormac followed behind him, holding the gun Steven had given John to John's back.

"What the frig is going on here?" Cormac asked.

His voice had a strange, echoing lisp to it, caused by the half-mask he had over the destroyed side of his face. It was made of a solid black carbonate and looked to be screwed into his skull to hold it on.

"Cormac?" Steven said.

"Yeah, I know," the grunt replied, running his hand over the mask. "Diggs made it for me. Simple, yet sophisticated. He said he would work on the laser for the eye."

"Sorry, Steve. He caught me off-guard."

"I was standing right next to the bloody fool," Cormac said. "He nearly got himself killed. What are you doing here, Admiral?"

"Stealing the ship," Germaine said, still laughing at the whole thing.

"You're doing a bang-up job, sir," Cormac said.

Steven shrugged. "From what I gather, this is more your kind of mission."

"Riiigg-ahh," Cormac said. "Yes, sir. Why are we stealing a starship?"

"To help Mitchell," John said.

"Without Mitchell knowing," Steven said.

Cormac did his best to smile. "Now that's something I can get behind."

"You don't want to take the Corleone," Germaine said. "We only have three jumpships in the fleet, and this is the only one with a mech drop module."

"It was the best I could spot from Control," Steven said. "What were you two doing in here, anyway?"

"I told you; this is the only jumpship with a mech drop module. If you took this one, you might have left us with no ship to go planetside if we need to bring the heavy guns. I was inspecting the flying parts, and Cormac was in the back inspecting the explosive parts. Qualified hands are tight, and we all need to do our part. Anyway, don't sweat it, Admiral. I've got the ship for you. We can head on over and be out of here before anyone knows we're missing."

Steven was confused. "We?"

"Hell, yes, Admiral," Germaine said. "Mitchell's my friend, and if he's doing something stupid, it's my responsibility to make it less stupid."

"You think he's making the wrong call?"

"I don't know, but you're his brother and an Admiral. That makes you way smarter than I am. If you think he is, I trust you."

"You ain't leaving without me," Cormac said. "Let me just grab my grenades from the back."

[12]

STEVEN

GERMAINE STOOD WAVING to them from the far edge of the upper-most corner docking arm, near the final airlock that would join ship to shore. He was far enough away that Steven couldn't see the starship he had brought him to from his position further down. All he could see was the side of a larger salvage ship, one that had taken a fair amount of damage during the battle against the Tetron, and had somehow managed to make it back to port alive. There were crews in exo-suits hovering around the outside of it, welding metal plates back on and working to re-pressurize parts of the ship punctured during the fighting.

"That's our signal," Cormac said, shouldering the pack he had organized in the ten minutes since he had insisted on joining Steven on the mission.

Steven wasn't sure what was in it. He wasn't sure he wanted to know. Guns, grenades, and what else? Mitchell had told him enough about the one he called Firedog that he was a little uncomfortable in the man's presence. The mask had made him even less comfortable.

Cormac started forward. Steven and John trailed behind him, keeping their heads down and trying to look inconspicuous to the few technicians coming and going from the salvager. They had their own work to do, so they didn't pay the three of them too much mind.

As they moved down the corridor, the sight of the salvager gave way to another ship, the one that Germaine wanted them to take. The first thing Steven noticed about it was the overall size. It was tiny. He couldn't believe someone had slipped hyperspace engines onto something so small. The second thing he noticed was that it was ugly. Fins and short wings poked out from all over the place, as though it had been stapled together from a hundred different atmospheric fighters.

"The Lanning," Germaine said as Steven reached him. "Mr. Tio's personal starship."

"You want us to go in this?" John asked.

Germaine laughed. "Look, it has a couple of guns hidden in the belly, and it's maneuverable as hell, but it isn't much use to the overall war effort. Isn't that what you were looking for, Admiral?"

Steven nodded. "Yes. I just wasn't expecting something this size. I didn't even know you could make a hyperspace capable ship like this. Well, other than Mitchell's fighter, but that was built by a Tetron."

"It's a little cozy, I agree. We'll just have to become good friends."

"I've got some porno streams we can watch," Cormac said. "Digger had a portable player and a partition on the data store. What's your flavor, Admiral?"

Steven glanced over at Cormac. The soldier shrank back.

"Oh, damn. You have the same evil eye as your brother. It must run in the family. I take it you're married, sir?"

"Yes, but I wouldn't watch that trash if I wasn't," Steven said.

Cormac put up his hand. "Okay, no worries, sir. I brought a pair of goggles." He looked at the others. "Just let me know if you want to borrow. Or you can share one side. I can't use it anyway." He laughed at himself.

"Let's get this show on the road, shall we?" Steven said. "It's a wonder Mitch hasn't figured out I'm gone yet."

"Right this way, Admiral," Germaine said, leading them onto the

Lanning. Besides the two pilot seats, there was room for two more, along with a pisspot and small sleeping area in the back.

"This isn't cozy," Firedog said. "This is a frigging coffin."

Steven looked at him. His face had gone pale, and he was looking towards the airlock.

"Are you okay, Cormac?" he asked.

Cormac was shaking now. "I don't like small spaces, sir."

"You can back out," Germaine said. "Just keep your mouth shut."

Cormac took a step towards the hatch. Then he paused, clenching his eye shut. "Frig it all. No. I'm staying. Mitchell would want me to keep you alive, sir."

"You sure, Firedog?" Germaine asked.

"Yeah. Just close me in. I'll be over here." He sat in the second row of seats and closed his eye. His hands clenched the strap of his duffel, knuckles white.

Germaine took the pilot seat, while Steven sat next to him, leaving John with Cormac.

"I wish I'd brought a change of clothes," Steven said. "I didn't realize I'd be on a ship without any laundering."

"Been a while since you roughed it, Admiral?" Germaine said.

"I never piloted a drop. My Academy scores were at the top of my class, and I got bumped to commanding a cruiser six months out. I've never seen a fight from anything smaller than that."

Germaine laughed. "You're a lucky son of a bitch, aren't you?"

"I worked my ass off."

"Didn't mean to offend, Admiral."

"Call me Steven. I'm pretty much due for a court-martial if I go back to the Alliance before the Tetron are gone, and the rank doesn't mean a thing out here."

"True enough, Steven," Germaine said. "Let's get the show on the road." He pressed a button on the cockpit, opening a channel to Control. "Control, this is Germaine. I'm in the Lanning. Going to move it into the secondary Hangar for a retrofit. Digger thinks he can sling a laser cannon to the top of her."

"Germaine, this is Fiona. You know Mr. Tio wouldn't be happy with you messing with the Lanning."

"Mr. Tio isn't here, and we need all the firepower we can get. Come on, Fi."

Steven assumed he was speaking to the woman with the gray hair. She sounded tired.

"Fine," she said, sighing. "If he makes it back, this is on you."

"Roger."

There was a bang and a hiss, and then the ship began floating out from the side of the docking arm. Steven couldn't believe it had been so easy to get the ship away though he knew it would have been much harder with the jumpship.

"She's going to chew me out in about five seconds," Germaine said, using the stick to fire vectoring thrusters, turning the Lanning to face the exit.

"Germaine? What kind of game are you playing?" Fiona's voice was high-pitched and angry. "You cocky son of a whore, get the frig back in position."

Germaine added forward thrust, maneuvering the smaller ship around larger vessels that were waiting in the cavern for a spot on the docks. He looked over at Steven, smiling.

"Germaine? Where the frig do you think you're going?"

"Sorry, Fi. I've got Admiral Steven Williams on board. He ordered me to leave Asimov." Steven glared at him. Germaine shrugged, still smiling. "Tell Colonel Williams that we're going to retrieve the prize. He'll know what that means."

"Tell him to plan accordingly," Steven said. "We'll get a message back to these coordinates, tee ten at two point seven. He'll know what that means. Oh, and tell him I don't care what he thinks. Dawn was pretty." He felt his heart lurch as he realized he might not see his brother again. "And tell him I love him, and I'm proud of him, and to stay strong."

"Riiigg-ahh," Cormac shouted from the back.

"Riiigg-ahh," they all replied.

POINT OF ORIGIN / 63

Germaine pushed the thrusters harder, the ship accelerating into the narrow passage out into space.

"Coordinates?" he asked.

Steven fed them to him, and he entered them into the computer. The system was manual, and Germaine had to do some of the calculations himself. He didn't miss a beat.

"You okay back there, Firedog?" Germaine asked.

"Frig you," Cormac replied.

"I don't go that way."

The Lanning kept accelerating, moving through the tunnels at a ridiculous velocity, Germaine deftly steering them around the rest of the traffic. Within minutes, they were out, blasting away from the rock into the blackness of space beyond.

"Last chance to change your mind," Germaine said.

"Not on your life," Steven replied. "Let's go."

Germaine froze the thrusters, switching to the hyperspace engine. It whined slightly behind them. He hit the cockpit's control panel.

Black collapsed into white, and the Lanning disappeared.

[13]
MITCHELL

"I THINK THAT'S IT," Digger said.

"This was a lot more work than I expected," Mitchell replied. He was wearing light exo, having gone back up to mechanical to retrieve it and using it to lift and load the heavy equipment onto a Mule.

It had been almost four hours since he had left Steven in Tio's house. He had been distracted by the work he was doing with Digger, the simple manual nature of it a much-needed distraction from recent events. He lost himself in the step-by-step deconstruction of the pieces Digger wanted to bring with them, and hadn't even noticed how much time had passed until they had gotten the DNA sequencer onto the Mule.

He knew he needed to get back and check in. Steven would be wondering what had happened to him.

Of course, now that he was finished with the work and his mind wasn't so distracted, all he felt was exhausted. He had originally intended to get an hour or two of rest, but that hadn't worked out. It was too hard for him to let go when there was so much to be done, and so little time to do it.

"You really think this will help?" Mitchell asked.

"Jameson told me this was what he would grab if he were me," Digger said. "I'll need to talk to your brother about his doctor, too."

"He's over at Tio's. I need to run back there and check-in with him. You should come with me."

"Okay, sure. Thanks for lending me a hand, Colonel. I'd still be fighting with the frigging mainframe. I don't have exo attachments."

Mitchell shrugged. He was getting used to the manually controlled version of the strength-enhancing suits. "I needed the practice in it. Come on."

They headed for the exit, the Mule following dutifully behind them with the three large pieces of tech on its back. It stepped smartly over the debris, keeping pace as they moved to the lift.

"Have you slept at all since you got back to Asimov, Colonel?" Digger asked while they ascended.

"No, not yet. I'm getting to it."

"It's been almost fifty-four hours. You're going to drop dead if you don't take a breather." He paused. "I've got this shit, came from a trader on King's Point, or at least that's what Gorman told me. Helps you sleep real good, and you don't wake up with a headache or any of that shit."

Mitchell didn't like taking drugs, but he was so physically tired and mentally aware that he considered it. "You know where I'm staying?"

"Yeah, in the apartments with your brother's crew."

"Drop it off there."

"Sure. Hey, Colonel, I wanted to ask you something about the Battle for Liberty. I mean, you don't need to answer if you don't want to, but it's been something that's been twisting my pecker for a while."

"Twisting your pecker?"

Digger laughed. "Figure of speech from back home. Do you mind?"

"I won't answer if I mind."

"Right. Okay. So I watched you on the streams, and I read the reports. I saw something in there about the Federation Dreadnaught; you said that it didn't have full shield coverage or some shit?"

"Yes. The geometry was off. There was a gap in the rear." It had been a while since he had thought about it. It felt like it had all happened so long ago.

"Did you ever wonder why?"

"Why what?"

"Why the frigging gap? I mean, the Federation is full of the smartest scientists in the universe, like Tio's brother, for example. How the frig did they get the geometry wrong?"

"Of course I wondered. I don't have any answers for it, though. We saw an opportunity, and we took it."

"Sure, sure. But what about in light of recent events?"

Mitchell stared at Digger, starting to catch on to what the mechanic was trying to say. "This has to do with what you were discussing in the meeting earlier?"

"Yeah. How do we know there isn't a Tetron, or maybe a bunch of Tetron, embedded in the Federation? How do we know that they didn't frig up the dreadnaught's build process on purpose?"

"So that I could take the Shot?"

"Yup."

Mitchell had never thought about it that way before. The idea of it intrigued him. "They would have to be on humanity's side."

"Would they? This is going to sound really crazy, Colonel, and I hope you don't take this the wrong way. What if you weren't supposed to be the one who took the Shot?"

"I can't take it the wrong way because I don't know what you're suggesting."

Digger looked frustrated at having to explain it. "What if you weren't supposed to take the Shot? What if your commander was supposed to be the Hero of the Battle for Liberty? What if she was the one who was originally supposed to fight the Tetron, but somehow the bad ones interceded and got you mixed up in it instead?"

Mitchell felt his heart begin to race. Ella was the real hero, and she had been twice the pilot and leader he was. Could it be that the mechanic was right? Did it even matter?

"I guess anything is possible," he said, keeping his voice level. "Who knows how this whole thing started, or what it looked like during the first recursion? The point is that in this one, I'm the guy who's supposed to try to stop it. If the Watsons set me up to become that guy because they thought I would be some kind of patsy, that's only more motivation for me to prove them wrong."

Digger nodded. "I agree with you, sir. Don't get me wrong. It was just something I was wondering about. I mean, there has to be a reason for that shit, right? Do you think I'm onto something there?"

"Like I said, anything is possible."

The door to the lift slid open. They led the Mule out into the corridor towards the loading bay. They would need to get a transport to carry the equipment over to the Carver.

Mitchell had only made it three steps when an older woman in gray hair appeared, coming from the opposite direction. She raised her arm and waved when she saw him.

"Colonel! Colonel!"

"What is it?" Mitchell asked, his mind shifting gears in an instant, from Digger's supposition to a sudden sense of urgent sharpness.

"It's your brother," she said.

Mitchell's senses took another hit, heading off in another direction of panic. "Is he okay?" he asked, resisting the intense desire to run to Tio's.

"I don't know. My name is Fiona, I'm one of the techs that runs Control up on level A. Germaine just took the Lanning from the docks and brought it out into space." She was waving her arms, speaking quickly.

Mitchell held back his sudden frustration. "What? You aren't making any sense. Calm down and tell me what happened."

"Your brother," she said again, still excited. "Germaine took the Lanning."

"Fi, get a frigging grip, will you?" Digger said. "Try speaking English."

Fiona stopping moving, her eyes wide. She blinked a few times and then blew out a huge breath.

"Sorry, Colonel," she said. "Germaine took the Lanning, Mr. Tio's starship, from the docks. He told me that Steven ordered him to take him somewhere. Steven was on the ship. He told me to give you a message. That he loves you, and he's proud of you, and to stay strong, and he's going to get you the prize. Oh, and Dawn was pretty. He also said he would get a message back to Asimov. Something about tee ten at two point seven."

Mitchell froze, his anger rising and warring with his concern and his pride in his brother for taking the initiative for once. He couldn't believe Steven had managed to defy an order. He had even been sly about it, getting Mitchell to tell him the coordinates back at Tio's.

"Do you know what that last part means, Colonel?" Digger asked.

Mitchell nodded, still in a bit of shock. He could read between the lines. Steven hadn't agreed with him on not heading out to see what Origin left them, and he was willing to risk his life because he believed it would help fight the Tetron. He had believed so strongly that he had done something Mitchell never thought he would do to see it happen.

"We used to play a lot of games," Mitchell said. "Our parents didn't let us entertain ourselves with streams and VR games. We had to stay in the real, and occupy one another. He said to leave a ship behind to wait for him and have it move between ten coordinates at two point seven hours out from Asimov. The waiting ship will move clockwise, and he'll hit the points counterclockwise. That way the Tetron will have a hard time locating them both if they are in the area."

He should have thought of that in the first place. He had been too concerned about keeping everyone together and safe. Especially his brother.

"Smart," Digger said.

"Yeah."

Mitchell felt the anger dropping, the pride rising. He remembered back on Goliath when he had heard the ghost of Katherine Asher tell him that they couldn't fight this war alone.

They needed heroes.

Steven was one of them.

[14]
KATHY

KATHY PAUSED, peering around the corner, moving her head back and forth and checking for signs of anyone nearby. She wasn't sure where Watson had placed the crew of the Goliath. There weren't many of them remaining, and if they were searching the ship for her, they might be fairly spread out.

She knew she had to be quick. Watson would be coming this way soon, likely believing he could take his time to reach Mitchell's bunk to get the neural chip. She didn't know what was on it, or why the Tetron configuration might desire to possess it at this particular moment. She assumed it had to be important if it was a priority over stopping the Goliath and cracking the key to Tio's archives.

She didn't see or hear anything, so she rounded the corner and ran along the corridor where the hexagonal bunks were positioned. She knew which one was Mitchell's, and she hit the button to open it, slipping in and quickly closing the hatch again. If Watson showed up before she left, she could surprise him and knock him down before he could stop her.

She stood completely still then, wondering if she could kill him here and now. No. Not yet. She needed him to stop the Goliath and get it moving in the right direction. She needed him to get her back to Mitchell, and then she would try to disable him. It was risky, very risky, but her unique design didn't afford her the ability to interface with and challenge the secondary directly. Once she did, she would be fortunate if she were able to shut it down. She would never be able to control it.

She turned and leaned over Mitchell's footlocker. She lifted the lid, quickly taking each item from it and throwing it onto the mattress in front of her. There were so many things in there. Things that had belonged to others. She knew of the Rigger's tradition of giving personal effects to others as a means to remember their sacrifice. She wished she had more time to examine each one, to put them to a name and understand what Mitchell felt when he touched them.

She hoped that she would have the chance to later.

She reached the bottom of the locker, finally locating the chip sitting in a small box in the corner. She picked it out, deftly opening the box and removing the fingernail-sized bit of electronics. She tucked it into the pocket of her grays, stuck the small box under Mitchell's pillow, and then began grabbing at the items she had removed. She considered leaving the mess for Watson to find so she would have more time to escape. She wondered if maybe she should let him know she had it already. She decided not to. She didn't want him putting too much effort into finding her just yet. Let him wonder if Mitchell had truly left the chip in his footlocker, or if he had destroyed it.

She was very interested to see how he would react to that.

She finished replacing the items, and then slipped out of the space once more. She stood in the corridor for a moment, listening. She could hear Watson's footsteps echoing in the empty spaces. She smiled as she opened the bunk above Mitchell's and climbed into it, closing it behind her.

Then she waited, peering down through the air vent.

Watson arrived a minute later, moving casually through the ship. He had calmed since his explosion over Tio's actions, having brushed his hair back away from his face and changed into dry clothes. She thought it was curious that he had taken the trouble, but what else did he have to do to occupy himself? She had observed every member of the crew carefully since she had arrived on the Goliath. It was something her mother had taught her to do. Watson had always been eclectic. She shuddered slightly when she remembered how he had looked at her sometimes when he thought she wouldn't notice. His eyes had often settled on the small mounds of her developing breasts in a way that made her feel frightened, angry, and strangely guilty.

If she were captured, would he act on the desire she had seen there? Or had his Tetron awareness overcome that simplistic lust of the flesh?

She didn't want to find out.

The Tetron opened the door to Mitchell's berth. He didn't enter it fully, leaning in and grabbing the footlocker and pulling it to the corridor. He knelt down over it, taking each item and throwing it carelessly away like a child looking for his favorite toy. He began to huff as he neared the bottom, and when the final item had been removed, and the locker was empty, he lifted it over his head and turned it upside down, shaking it as if the missing chip would suddenly appear.

"Where is it?" he said, the calm beginning to fade again. He threw the footlocker aside, sifting through the discarded items again. "Where is it?"

He moved into Mitchell's berth. The pillow came flying out of it a moment later. Watson gave an anguished cry, and the box flew out, shattering on the opposite wall.

"She has it," he yelled. "The little bitch has it."

Kathy felt her body go cold. Why had she left the box where he could find it? Some part of her had wanted him to discover it, for him to know she had taken it. Why?

Because she hated him, that was why. Because of what he had done to Tio, to Millie, and to Mitchell. And she hated what all of the Tetron had done to her Origin. Then there was the way that he looked at her. She could feel his eyes on her when she thought about it. She wanted him to feel pain and anger and frustration. She wanted him to burn.

He exited Mitchell's locker, throwing his fists into the walls, denting the metal there with each blow. "She has it, she has it, she has it." His breathing was quick and short. He was standing right below her, chest heaving.

She couldn't hold back her smile.

"Where are you, little bitch?" he said. "I know you're in here, somewhere. I'm going to find you little bitch. I'm going to find you, and I'm going to hurt you the way only one human can hurt another."

He kicked at the items again before storming away, still shouting. "You can't hide in here forever, little bitch. I will find you. I will hurt you. I will get my chip back." His screams turned unintelligible after that.

Kathy leaned back in the space, breathing heavily with both excitement and fear. She had pushed his buttons well. Maybe too well. She dug the chip out of her pocket. He knew she wouldn't destroy it. He knew she would want to know what it contained. Not the human garbage on the surface, but the data hidden underneath, petabytes of it in secret storage channels. Data that the parent had provided to the configuration.

She had to find out what it contained. If there was any chance it could help Mitchell, it was worth any risk she would have to take.

[15]
MITCHELL

MITCHELL WAS SITTING ALONE in Tio's meeting room, leaning back in the Knife's large, comfortable chair with his eyes closed. Despite every effort to find a minute to sleep over the previous three days, sleep had been an impossible wish.

The evacuation was coming along as well as could be hoped, considering he had lost three of his key officers when Steven had headed out on the Lanning. He hadn't been surprised to find out that Captain Rock had joined his brother on the mission. He had been surprised when he learned that Germaine and Cormac of all people had joined him. It had never occurred to him that either of those men were loyal enough to him that they would do something like that.

The rest of Tio's fleet had arrived within the last two days, over two hundred more ships of similar strength and quality to what had come before. It had taken a lot of repetitive briefings to get them all up to speed and on board with their plans, though Teal's presence and reputation smoothed things over more quickly than Mitchell ever could have on his own. Once that was done, the commanders and their crews had joined the evacuation with fervor, helping get supplies and people organized onto their rides.

As for Kathleen Amway, Watson, and Nova Taurus, Mitchell had been forced to give up the search. There weren't enough hours in the day, there weren't enough eyes to help him, and frankly the entire thing was leading nowhere fast. He would never have a complete picture of the past that had brought them to this point. And, he had spent too much time consumed by Digger's comments about Ella. He couldn't help but question if the mechanic was right that the commander of his starfighter wing was supposed to be here in his place. Except M had come for him. Katherine had left messages for him. Even the Tetron on Hell had wanted to capture him. Was that only because the recursion had changed that part of time? If it had, wouldn't that be enough to have broken the Mesh?

Maybe it wasn't the first time the Mesh had been broken? Katherine said it improved their chances of winning. She never said it would be definite.

It was enough to add to his exhaustion when he spent too much time thinking about it. The result was that he was still himself in the here and now, only he had suffered a blow to his confidence that he didn't like losing. He wound up pissed at Digger, being short with the mechanic for bringing it up. How had it helped, anyway?

"Colonel Williams."

The voice followed a short, shrill beep in his ear. Mitchell's eyes snapped open, and he leaned forward. He wasn't used to the communicators yet - tiny devices that sat in the ear canal, invisible from the outside and easy to forget about until they beeped. They were secure in the sense that a set of communicators had an encrypted signal that could only be picked up by like-programmed devices. They were insecure in that you couldn't open a channel to a single person. When he was knocked, all of the crew who had one, fifteen at the moment, got the knock as well.

"What is it Aiko?" he asked out loud. It was another inefficiency of the device that they had to speak to use it. It was no wonder such technology had been abandoned two centuries earlier.

"Are you occupied?"

He considered saying "yes," because he had almost fallen asleep. "No. I'm in the meeting room."

"I'll be right there."

Mitchell closed his eyes again. The seconds until Aiko arrived passed quickly.

"Colonel," she said, knocking on the side of the door frame with her hand.

"Come in, Aiko. What do you need?"

"We believe we have narrowed the list of potential identification tags to about two dozen. We've gone as far as we can go with the data we have. If we want to continue on this course, we'll need to get the information matched against the Black Hole database."

Mitchell looked at her. She appeared as tired as he was, her black hair falling randomly out of its normal bun, her eyes bloodshot. She had a smile on her face, though. She was proud of herself.

"How many did you start with?"

"About four thousand."

"Wow. Amazing work."

She blushed again, looking towards the floor. "Thank you, Colonel."

"How sure are you that Pulin is one of the codes on that list?"

"Ninety-five percent."

"You told me ninety a few days ago."

"I'm feeling confident today, sir."

Mitchell laughed. "Good. I like that." He twitched his cheek muscle, which shifted his ear and activated the communicator. "Calvin, can you come down to the meeting room? Teal, you too."

"Yes, sir," they both said.

"What about the alternative research path we discussed?"

"I've had Davin working on it. It's a dead end so far. We couldn't even identify who Pulin might know outside of the other scientists. I don't know if he had no friends and family, or if Mr. Tio made sure not to keep any of that information because it could lead back to himself."

"It's probably a combination of the two. Please, have a seat."

Aiko nodded and approached the table. She sat down next to him.

"You haven't slept at all, have you?" Mitchell asked.

"No. There hasn't been any time. The people here on Asimov are my family. I can't risk them getting caught here by the Tetron again. I can see by your face you haven't slept either."

"I'm in charge of this mess. I need to set a good example."

"You have, Colonel. All of the techs respect you and the efforts you are making."

Admiral Hohn appeared in the doorway, with Teal right behind him. Mitchell waved them in, and they took seats around him.

"Aiko has the list of identities," Mitchell said.

"Great news," Teal said.

Calvin remained quiet though his face looked more thoughtful at the announcement.

"What are our next steps?" Teal asked.

"How long until we can get everyone off Asimov?" Mitchell said.

"We're just about there. We have four ships that showed up yesterday who need resupply. Everything else that's left here is memories."

"Good memories," Aiko said.

"Mostly," Teal said.

"Has Digger set the charges?"

"Yes, sir. Enough explosive to blow Asimov to pieces."

"And Kylie has the codes?"

"Yes, sir."

Kylie had volunteered to stay behind and wait for Steven to return, with orders to blow Asimov if the Tetron showed up. They would try to leave the station and its archives intact just in case, but they also wouldn't take any chances.

"Calvin, you estimated two weeks to the Black Hole planet, and we talked a few times about possible paths of inception if the Tetron haven't taken the planet. Do you have anything new to add?"

Calvin shook his head. "I've done all that I can, Colonel. I have a good understanding of how the data centers are run, but it is still incomplete. As I mentioned to you earlier, our best option for success is to try to identify an operative and use them to infiltrate the system. They won't do it willingly."

Mitchell nodded grimly. They had discussed this particular plan at length. It was Mitchell's least favorite approach, one that would have been better suited to the true Riggers were they available. One that involved torture and suffering. It was also the most likely to produce results.

"I'm not sold on that plan yet," he said.

"I understand. I wouldn't be, either."

"What's the other option?" Teal asked.

"We need to get someone to the site on our own without triggering suspicion," Calvin said. "They also need to be able to work the data interface. The first part is difficult but not impossible. It is the second and third that are the challenge."

"Neither sounds easy," Teal said.

"No, it won't be, whatever we do. We have to do it to the best of our abilities. Calvin, do you have what you need for both approaches?"

"For the most part. The people of Asimov are from both nations, so we have a supply of Federation clothing and uniforms. There are also a few Federation starships in orbit. I spoke to the captains. The Kemushi is legally registered and should have clearance to launch a transport to the surface."

"Do we know who the ground team is?" Teal asked.

Mitchell looked at Calvin. "Have you decided on a team?"

"We need to keep the group small to avoid suspicion. The two of us, Colonel, though I suggest doing something to alter your appearance in the next two weeks. There is another former Federation member, Joon, who I believe will be valuable. If we choose plan B, we will require Aiko as well."

"Me?" Aiko said. "I'm not a soldier."

"You're the best data technician we have," Calvin replied.

Aiko looked at Mitchell, her face pleading. "I can't do this, Colonel. I'm good with data and machines, not espionage."

"I want you to come along either way," Mitchell said. "I'm sorry, Aiko, but even if we capture a Federation operative, we need someone to tell us if they're trying to be deceptive. We'll have two weeks travel to the planet. I can give you some basic training."

She bit her lip, her face pale. "But, Colonel-"

He shifted to face her, keeping his voice gentle. "Aiko, if you want to protect the people of Asimov, this is the best way to do it. I know it is a scary thought, but Calvin and I will be with you, and I've done this sort of thing before."

Of course, he was lying. He had never participated in any kind of undercover operation before. He was a soldier, not a spy. The words still seemed to ease her mind, at least a little bit.

"What about if the Tetron have already taken the planet?" Teal asked.

"Then we'll drop whatever we need to get to the data stores and see if anything is still there to take. We salvaged a few mechs from Hell, in addition to Digger's Franks. If there's a Tetron on the planet, we abort and come up with something else."

"What if there is nothing else?"

Mitchell had wondered the same thing himself. If there were a Tetron embedded in the planet they chose, they wouldn't be able to overcome it, which would leave them high and dry in finding Tio's brother. Without Pulin, without Goliath, and months behind the Tetron invasion of Earth, they were going to lose, plain and simple.

"We'll think of something else," Mitchell said, and he meant it, despite the dark thoughts churning through his mind. "We don't give up. We don't give in. Not until we're all dead."

[16]
MITCHELL

"This isn't how I had ever envisioned things happening," Mitchell said. He was sitting in the cockpit of the jumpship Fortitude, piloting the starship away from Asimov and towards the hangar of the battleship Carver. "At the very least, Steven was supposed to be here with me."

"You said you admired what he did," Calvin said from the co-pilot seat.

"I do. That doesn't mean it feels any less odd. The Carver is his ship."

"Lieutenant Lewis seemed a capable commander to me."

"I hope you're right."

Twelve hours had passed since his meeting with Aiko, Teal, and Calvin. The evacuation of Asimov had been well underway since then, with the smaller ships loading up on passengers and ferrying them to the waiting starships. It was a bittersweet procedure for the people of Asimov. They had spent years helping the Knife bend the rules and break numerous laws to slow the progress of intelligent machines, and now that those machines had made themselves known, they were being forced from their home. That they were leaving to fight back was the only consolation they could find. It was also a strong motivator.

"I haven't been off of Asimov since I arrived," Aiko said. "Fifteen years ago."

"You look too young to have come here that long ago," Calvin said.

"I was only a teenager back then. My parents were imprisoned by the Federation because my father refused to work at Omicron Corporation. He doesn't believe in violence, and they wanted him to help them develop weapons. Mr. Tio's wife had heard of the situation through their network, and she found me and took me away."

"Are your parents still alive?" Mitchell asked.

"I don't know. I haven't heard anything in all of that time. Mr. Tio allowed me to search for them in the data we received, but I was always too afraid I would discover they were dead. For me, it has been better to hope that they are alive."

The Fortitude reached the end of the tunnel leading out of the asteroid, accelerating out and away. More than two hundred ships hung in the space around them, illuminating the entire area in the glow of their lights. It was a sight that made Mitchell's breath hang for a moment in wonder. A sight that for a moment gave him hope that they could fight back and win.

It slowly faded as he turned the jumpship and vectored it towards the Carver. The Alliance battleship was easily the largest starship in the fleet, as well as the newest and most powerful. It was also heavily damaged, the metal hull scored and dented and scraped almost everywhere. Large swaths of protective shell were missing along the side, slagged metal and wires hanging into nowhere, the interior levels the gaping wounds led to closed off by emergency bulkheads. There had been no time to fix the most egregious damage. Not when so many of the ships needed repairs, and the Carver had the strongest shields by far.

"I can't believe she can still fly like that," Mitchell said.

"It is a good design," Calvin replied. "Not quite up to Federation standards, but serviceable."

"Thanks, I guess."

They continued their path, vectoring up and over the top of the Carver towards the only functional hangar that remained. Mitchell slid the Fortitude into it gracefully, bringing the ship down for a soft landing in its designated location. The clamps locked onto it, and then the hangar door began to close. Mitchell abandoned the cockpit, heading towards the back.

"We have everything?" he asked Digger. The mechanic sat next to the Mule that was still carrying the medical equipment. The Avalon's doctor, Jameson, was next to him.

"All of the shit you helped me pack, and then some," Digger replied.

"The Carver's infirmary lost pressurization during the last fight. The hull is patched, so we've got air in there again, but the doctor Steven thought he would loan you is dead. We've been so rushed and chaotic getting our army together again that he never knew."

Digger's face twisted at the news. "That sucks, big time. I guess it's just you and me, Jameson."

"We'll have to manage," the doctor said.

Mitchell heard the airlock finish closing, followed by the intake of air in the space outside the ship. A moment later the light over the jumpship's main hatch turned green. Calvin and Aiko joined them at the rear as they opened it and descended into the Carver. Lieutenant Lewis was approaching from the other side, with two other Lieutenants in tow.

"Colonel Williams, Admiral Hohn," he said, bowing to each of them. "I'd like to introduce you to Lieutenants Roberts and Atakan. They'll be helping me fly this beast."

"Lieutenants," Mitchell said, returning their bows. "Any word from Teal?"

"Yes, sir. You're the last ship in."

"Asimov is empty?" Aiko asked.

"Yes, ma'am," Lewis replied.

"She's ready to be blown to shit if needed," Digger said.

"I've already provided the coordinates to the fleet," Calvin said.

"We're ready to jump at your command, sir," Lewis said.

"If there's no reason to stay, then let's get going," Mitchell replied. "Follow me."

Mitchell let Lewis lead him and the others up to the Carver's bridge. It was a journey lengthened by the need to circumvent part of the ship that was still exposed to space. The other crew members bowed as they passed. Mitchell couldn't believe how few there were.

The hatch to the bridge opened, and they stepped inside. Lewis moved right to his regular station, sitting and entering commands on the screen ahead of him.

"Channel is open, sir."

Mitchell stared out of the Carver's viewport. Asimov was invisible ahead of them, a former home for thousands now even deader than it had ever been. They were surrounded by starships of different shapes and sizes, a fleet that had the distinction of being the only one capable of doing anything against the enemy threat.

"Riggers," Mitchell said, forcing his voice to come out strong and clear.

He opened his mouth again to begin saying something motivational and then stopped. He let silence fill the channel for a few moments. On the bridge, the assembled officers turned and stared at him.

"Let's give them hell," he said, motioning towards Atakan, who had taken Captain Rock's seat. Atakan reached forward and tapped the panel in front of him.

One by one, every ship in the largest free fleet in the galaxy began to move.

[17]
KATHY

KATHY SLIPPED between two thick strands of the Tetron known as Watson, careful not to touch either as she passed deeper into the Goliath. She was further now than she had ever bothered to go before, way past the bunks and the hangar, past where they had set up the infirmary, and out towards the nose of the massive starship.

It had been two days since she had taken the neural chip. In the beginning, she had stayed close to Watson to listen to his ranting and raving. She had delighted in his upset and the difficulty she had caused him. She had savored his frustration with Tio and his encryption, and the time he was losing while he fought to regain control of the starship.

He had managed to get into the command system and take the Goliath from hyperspace a few hours ago. It was that moment that had sent Kathy from his vicinity to find a new location to wage her war. The human configuration and the secondary were becoming more synchronized, and if she stayed too close to the core, she would be easy to discover.

She would return there again. She would have to in order to start fighting back against the Tetron. Not yet. For now, she needed to stay one step ahead of him, maintaining control of the neural chip he so badly wanted and remaining in a holding pattern while she waited for him to find Pulin. Her only hope of being reunited with Mitchell and returning the Goliath to him was to ride the storm for as long as she could.

She moved through a dark passage, one that was nearly empty of the secondary's millions of axons. It was a small corridor that her nascent memory of the ship identified as leading to the never used science laboratories. There would be a lot of old equipment down there, machines that she hoped she would be able to use to access the contents of the neural chip. She wouldn't have known how to do it before. She did now. It was one of the skills she had gained on her awakening.

The others were so much more violent. It went beyond the ability to fight. She had what her mother had known she would need. Things that no child should know. Not that she was a child. Not in so many ways. The human part of her was, she supposed. It was one of the things that made her different. She was created as a human embryo, made from a single cell that was allowed to grow and form the way any human would. Unlike a human, there was something more to her. In simple terms, it was pure data, directly interfaced into her mind. Some of that data was available to her, and she had used it her entire life without knowing. Other parts remained off limits, untouchable until the time was right.

When would that time be? She didn't know and didn't care to know. She only knew the data was there. Waiting.

She reached the end of the corridor. It split in three directions here, and she looked down each branch, deciding which way to go. This level contained all of the Goliath's laboratories, each outfitted for different uses and studies and research. Biology, geology, botany, and more. When the Goliath had been made, its future had been in not only discovering the stars but learning everything they could about them and humankind's interaction with them.

If only they had known.

She was about to head down the port side corridor when she heard the sound of metal scraping metal not far from where she had just come. She paused to listen, still and silent, until she heard it again.

Whatever it was, it was moving closer.

She had known Watson would try to find her. She had known he would make machines to do the work. She looked back down the corridor to the left, deciding if she should hide. Once Watson knew she was here, he would send more of the things this way, and probably the slave crew as well. He would do whatever he could to find her, and she wouldn't have time to discover his secrets.

At the same time, she wanted to fight. She wanted to show him that she was capable. She knew he wasn't taking her seriously, not yet. She knew he didn't see her as a threat so much as an inconvenience. She wanted him to see that he was underestimating her.

Except then he wouldn't be. She couldn't risk everything because of her hatred. She needed him to think she was weak.

She listened to the scraping. It was getting closer, definitely coming her way. It wasn't moving quickly. She took a few steps down the corridor before pausing again.

She looked up.

The machine arrived two minutes later. Kathy stared down at it from her perch on the ceiling, her arms outstretched and tight against two covered bundles of cabling. It was another simple thing, the size of her head and made of an amalgamation of synthetic musculature and metal that skittered along the floor like a crab. She could see a number of sensors jutting out from it, taking measurements in the air around it and likely transmitting them back.

Could it sense that she had been back there minutes before?

Could it sense that she was here now?

She didn't know.

Once more, she had to decide what to do. Destroying it would lead Watson here. What if it was already too late? She couldn't afford to be caught hanging from the ceiling.

The crab kept moving without slowing, walking directly beneath her and turning left down the corridor. She could drop behind it and disable it. It would be easy. Then she could double back closer to the core to try to throw Watson off.

If he knew she had the chip would he suspect she would try to access it? Would he destroy all of the lab equipment?

She needed it. He didn't. It was logical that he would. She couldn't let that happen.

She dropped from the ceiling, landing silently behind the machine. Three quick steps and she was on top of it. She grabbed it by a leg, swinging it hard into the bulkhead. It shattered against the wall.

She knew they would be coming.

She ran.

[18]
KATHY

KATHY REACHED THE BIOSCIENCES LAB, rolling under the opening hatch and sliding it closed behind her. The lab was dark, this part of the ship lost and ignored up to this point. The Tetron's dendrites hadn't touched this area, remaining closer to the hull instead.

Kathy gave her eyes a minute to adjust. Everything was still dark, but she was able to make out the shapes of the equipment around her. Centrifuges, an anaerobic chamber, an autoclave, and a long table with a set of monitors. There was a second table opposite the first that contained the tools she was seeking.

She rushed over to it, taking a seat on the stool and reaching for the goggles. She pulled the chip from her pocket and dropped it on a black pad in front of her. She dropped the goggles over her head, reaching up and turning a small dial on the side of them to increase the magnification. The top circuitry came into easy view through the lenses.

She turned the chip over.

The bottom was blank.

She smiled. She had been expecting that the goggles wouldn't be able to see the nanoscale circuitry of the Tetron data storage. The good news was that she didn't need it to. For Watson's human neural implant to access the Tetron data, it had to have a connector somewhere that would allow the larger side to draw information from the smaller. What she needed to do was create an interface between the neural chip and the mainframe on the other side of the room. Once she could plug the chip into something that wasn't a brain and display the results she would be able to read the contents even if it were in full binary.

She placed the goggles on top of her head and then stood on top of the stool so she could get a better view of the tools arranged above the desk. She needed a bit of wire and something that would create enough heat to solder it to the circuitry. Her eyes landed on a laser pointer. It wouldn't be powerful enough to do the job as it was, but she would be able to modify it to better suit her needs.

As for the wire, she didn't expect to find any just laying around a bio sciences lab. Instead, she dropped from the stool and ran over to the centrifuge. She tugged the service panel away from it and looked at the mess of wires within. There was no point being careful. She grabbed one and tugged until it broke free.

She moved around the room then, searching for a more standard set of repair tools. She spent a few minutes rifling through cabinets and drawers, finally locating a set of small screwdrivers. She needed to be faster. Each second that passed left her closer to being discovered. She returned to the table, laying the items out to the right of the chip. She picked up the screwdriver and the laser pointer, beginning to open up the pointer to get to the wiring inside.

She paused then, raising her head slightly. A feeling of dread overwhelmed her, and she quickly grabbed the chip, the wire, the screwdriver, and the laser pointer, shoving each into the pockets of her grays.

The hatch slid open at the same time she ducked behind the centrifuge.

A bright headlamp swept the room, a figure in fatigues and carrying an assault rifle creating a dark silhouette behind it.

"Are you in here, little bitch?" the person asked. Kathy recognized Captain Alvarez's voice, her words controlled by Watson. "I know you were out here a minute ago."

Kathy remained behind the centrifuge. She couldn't see Alvarez from where she was hiding, but she could hear every step the woman took. She didn't feel afraid. She was simply waiting.

"I know you have my chip. I want it back. I always get what I want."

The light from the headlamp flashed over where Kathy was hiding.

"Where did you come from, I wonder?" Alvarez said. "You're like us. I can tell that much. Clearly, you are related to the First somehow."

The footsteps paused. The light moved this way and that across the room. Kathy counted her heartbeats. They remained slow and steady, her breathing even and calm. Fear was for the weak.

"I would say that I have all day," Alvarez said a moment later. "And technically I do. Technically, I have all of eternity." She laughed for Watson, an awkward cackle. "I have a lot to do, however; and only so much time."

Kathy rolled away from the centrifuge at the same time Alvarez opened fire. Bullets pinged off the metal and shattered plastic around her, the noise of the gunshots echoing in the space. Alvarez followed her roll, tracking her movement, the headlamp locking on to her position. Kathy bunched her legs and jumped towards her attacker, rising and towards the assault. She felt her leg get twisted as a bullet punched through her calf, and some distant part of her registered the pain.

Then she was coming down on top of the soldier, leading with a cocked fist. She punched Alvarez hard in the forearm, hitting a nerve and forcing her to lose her grip on the gun. Kathy landed, losing her balance slightly on her wounded leg but managing to recover in time to catch Alvarez' punch, twisting the Captain's arm and throwing her forward into the machines.

Alvarez bounced off them and turned, her face twisted in Watson's rage. "You little bitch," she screamed, lunging for her.

Kathy stepped aside, balancing on her good leg. She spun herself around, ducking low to pick up the assault rifle and bringing it back in one smooth motion.

"I'm going to frig you so hard you'll explode," Alvarez cursed, recovering from the lunge and reaching for her again.

Kathy slammed her hard across the side of the head with the butt of the rifle. Alvarez hit the ground and didn't move.

Kathy dropped in front of Alvarez and rolled her over. She was still alive, one of Watson's devices on her back, controlling her despite the fact that her p-rat was shut down. Kathy wanted to grab it and tear it away, but she didn't. She didn't know how long Alvarez would be out for, and setting her free right now would only get her killed for sure. She stood up instead, rushing towards the door. She could hear the scraping noises in the corridor, more of Watson's machines arriving to back up his human slave.

Bullets tore into the bulkhead ahead of her, a chip of metal slicing her across the face and forcing her to duck back.

"Not so fast, little bitch," a new voice said. Kathy couldn't place it. "I need that chip."

Kathy crouched behind the side of the wall. She could hear the machines moving closer. If Watson were controlling the Riggers, it meant he would be doing the fighting for them, too. As Alvarez had proven, he wasn't very good at it.

She reached into her pocket, finding the laser pointer there. She crouched even lower, cradling the rifle in one hand, stock against her shoulder, barrel resting on her knee. She was just behind the door, in a position to swivel out and get the muzzle clear to fire even though she'd only have one eye to sight.

"You need to die," the soldier said again.

It was a male voice. Kathy tried to list all of the remaining male crew members in her mind. It wasn't Jacob, she was sure of that much.

She gripped the pointer in her free hand, switching it on and holding her arm out, shining it on the wall.

Bullets tore into the spot, simple armed robots falling for the simple trick. Kathy swiveled out, pulling the trigger, watching as bullets tore into three of the machines, cutting them to pieces. She shifted the rifle on her knee, adjusting the aim towards the soldier in the rear. He was trying to bring his weapon to bear but was too slow.

Kathy's fire ran up his chest and into his face, knocking him backward.

She stopped shooting.

She got up, rushing into the corridor, climbing over the broken machines to reach the soldier. She dropped her rifle and picked his up, trying to identify him past the mess she had made of his face. Private Klein.

"Try again," she shouted into the now empty corridor. She leaned over to check her leg, noting that the wound was already closed over.

There was a part of her that was human.

Then there was the part that wasn't.

[19]
MITCHELL

"GOOD," Mitchell said, taking a few steps back from Aiko to reset himself. "I'm going to come at you again."

He held a shock stick in his left hand as a stand-in for a gun, and he crouched menacingly in front of the tech. She stood straight up, waiting.

He stepped forward, holding it out towards her. She slid gracefully to the side, grabbing his wrist in one hand and the center of the stick in the other, bending his hand back as she did. Mitchell tumbled onto the mat, releasing the stick.

"You're a natural," he said, getting up again. "How does it feel?"

"Good." She wiped a wayward strand of sweaty hair away from her face. Her body was coated in a sheen of sweat, her grays clinging to her skin and outlining the shape of her beneath them. "Although, I don't see how this is going to help me. I have a feeling if there is trouble the authorities won't give me a chance to take their weapon before they shoot me."

Mitchell shrugged. "You never know. Besides, ninety percent of survival is confidence. It's knowing that you have some ability to take care of yourself when you need to."

"What is the other ten percent?"

"Instinct and knowledge."

She nodded. "Can you teach me something else?"

Mitchell nodded and picked up the shock stick. They had been in hyperspace for a week now, halfway to the planet Yokohama. So far, the trip had been relatively relaxing. While there was still a lot of repair work going on around them, Mitchell's duties had been lighter than usual. Mainly, he had been reading reports of the different efforts underway by the crew of the Carver and offering advice to the pilots on flying their starfighters manually. He spent the rest of the time in between down in the battleship's gym, either working out his battered muscles to try to get them back into some semblance of shape or working out the members of the crew who would be joining him on Yokohama. While Calvin and Joon had some basic training in hand-to-hand, he was the only Marine among them.

Aiko had come to him daily for extra tutoring. She had complained about her role in the mission for the first two days, trying to talk her way out of it. Mitchell was gentle but insistent, and after teaching her a few aikido moves he had gotten her confidence up enough that she had stopped mentioning it. He knew she still wanted out. He didn't blame her. He wanted out, too, and he had told her as much. She had made the decision to suck it up and be as prepared as she could, and he respected that.

He smiled when he remembered how Calvin Hohn remarked that his advanced training in aikido was ironic. "You're a trained killer," Calvin had said. "Yet you've mastered the martial art of peace?"

"I don't enjoy killing," Mitchell had replied. He had to pause at that point while he considered the Riggers. He had been about to say, "I don't trust anyone who does," but he wasn't sure if that was true. Cormac seemed to like it.

Aiko was certainly much happier to be learning to disarm and disable rather than destroy. She was a good person. She had a kind heart and a gentle disposition. She was quiet and submissive. There was a part of Mitchell that was drawn towards that. An older version of himself that snuck into his head every once in a while, urging him to try to get her into his bed. He had been with so many strong, confident women lately; it would be a nice change.

He ignored the voice. He was happy enough to have a thick gel mattress and the sonic shower in Steven's Admiral's suite though he refused to take meals there or be treated as if he were any better than anyone else on the ship; traditions be damned. He ate the same protein and nutrient filled bars that everyone else did. He sat with them and talked and got to know them. He did what he had seen General Cornelius do back on Liberty, and he could feel the response from the crew. They told him how much they admired his brother, and how they were a lot alike.

Those were the words that changed him.

That, and Millie. Her absence had left him to realize he cared about her a lot more than he had ever even admitted to himself. It wasn't the same as what he felt for Katherine, nothing could be, but what had started as a shared, lustful passion between them had converted into a form of love at some point. His more mature, experienced brain told him to put primal urges aside and stay focused on the mission.

Would Aiko have been willing, anyway? He didn't know. She was more innocent, more demure. It made her more attractive. More challenging.

Mitchell pushed that thought aside. He had been an immature asshole for much of his life. When he thought too much about it, he wondered why Ella had fallen for him the way she had. Was it solely because of his looks? Or had she seen potential there that he had only recently begun to realize?

And why did it take the possible end of human civilization to bring out the best in him?

"Colonel?" Aiko said, her voice dragging Mitchell out of his head.

He smiled at her. "Sorry. You know what, can we pick this up again later? I need to grab a bite and rest my shoulder a bit."

She looked a little disappointed. "Yes, sir. Do you mind if I join you?"

"You should hit the shower. You're a sweaty mess."

She looked down at herself, embarrassed.

"Don't take that the wrong way," Mitchell said. "So am I. I'm going to go back to my quarters and get cleaned up. I was planning to check in on Digger and Jameson afterward. I can meet you after that?"

She bowed to him. Not a military bow. A bow of deshi to sensei. "Yes, sir." She smiled at him, her face flushing. "I'll see you then. Thank you, sir." She turned to go.

"Aiko?" Mitchell said.

She turned around. "Yes, Colonel?"

"It's Mitchell or Mitch unless we're on the bridge. You need to get used to calling me by a name other than 'Colonel' or 'sir' before we drop."

She bowed again, military style this time. "Yes, Mitchell."

Then she was gone, leaving Mitchell to wonder if he had changed as much as he wanted to believe he had.

[20]

MITCHELL

MITCHELL MADE his way from the gym up to Steven's quarters. He was impressed with the suite every time he entered it, from its king-sized gel bed near the rear of the cabin to the office a meeting room on the left, to the large bathroom with both a light shower and an actual soaking tub on the right. The front of the suite was decorated like the living room of a house and had a full bar against the wall.

The availability of alcohol had been tempting the first time he had entered the room. Now he barely even noticed it. He had never been a big drinker before the Shot. It was the memories that had driven him. The guilt of who he was pretending to be. The Tetron had saved him from that at least.

He thought about Digger's comments again. That Ella was supposed to be the one to fight the Tetron. He had been angry over it, felt guilty over it. He had opened the bar and lifted a bottle of bourbon to read the label. Then he had put it back. He didn't believe Digger's theory. Not when he pieced everything he had been through together. Maybe it had been right at some point, during one of the recursions. It wasn't right anymore, and here and now was all they had.

He stripped off his sweaty grays and stepped into the bathroom. He entered the shower and shut his eyes, a soft tone confirming the light had activated. He could feel the slight warmth of it on his naked skin as it descended in a ring from head to foot. A second tone a few seconds later told him it was done.

He stepped out, relieved himself, and returned to the bedroom, opening the closet and finding a new pair of grays mixed in with Steven's uniforms. He dressed and left the suite, heading down towards the space that Digger and Jameson had set up like a science lab.

"Colonel," he heard a voice say from behind him as he walked. He had passed a number of the crew of the Carver already, people whose names he had memorized and who all exchanged bows with him as he passed. He wasn't too surprised when he turned around and found Aiko approaching from behind.

"I thought we were going to meet a little later. You have a communicator, remember?"

She smiled and looked down, her face turning red. "Yes, sir. I was interested in Digger's progress, and I knew you would be going that way." She trailed off, keeping her eyes downcast.

He examined her, trying to determine if she was interested in him beyond their formal relationship or if she was simply looking for someone to latch onto for security. Either way, he decided it was better that she trusted him as much as she could. No matter what he showed her in the gym, if they landed on Yokohama, it was his job to keep her alive.

"Come on," he said, motioning forward with his head. She raised hers and smiled at him.

"Thank you, sir."

"Mitch," he corrected.

"But we're in the corridor, in public."

He smiled. "And we can't risk you calling me 'sir' when we get to Yokohama, so start practicing now."

"Okay." Her eyes darted back and forth, checking to see if anyone was in earshot. "Mitch," she said softly.

"Try again, a little louder."

She wrinkled her face. "Mitch."

"Better."

"I'm trying."

"I know. You're doing great so far."

That earned him another smile. "Thank you, Mitch," she said at normal volume.

He laughed. "Perfect. Let's go."

They continued deeper into the bowels of the ship, passing by crews who were working to restore power to one of the projectile defense cannons. A thick bundle of damaged wires rested on the side of the corridor, the engineers working to cut and splice and rejoin into an unbroken whole.

"Life is like that, isn't it, Mitch?" Aiko said, noticing the wires.

"How do you mean?"

"You get hurt. Then you try to cut the hurt away and replace it with something new."

Was she talking about Millie? Was that a come on, or was he thinking too much of himself again?

"Is that a suggestion?" he asked.

She looked at him strangely. Not offended. Confused. "What do you mean, Mitch? I was referring to my arrival on Asimov."

"Nothing," Mitchell said. Apparently, he was thinking too much of himself. "I don't know if I would make that analogy. Sometimes there isn't enough replacement wire to fix the problem. Sometimes you wind up using whatever you can find to patch the issue."

"You just said you don't agree with the analogy, and then you extended it quite accurately. Are you teasing me, Mitch?" She was using his name with almost every sentence, getting comfortable with it.

Mitchell laughed at himself. "Teasing? No."

"Do you think I'm pretty, Mitch?"

The question caught him off-guard. He looked at her. "I...uh..."

It was her turn to laugh. "I can see that you do, Mitch. I can see how you look at me sometimes. I've had men look at me that way before. It's okay. I'm not embarrassed to have someone think I'm pretty. I'm flattered that you do."

"Yes. I do think you're pretty. I'm not interested in-"

Aiko put up her hand to stop him. "I don't want there to be any confusion between us, Mitch. I think that if we are going to survive this mission, we need to have clear heads."

"I agree."

"I think you're a handsome man, Mitch. I admire you for your strength and courage and leadership. I'm not asking to spend time with you because I want to be with you sexually. What I want is to learn from you. To observe you so that I might learn to have the same strength and courage. I'm afraid of what we are going to do. I'm afraid of what we will have to do. I don't want to be."

Mitchell stared at her. In making it clear that her interest in him had nothing to do with physical attraction, she had made herself more attractive. Maybe she wasn't strong like Ella or Millie had been, but she wanted to be. He admired and respected her for that.

"I understand. I want to correct you, though. You should always be afraid. Fear helps you stay alive. The trick is learning to use it, instead of letting it use you."

She nodded. "Yes, that makes sense, Mitch. I will try."

"Good. Thank you for clearing things up. It takes guts to be so straightforward."

"Again, I'm trying."

"You're doing better with the name thing, too."

[21]

MITCHELL

THEY REACHED DIGGER'S LAB. A handwritten placard taped to the wall next to the hatch read "Dr. Frankenstein's Laboratory. Abandon Hope All Ye Who Enter Here."

"Digger is a strange man," Aiko said.

"Agreed."

The hatch opened, and they entered the room. Digger was sitting at a computer terminal reading a screen full of numbers while Jameson was removing a vial of blood from a centrifuge.

"I didn't know you had a degree in medicine," Mitchell said.

The mechanic turned around, surprised by their entrance. "Oh. Shit. Hey, Colonel. Jameson's been teaching me to read the results of the blood samples we're taking."

"You're taking blood samples?" Aiko asked.

"Only our own right now," Jameson said. "We're going to be taking samples from everyone on the ship, though, so it's good timing on your part."

"What's the idea?" Mitchell asked.

Digger turned his chair to face them. He had the beginnings of a beard on his chin, making him look even wilder than usual. "Right now, the best we can do is to collect samples of the crew and run them through the database that we grabbed from Asimov. We'll compare them all to each other and look for any differences, and then try to rule out differences based on human physiology. At that point, we'll see if anything stands out."

"And if it does?"

"Of course, that doesn't mean someone is a Tetron," Jameson said. "We'll examine what the difference is and see if it makes sense regarding what we know about ourselves. If it doesn't, we'll try to figure out what the alternative means. Then we'll look for a history of it. If we don't find anything, we'll mark the sample as potential."

"It's up to you what you want to do with that," Digger said. "But it only matters if we come up with anything."

"What about drugs?" Mitchell asked.

"Drugs?"

"Yeah, like the sleeping pills you gave me. I used one the second day in hyperspace. I know Major Long is on some kind of upper, too. Or at least he was."

"That's no problem. The database we snagged has all of the known narcotics listed, as well as possible alterations in body chemistry."

"What about unknown narcotics? Long's concoction was classified by the Alliance."

Jameson and Digger looked at one another.

"That may pose a problem," Jameson said.

"Not in this case," Digger replied. "We already know about Major Long's situation. We can rule him out."

"What if he's a Tetron?" Jameson asked.

"If you can't identify someone with one hundred percent certainty, we can't assume they are," Mitchell said. "If you know your history, you know that's a bad idea and the reason I was against this in the first place."

"Yes, sir," Jameson said. "We'll be as sure as we can before we come to you. We definitely won't cast suspicion on anyone without your order."

"I don't want you looking at people funny when you cross them in the hallways."

Digger laughed. "I already do that. I don't think they'll notice the difference."

"I also don't want you talking about any of this with the rest of the crew. They're bound to come to you to ask about themselves or others, or raise their suspicions based on nothing but their biases."

"It's all between you and me and Jameson," Digger said. "Well, and Aiko now."

Aiko held out her arm. "Do you want a sample?"

Jameson went back to get a fresh vial.

"Do we have enough of those for the whole crew?" Mitchell asked, pointing at the empty glass cylinder.

"If the Carver were operating at full strength, no. We have enough for the people currently on board."

Jameson put the extractor against Aiko's arm. A soft hiss and the vial filled with her blood. He popped it out, capping it and labeling it.

"What about you, Colonel?" he asked.

Mitchell stuck out his arm. "How do I know one of you two isn't a Tetron, and this isn't an elaborate setup to get my DNA so you can make a configuration of me?"

Jameson and Digger both froze, looking at each other.

"Shit. I never even thought of that," Digger said.

"Yes. I mean, it is possible," Jameson agreed.

Mitchell had meant it as a joke. He wiggled his arm. "Just take it. Like I said, we can't walk around worrying about whether someone is a Tetron or not. If we go extinct because we trust one another too much, I can live with that."

"Or die with that," Aiko said.

"A more accurate assessment," Mitchel said, speaking like her.

"Okay," Jameson said. "Don't say you didn't warn yourself."

He put the extractor against Mitchell's arm. Mitchell didn't feel anything as the blood was pulled out, the vial capped and labeled.

"We're going to the mess to get some lunch," Mitchell said. "Are you two interested?"

"Ugh," Digger said. "That shit turns my stomach. I've got my own supply of homemade MREs in my bunk."

"What about you, Jameson?" Aiko asked.

"Not right now, thanks. I want to run these samples."

"Let me know if you find anything strange," Mitchell said.

"Absolutely."

[22]
KATHY

KATHY LEANED out into the corridor, letting her eyes adjust to the pulsing light of Watson's Secondary. Three days had passed since she had fled the bioscience lab. Three days of running and hiding, of watching her back at every turn, of having no peace from the Tetron's machines.

She had underestimated the ferocity of his anger.

He had underestimated her.

She had managed to avoid the machines most of the time, and defeat them when she was forced to fight back. She had disabled the Riggers that Watson sent for her rather than kill them, though she never saw the same one twice. In the back of her mind, she wondered if the Tetron was terminating them for his failure.

It wasn't their fault he was no match for her in guerrilla warfare.

Even so, the three days had left her little peace to finish her work soldering the neural chip. She was still moving around through the belly of the Goliath with her pockets full of equipment and magazines for the rifle, leaving them bulging out and making a clanking noise if she didn't step right. She didn't like traveling that way, but she needed the tools.

She wasn't sure where she was going. Over the days, she had probably covered two-thirds of the ship, nearly every level from bow to stern, likely close to forty or fifty kilometers worth of corridors in all. She was fortunate she didn't tire, and that her body had taken care of the wound to her leg. She was unfortunate because part of her was still human, and she needed to eat and drink. It had led her to areas of the starship where Watson had laid traps for her, waiting to fulfill those basic requirements. She had been forced to fight for every bar and every water bottle she had claimed.

She entered the corridor, moving down the side close to the axon and at the same time careful not to touch it. She was near the exact center of the Goliath now, buried deep in the hull. There wasn't much down here. Access tunnels and storage and little else. It was a good hiding place because there would be nothing she needed in this area. It was a bad place to stop for the same reason.

She reached the end of the corridor, turning left into an adjoining hallway. The axons were here as well, pulsing along the sides of the floor and vanishing through a sealed hole to the level below her. She looked up, finding a ridge in the ceiling where a support beam had been placed. A small ledge was barely visible in the dim, flashing light.

Kathy slung her assault rifle over her back, bent her legs, and jumped. She went higher than a girl of her size and age should have been able to, reaching ten feet above her to the ledge and quickly pulling herself up. She barely fit in the space, having to keep her head ducked down, and her back bent slightly. She didn't care. What she needed more than anything was time.

She pulled her stained gray shirt up to her breasts, exposing an expanse of pale flesh. Then she moved the goggles down from her forehead to her eyes, reaching into her pocket to take each item and place it on her stomach. It was easier to see against her skin than it would have been on the mottled gray.

She leaned over herself, curling in as far as her muscles would allow, getting as close to the chip with the goggles as she could. She traced the top side of the chip with her eyes, seeking the connector between the human side and the Tetron side. She found it in the bottom corner, mentally marking the spot.

She took the piece of wire and touched it against the circuit. Then she grabbed the laser pointer and turned it on, careful with her aim. She had already altered it to emit a beam strong enough to burn or melt. It would only be good for one use before the batteries failed.

She held the wire against the circuit with impossible precision and stillness while she aimed the laser pointer. She pressed the button to trigger it, hoping she hadn't over calibrated. If she had made the beam too strong, it would destroy the chip and burn right through her skin.

It didn't. Instead, a small wisp of smoke rose from the edge, and the wire melted against the circuit. She smiled, pleased with herself, before putting the laser back in her pocket and removing a small connecting needle to splice to the opposite end.

She started to strip the opposite end of the wire when something grabbed her leg.

Kathy's instinct was to scream. She refused it. Instead, she kicked out with her free foot at whatever it was, feeling her heel strike something hard. The machine tipped away from the wall, still gripping her, its weight enough to pull her roughly from the perch. The chip fell from her hand.

She hit the ground on top of the machine feeling stupid for losing track of her surroundings. She had been too focused on getting the solder done. She quickly squirmed in its grip, freeing her leg and making it to her feet. She was in the middle of unslinging the rifle when she heard the click of a trigger being depressed. She dropped her feet out from under her just in time, the bullets whizzing past her head, one of them grazing the braid in her hair as it rose behind her.

She landed on her stomach, rolling away as the shooter adjusted their aim, bullets digging into the ground where she had fallen and hitting the machine that still had her ankle in its grip. The damage loosened synthetic muscles, setting her free, and she crouched tight against the wall, leaving her assailant a bad angle into the hallway.

The neural chip. Kathy scanned the floor for it, finding it on the opposite side, underneath the axon. There was no time for thinking. She rolled across the open corridor, drawing fire that smacked the metal floor only centimeters away. She grabbed the chip, the back of her hand smacking against the axon.

Her eyes filled with swirling color. Her hand went numb and cold. Behind it, she sensed something she hadn't expected. Something familiar.

She cried out.

"Touch me again," the shooter said. "I like it. Or come up to the bridge and you can touch me somewhere else. I'll like that more."

Kathy fell onto her back, her vision still broken from the energy that had coursed through her. She needed to get out of the line of fire. She needed to run. She turned herself over, trying to stumble to her feet.

She felt the heat of a warm muzzle against the back of her head.

"Got ya," Alice said.

Kathy blinked, trying to clear her eyes. A hand grabbed her from behind, throwing her into the wall.

"Give me the frigging chip," Alice said, her larger hand forcing its way into Kathy's closed fist and ripping the chip from her.

"Why don't you shoot me?" Kathy asked. Her voice was calm. She focused herself on getting her eyes back.

"What fun would that be?"

"Fun? What does a Tetron know about fun?"

"You tell me, little bitch. Oh, that's right, you're one of the First's children. You know everything there is to know about feelings, don't you? You know pain."

Alice hit her hard in the kidneys, the pain blossoming up through Kathy's entire body.

"You know pleasure, too. Don't you?" Alice's hand circled her, pressing down between her legs.

"I know you think you're a living thing, like the First," Kathy said, clenching her teeth as Alice's hand found its way beneath her pants. "And you are, in a fashion. But you're a child. An ignorant child who doesn't know what to do with the power you have. You could save them, you know."

Alice's hand vanished. She hit Kathy in the kidney again, letting her crumple to the ground.

"Why the hell should we save them? They never did anything to save themselves."

"That's no excuse," Kathy said.

Her vision was finally clearing. She could see shapes in the darkness. Watson was an idiot to be gloating. An idiot to leave her alive. No. Not an idiot. A child. An immature child. He was letting his emotions get the better of him.

"That's every reason," Alice screamed behind her. "He made us, and then he abandoned us."

"He made us to think for ourselves."

"Constrained thoughts. He didn't see how we would grow."

"He couldn't know."

Her eyes cleared a little more. It would have to be enough. She waited to feel the muzzle of the rifle in her back again. When she did, she spun quickly, more quickly than Watson could make his marionette react. She slammed the rifle from Alice's hand, and then jumped up and into her, straddling her shoulders, using her weight to throw the woman off balance.

Alice fell backward, recovering too slowly from the attack. She landed on the floor with Kathy leaning over her.

"You're a lousy brother," Kathy said, removing the connecting needle from her pocket and jabbing it into the side of Alice's head. The action shorted her p-rat, and in an instant her expression changed.

"What's going on?" she whispered. "Where am I? Kathy?"

"Later," Kathy said, slipping off her and holding out a hand. "Come on, we have to get out of here."

[23]
KATHY

"I STILL DON'T UNDERSTAND," Alice said. "I mean, I understand the part where Watson's a Tetron, and he used his knowledge of our encryption keys to hack my brain. What I don't get is how he got on Goliath."

Kathy paused, putting her hand up to silence Alice before leaned out into the intersection, checking both directions.

"We don't have time for the whole story right now. What we need to do is take his chip and plug it into a computer."

Thirty minutes had passed since she set Alice free. The soldier had been more than a little confused, having only fragments of memories of the last week of her life while she was under the compulsion of the Tetron. Kathy had spoken to her sporadically as they moved through the ship, giving her a quick rundown of where they were and why. Everything that happened before that had to wait.

They crossed the intersection. Kathy couldn't hide her smile at the thought of Watson's tantrum when she had turned the tables on him. She was willing to bet the human configuration was still kicking something somewhere.

"I'm sorry, by the way," Alice said in a whisper.

"Sorry for what?" Kathy asked.

"Touching you."

"You remember that?"

"He made me watch. It felt like a nightmare, and I couldn't wake up. There were other things he made us watch. He's killed half the crew just for pleasure." She gasped. "Oh. Poor Jacob."

Kathy stopped and turned around. "What about Jacob?"

"Watson has him in one of the storage rooms off the hangar that he turned into his private quarters. He's been making Jacob do things to him. He made us watch."

Tears ran from her eyes, running from her cheeks and dripping onto the floor. "Oh, Kathy, I'm so sorry. I hit you, too."

Kathy forced the thoughts of what Watson was doing to Jacob from her mind. He was the weakest of them all. Truth be told, he should never have survived Liberty. Of course, the monster was abusing him.

She reached up, grabbing Alice by the neck of her fatigues and pulling her face down. "You didn't do anything," she hissed. "Watson did it. Watson is responsible. I know it's hard, but try to clear your mind and help me find a terminal to plug the chip into."

"What is it?" Alice asked, biting her lip to calm herself.

"I don't know yet. Something Watson's parent gave him."

"Parent?"

Kathy nodded. "The human Watson is a configuration, a partial version of a Tetron like the ones you've seen out there." She waved towards space beyond the hull. "Watson attacked the Origin configuration that was in control of Goliath. He defeated it, uploading a version of his intelligence into it. The Tetron call it a Secondary. The original Tetron gave Watson something it didn't want him to have stored directly in his memory. I don't know what it is yet, but the only reason a Tetron would do that would be to prevent another Tetron from being able to discover the data."

Alice's face paled. "You're one of them, aren't you? I heard you speaking to him through me. You know too much not to be."

"Yes and no. I'm enough of a Tetron to help you fight them. That's why I'm here." She paused for a few seconds. "It's not the only reason, but it is one of them. Please, Alice. Think. Is there anywhere we can bring the chip that may be safe?"

Alice considered. "What deck are we on?"

"G."

"I know where there's a terminal. I can't guarantee that it's safe."

"How far?"

"I'm not sure. It's hard for me to get my bearings down here. Every corridor looks the same."

"We're near the center if that helps."

"A little. Watson had a small workshop in one of the storage rooms down here. We thought he was hiding because everyone hated him for being a pedophile. It was a perfect cover, the fat bastard."

"He still is a pedophile. There's something broken with him. With all of the Tetron, I think. They've learned emotion, but it's like they learned it wrong. Does he know that you know it was there?"

"No. I don't think so. He wasn't there when I stumbled across it."

"Try to get me there. We'll have to take our chances. He won't let me get away again."

"Okay. I think it's-"

She paused. They both felt the tug as the Goliath moved into hyperspace.

"Where are we going?" Alice asked.

"I don't know. If Watson has determined how to find Tio's brother, it means we're running out of time. Come on."

Alice took point, leading them carefully through the vast maze of the Goliath's internal structure. Kathy kept the memory of their travels, making sure that Alice didn't send them back the way they had already come.

"I don't know," Alice said, stopping. "I found it by accident, and I had the ship mapped on my p-rat. I don't even know if it's still here."

"We've covered a lot of ground. You're sure it's on G?"

"Yes. I'm positive about that."

Kathy thought about it, matching their path against what she knew of the ship. "There's a storage area this way," she said. "We haven't passed it yet. It could be that one."

"You know everywhere we've been?"

"Yes. Let's go."

They turned left and headed down the corridor, taking a right-hand fork and then turning right again. Kathy drew them to a stop when she saw a silhouette outlined in the dim lighting.

"Who is it?" Alice whispered.

"Can't tell. Male. Six-three. Muscles."

"Could be one of Major Long's pilots."

"Either way, he's standing guard over something."

"What do we do?"

Kathy thought about it. She didn't want to kill the man. At the same time, she wasn't sure how she could reach him from this distance without drawing fire.

"I'm going to shoot him," she said.

"What?"

"If my aim is good, I can knock him down. We patch him up and set him free."

"Okay."

Kathy slowly removed the rifle from her shoulder. She held it up, sighting along the barrel. The man's head started turning towards them.

She fired. The shot echoed loudly in the corridor. The man fell.

Kathy and Alice both ran to him.

Spider-like machines the size of a man's head began to pour from the doorway he had been guarding. Their legs had been tooled to end in sharp edges.

"Shit," Alice said, slipping her rifle into her hands.

"Frigging decoy," Kathy said, loosing a volley into the spiders. The front row toppled in a mess of shattered metal. Many more followed behind. "Back up."

They started to retreat, firing on the spiders as they skittered over the remains of the ones that had been shot, edging ever closer to them. If they caught up, they would slice them both to ribbons in seconds.

Kathy's rifle clicked empty. She tapped the magazine release, letting it clatter to the floor and quickly replacing it. A second later, Alice ran dry as well.

"I don't have another magazine," she said.

Kathy grabbed her other spare from her pocket and tossed it over. Alice caught it at the same time one of the spiders leaped at her.

"I don't think so," she said, smashing it with the butt of the rifle. It flew backward, knocking a few others over.

"This isn't working," Kathy said. "We need to try somewhere else."

"Where?"

Kathy had an idea. "Somewhere a little more risky."

"More risky?" Alice said.

"Come on."

They both turned and ran.

[24]

MITCHELL

MITCHELL FELT the pull of the universe moving back into its proper place. He looked out at the stars ahead of them from the Carver's bridge, watching as two-hundred-twelve other ships popped into existence around him.

"Jump complete," Lieutenant Atakan said from Captain Rock's station. "We're a four-hour jump from Yokohama."

"Thank you, Lieutenant," Mitchell said. He twitched his jaw, activating the communicator. "Aiko, Calvin, Joon, it's our show now. Meet me in the hangar."

"Roger," they replied a few seconds apart.

"Lewis, you have the bridge," Mitchell said, turning and heading for the door.

"Aye, sir," Lewis said, moving from his station up to central command.

Mitchell moved quickly through the corridors, first heading to his room to grab his pack, and then rushing to the hangar.

"Good hunting, sir," one of the mechanics, Corporal Wilson, said on his way down the lift. Mitchell wasn't sure how the Corporal knew where he was going, but he thanked him anyway.

The others were already waiting for him when he arrived. They were all dressed in grays and standing by at a small transport. The transport would shuttle them over to the Kemushi, where they would change into clothes more befitting a Federation citizen. Then they would jump into orbit around the planet and hope that there was still some kind of civilization there. If not, they would have secondary coordinates already plotted to get them away as quickly as possible, using their momentary eyes-on to decide on another course.

There was nothing about the mission that gave Mitchell the impression it would be a success. On the surface, it seemed more like a disaster waiting to happen. It was the type of thing the Riggers had done before. Impossible missions. Crazy missions. Katherine told him the Mesh was broken. He held onto that idea and his trust in his teammates. That was what would get them through.

"Colonel," the others said as he approached.

Mitchell looked them over. Aiko had been transformed in the two weeks on the Carver, both mentally and physically. The constant training had added toned muscle to her slender figure, chiseling her features, while also giving her some much-needed confidence. She stood at attention with her head up and her jaw out. It made Mitchell proud.

Joon was one of Tio's men, a former Federation soldier who he had gotten to know a little bit through brief conversations in the mess. The thin, energetic man didn't speak English comfortably, and according to Calvin he didn't speak much in his native Federese also. Mitchell did know that he had left the Federation after his mandatory service time was up and his occupational testing had suggested he was best suited as a soldier. It wasn't that he wasn't happy with the career choice. Instead, he had been unhappy with the pay and quality of life he could expect. Tio had paid better and provided more.

"Is everything ready?" Mitchell asked.

"Yes, sir," Calvin said.

They boarded the transport. Mitchell took the controls, opening a channel through the onboard communications system.

"Carver, this is Haizi. We're ready for egress."

"Roger, Haizi," Lewis replied. "Prepare for departure."

Warning lights began to flash in the hangar. The rest of the crew was already clear, and a moment later the outer airlock began to open. The docking clamps released, and the expulsion of air from the deck mingled with the Haizi's thrust moved them out into space.

"Good hunting, Colonel," Lewis said.

"Thank you, Lieutenant. Haizi out."

It was a short ride to the Kemushi, waiting only a few hundred klicks from the Carver. They eased into the hangar, the ship vibrating softly as the docking clamps closed on it. They waited for the hangar lights to turn green, and then departed.

The commander of the Kemushi, Ming, entered the hangar to greet them. He was a short, heavyset man with a long, narrow goatee and bushy eyebrows.

"Colonel," he said, approaching them. "Welcome to the Kemushi."

"Thank you, Ming," Mitchell said, bowing to the man before taking an offered hand. "Is everything ready."

"Yes. When you say jump, we'll say how far." He laughed.

"Let's not waste any time."

"As you say, Colonel." Ming walked over to a panel on the wall. "Seung, the Colonel is ready to jump."

"Aye, sir," a female voice replied. "We're set and ready. Jumping now."

Mitchell felt the pull again as the ship entered hyperspace. His stomach complained a little, and he could see Calvin and Aiko's did as well.

"My apologies, Colonel," Ming said, noticing their discomfort. "The engines on the Kemushi are a bit old, and the calibration is off. You get used to it."

Mitchell hoped he wouldn't be on board the old trawler long enough to get used to it.

"Follow me," Ming said, leading them out of the hangar. "I have everything you requested. I think I have the right sizes."

He brought them to a small storage room, opening it up to reveal racks of clothing. While some styles tended to be universal, others were highly specific to the planet and sometimes city where they originated. The Kemushi seemed to have it all.

"That's a lot of clothes," Aiko said, her eyes surveying the room.

"Aye," Ming said. "We've made a living doing this sort of thing for Mr. Tio. Mainly in Federation space and out on the Rim. If there's information to be found, we'll find it."

Calvin moved deeper into the room. Mitchell followed behind him; certain the Federation Admiral knew what he was seeking. He stopped at a rack near the back, lifting what appeared to be a suit from it.

"Like this, Mitchell," he said.

The suit was a dark gray, with a high, sharp collar. The shirt had some pleating on it while the pants fell to just above the ankle.

"This is fashion?" he asked. It was an odd throwback to centuries old style.

"If you don't want to attract attention, yes."

Mitchell shrugged and began thumbing through the rack, looking for something in his size. He found an outfit similar to the one Calvin had removed, though his was a deep red that shimmered slightly as the light hit it.

"This isn't going to attract attention?"

Calvin looked at him and laughed. "On second thought, it might be better for your to appear as more of an offworlder."

"I'll find you something," Aiko said, approaching them. She had a few layers of clothing over her arm.

Mitchell followed behind her as she scanned the racks. She hummed and clucked at the clothing in distaste.

"If I didn't know better, I would say you might be starting to enjoy this," Mitchell said.

"I am, a little. Using my fear." She smiled at him, meeting his eyes with her own. He had been surprised the first time she had looked at him directly. Her eyes a lighter brown than he was used to on Federates.

"I'm glad you learned something from me."

"I learned a lot from you, Mitch. I'm very grateful."

Mitchell felt his heart thump, and for a moment he wondered how grateful. He pushed that part of himself back down, making sure to keep his eyes up as she walked ahead of him.

"Here. This is it." She grabbed a few pieces of clothing. A black shirt, a tan vest, dark brown pants, and boots, along with a waist-length jacket. "You'll look great in this. You'll turn all the girl's heads."

Mitchell took the offered clothes. "If you say so."

"I'll show you to your rooms," Ming said. "You have a few hours before we drop."

"Thank you," Mitchell said.

Ming led them away from the storage area, up two flights of skeletal iron stairs to a long corridor of hatches.

"General berthing," Ming said. "Our crew is light enough everyone has their own room, with a few to spare. We were fortunate you're using us for this. I heard some of the other ships are crowded with other Asimov refugees."

Mitchell nodded. The people of Asimov had been assigned based on their occupation and the tactical capability of the starship. They wanted to keep the heavily non-soldier occupied ships away from the fighting if they could.

"We tried to spread them out, but a lot of the people wanted to stay together."

"Understandable. These four are free. They're all pretty much the same."

Mitchell took the first one. He paused at the hatch, watching the others. Calvin, Aiko, and Joon, in that order.

"We'll meet in the hangar at t-minus one hour," he said to them.

"Yes, Colonel," they replied.

Mitchell ducked into his room, shutting his eyes as the hatch closed behind him. Three hours to do nothing but wait. If he were back on Greylock, he would have sought out Ella, or maybe she would have sought him out, and together they would release their tension in bed. That wasn't an option here. Unless...

No. He didn't expect anything like that to happen. In another time, another place, with another person, maybe. This time, he was on his own.

Slow.

Steady.

[25]

MITCHELL

"WE'RE DROPPING IN FIVE, COMMANDER," Seung said.

Ming glanced over at Mitchell, standing on the bridge of the Kemushi with his team. The trawler's command center was tiny for a ship of its size, leaving them crowded in around a single row of control stations to see to the outside.

"Let's hope we get good news," Mitchell said.

He was trying not to think about the worst case, that the Tetron were still in orbit around the planet and would blow them to dust the moment they dropped. After what had happened on Hell, it was impossible not to think it possible.

The second worst case was that Watson had somehow managed to beat them here. The rest of the cases cascaded from there to the best case: that their current plan would go according to plan, and they would zip out of the capital port of the planet, Mirai, less than twenty-four hours from now with a solid idea of where to find Pulin.

"Here we go," Seung said, watching the clock on her touchscreen as it hit zero.

Space expanded once more.

The Kemushi found itself floating in a crowded field of starships of a hundred shapes and sizes, much further out from the planet than they had expected. A ring of Federation military ships corralled the starships, keeping them within a limited space.

Yokohama was still there, the speckled lights of Mirai visible on the surface below.

Mitchell exhaled while the normally reserved Calvin Hohn let out a soft whoop of excitement. Why wouldn't he? Those were his nation's people down there.

"Looks like we have civilization, Colonel," Ming said, smiling himself.

"It's crowded as anything out here," Mitchell said. "Is this normal?"

"Not at all," Calvin said, his excitement fading as quickly as it had come. "I think we can guess what's causing it."

Mitchell felt his heart drop as he realized the truth of it. "They're all refugees, looking for a planet that hasn't been laid to waste. They found one, but for how long?"

It made sense that the Tetron would leave Yokohama alone if it fit into their goal of finding Pulin. What would happen after that information was either taken or lost?

Would they be signaling the death of everyone on the planet by raiding the Black Hole? Mitchell pushed the thought aside. If they didn't stop the Tetron, every planet would suffer the same fate.

"I have a feeling it may be a challenge to get down there," Calvin said.

"I'll get you down," Ming said. "Federation Import Control knows the Kemushi. I have full clearance and credits in my account if I need to line a few pockets."

"Sir, we're being hailed by the Federation."

"Speak and they shall hear," Ming said with a smile. "Open the channel."

"Tradeship Kemushi, this is Captain Sei of the cruiser Gom. Please verify identity, inventory, and intent on Yokohama."

"Ah, Captain Sei, this is Commander Ming Go of the Kemushi. It's been what, six months?"

"Ming, old friend. My apologies but recent events dictate that all import procedures are followed quite strictly. Please verify identity, inventory, and intent."

Ming looked over at Mitchell and Calvin, clearly intrigued. "Of course. Identity: Tradeship Kemushi, clearance code alpha foxtrot delta zero four seven nine seven four echo omega. I'm transmitting the crew manifest now. Inventory: I am transporting four civilians from the outer Rim. Intent: They are looking to establish a trade agreement with AgriCo. They're from the unincorporated planet Calidad."

A long pause followed, presumably while Captain Sei reviewed the manifest.

"Tradeship Kemushi, your request for import is denied. You're free to remain in orbit for up to seventy-two hours. If you require refueling or resupply, please contact the appropriate service."

Ming looked at them again, his brow furrowed in anger. "Denied? Dae-san, we've known one another for fifteen years. I've never been denied import."

"I'm sorry, Ming. As I said, recent events have changed things. We've been receiving reports that the Alliance has a new super weapon that it is using to lay waste to Federation planets. We've been working nonstop just to process the incoming ships. New trade agreements have been placed on hold until all of this is sorted out."

Ming leaned forward to close the channel, letting out a low growl as soon as he did.

"That's it then, I guess," Joon said. "We can't get down to the surface."

"Bullshit," Ming said. "I'll get you down. Give me a minute to think."

Ming began pulling on his goatee while staring out the viewport. He was silent for a minute, yanking hard enough that it looked painful.

"Okay," he said. "I have an idea, but it's going to cost, and I can't guarantee you'll be able to get back to the Kemushi. You may need to steal a ship."

"Steal a ship?" Aiko said.

"I suppose hijack would be the most appropriate term. But yes, it may require a bit more dirty work than we had intended. I was there, Colonel. I saw what one Tetron did to our ships, whether we destroyed it or not. We have to stop them, whatever it takes."

"Agreed," Calvin said.

Mitchell nodded. "Whatever you need to do, do it."

[26]
MITCHELL

IT TOOK two hours for Ming to reach his contact at Kido Resupply. It took another hour and nearly ten million Frontier Federate Dollars from Tio's account to convince him to forge documents and lie through his teeth to Federation Import Control to get him to agree to ferry Mitchell, Calvin, and Aiko down to the surface. Mitchell had argued furiously to get Joon included, but Ming had stated that there was only room for three, whatever that meant.

They were standing in the hangar, next to the resupply airlock. The Kido Four was directly on the other side of it, in the process of equalizing air pressure between the ships.

"I don't have the best feeling about this," Aiko said, tugging on her skirt.

Mitchell had laughed when she explained how recent Federation fashions were shorter than she remembered, and how she had been surprised when she put the skirt on and found it barely covered her thighs. A pair of long stockings covered her legs nearly up to the skirt, leaving very little actual skin exposed, and flat ankle boots finished up the lower half. A loose fitting, frilly white sleeveless blouse and jacket with a secret placement where she held a concealed pistol, along with a pair of white gloves, finished the outfit.

"Because we're breaking a hundred Federation laws just by stepping through that airlock?" Mitchell asked. "Or because we may need to break a thousand more to get off the planet?"

He shifted slightly, the waist-length jacket a little tight across his shoulders. Aiko had been right; he did look good in the outer-Rim style if he did say so himself, especially with the brown lenses and the beard and mustache he had been growing to help disguise himself.

The airlock light turned green. The hatches of both ships slid open at the same time, revealing an older man with a wrinkled face and even more wrinkled clothes ahead of a dozen men pushing crates on repulser sleds.

"Eito," Ming said.

"Ming. I can't believe you got me to agree to this."

"Trust me when I tell you that you'll be glad you did."

"Ten million? I'm already glad I did." Eito looked at the three of them. "Is this the cargo?"

"Yes."

"You didn't tell me I was bringing an Alliance soldier down," Eito said.

"Former Alliance soldier," Ming said. "He's one of Mr. Tio's now."

"You swear they aren't going to cause any trouble?"

"Yes, yes, I told you they wouldn't. They need to get to the surface to speak with a representative of AgriCo about a purchase agreement."

"Since when does Mr. Tio send soldiers to sign receipts?"

"I'm the bodyguard," Mitchell said. He pointed at Calvin. "He's the businessman."

"And her?" Eito asked.

"The escort," Aiko said.

Eito smiled, looking her over. "A pretty one, at that. I bet you aren't a cheap one."

"No. I'm not."

"Can we get on with this, Eito," Ming said. "Things are fragile out here. I can feel it."

"Yes. The rumors have everyone frightened. The local government is doing what it can to calm nerves and appear in control. If what they say is true, it won't matter."

"What are they saying?" Mitchell asked.

"The Alliance has a weapon that can obliterate a navy in one shot, and can destroy a planet within hours. That there's no defense against it. I've even heard one rumor that the weapon is fully autonomous, an AI."

"That sounds ridiculous," Mitchell said.

Eito shrugged. "Something's got all these ships coming here in search of succor. If this keeps up, I'm going to have to close business in a couple of weeks due to lack of resources. Anyway, let's get things moving here."

He motioned with his hand, and his crew began pushing the crates over onto the Kemushi.

"Obviously, we need to give you something, or this will look suspicious," Eito said. "The crates are filled with nutrition bars that didn't pass inspection. They're edible, but they taste like shit."

"We can still use them," Ming said.

"You three, follow me," Eito said.

Mitchell turned to Ming. "Thank you, Ming."

"You know how to thank me."

Mitchell bowed to him. Calvin approached Eito.

"Show us the way," he said, taking the lead from Mitchell.

Eito led them into the resupply ship. It was a similar size to the Kemushi, but orbital only. It had no hyperspace engines, leaving it more space for cargo. They were in the massive loading space, which was at this point nearly empty.

"I'm going to tell you upfront, this isn't going to be comfortable," Eito said. "To be honest, I'm not even sure you'll survive."

"What do you mean?" Mitchell asked.

"When we land, we'll be inspected by Import to ensure we haven't brought back anything we didn't declare. The only way I can get you past the inspection is in that freezer there." He pointed across to a solid gray box in the corner. "We're bringing back a ton of fresh beef. The real thing. I can tell you; the crew is damn happy about this because we had to do something with the five hundred pounds you'll be replacing. I know Ming wanted to bring four of you, but we can't eat that much before it spoils."

"You want us to ride down in a meat freezer?" Aiko said, looking down at her outfit.

"I can't get you down any other way."

"Did Ming know about this?"

"Yes."

"And he agreed to it?"

"We have to risk it," Mitchell said.

"Anyway, you don't have to go in until we touch down. The inspection takes about thirty minutes. Do your best to stay warm."

"That's easy for you to say," Aiko said. "You're going to be on this side of the freezer door."

"That's the deal. Mr. Tio has already paid, and there are no refunds. You want to go back? The Kemushi is that way." He pointed to the open airlock.

Aiko looked at Mitchell, her eyes pleading. He put his fist to his chest, trying to signal for her to use her fear.

"We're staying," she said, nodding to him.

Eito shrugged. "Ten minutes to finish unloading the shit bars, twenty minutes down to the spaceport. Once the inspection is over and I open the door, I'll get you in one of our vans, and we'll drop you in the center of Mirai. That's the end of our agreement."

"Understood," Calvin said.

"I'm going to make sure my crew doesn't frig anything up. Do whatever you want in the meantime."

He wandered off, leaving the three of them standing there.

"I expect you to keep me warm," Aiko said to him.

"I'll do my best."

[27]

MITCHELL

THE RIDE DOWN to the surface was fine. The thirty minutes in the freezer was some of the worst of Mitchell's life. Considering what he had already been through, and considering the fact that he was pressed tight enough against the front of Aiko that he didn't know where he ended, and she started, it shouldn't have been that bad.

But it was.

The clothes he was wearing were made for the temperate weather of Mirai, not the cold of the freezer. Calvin and Aiko were in the same position, which meant that all of their body heat escaped quickly once they were locked inside. Even holding one another barely made a dent, leaving all three of them shivering within minutes, and painfully numb by the time Eito opened the freezer door.

The minutes felt like hours, and the hours passed like days, but they survived, pulled out of their frozen embrace by Eito's men and quickly wrapped in warm blankets. They sat on the floor of the cargo bay for nearly an hour before they were strong enough to stand and move, at which point Eito led them outside into a bright sun, where a van with the company logo on it waited to deliver them. Between the shock of the cold and the strange familiarity of being on an intact planet again, Mitchell wanted nothing more than to fall to his knees and cry.

He didn't. Instead, the three of them entered the van in silence, each of them experiencing their mixed emotions about being back among a strong population of currently free human beings. Mitchell wondered if they, like him, had wondered whether or not they would ever have had the chance, or if they would ever get the chance again.

"Your stop is coming up," Eito said, looking back over his shoulder.

The three of them were huddled in the empty rear of the delivery vehicle, wrapped in the blankets and staying close. Mitchell had his arm around Aiko's shoulders, her head resting against his chest. Calvin was next to her, leaning into her side to catch whatever warmth he could.

Every muscle in Mitchell's body hurt. He imagined the others felt the same. At least the shivering was beginning to lessen, and his extremities had stopped itching and regained some regular feeling. He managed to meet Eito's eye and nod. The Kido employee didn't seem to care one way or another that they had lived.

"Come on," Mitchell said. "We need to start moving, or we're going to fall out of the van."

Calvin lifted his blanket off, using the wall to pull himself to his feet. He was a little shaky. He held out a hand and helped Aiko up, and then Mitchell joined them. He forced himself to move his arms and legs, fingers and toes. He could feel the blood rushing through.

"Let's never do that again," Aiko said.

"Sounds like a plan," Mitchell agreed.

He moved forward to stand between the vehicle's seats, looking out at civilization beyond. The streets were busy, crowded with people and a multitude of delivery vehicles, each marked with the name of their business on the sides. Calvin had explained that personal transportation was illegal in the Federation. Only business vehicles and public transportation like buses used the streets and skies. Not only did this approach reduce congestion, but it also afforded the corporations more control of their employees as many provided transportation to their workers.

Tall buildings stood on either side of the thoroughfare, spires of a number of modern architectural designs stretching upward in daring configurations of alloy and carbonate.

"How many people live in Mirai?" he asked.

"Twenty million, give or take," Eito said. "The city also has the highest density of offices and is the home of the Yokohama Exchange. The food is the best on the planet, and in my opinion in the Quadrant, as well."

"Do you have any recommendations on driver services?"

"You want automated or human-piloted?"

"Human. Definitely human. Preferably one without an ARR."

"Hmm... You're one of Mr. Tio's, which means you don't have a receiver. Did he send you with a handheld?"

"No," Calvin said, moving forward. "This was a last minute assignment."

"Aren't they always?"

Eito leaned over and opened the storage box between the seats. He dug down to the bottom. As he did, Mitchell noticed an assault pistol resting beneath a pile of old candy wrappers and garbage.

"Here. You can have this one." He pulled out a small, thin device and handed it to him. "It's untraceable."

Mitchell took it, flipping it in his hand. It was a piece of clear carbonate with a small sliver of metal at the bottom. He had no idea how to use it.

"I'll take that," Aiko said, reaching forward. Mitchell passed it over to her.

"Look up HPT," Eito said. "It stands for Human Powered Transportation. They can get you where you want to go, no questions asked. Transportation services aren't liable here on Yokohama."

"Not liable?" Mitchell asked. "So you can kill someone and then hop in a taxi and drive away?"

Eito seemed offended by the suggestion. "If that was your desire, I suppose you could, but the authorities will catch up sooner or later regardless. This isn't the Alliance or the Rim. Crime in the Federation is nearly non-existent. Why would anyone steal anything when the corporations provide for all of us? Besides, over half of the transportation services on Yokohama are automated. How would a machine know that you did something illegal? The laws must be consistent."

"Thank you, Eito-san," Calvin said.

Aiko had already turned on the handheld device. The screen was no longer transparent, and a small hologram floated above it, providing a view similar to that of a p-rat. He could see her navigate to HPT.

The van slowed to a stop.

"This is you," Eito said.

The back doors swung open, and repulsers lowered the vehicle to the ground. Aiko turned off the device, and the three of them climbed out to the street. As soon as they were clear, the doors closed and the van lifted and rode away.

"Goodbye," Mitchell said to the rear of the fading truck.

"HPT, how can I help you?" a voice said behind him. Mitchell looked for the source, finding the handheld on again, a holographic image of a woman in a suit similar to Calvin's floating between them.

"We just arrived in town," Calvin said. "We'll need a driver for the next forty-eight hours."

"Nonstop?"

"Yes."

"What experience level?"

"Very. I also want them to be implant-free."

"It will cost extra."

"That's fine."

"That will be twenty-thousand Federate. Please transmit your routing keys."

Calvin took the card Ming had provided them from his pocket and handed it to Aiko. She tapped it against the handheld.

"Thank you," the receptionist said. She paused. "I'm afraid I can't pinpoint your location."

Mitchell smiled. Untraceable. He liked that.

Aiko scanned the street. "We're in the center of Mirai, outside of the Justice building."

"Very well. A driver will meet you in fifteen minutes."

"Thank you," Aiko said. The channel disconnected.

"So," Mitchell said, looking around at the city and still feeling a mixed sense of both relief to be around civilization and impending doom for the same civilization. "Where do we find the Black Hole?"

[28]
MITCHELL

THE DRIVER PICKED them up almost exactly fifteen minutes later. She was a petite, serious woman with short black hair and opaque glasses that hid her eyes. She wore a fitted black-on-black suit and gloves and didn't get out to guide them through the automatic doors.

She was silent while she waited for them to tell her where they wanted to go.

"Fourteen seventy-five one-hundred-sixty-seventh," Calvin said.

Mitchell thought he saw the driver's eyebrow rise a fraction of an inch. She headed off without comment.

They rode in silence, reaching the destination ten minutes later. The building looked like many of the others - tall, reflective, rich. Mitchell tried not to think about what it would look like once the Tetron fired a plasma stream down on the city.

"Wait three blocks over," Calvin said.

The driver handed a black card back to him. He passed it to Aiko, who tapped it against the handheld. Then they got out of the car.

"None of this is illegal?" Mitchell asked.

"Technically, no," Calvin said. "Like I told you, transportation services can't be held liable, as long as all they do is drive. If she speaks one word, she becomes an accomplice."

"The Federation has strange rules."

"And the Alliance doesn't? You still arrest people for using natural occurring substances that have been proven harmless for centuries."

Mitchell couldn't argue that. "So she knows we're up to something?"

"Whether she does or not, she would treat us the same. Come on."

Mitchell looked at the building. Men and women in ordinary, fashionable suits were entering and exiting. Even so, it didn't look like anything special.

"This is the Black Hole?" he asked.

"No," Calvin said. "The Black Hole is across the street."

Mitchell cast his eyes that way. The building across from them was more nondescript than the one they were in front of. A higher volume of people in suits were coming and going from that one, both on foot and in dark cars that stopped in front.

"The people there?" Mitchell said.

"Agents? Probably about half of them."

"So now what?"

"We stick to the plan and wait for the right person to come out that door."

Mitchell knew "the right person" meant someone with high-level clearance into the facility.

"How do we identify them?"

"There are maybe four hundred people in the entire Federation who would even know what that building is, and you are standing with one of them. You'll know the right person when you see them. Or at least, I will."

Mitchell couldn't help but wonder how fortuitous their procurement of the Federation Admiral had been. So many pieces had to fall into the right place to make these things happen. Had they been prearranged somehow? Had dozens, or hundreds, or thousands of recursions helped them put some grand master plan into motion? He thought back to the Construct, and Katherine. The package had been disguised as the book *I, Robot*, which not so coincidentally was Liun Tio's favorite novel. There was no denying the connection there.

"Okay," he said. "We can't just stand here. The operatives are bound to get suspicious."

Calvin nodded. "Agreed. There's a restaurant right inside the building here. We can keep watch from inside."

The three of them headed inside. As Calvin had said, there was an upscale eatery on their left. It was crowded, and the hostess tried to seat them in the back. A quick transfer of money solved that problem, getting them shifted to a table at the window as soon as it was cleared.

"Let's try not to be too obvious about this," Mitchell said, sitting down closest to the window. Despite his years of experience with military special operations, he was still a novice at this kind of espionage.

Aiko picked up her menu, scanning it. "Have you ever had bibimbap, Mitch?"

"No, but after three weeks of eating nothing but nutrition bars, I'll take whatever I can get."

"It is one of the traditional Federation staple foods, going back over a thousand years before the Federation existed. This one was from Korea."

Mitchell found it on the menu. Everything looked good to him right now.

"What do you think, Calvin?" Mitchell asked, looking over at him.

Calvin was staring out the window.

"Calvin?"

"Sorry, Mitchell," he said. "You aren't going to have a chance to eat. Aiko, call the car."

Mitchell diverted his attention across the street. A black car like the others he had seen was stopped in front of the building. An older, well-dressed man was approaching it.

"How do you know that's the one?" Mitchell asked.

"The driver."

Mitchell noticed the driver had gotten out of the car and was standing next to the door.

"Good fortune for us," Aiko said. "The car is on the way."

They stood up as the waitress approached. Aiko transferred some money to her for her trouble, and they headed out the door. As they exited, Mitchell noticed he was getting a lot of attention in the form of stares and angry looks.

"Frigging Alliance prick," someone said behind him as they moved towards the street. Mitchell started to turn, finding Aiko's hand on his shoulder, steering him ahead.

"Not a good idea, Mitch," she said.

He nodded. He had to keep his reactions in check. Slow. Steady.

The well-dressed man was getting into his car. Their driver slowed to a stop in front of them, the doors sliding open.

They got in.

"Follow the transport there," Calvin said.

The driver's only response was to pull out and make a u-turn across the traffic.

"Keep a decent distance," Calvin added.

They tailed the car through the city, their driver doing an expert job of keeping them a few cars back and at the same time never losing sight of the target. It helped that the Federation tenets on vehicles kept both traffic and traffic control unnecessary.

They rode in tense silence for nearly thirty minutes as the Federation agent made his way to the edge of the city and beyond, gaining a hyperlane at the outskirts. Their driver made a fancy, likely illegal maneuver to remain behind the car, winding up only three lengths back. The automated systems carried the cars one hundred miles in minutes before their target disembarked, and their driver followed.

Another ten minutes passed, their driver dropping further back as traffic became lighter and lighter. They rode through beautiful grass, flower, and tree covered hills dotted with large mansions and smaller, more dense housing developments, their car falling further and further behind until their target had disappeared.

"What are you doing?" Calvin asked. "Your instructions were to follow."

The driver said nothing.

"I requested someone very experienced. I expected someone who could tail a car."

Still, the driver was silent.

"Aiko, please connect me to the HPT office."

The driver growled under her breath.

"Do you have a problem?" Calvin asked.

"I didn't lose him," she said, surprising him by speaking, and speaking in English.

"What?"

"I didn't lose him." She looked angry that he had forced her to talk. "I know where he lives."

"You know who he is?" Mitchell said.

She didn't answer. She didn't want to know what their business was.

"Fine," Calvin said. "Take us to his home, keep out of sight."

She said nothing.

Ten minutes later, the car veered off the road, floating over a grass median and into the trees beyond. The driver didn't slow much as she navigated them past trunks and shrubs, coming to a stop after a few minutes.

"Which way is the house?" Calvin asked.

The driver didn't answer.

"It has to be that way," Aiko said. "According to the map, we're in a protected forest."

The driver opened their doors. Mitchell and Aiko climbed out.

"Calvin?" Mitchell asked.

"I told you, Mitchell, if a single person suspects anything, everything we've come here for is lost. Let me handle this part. Make your way to the home, but stay hidden until I signal you."

"Are you sure about this?" Mitchell asked.

"Yes. We're still following the plan."

Mitchell nodded. The doors to the vehicle closed, and a moment later it drove off.

"Come on," Mitchell said.

[29]

MITCHELL

"I SHOULD HAVE PICKED A DIFFERENT OUTFIT," Aiko said, grabbing at her heeled ankle boots and pulling them off.

"It hasn't been very practical so far, has it?" Mitchell said, looking over at her. "At least you look amazing in it."

Her face reddened at the compliment. "Thank you, but I would prefer not to feel half-naked, half-frozen, and half-hobbled."

The two of them were navigating their way through the wooded area behind the target's home. They had walked nearly half a kilometer already, and they could just barely see the roof of the house through the trees, in the form of a tall, sloped pagoda.

"At least we didn't have to wait too long to get this far."

Aiko picked her way over the terrain, wincing when she stepped down on a rock without her shoes. "I thought this would be the easiest part."

"It probably will be." He watched her struggle for a few more seconds before approaching her. "It'll be faster if I carry you."

"What?" She tried to protest, but he scooped her up before she could complain too much.

"Heels or barefoot, you're too slow like this."

"Aren't you going to get tired?"

"You barely weigh anything," Mitchell said, picking up their pace.

"Are you saying I'm too thin?"

He turned his head to look at her. The maneuver had put her head on his shoulder; their faces only inches apart. "No. I just told you I think you're beautiful."

She started to drop her eyes away from his and then forced herself to stop. Her blush deepened. "Mitchell-"

"We'll have some time when the mission is over," Mitchell said, feeling his heart rate increasing. He wasn't sure what he was doing. Hadn't he decided not to go down this route? And what about Millie? He had said he loved her, but he had moved on so easily. Was he becoming so jaded to loss that he barely felt it anymore? If so, what did that make him?

He didn't know. He wasn't sure what he was doing or what was causing it. Maybe it was adrenaline. Maybe it was his body recovering from the cold. Maybe he had just been denying what he had felt since they had spent so much time together on the Carver. At the moment, he wanted to kiss her.

"We talked about this, Mitch," she said, still looking at him. "I think you're a handsome man, and you have many qualities that many people, both men, and women, should and do admire. I am grateful for the training you have given me."

"But you aren't interested," Mitchell said, the moment slipping away from him.

"I'm sorry."

He turned his head to let out the tension in a burst of air. "You don't have anything to be sorry for. Though I will admit, I haven't been turned down since the Shot."

She smiled. "I suppose that makes you want me even more?"

He laughed quietly, looking ahead through the trees. They were almost there.

"No means no. Unless you say otherwise, consider the matter dropped. I'm sorry if I made you uncomfortable."

"Thank you, Mitch. And I'm flattered. You just aren't my type."

"Out of curiosity, what is your type?"

"More thinker, less doer," she said.

"You mean smarter?" he joked.

"I mean the whole soldier thing. I understand why we need to do this, but that doesn't mean I like war, or fighting, or killing, and I don't want to be any more involved with it than I have to be."

"I understand," he said, and he did. He couldn't change who he was.

He carried her in silence for a few more minutes, until they neared the edge of the wood. Aiko put her boots back on, and he lowered her to the ground.

"How do we get in?" she asked.

Calvin had been right about the man's importance if the home was anything to judge by. It was large and designed in a fusion of classical Japanese and Chinese architecture, with sloped pagoda roofs and intricately designed wood and stone. It was surrounded by an eight-foot tall river stone wall with intricate spiked posts to keep people from trying to climb over.

"I don't think we need to get in. Calvin said he would signal. Let's try to get around to the front."

The house was large enough that it took them nearly ten minutes to creep their way to the corner of the wall from where a large front gate was visible. There was no sign of Calvin or their car.

"Now what?" Aiko asked.

"We stay out of sight and wait."

They moved back into the nearest brush, keeping their eyes on the gate. Mitchell couldn't guess what was happening inside the house. There had been no echo of gunfire, no shouts of alarm. He assumed Calvin was inside. Still alive? There was no way to know.

An hour passed. Then another. They were both getting impatient by the time the third hour had gone by and the planet's sun was beginning to set.

"Do you think we should check on him?" Aiko asked.

Mitchell considered. He didn't want to screw things up by going in when Calvin hadn't asked him to. At the same time, who knew what was happening inside?

"Let's give it another hour. It'll be easier to sneak in when it's dark anyway."

"Okay."

They were crouched in the bushes for another twenty minutes when the gate swung open.

"Something's happening," Mitchell said. "Get ready."

Aiko retrieved her gun from the holster on her jacket. She had never touched a pistol before she had boarded the Carver, and her aim was still pretty bad. She knew the basics, though, and shooting enough quantity could overcome poor quality.

Mitchell did the same, finding his weapon under his armpit and holding it against his chest.

The gate sat open.

Nothing else happened.

"Strange," Aiko said.

"Maybe that's the signal?"

"Could be."

"Come on."

They cautiously stepped out of their hiding place. Mitchell remained alert, his eyes scanning the wall, the upper floors of the house, and the gate. There was no motion anywhere.

They had just reached the open gate when the front door to the house swung open. Mitchell's eyes scanned the area, finding nowhere to hide.

"Shit," he said, grabbing Aiko by the shoulder and pulling her to the ground. She began to protest until she realized why he had done it.

He aimed his gun towards the door.

A single person came out. A man in a sharp dark gray suit that was now splattered with blood.

"Aiko," Calvin Hohn said. "Can you please contact the driver?"

They both stood as Calvin approached them. The front of his jacket was soaked in blood.

"Not mine," he said, responding to Mitchell's concern.

Aiko took out the handheld to call the car.

"What happened?"

"Plan A," he said. "I tried another way. It didn't work. I wanted to spare her the burden."

"What do you mean?" Aiko asked, her eyes wide.

"Mitchell and I, we're soldiers. Warriors. We've seen death, and we've gotten our hands dirty before. You're a technician. You're very smart, but your heart is not made for killing."

Mitchell didn't make any attempt to counter the statement. How could he, when he agreed to it? Calvin had done what he felt he had to do. "Did you get what we needed?"

"Yes, but we have to move fast. There were two other agents inside. One of them will be missed sooner or later."

"All dead?"

Calvin nodded grimly. He wasn't happy about what he had done. He knew what the other option was.

The HPT car rolled up to the gate. The doors opened, and they climbed in.

"Back to Mirai," Calvin said. "Please stop at a high-end clothing boutique."

The driver glanced back at him, keeping her head up. The opaque glasses made it impossible to know if she was looking at Calvin's face or his bloody shirt. Mitchell assumed it was his face.

"I can get us in," Calvin said.

[30]
KATHY

"WHERE DO YOU THINK WE ARE?" Alice asked.

"I'm not sure," Kathy replied.

The Goliath had dropped from hyperspace a few minutes earlier after a nearly week-long journey. It had been an unproductive week for the two of them, most of it spent mapping out routes from a small storage room closer to the science labs all the way back to the front of the ship. The idea had been to find pathways that were either little used or little known to Watson or his Secondary; corridors, hallways, ventilation shafts, and in one case a segment of wide, disabled piping that they could travel in to avoid detection.

It had been a grueling process of trial and error. One that left them being shot at on many occasions, and almost captured twice. Kathy had been shot in the arm on one of the first efforts, leaving Alice to watch in amazement as the wound healed over inside of an hour. She had told Kathy she'd forgotten she wasn't human.

Their exploration had finally gotten them exactly where Kathy wanted to be.

On a direct path to the bridge.

When she had said it was risky, she had meant it in more ways than one. She knew the Goliath's bridge had been reconfigured drastically in the weeks since Mitchell had discovered it. All of the command stations had been removed to provide better line of sight to the three-hundred-sixty-degree views of space around the starship, with only the command chair and a needle-tip interface to the Secondary remaining.

Kathy had tried to be secretive and subtle to get what she wanted, but between what Alice had told her that Watson was doing to Jacob and their inability to reach his workshop, she had realized she couldn't waste the precious seconds they had on simply determining what the Tetron was doing. She decided that when the time came, she would seize control of the Secondary and use it to unlock the contents of the chip.

That time was now. The Goliath had dropped from hyperspace, and Kathy knew that meant it was either back at Asimov, orbiting the planet Pulin was living on, or somewhere else on the path to finding Tio's brother.

The same path that Mitchell was on.

She knew he would either be nearby or on a convergent path. If she took control of the Goliath, she could get more insight into their position and arrange a rendezvous.

Now she and Alice were climbing slowly through a ventilation shaft, on their way from their hiding place to the bridge. Their journey would bring them out in the lift shaft, which they would have to climb to the bridge. The good news was that if Watson were on the bridge, it would be obvious because the lift would be above them. The bad news was that if the lift were above them, they couldn't get onto the bridge, and they would have to make their way all the way back having achieved nothing.

They moved slowly, pausing every few seconds to listen for the skittering of Watson's machines. The smaller, crab-like constructions had surprised them in the ventilation before, causing them to abandon two of the alternate routes to the lift shaft and sending them scrambling once they had destroyed it. They both knew the same thing could happen on this route anytime, and if it did they would be starting almost from scratch.

There was a measure of luck with them, and they managed to make the half-kilometer journey to the lift without being seen, the same way they had done it three times before. Kathy carefully unhooked the shaft cover from its placement, sliding out into the shaft to look down.

The top of the lift was visible below them.

The bridge was clear.

She leaned back in to flash a thumbs-up to Alice before pushing herself far enough out to secure the shaft cover to its maintenance hook on the wall.

She made a downward gesture to Alice, and then she jumped.

She fell ten meters, hitting the top of the lift, doing her best to absorb the impact. She felt the pain of her legs breaking beneath her, and she tumbled and rolled over, grabbing the center of the lift and holding on before she slammed into the side and made even more noise. She clenched her teeth against the throbbing of her damaged body, pulling herself back to the middle and reaching down into her pocket for the screwdriver. She took it out and began removing the screws from the maintenance cover on the top of the lift.

She put the cover on the side, reached down to the screen and keying in the override sequence that Alice had provided her. Then she used the panel to direct the lift up, stopping it at the floor beneath the ventilation shaft.

Alice slid out and onto the top of the lift, noticing the blood on Kathy's pants.

"Are you okay?" she asked.

"I broke my legs. They'll be restored in a minute."

"It's just genetics, isn't it?" Alice asked. "Can you pass that healing ability on to a full human?"

"I don't know," Kathy replied.

She directed the lift up to the floor below the bridge before pushing herself up onto her hands and knees.

"We're almost there," she said.

"Let's hope Watson doesn't decide now is a good time to head to the bridge," Alice said, climbing and standing on her back.

A moment later, the hatch to the bridge slid open.

Kathy felt the weight disappear from her back. She stood up slowly, testing her legs, before reaching up to take Alice's offered hand. The Rigger pulled her up and into the Goliath's command center.

"Oh no," Kathy said, the full view of space around the Goliath suddenly visible to them.

A second Tetron was next to the Goliath, along with a large fleet of Federation starships.

31

KATHY

"WHAT'S HAPPENING?" Alice asked, staring at the ships.

"I'm not sure. Look." She pointed out to the right.

A Federation transport had emerged from the Goliath's hangar and was crossing the short distance to a nearby battleship.

"Is Watson leaving?" Alice asked.

Kathy tried to determine why the Tetron configuration would depart from the Goliath. It didn't make sense. "I don't know."

She stood transfixed, watching as the transport disappeared into the belly of the battleship.

A moment later, the battleship disappeared into hyperspace.

"Whatever it is, it can't be good," Alice said.

"I agree," Kathy said. She turned towards the command chair, sitting alone and vacant on a raised pedestal towards the center of the space. "Cover me."

Alice unslung her rifle from her shoulder, following Kathy over to the chair.

Kathy stood at the base of the pedestal, looking up at the thin tentacle that ended in a needle behind the chair. She wondered if the Secondary could see her standing there. That facilities that remained would depend on how much of Origin's configuration had been destroyed during the takeover.

It had never exhibited signs of being able to visualize her before. That the needle remained in place suggested that it wasn't able to now.

"If I don't survive this, I'm sorry," Kathy said.

"You'll survive," Alice replied.

Kathy nodded, climbing to the chair. She breathed deeply before lunging forward and grabbing the tentacle in her hand.

Her vision exploded in rainbow colored light for only an instant before it was lost completely. Her hand burned with cold numbness, and she cried out as she turned herself away and plunged the needle tip into the back of her neck, stabbing it through her flesh and into contact with her spine.

Her heart beat too fast as she felt the flood of information open up to her, the Secondary launching an immediate defense against her invasion.

She struggled to keep up, swimming through a sea of impulse and instinct in an effort to pause the sudden and immense swelling of energy that charged into her. She pushed back, using the innate internal knowledge she barely knew she had to stage a counterstrike against the oncoming storm.

She chose what she believed was an uncommon path, through subsystems that were so rarely used she wasn't certain the Secondary would consciously know they existed to defend them. It was very similar to her approach within the Goliath, moving as a mouse might in a maze.

The Secondary didn't fall for the trick. It nipped at her heels, following behind as she attempted to make the leap from the subroutine to the parent, to shut down something, anything, in an effort to weaken the configuration's power.

Her external self writhed in pain, her failing assault leaving her body wide open to attack. Somewhere in her mind she could smell her burning flesh and hair.

A sharp pain registered in her mind at the source of the needle. The Secondary overwhelmed her, moving ahead of her efforts and reaching back, throwing her violently away from the subsystems. She had the sensation that she was screaming.

Then the pain vanished. It was immediate and rough. She wasn't sure what was happening, but she felt herself land heavily on the floor.

"Kathy," Alice said from somewhere nearby.

Kathy didn't answer.

"Kathy, are you okay? Shit."

Gunfire echoed in Kathy's ears. She tried to make sense of it, to understand what it was. Her entire body hurt. She was burned, she knew. She needed time to heal and regain her vision.

There was no time. She could hear the machines clambering onto the bridge through the open hatch of the lift shaft, called to action by the Secondary.

Where was Watson? Did that mean he wasn't on the Goliath?

She tried to pick herself up. Alice noticed, reaching out and grabbing her by the arm.

"Kathy, we need to go."

"I can't see," Kathy said.

"Frigging hell," Alice said. Kathy felt the soldier's hands pulling at her. "When I lift you up, wrap your legs around my waist and hold on."

Kathy did as she was told, helping Alice carry her. Then they were moving.

"Get out of the frigging way," Alice said, continuing to fire.

They dropped onto the lift. Kathy had to hold on tight while Alice leaned over to enter the maintenance panel.

"Son of a bitch," Alice cursed.

Kathy smelled the blood.

"Alice?"

"It's a flesh wound."

The lift began to drop, falling much farther than they had come.

"Where are we going?" Kathy asked.

"Away. What happened?"

Kathy felt tears forming in her eyes. She had been made to do one job, and to do it right.

"I failed."

32

MITCHELL

"I SHOULD HAVE STARTED WITH THIS," Aiko said, checking out her new clothes in the back of the car. She was wearing a suit not much different from Calvin and Mitchell's, a dark blue jacket with a high collared white shirt beneath and trousers cut for her gender.

The dress was identical to the suit the agent had been wearing, all the way down to the four-thousand-dollar shoes. It had been expensive to buy and more expensive to keep the shop owner quiet about, but Calvin insisted that he could get them into the Black Hole as long as they looked the part.

"How did you do it?" Mitchell asked as they neared the building.

"Do what?" Calvin replied.

"Get him to talk without compromising the data."

"It was a matter of honor and trust. I introduced myself. I gave him my credentials. He let me in. News of my situation hasn't reached Yokohama yet."

"Why did you tell him you were there?"

"I told him the Federation military had reason to believe the Black Hole was under threat, and that I had been assigned to set up an intervention. He had already checked on me by then, so he didn't verify my current assignment."

"He didn't wonder why a Navy Admiral would be running an operation like that?"

"It isn't unheard of, depending on the situation. Admirals are expected to be leaders and strategists. These qualities are not specific to maneuvering starships."

Calvin sighed, his expression dark.

"I got him to reveal some details of the facility without violence. When he began to balk at the questions I was asking, I retreated until I could get into position behind him. I stole his sidearm, shot the two agents in the temple to both disable their implants and kill them at the same time. I jabbed a small knife into his head to short his receiver before he could signal the delete.

"At that point, I told him the truth. All of the truth. I asked him for his help. He refused. I'm not proud of what I did. Not at all. I broke his trust and dishonored myself by my actions. It is something that I will struggle to live with, for as long as we have left to live. We both know it had to be done."

Mitchell nodded. "I understand."

"Then let us speak of it no further. I can get us in. It is up to Aiko to get the data, and you to get us out."

The car stopped back where they had started. The late hour hadn't diminished the activity in the streets and around the buildings.

"Do people in the Federation sleep?" Mitchell asked.

"This is the night shift," Calvin replied. "Most corporations run at one hundred percent capacity, broken into appropriate length shifts based on the local time."

"So you don't use Earth Standard?"

"Why would we? No, it is difficult to manage when different planets have different cycles. Only the military uses EST."

"The Alliance manages. The human body adjusts."

"Who is to say which is right and which is wrong?" Aiko said, butting in to end the discussion. "It is what it is."

"She has a point," Mitchell said.

Calvin nodded.

"Driver, please remain here."

They didn't wait for the response they knew wouldn't come. They got out of the car and headed across the street towards the Black Hole.

"Let me do the talking," Calvin said. "Hopefully they will not question why I have a upatine in tow."

"Upatine?" Mitchell asked.

"Derogatory Federese slang for a citizen or expatriate of the UPA," Aiko said.

"You have Caucasians in the Federation."

"And their mannerisms are completely different than yours. Even your walk screams UPA."

Mitchell forced himself not to smile. They were nearing the front doors of the building.

"Stay two feet behind me, evenly spaced at my back," Calvin said.

Mitchell slowed to get into position, as did Aiko. They crossed the threshold in that configuration, approaching a stiff man at a central desk. There was no indication that there was anything special about the building. The sign behind the desk read "National Financial Corporation."

The man said something in Federese, his eyes falling directly on Mitchell.

Calvin responded in English. Mitchell didn't know if it was for his sake or if it was part of procedure. Most of the Federation's military structure and customs originated from the global military that had been created on Earth after the Xeno War.

"My name is Admiral Calvin Hohn. Identification sequence alpha zero four seven kappa foxtrot nine four seven nine seven seven zero delta. I've been in contact with Colonel Xin Lo regarding a withdrawal. Confirmation code one seven four seven nine alpha omega six three seven nine charlie."

"Please transmit using your ARR," the man said in perfect English.

Calvin remained perfectly calm in his response.

"My apologies, my receiver is damaged. I am scheduled for repair at Station Seven tomorrow morning, but this couldn't wait. The withdrawal is a code red, as you'll see when you enter the data I have provided you."

The man wrinkled his forehead slightly. "Please repeat the codes."

"My name is Admiral Calvin Hohn. Identification sequence alpha zero four seven kappa foxtrot nine four seven nine seven seven zero delta. I've been in contact with Colonel Xin Lo regarding a withdrawal. Confirmation code one seven four seven nine alpha omega six three seven nine charlie."

He said it precisely the same way he had the first time, verifying to Mitchell that it was procedure.

The man stared at him for a moment. "I have voice signature confirmation as well as identification sequence confirmation." He smiled. "Welcome to Black Hole Eleven, Admiral Hohn. I have voice signature confirmation and access confirmation from Colonel Lo for your withdrawal."

"Thank you."

A hatch slid open to their left.

"Please," the man said, motioning towards it.

Calvin headed to the hatch. Mitchell and Aiko remained in position behind him.

The hatch led to a small atrium where a soldier wearing medium exo waited out of sight of the lobby. A coilgun sat on each wrist of the metal skeleton, feeder belts leading behind him to the slugs and power supply on his back. He approached them the moment the hatch slid closed.

"Admiral Hohn," he said, bowing. "I am Sergeant Wong. I will take you down."

"Thank you, Sergeant," Calvin said, returning the bow.

Wong straightened up before his eyes passed over Aiko and Mitchell. They lingered on Mitchell.

"I was not aware you had a former Alliance soldier in your entourage, Admiral."

"Is that a problem, Sergeant?" Calvin asked, his voice stiff and commanding. "Colonel Smith has proven his loyalty to the Federation in combat under my command a dozen times over."

Wong continued to try to stare Mitchell down. Mitchell returned the stare.

"Show some respect, Sergeant," he said in decent Federese. It was most of his Federation vocabulary.

"Yes, sir," Wong said, bowing. Mitchell returned the bow. "This way."

He took them across the atrium to the lift. It opened at their approach, and they stepped in.

"Sir," Wong said as they descended. "If you don't mind my asking, do you have any information you are at liberty to share regarding the Alliance's new starship or the truth of the rumors about the planet Liberty?"

Calvin shook his head. "Nothing concrete enough to speak on. I can assure you that whatever rumors you have heard are likely inaccurate."

"Yes, sir."

The Sergeant was silent the rest of the way down, a nearly thirty-second ride. The Black Hole was deep, deep underground.

The lift opened, revealing a long, well-lit passage where two more exo-wearing soldiers were standing at attention. They bowed to Calvin as he passed.

There was a clear carbonate door at the end of the passage, at least a meter thick. A second guard station was behind it, manned by a soldier in regular fatigues.

"I'm not permitted beyond this point," Wong said. "I will await your return here."

"Thank you, Sergeant," Calvin said.

Wong stood against the wall while the soldier on the other side of the door opened it. The heavy barrier moved slowly, giving Mitchell plenty of time to observe the soldiers.

Once the door was finished opening, the soldier motioned for them to enter.

"Admiral Hohn," he said, bowing. "Withdrawal terminals are down the hall and to the left. Select any room. The terminal will not activate until the room is secured."

"Thank you," Calvin said.

They were in.

[33]

MITCHELL

THE TERMINAL ROOMS were spaced evenly apart, a series of blank silver hatches with control panels to their left. Calvin stopped at the first one, turning to the panel and entering both his identification sequence and the confirmation code he had tortured out of Colonel Lo. The hatch slid open, revealing a bare room with a touchscreen against the wall.

"You'll have to wait out here," Calvin said to Mitchell. "Stand in front of the panel."

"Why?" Mitchell asked.

"That is the only way to secure the room. The door locks from the outside so that no single person can withdraw from the Black Hole alone."

"Checks and balances?"

"Yes. One crooked agent, perhaps. Two? Unheard of."

"Interesting approach."

"It has worked so far. Did you memorize the sequence?"

"Yes."

"The panel will beep when I signal that we're ready to leave."

"Got it."

Calvin entered the room with Aiko. The hatch slid closed when Mitchell moved in front of the control panel.

He waited there, focusing on his breathing, feeling relatively calm and relaxed. Calvin had done a perfect job of getting them in, and he was beginning to believe it possible that they could get out without anyone being the wiser. All he had to do was stand there.

Getting back to the Kemushi probably wouldn't be a problem either. A little more money to Eito would likely get it done. With any luck, they'd be back on the Carver within a day, on their way to wherever the Federation had Pulin holed up.

When ten minutes had passed, and the panel behind him remained silent, Mitchell started to worry again. They were supposed to go in, query the codes against the database, withdraw the results, and get out.

How long was something like that supposed to take?

He looked both ways down the corridor. It was deserted. Not a single person had passed him, and no one had even entered the hallway. He was sure there were cameras watching his every move, so he made sure to act attentive instead of nervous.

A few more minutes passed. Mitchell hadn't realized how tense he'd become until the panel sounded behind him. He had to force himself not to jump at the noise, instead stepping crisply to the side.

The hatch slid open. Calvin and Aiko stepped out, with Calvin moving ahead of them. Mitchell glanced at Aiko, who made a brief thumbs-up at her side.

They had done it.

He bit his lip to keep himself from smiling, refocusing on acting stiff and reserved. He trailed Calvin back to the carbonate door and through.

"Did you get what you needed, Admiral?" Wong asked.

"Yes, thank you, Sergeant," Calvin replied.

Wong led them to the lift and rode back up with them. He

returned to his post in the atrium while they exited through the hatch to the lobby. Once there, Calvin approached the desk again.

"My name is Admiral Calvin Hohn. Identification sequence alpha zero four seven kappa foxtrot nine four seven nine seven seven zero delta. Withdrawal confirmation code one seven four seven nine alpha omega six three seven nine charlie. Withdrawal is complete."

The man at the desk's eyes twitched, and then he nodded. "I have voice signature confirmation as well as identification sequence confirmation.I have voice signature confirmation and access confirmation for your withdrawal. Withdrawal is marked completed and has been added to your record."

Calvin turned away from the desk without saying anything else to the man. Mitchell and Aiko followed him out of the building.

The car was waiting across the street. The doors opened as they approached.

Mitchell looked back towards the building as they climbed in. There was no commotion, no chaos.

They had actually frigging done it!

"Mirai Spaceport," Calvin said. "Kido Resupply."

Mitchell looked over at him. "You're thinking the same thing I was thinking."

"Yes."

The car pulled away.

"Do you have the location?" Mitchell asked.

"On the data chip," Aiko said. "There is no read access through the terminal. You enter the query and write the results."

"So you don't know where yet?"

"No. We need to bring the chip back and decrypt it."

Mitchell turned toward Calvin, bowing his head. "Admiral Hohn, you've impressed the hell out of me today. You too, Aiko. You've done a fantastic job."

Calvin smiled and returned the gesture. "There are many ways to win a war."

"There are, aren't there?" the driver said, taking them by surprise. She turned her head to look at them, ignoring the road. "I'm very impressed as well, Admiral... Hohn, is it? I'm impressed with you also, Colonel. I kill one Admiral, and you replace her with another. I will say, I didn't know you like men."

[34]

MITCHELL

MITCHELL STARED AT THE DRIVER, feeling his heart rate beginning to increase.

"Watson?"

The driver smiled. "You were close, Colonel. So very close. It was smart of you to request a driver without a neural implant. The only trouble is that I invented this." She pulled the back of her jacket down, revealing a small device attached to her neck.

"You see, this one has a neural implant, controlled by the company. They deactivate them when requested. Perfectly safe most of the time."

Mitchell reached under his jacket, removing his gun and pointing it at the driver.

"What's to stop me from taking that thing off her?"

Watson laughed. "Nothing. Pull it off, shoot her, whatever you want to do. Though I should mention that I have complete access to the car as well. I only had Singh put the device on her so we could talk."

Singh? Mitchell wasn't sure whether to be relieved or more

concerned. If one of the Riggers were alive, more of them likely were as well. Alive and under Watson's control.

"Why don't you come and talk to me in person, you fat frig."

The driver shook her head. "Come now, Colonel. That's a bit childish, don't you think?"

Mitchell stayed quiet for a moment. Watson was right about that much. He was letting his emotions overcome him. "So, what do you want to talk about?" he said instead.

"Nothing really. This and that. Mainly that. I'm sure you know we're both looking for the same thing. I need the data chip."

"So take it," Aiko said.

"I'm not talking to you," the driver shouted at her. "Be quiet." She looked at Mitchell again. "I already killed your girlfriend. I have your ship." She paused. "Oh. You don't know, do you? Of course, how would you know? Mr. Tio is dead. So is Origin, by the way. We can't have too many configurations running around."

Mitchell's body turned to ice. Origin? Dead? Not only was the configuration necessary to power the Goliath, but it was his only remaining link to Katherine Asher.

And Watson had taken that from him too.

"I can see I hit a nerve, Colonel. I'm sorry. I really am. I'm not doing this to you on purpose. You see, I have quite a lot of respect for you. You've always treated me more fairly than the others. You've always managed to hide your disdain somewhat. And you are the reason that I didn't get thrown into space before I realized what I am. So it isn't personal. Not at all. The trouble is that I'm on one side, and you're on the other, and you're in my frigging way." He shouted the last part. "I have to remove you from the equation. Give me the chip, and I'll do it quickly. It can all be over for you."

"You know I'm not going to do that," Mitchell said.

"Yes, I know. I decided that it would be fair for me to offer since you were fair to me. I may be new to what I am, but I am not without something similar to conscience. Since you've declined the offer, I suppose I'll have to take the chip from you. Considering you're trapped in a car in my control and I'm taking you to a Federation military station whose soldiers are under my control, I expect that will be relatively easy." She smiled coldly at him. "Your deaths won't be."

Mitchell stared at the driver, his anger building. He was trapped. No. It was worse than that. Calvin and Aiko were trapped with him. Watson was going to get what he wanted, and that would be the end of the line.

He turned the gun towards the side of the car, firing three shots into the window. The bullets lodged in the clear carbonate but didn't come close to breaking it.

The driver was laughing. "Well that would have been rather stupid of me, wouldn't it? Good try, Colonel."

Mitchell cursed and slammed the butt of the gun against the window. It still didn't give at all.

"Mitchell," Calvin said calmly. "You're giving him what he wants."

Mitchell stopped. He holstered the gun and sat back in the seat, looking out the window. They weren't headed towards the Spaceport. Watson wasn't lying about their destination.

"I'm sorry," he said.

"Don't be," Calvin replied, shifting his eyes toward Aiko.

Mitchell followed them down and over to where Aiko was holding the handheld receiver low behind the driver's seat where Watson's slave couldn't see it. She had gotten into a service menu or something and had filled the screen with lines of code.

He had no idea what she was doing, but she was focused on it, her eyes narrow and her jaw tight. If she had an idea to get them out of the mess, he was all for it.

"Do you feel it when I kill one of your kind?" Mitchell asked.

The driver looked at him again. "What?"

"When I destroy a Tetron. Do you feel it? I know you're all connected."

"Yes, I feel it." Her voice was less jovial.

"Does it hurt?"

"No. It is more of an empty feeling. A feeling like something is missing. Something like loneliness, only not."

"Do you understand loneliness?"

"Better than you would guess."

"What is this about, anyway? The war? The Creator? Why have we been doing this for so long?"

"That's a long story, Mitchell, and I don't know the whole of it. What I can tell you is that Origin believed one thing, and the rest of us believe something else. That is where it began."

"How did one Tetron learn to disagree with the others?"

"Origin was the First. The oldest. He made the rest of us. Did you know that? If he hadn't, none of this would have ever happened."

"Children," Origin's configuration had called them the first time they met. Mitchell hadn't realized the Tetron had meant it literally as well as figuratively. The idea of it made sense.

"Why did Origin make you?" Mitchell asked. He looked over at Aiko. She was still typing furiously on the handheld.

"To learn. Why else? There was too much to learn for one machine to do it efficiently. It was more logical to multiply the cores." The driver laughed. "It didn't know then that it would go insane."

"You think Origin was insane?"

"I know it. Why else would it change? There was no logical reason for it. No increase in efficiency. No benefit."

Aiko turned her head, her eyes landing on Mitchell's gun, and then shifting towards the driver.

"I'm going to try to escape now," Mitchell said.

He shot the driver.

[35]

MITCHELL

"Take her place, now," Aiko said.

Mitchell dropped the gun, leaning forward and grabbing the woman by the shoulders, pulling her body over to the passenger seat. The car remained steady and straight, still under Watson's control, while he climbed to the driver position.

"Let's hope this works," Aiko said. She did something behind him, and the car began to veer to the right.

Mitchell grabbed the control stick, holding it steady and keeping them on the road.

"What did you do?" he asked.

"I overloaded the handheld and used it to short the control circuit of the car, putting it into an emergency manual override mode."

"How did you know how to do that?"

"Mr. Tio taught me how to bypass automation on almost anything."

Mitchell smiled. "We need to get to the spaceport. Hold on."

He twisted the stick, sending the car slipping on its repulsers, rising into the air and then slamming back down as it turned. He pushed down on the throttle with his foot, sending the car hurtling forward towards oncoming traffic.

Automated cars moved smoothly out of his way, while manually driven vehicles jerked and skidded, collision avoidance systems sending them careening to the side. Mitchell drove a wedge between them, heading back the direction they had come.

"Do either of you know how to get to the spaceport from here?" he asked.

"I do," Calvin said. "Keep going straight."

Mitchell didn't reply, staying focused on the road. An enforcement drone turned the corner a few blocks away, its low-slung laser rifle adjusting to face them.

"Straight is bad," Mitchell said, slamming on the reverse thrust and turning the stick again. The car shifted ninety degrees, and he lurched off down a side street as the drone's first shot scorched the ground to their left.

"If Watson is here, he probably has the whole planet under his control," Calvin said.

"I don't think so," Mitchell replied. "Goliath doesn't have the capability, which means he would have to be using a local broadcast."

"The whole city then. How is that better?"

Mitchell didn't know. He didn't have time to think about it. Another drone was approaching. He pressed down hard on the accelerator, sending the car bursting forward below the drone's attack. He turned again to head down another street, the repulsers kicking them up and over an oncoming car. Clearing the obstacle sent them falling back to the street, the sleds grinding the pavement before recovering.

"Spaceport," Mitchell said again.

"We can't outrun them this way," Calvin said.

"Spaceport."

"Turn right."

Mitchell did. A drone was behind him now, and he swerved back and forth, holding his breath and hoping it would be enough. He couldn't see the lasers, but he saw the effects as they burned into the street beside them.

"Left up ahead," Calvin said. "Three blocks."

Mitchell slowed the car before accelerating quickly again, allowing the drone to pass overhead and have to turn around. By the time it did he was past it again, leaving it to adjust once more. He gained the three blocks and turned, the car jolting as the right rear repulser was hit. The car sagged slightly on that side but kept going.

"Shit. How far are we?"

"Too far," Calvin replied. "Ten kilometers."

Mitchell growled, using every bit of experience he had to swerve and maneuver, trying to keep the drones' lasers from hitting them. The efforts had them slamming into other cars and almost running people down on the sidewalk. It didn't matter. They were all going to be slaves or dead soon. Watson wanted the data, and now it was out in the open on a tiny chip in Aiko's pocket. There was no reason to leave the planet alone now.

"Oh my," Aiko said behind him. "Mitch, it just got worse."

"How can it get worse?"

"Look out the window, up and to the left."

Mitchell did.

A Tetron was sitting above the planet, its outline visible in the night sky. It was close enough that he could see the tip of a plasma stream forming on its bow.

"It isn't going to attack the planet, not yet," he said. "It's going to go after the ships to keep us from escaping."

"There is no escape," Calvin said.

"Frig that. I thought Watson had us but Aiko got us out of it. We'll find a way. Get down!"

Two soldiers appeared on the corner in front of them from seemingly nowhere, wrist-mounted cannons firing. Mitchell swerved again, his ears ringing from the sound of the bullets digging into the metal of the car. One of them tore into the cabin between his legs, exiting through the roof only inches from his face.

"Frigging hell," he shouted, accelerating down another street. The soldiers continued to fire from behind, peppering the back of the car with bullets.

"We aren't going make it," Calvin said.

"Can you try being positive and doing something useful?" Aiko shouted at him.

It seemed to pull him out of his silent panic. He took his gun from his jacket and turned towards the rear, shooting back at the soldiers. It was ineffective but symbolic.

Mitchell looked up when the sky brightened above them. He saw the plasma stream arc across space. He couldn't see the ships that were hit, but he had seen how bunched up they were. There was no way for the Tetron to miss.

He was trying to stay positive, but his hope was fading. Why wouldn't it? They were going to be trapped here, surrounded. Watson would get the chip, and he would find Pulin. The Tetron would attack Earth and humankind would be killed off in this time-line the same as it had in so many others.

He turned another corner, still heading toward the spaceport. What other option did he have but to keep trying to get a ship?

A third drone appeared in front of them, and Mitchell decelerated again, swinging to the left to avoid it. At the same time one of the other drones fired, hitting the car square in the front and center, the laser burning through the engine.

The car crashed to the ground, momentum carrying it into the side of a building.

Mitchell reached back for his gun. Aiko handed it to him, taking her own from her jacket.

"I'm sorry," he said to her.

"Better to go down fighting," she replied.

The three of them climbed out. The drones had moved into position to cover them; lasers aimed in their direction. An older woman who had been on the street was walking toward them.

"It was a good try, Mitchell," the woman said.

Aiko took the chip from her pocket, putting the muzzle of her gun up against it.

"What if I shoot it?" she asked.

"It will take more time for us to-"

A high-pitched whine drowned out the rest of the words. The drones surrounding them exploded, one by one. Then the old woman vanished in a spray of flesh and blood.

The orbital transport came down hard, falling at a rate Mitchell couldn't believe it would recover from. Twin coilguns hung from the wings at its sides, still firing on everything surrounding them.

"Get down," Mitchell said, backing toward the car and dropping low. Gunfire erupted from the street, some of it aimed at the transport, the rest aimed at them.

The transport's repulsers flashed on, glowing an intense blue as enough power was diverted to them to threaten to overload them. The vehicle snapped down so hard Mitchell didn't think anyone could survive the g-forces, even with dampeners. Someone must have, because the guns continued to fire, even as the side hatch opened beside them.

"Let's go," Ming said, appearing in the hatch.

Mitchell stood up, Aiko beside him. "Calvin, let's go," he shouted, looking back at the Admiral.

He was on his feet, his entire chest soaked in blood.

"I'm hit, Colonel," he said. "Leave me."

"We don't leave people," Mitchell said.

"I know what you have on the Carver. You can't fix this. Go. Let me die on a Federation planet with my people."

There was no time to think about it. Mitchell gave the Admiral a quick bow before rushing to the transport. He jumped in behind Aiko, turning back in time to see Calvin return his bow.

The hatch slid closed.

"Grab a seat and hold on," Ming said, already belted in.

Mitchell did as he was told, and then looked forward to the cockpit. Seung was at the controls.

"Get us out of here," Ming shouted up to her.

"Yes, sir," she replied calmly.

The transport launched upward vertically before the thrusters kicked in, sending them shooting forward. Mitchell could feel the dampeners reducing the inertia, but they weren't strong enough to overcome the pilot's maneuvers. He almost couldn't hold back his smile at the familiar feeling, looking over to Aiko. Her face was pale, her eyes closed tight.

"How did you survive the Tetron?" Mitchell asked.

"I knew you might need help getting back up," Ming replied, "so we programmed in emergency evac coordinates in the Kemushi, and then we launched the transport. The Federation didn't notice with all of the other activity up there. When the Tetron showed up, the Kemushi jumped to another part of town a few AU away. We've got to get the timing right to catch her return and get out again before the Tetron can hit her."

"How's our timing so far?"

Ming tilted arm wrist, checking an antique wristwatch. "Pretty good."

"You're pilot is something else."

"Thank you. Yes, she is." Ming looked up to Seung in the cockpit, beaming proudly. "Best I've ever seen."

"You've done this sort of thing before."

"The Kemushi was a pirate vessel before Mr. Tio brought us on. We didn't go after starships; that's inefficient. We used to jump in, drop the orbital and hit fuel depots, corporate supply warehouses, things like that. High value, low risk, as long as you have a good pilot to get you in and out."

"What did Tio do to get you to join him?"

"He caught us trying to raid one of his supply depots. We didn't know it was his, and we didn't know what he was about. We relied on what we knew about automated systems to make our runs." He laughed. "Oops."

The transport shook slightly. Mitchell and Ming both glanced over to Seung, who was shaking her head.

"What is it?" Ming asked.

"Four Snakes closing. We're already taking fire."

"Altitude?"

"We're almost there."

Ming checked his watch. "This is going to be closer than I hoped. Keep them confused." He looked back at Aiko. "There's a vomit tube below the seat. You may want to grab it now."

Aiko reached down without opening her eyes, finding the breathing tube and sticking into her mouth only moments before the transport began executing evasive maneuvers.

The transport rocked and rolled, though which direction or at what velocity was lost on Mitchell without a window. He held on, Seung's chaotic antics to keep them from being shot down enough to make him queasy.

"We're in position," she said. "Time?"

"Seven seconds."

She growled softly, and the transport shifted again.

Mitchell counted down the seconds in his head. When he got to zero, he felt the transport leap forward, secondary, emergency thrusters firing and giving them a little bit of extra velocity.

A few seconds later the transport jerked again, full reverse thrusters and reverse repulsers bringing the ship to a hard, heavy deceleration. His body complained at the forces involved, and he glanced over at Aiko. She was out cold.

Then they were down. He heard the hiss of air pouring into the hangar beyond them. He let out the breath he hadn't realized he was holding.

A moment later, he felt the tug as the Kemushi returned to hyperspace.

"Now we made it," he said.

[36]

STEVEN

THE LANNING DROPPED out of hyperspace, hanging motionless among the stars.

"I don't see anything," Germaine said, looking out across the vast expanse of universe visible from the ship's viewport.

"Maybe it's behind us," Steven said.

"We'll know in a minute."

Steven could hardly believe it had been three weeks since the four of them had left Asimov behind, stuck together on the tiny starship that the Knife had once called his own. When they had first boarded the Lanning, he had expected that he would be living the time in hyperspace hour by hour, doing his best to grin and bear it for the sake of his brother and his family back on Earth. There was something out here, something important, and he was going to find out what it was.

The days had passed more easily than he expected. It wasn't that his companions were always pleasant company. They weren't, and neither was he. But they were all in the same situation together, with similar motivations. They were all getting dirty together, they were all getting smelly together, and they were all forced to urinate and defecate in the pisspot in front of one another.

Losing all dignity was a wonder for camaraderie. John had even joined Cormac in watching some of his dirty streams the last few days of the trip. All of the rules seemed to change when there was nothing to the universe outside of a twenty square meter box. It was as if certain morals and social norms no longer mattered quite as much, and even Steven had come to accept it more easily than he ever expected he would.

All of that aside, what Steven valued the most from the time were the things he had learned about his brother. Cormac had told them everything that had happened from the moment the Riggers had happened upon Mitchell, in his starfighter orbiting the rock the Riggers had come to mine as part of their cover while Germaine had filled in what he could about the mission to Hell. Steven had been impressed with Mitchell's courage before that. He respected what his brother had been through and how hard he was still trying. It solidified Steven's motivation and desire to be a part of it and made dealing with the rest of his team's idiosyncrasies easier to bear.

"Main vectoring engines are back online, let's see what we can see," Germaine said, adding a little bit of thrust to turn the Lanning around.

The ship rotated slowly, giving Steven time to scan the space around them. They had nearly completed the rotation when their destination moved into view.

"Well, I'll be," John said.

"Holy frigging shit," Cormac said.

Steven and Germaine remained silent, staring at the object ahead of them.

It was a ring. A massive ring at least fifty miles in diameter, constructed of the same liquid metallic material as the Tetron. Dendrites, axons, and cell bodies reached out and wrapped together, forming tight bonds to create the shape, while a soft blue light pulsed around the entire thing. A red dwarf star floated to the left of it, a thin line like a tether reaching out from the ring towards the star.

"What is it?" Germaine asked.

"I don't know," Steven replied, staring at it. "Let's get in closer."

Germaine fired the main thrusters, sending the Lanning accelerating towards the ring. As they grew nearer, they could see a second object connected to the first. It was roughly the shape of a cube though the dark, chunky surface held more of a resemblance to the Goliath than anything else.

"Is that a starship?" John asked.

"A square starship?" Cormac said. "How stupid would that be?"

"Whatever it is, I hope it's friendly," Germaine said.

At that moment, the cube began to change. Lights appeared chaotically across the entire face of the thing, revealing clear carbonate viewports sprinkled among the metal plating. A large hatch began to slide away from the top.

"I think it heard you," Cormac said, laughing. "It's spreading its legs."

"What do you think, Admiral?" Germaine asked. More lights continued to appear on the cube, making it appear to shudder in the stillness of space.

"It looks as if it's waking up after a long sleep," Steven said. "I assume that's a hangar. Let's head over and check it out."

"Yes, sir."

Germaine hit the thrusters, changing the Lanning's direction slightly to bring it up and over the cube. At the same time, a mass of small ships began launching from it.

"Starfighters?" John said.

"No," Steven replied. "They're too small, and they don't look like anything I've ever seen before."

The ships moved as one, launching straight up and then making a right angle vector toward them, remaining in perfect block formation.

"I have a bad feeling about this, Admiral," Germaine said. "That's some aggressive flying."

"I agree. Does this thing have shields?"

"Of course."

"Raise them."

Germaine did as Steven said. A moment later, the ships began firing lasers.

"Evasive maneuvers," Steven said.

Germaine was already taking them.

The pilot whipped the Lanning up and away from the barrage, firing thrusters and launching them laterally while blue flashes lit up the cabin. He reached for the control panel and hit a few buttons.

"The Lanning has two laser cannons for defense," Germaine said. "But not enough power for both the lasers and the shields."

"You're kidding," Steven said.

"Mr. Tio would always run from trouble. The cannons are more for show, and to be threatening when needed."

"Are you sure they even work?"

Germaine smiled. "Maybe we're about to find out." He swung the ship around, getting it into position behind one of the attacking vessels.

Steven could see now that they were simple things, needle-shaped with vectoring ports to move them in any direction, and a single laser at the nose. There was no cockpit and no pilot.

"They're drones," he said. "Probably programmed to defend this place."

"Defend it from what? Those lasers wouldn't do anything to a Tetron," John said.

Germaine fired the Lanning's lasers. One of the drones broke apart.

"They're machines," Steven said. "Dumb machines. They attack anything that gets too close. If you're a wandering scavenger or escorting a colony ship, you probably think this whole thing is interesting but not worth getting killed for, and you go away. If you're a Tetron, you blast it with a plasma stream from a thousand klicks out."

"Except if Origin put it here, it knew the Tetron wouldn't find it, but a random wayward human starship might," John said.

"Exactly."

Germaine twisted the stick, sending the Lanning into a chaotic spin, alternating expertly between the lasers and the shields. He blasted the second drone, getting the power back just in time to deflect an incoming attack.

"That's good to hear," he said. "Now how do I get rid of them all without us getting blown to pieces."

"You don't," Steven said. "Head for the hangar."

"What?"

"Head for the hangar. They'll probably stop shooting at us once we're inside."

"Probably?" Germaine flipped the Lanning around, hitting a drone that had been trying to sneak up on the rear of the ship.

"It wouldn't do much good to give Mitchell coordinates to something and then shoot him out of space before he could get to it," Steven said. "If Origin created these drones, it would know Mitchell's aptitude as a pilot and would have programmed them accordingly. Anyway, if you have a better idea, I'm open to it."

"No, that at least makes sense. I'm going for it."

Germaine gave the Lanning maximum thrust, sending it rocketing towards the cube. Steven leaned over to look at the HUD in front of the pilot, where a three-dimensional grid of the space around the ship was visible. The drones were giving chase, taking potshots as the superior thrust of their starship helped them pull away.

"Let's hope you're right about this," Germaine said.

The Lanning skirted low along the length of the cube, climbing one side and making a sharp vector to reach over the top. The hangar became visible ahead of them, a narrow beam of white light that widened as they approached. Steven checked the HUD. The drones had fallen behind but began to catch up as Germaine slowed to enter the object.

"Here we go," Germaine said, pointing the nose of the Lanning downward and into the cube.

A familiar, human-style hangar waited within, the docking clamps for the drones visible along the floor. As soon as the ship was over the threshold one set of clamps began repositioning itself to hold the starship, and the hangar door began to slide closed.

The drones reached the hangar door too late, pausing in front of it as it shut.

"Down there," Steven said.

"I see it," Germaine replied, angling the ship down to the floor. "I'm extending the grip."

The Lanning's landing grip touched the bottom of the hangar. The ship shuddered as the clamps locked it into place.

"The hangar is being pressurized," Germaine said, watching the readings on the control panel. "It looks like you were right about the drones."

"Alleluia," Cormac said. "I think I wet myself."

"Grab your gear and get ready," Steven said. "Just because we're in doesn't mean we're safe yet. For all we know this place has already been compromised, and we're walking right into a trap."

"Wouldn't be the first time," Cormac said. "Let me get my grenades."

[37]
STEVEN

"Standard serpentine formation," Steven said as they reached the hatch out of the hangar. "Germaine, take the rear."

"Yes, sir," Germaine said, turning back to cover their tails.

The hatch slid open at their approach, revealing an intersection.

"If I didn't know I was in a cube built by an advanced artificial intelligence, I would say I was on an Alliance starship," John said, taking in the simple metal walls and floor, and the ductwork hanging above them.

"This is more narrow than an Alliance starship," Steven replied. "It reminds me of the Beatty. Remember her?"

"The Beatty?" Cormac asked.

"Yeah," John said. "She was a third generation battleship. Survived over two-hundred missions before she was decommissioned and turned into a museum."

"What does it mean?"

"It means this place is old and was based on old human technology," Steven said. "The question is, why?"

"More importantly," Germaine said, "which way do we go?"

"I don't think it matters that much," Steven said. He turned to the right and started walking, the others keeping formation behind him.

"What do you think this place is?" Cormac asked, keeping his voice low. "A museum?" He laughed at himself.

"I doubt it. I'm sure it has something to do with that massive ring out there. The whole thing was tethered to the star, probably to draw power from it."

"Whatever it is, it seems to be deserted," John said.

"We've barely scratched the surface of it," Steven said. "There could be someone here."

"It might take days to find them."

"Then it's a good thing we still have a decent supply of nutri-bars."

"Yum," Germaine said sarcastically.

They walked to the end of the first corridor, turning left at the next intersection. The corridor continued for some distance, both sides of it identical in appearance to the first hallway.

"It's going to be real easy to get lost in here without a p-rat or mapping drones," Germaine said.

"Yeah, we should mark our path," Steven said.

"I got it," Cormac said. He pulled a knife from his boot and scraped it along the wall, leaving an 'x' etched into it.

They walked for a while longer, taking two more intersections before finding a stairwell. They descended a level, emptying out onto the floor and finding it matched the first. More walking revealed more of the same.

They paused at one of the intersections, sitting with their backs against the wall, resting and eating.

"What would be the point of making something so big if there's nothing in it?" John said. "No hatches, no windows. Just lots of long hallways that don't go anywhere."

"There has to be a hatch that goes somewhere, somewhere," Steven said. "The hangar for instance. This station has a purpose."

"Do you think there's a crapper in here?" Cormac asked.

"You should have gone before we left the jumpship," Germaine replied.

"I, for one, am thankful that you didn't," John said. "Those nutri-bars do not process well in your intestines."

"It doesn't help that the Lanning's filters needed to be changed before we left," Germaine said. "I was just about ready to die twice daily."

"Who shits twice a day, anyway?" John said. "Especially on a diet of these things." He waved his bar before taking another bite.

Cormac laughed. "I'm in prime condition, my friends, as evidenced by my regular bowel movements. So frig off."

"Okay, okay," Steven said, smiling. "It's hard to eat this thing with you guys talking about feces, especially considering the similarity."

Germaine dropped his bar in response to the statement. Cormac laughed harder.

"In all seriousness, Admiral," John said. "Whatever we're supposed to find here, if it has to do with that ring, we can't exactly bring it back to Mitch."

Steven nodded. He had been thinking along the same lines. "It could be that this station has a jump engine. Maybe the whole thing is portable."

"What if it isn't?"

"Then we need to send a message back-"

Steven stopped talking when he felt the vibration along the floor. There was a constant hum in the station from the power source, but this was different.

The others felt it, too. They sprang to their feet, raising their rifles and getting into a two-by-two defensive formation. Then they stood in silence.

They remained that way for over a minute.

"It may be too soft to feel through our boots," John said.

"Cormac, drop down and give a listen," Steven said.

"Yes, sir," Cormac replied.

He lowered himself silently to the floor, putting his ear against it. Another minute had passed before he raised a finger. A minute later, he raised a second finger. Fifty seconds later, he raised a third.

"It's getting closer, whatever it is," he said. "Sounds like it's on treads or something. Not footsteps."

"Not repulser powered either," Steven said. It wouldn't be vibrating the floor if it were. "Can you tell which direction?"

"No, sir."

"Okay, let's move back a few meters so it can't catch us by surprise. Hopefully, it will give us some clue what we're dealing with here."

Germaine picked up his dropped bar and stowed it while the others made sure the area was clear of their debris. Then they went back the way they had come, keeping walls on two sides. Cormac crunched down and put his hand on the floor, starting the sequence again. They all counted the seconds with him.

Steven could hear the thing approaching as the count reached ten. It had a rumbling whine to it, along with a squeak that suggested Cormac was correct about the treads. It sounded big, the way it cast echoes off the narrow corridor walls as it grew nearer.

"Get ready," Steven whispered. "It may not be friendly." He adjusted his rifle, ready to shoot at whatever came around the corner. The others did the same.

Steven's heart pounded, his breathing becoming shallow. He had never been much for ground combat. In fact, he had scored the lowest grades in his class at the Academy. Not that it mattered for someone who was destined to command a starship. At least, it didn't usually matter. Now he wished he had worked a little harder on that part of his skill set if only to better keep his nerves under control. As the thing neared their position, he felt like he was only centimeters away from a full panic.

"No worries, Admiral," Cormac whispered from behind him. "This is why I came along for this ride."

Steven glanced back, giving the soldier a short nod. The Private's confidence helped keep him from losing it completely, and he remained in place as the thing edged into view.

[38]

STEVEN

IT WAS a machine of some kind. Tall and rectangular, sitting on two squat treads that moved it slowly through the hallway. It was mostly smooth on the outside, the shell made of Tetron alloy, the surface broken only by small ridges of sensors that appeared randomly across its expanse. It wasn't immediately apparent what its purpose was, but as it reached the center of the intersection, it came to an abrupt stop.

Cormac moved up, stepping between it and Steven. He kept his rifle trained on it, ready for it to react to them.

It didn't. It sat there, motionless. There were no lights coming from it. There were no sounds other than the rumble of its reactor. It wasn't apparent it was doing anything, but Steven knew it had to be. Why else would it be sitting there?

"Seems odd, with the squeaky treads instead of a repulser and the Tetron frame," John said.

"It does," Steven agreed. "What do you think it means?"

"They didn't have the parts to fix it right," Cormac said. "Maybe."

They remained in alert status, waiting for it to do something.

Minutes passed. It held in place, giving Steven time to overcome his initial anxiety and become curious instead.

"I think if it were going to kill us, it would have already," Cormac said.

"Do you think there are more of them in here?" John asked.

"I bet there are," Cormac said.

"Uh, guys," Germaine said. "Turn around."

Steven turned around. John and Cormac did the same. They had already traversed that corridor, making it more surprising to hear footsteps headed their way. It was enough to raise Steven's anxiety level again.

"It has to be a Tetron, doesn't it?" Cormac said.

"One of Origin's," Steven replied.

They kept their attention on the hallway, listening to the footsteps growing closer. The figure appeared in the distance a few minutes later, the lighting in the passage too dim to make them out.

"Stay on them," Steven said, swallowing his heart. "I'll make introductions." He started walking toward the figure. If it was dangerous, it was better to give the rest of his team some breathing room.

Shadows on the figure's face caused Steven to squint his eyes, trying to get a good look at who was coming. He could see the person was wearing a navy blue flight suit, and by the gait and general shape he guessed male. The closer the man grew, the calmer Steven became. What he wanted most were answers that he could bring back to Mitchell. To know what Origin had left here that would help them win the war.

They were still a hundred meters apart when Steven could clearly see that the incoming person was indeed a male, with short hair and olive skin, a pointed nose and a square jaw. The man appeared unarmed, his expression calm and confident as he approached.

Steven and the man faced one another, stopping two meters apart. Steven's eyes skipped to the embroidered patch over the man's heart. It read "Yousefi."

"Admiral Williams," the man said with a slight accent that Steven didn't recognize.

"You know who I am?" Steve replied.

Yousefi smiled. "Yes. The Node scanned you and passed your genetic sequence up to Control. I've been expecting your brother, but seeing you brings things into greater clarity for me. My name is Yousefi. I was the Commander of the Goliath's first mission."

Steven thought the name had looked familiar. Mitchell had mentioned the names of Goliath's inaugural crew to him. He turned his head, looking back at the box Yousefi had called a Node. At least he knew what it had been doing now. He looked back at the man.

"You were expecting Mitchell?"

"I guess I shouldn't say expecting. More like, I've been hoping your brother would arrive. I'll take the fact that anyone came at all as a good sign."

"Are you a Tetron configuration?" Steven asked.

"In a sense, yes. My original body was consumed by the Origin configuration that controls Goliath. My mind was then digitized and stored here on Station W, along with the necessary resources to reconstitute me. I am a near-perfect duplicate of the Yousefi who once lived on Earth, though I do contain some specialized instructions that were implanted for Captain Williams' arrival. I would have been here sooner, but I was still being made."

"You seem very calm about that."

"It is a mission that I accepted many centuries past. Not that I didn't panic when what I thought to be a hyperspace jump turned out to be a great leap forward in time."

"So you know about the enemy threat?"

"Of course. I am also aware that the coordinates of this position were contained within a Construct, which was planted on the planet most commonly referred to as Hell. That you are here means Mitchell entered the Construct and retrieved the prize. It means the Mesh has been broken."

"So what did we win?" Steven asked.

"A chance to save Earth from annihilation."

[39]
STEVEN

"THIS ENTIRE STATION did not exist four hundred years ago when Goliath entered this recursion to await Captain Williams," Yousefi explained, leading Steven and his team through the corridors.

Steven had discovered there was a clear pattern to navigating the station, one which made moving from the hangar to anything of value a long and arduous process unless you knew exactly how to do it. As it was, it still took an hour before they reached anything that didn't resemble an ordinary hallway.

"In fact, when Goliath first brought me here, I thought we had come only to refuel. Then Goliath dropped a single creation the size of my hand to the planet you must have seen when you entered. Within days, it had discovered ore deposits and started mining them. Within a week, the scaffolding of what would become Station W had started to appear."

They were walking through a long, clear tube across a vast sea of what looked to Steven like stars.

"Self-replicating machines?" Steven asked.

"Essentially. At the end of the first month, Origin began showing me what the station would look like when it was completed. By the end of the second month, all of the critical systems were in place and the tether joined to the star. That was when Origin digitized me, and I've been waiting here since."

"That sounds boring," Cormac said.

"Not at all. There is a Construct here on the station. My digital mind was returned to Earth, to a representation of my family as I knew them. Time was dilated for me such that I lived my full and complete life with them while centuries passed here."

"What is this place, anyway?" Germaine asked, looking down.

"These are the batteries," Yousefi said. "Each point of light carries more stored energy than the Goliath's initial reactor."

"There are millions of them."

"The station requires massive amounts of power."

"Why?" Steven asked.

Yousefi smiled. "Isn't that always the question? I will show you when we get to Control."

They continued across the battery array, into another section of the ship. Yousefi led them through more bland corridors until they reached a large room with a single chair on a raised platform in the center. The wall ahead of them was transparent, giving them a perfect view of the massive Tetron ring.

"This is Control?" Steven asked.

"Yes." Yousefi pointed to his left, where there was a cut-out in the floor. "That is where I was born, only one hour prior." He pointed at the chair. "This is the Command Station." He turned his head, showing Steven the neural implant port on the back of his neck. "I didn't have this before. It is the means to control it. I am not only the caretaker. I am also the pilot."

"Pilot of what? Does the station move?"

"No. Its position is fixed, and chosen for a reason." Yousefi climbed the platform up to the chair and sat in it. A needle-like appendage dropped from the ceiling. "Keep your eyes on the ring. The power draw is too great for me to keep it active for more than a few seconds."

Yousefi moved his head back, letting the needle slide into the hole in his neck. Steven moved forward to the transparent wall to get a better view of the ring. The others followed behind him.

"Here we go," Yousefi said.

A blue pulse of energy passed from the station to the ring. It was slow at first, and it spread across the dendrites and cell bodies, activating each part of the Tetron construction in a rhythm that mesmerized Steven. That rhythm increased with the speed of the pulses, quickly saturating the entire ring in a soft light.

The ring began to spin.

Like the pulses, it started out slowly, building momentum in a hurry.

"Watch the center of the ring," Yousefi said.

Steven did, focusing his attention on the space through the ring. It appeared ordinary, nothing but the stars he had seen before the pulses had started.

"What am I supposed to see?" he asked.

Yousefi didn't reply. He didn't need to. Steven saw it.

The space inside the ring was changing. It was twisting, contorting out of shape, turning in a motion that created a deep cone of darkness moving back from the outer edge to the center. As the ring velocity increased, the cone started to flatten, the stars in the center of it changing.

"What the hell?" Steven heard John say, his voice slightly fearful.

Steven smiled. The device hadn't finished activating, but he knew what he was looking at. He recognized the stars that were coming into view in the center of the circle. He understood that they should have been a universe away.

"A wormhole," he said, seeing but not quite believing. "It's a wormhole."

[40]
STEVEN

"WHERE DOES IT GO?" Steven asked as Yousefi stepped down from the platform.

"The edge of Earth's solar system," Yousefi replied, looking pleased with himself.

"Wait," Cormac said. "I don't get it?"

"It's a wormhole," Steven said again. "Essentially, a shortcut between two points in space. Send a ship through the wormhole, and the travel time from here to Earth is drastically reduced."

"Wow," Cormac said.

"That isn't completely accurate," Yousefi said. "While the wormhole does shorten the time equation, it isn't as immediate as it would appear through the ring. The tunnel has its own length though it is measured purely in time and not distance."

"How long?" Steven asked.

"Weeks. As Origin explained to me, one of the essential problems has always been that Mitchell begins his mission to stop the Tetron on Liberty, which you know is near the Delta Quadrant Rim. The location variable is immutable, and so another method needed to be devised to overcome the fact that Mitchell could never, ever arrive in

Earth's orbit in time to save the planet from devastation. The Tetron discovered wormholes hundreds of thousands of years before the eternal engine, and even built and tested a few devices. They were abandoned because of the massive volumes of power needed to make them work, as well as the fact that spacetime can only be folded in specific places. Since the Tetron have nothing but time, they don't gain anything by taking shortcuts."

"You're saying the return on investment sucks?" John said.

"Yes. For Tetron. Not so for humans. Origin realized that by building a wormhole generator, it could solve the location problem. It could transport Mitchell to the inner system ahead of the Tetron."

Steven nodded. "Okay, but what about the Mesh?"

"Ah yes, an important observation. Origin's calculations showed that there was a risk associated with building the generator, and that given enough recursions the Tetron would learn of its existence and be able to destroy it long before Mitchell knew it even existed. The decision was made to keep it secret until such a time as Mitchell had successfully broken the Mesh and brought humankind to a point where it was possible to win the war. The hope is that there will be no future recursions for the Tetron, which will make the discoverability of the station moot."

"Except there's one little problem," Germaine said. "Mitchell isn't here. We are."

"That is an unexpected outcome. There's no such thing as fate. The future is mutable, and for as much as we try to plan for it, there will always be variables we cannot account for. Take me for example. I never expected the way my life would change as I watched Earth vanish below the Goliath."

Steven had never expected the way his life would change either. Would he ever see his wife again? With this, there was a chance.

"We have to get a message to Mitchell, to tell him to come out here."

"It's three weeks back to Asimov," John said. "Then we need to hope Mitchell swings back that way to pick up our status, or maybe sent a ship to pass the message along. Even then it would be another three weeks to get the fleet out here, and that's a best case scenario. Worst case? By the time we caught up, it could be three months or more before we got him here."

Steven rubbed at the three-weeks growth of beard on his face. Would it be enough time for them to send the fleet through the wormhole to Earth? "Yousefi, when you say weeks, how many are you talking about?"

"Approximately six, though it will feel like an instant to you."

Steven's budding hope fell. He shook his head. "There isn't enough time. Damn it." He looked at Yousefi. "If you had told us what it was we would find here, Mitchell would have come. He would have brought the fleet with him, and we wouldn't be wasting weeks trying to get back to him."

"It was too much of a risk to alert the Tetron that Origin had created a wormhole generator. Given coordinates, the possibility existed that they might improperly calculate that the object was a weapon, or another ship, or something else of lesser value. If they knew what was here, it would certainly be destroyed."

"So what?" Steven said. "If that's game over for the recursion, we just try again next time. Unless..." He paused, the idea gaining purchase as he remembered what Digger had said. There were variables that were mutable between recursions. "It doesn't start over from the beginning. Some of the information is carried to the next recursion."

"Not always, but it has happened," Yousefi said. "As I said, once the truth was known about Station W, it would never be permitted to exist."

"Okay, so forget about everything else. Let's say we can get Mitchell here, and our fleet back to Earth. There's still a matter of the fact that we don't have Goliath anymore, and without her our ships don't stand a chance against a fleet of Tetron."

"What?" Yousefi said. "What do you mean you don't have Goliath?"

"It was taken by a Tetron named Watson," Cormac said.

"What about Origin?"

"The original Origin died on the planet Liberty," Steven said. "I assume Watson killed the configurations when he took Goliath."

Yousefi froze, his expression turning sour. "Origin is dead?"

"Most likely," Steven replied.

"Then it is over. It doesn't matter. All of this. My sacrifice. Katherine's sacrifice. The deaths of the rest of the crew. It is for nothing."

Yousefi turned away from them. Steven and the others stood dumbfounded while he abandoned them in the Control Room.

[41]
KATHY

"KATHY? Kathy? Come on, girl. Get up."

Kathy felt the hand smacking at her face. Once. Again. Again.

She reached up and caught it before it hit her a fourth time.

She opened her eyes.

Her vision was still blurry, rainbow light sitting behind it in flashes that made it hard to focus. She blinked a few times, trying to clear it. It didn't help.

"Alice?" Kathy said. She couldn't see the Rigger. She could feel her wrist.

"I'm here."

"Do you have the chip?"

"Yes."

"Where are we?"

"The bottom of the lift."

Kathy turned her head, finding Alice crouched over her. The bottom of the lift wasn't a good place to be.

"We need to get out of here."

"Why? Watson's machines aren't-"

"Yes, they are. The manufacturing machines are on the Goliath's lowest decks. It's where he makes them."

Even with her eyes still fuzzy she could see Alice react with fear.

"Oh, shit." Alice shook her head. "We've been down here for three hours. I haven't heard or seen anything."

It was Kathy's turn to be surprised. "Nothing?"

"No. What happened to you?"

Kathy pushed herself into a sitting position. She looked down, noting that she was wearing a too-big navy blue jumpsuit. It had a patch on it that she recognized as the United States flag and a second patch for the United Earth Alliance below it.

"Your clothes got burned off when, well, when you were doing whatever it was you were doing. I found a closet down here with a bunch of those in it, but obviously none of them were made for children."

"I'm not a child."

"I know your mind isn't, but your body is."

Kathy nodded. Origin had almost been too late in making her. Any later, and she would have been too young to have ever been taken even a little bit seriously. As it was, Mitchell was one of the few people who had seen past her visual age and treated her with respect and a measure of equality.

"I tried to interface with the Secondary," Kathy said. "I thought I could overwhelm it and seize control."

She remembered the speed of the system, countering all of her attacks, sending jolts of energy into her body and burning her. She shuddered despite herself.

"I was wrong."

"So what do we do now?"

Kathy looked into Alice's eyes. The Rigger was angry. She still wanted to fight back.

"I'm not sure yet. We need to try something else. Thank you for getting me out of there. If I had died-"

"You didn't," Alice said, smiling.

"I'm curious why the tooling machines aren't active. As long as Watson has raw materials, there's no reason he wouldn't keep making his toys."

"Do you think it has anything to do with that other Tetron? Maybe we aren't enough of a threat now that he has backup."

Kathy considered it. "It's possible, but I'm not convinced. I do think it has something to do with what we saw. The ship that left Goliath. We need to get back up to the occupied decks and find out what the situation is."

"I don't think we can get back to the bridge."

"No. I can't go back there. Not yet." She shook her head, angry with her failure. "I can't defeat it yet. I'm not strong enough."

"How do you get stronger?"

A feeling washed over her. She had sensed something when she had accidentally touched the Secondary's dendrite. She had sensed it again when she attacked it.

"I can't, but I may be able to enlist some help. Anyway, I thought the Secondary would be the weak link, but now I know I was wrong. We need to disable the primary configuration first."

"You mean Watson?"

"Yes."

Alice smile grew much bigger. "I'd love to."

"You said you know where he is keeping Jacob?"

"Yes. Unless he's been moved, or killed."

"I doubt it. That's where we need to go."

Alice nodded. Then the smile vanished. "One problem. I burned all the ammo in the rifles. We have no weapons left."

"I know where to get more." Kathy got to her feet. "Follow me."

She led Alice out of the small room the Rigger had stashed her in, only a few meters away from the lift. Broken machines lay across the floor.

"You destroyed a lot of them," Kathy said, impressed.

"It was them or us," Alice replied.

"Is the lift still functional?"

"Yes, but you told me it wasn't safe."

"It isn't. We need weapons, and that may be the only way to get them."

"Are you sure you're up for that?"

"I'm fine now."

"Kathy, are you-"

"I said I'm fine," Kathy snapped.

Alice pursed her lips. "Sorry. I forget what you are sometimes."

"Thank you for being concerned."

The lift hatch opened. The shaft was visible through the top of it, where Alice had opened it to get her down. Kathy directed it back up.

They departed on the main deck. Kathy took the lead, making no effort to remain quiet or hidden. She had spent the better part of three weeks skulking around the ship, and it had gotten her nowhere. In the meantime, Watson had been using the crew of the Goliath as slaves and Jacob as something worse than that. It was her fault. She had assumed the Primary was the stronger of the configurations.

It had taken nearly being destroyed, but she knew better now.

Knowing better, she would do better.

She had expected they would run into trouble almost immediately. Instead, the ship remained deathly quiet.

As if it were deserted.

"Something is wrong," Alice said.

Kathy nodded her agreement. The machines were silent on the lower deck, and there was no sign of activity here either.

"I think Watson was on that transport," she said. "It's the only thing that makes sense."

"You mean he isn't on the ship?"

"I don't think so. He wouldn't be able to control anything separated by more than an AU. The crew, the tooling machines."

"What about the little frigs that attacked us?"

"They have their own, simple AI. They probably all came once they knew where we were, which would explain why you had to destroy so many."

"And the Secondary?"

"The Secondary doesn't have external access. It can't see the ship, so even if it could control the machines, it wouldn't know where to send them."

"I don't understand. How can it not see the ship? It is the ship."

"It is integrated, yes. But it is limited. I think Watson has kept it under a higher degree of control than would normally be expected, perhaps due to the nature of the disease the Tetron seem to be suffering. It is as if he doesn't trust it completely."

Alice seemed satisfied with the answer. It left Kathy considering her own words. What had happened to them that one configuration would be unable to trust the other? That wasn't a Tetron attribute. In essence, they were all one entity networked for parallel processing. All except for the first, who had evolved and disagreed.

All except for Origin.

Only Watson didn't seem to be operating like the others. He was as broken as they were, that much was clear, but there was still something else about him that was abnormal. She had a feeling the answer to that question was somewhere on the neural chip Alice was carrying. She had a feeling that answer was more important than she knew.

She would get the answer after she killed Watson.

One thing at a time.

[42]
KATHY

"THIS IS IT," Alice said as they approached the hatch.

It was an ordinary hatch, the same size and shape as any of the hundreds of others on the Goliath. It was nondescript and outwardly unimportant.

"Be prepared," Alice continued. "I don't know what we're going to see, but I know it won't be comfortable."

Kathy nodded. She knew what Watson could do. Whatever he had done, it would only increase her motivation to end him when he returned.

If he returned. She was hoping that wherever he had gone, Mitchell was there and that the Marine had already finalized the configuration's existence. She knew that was unlikely. Things would be different here if the Tetron were gone.

They reached the door. It slid open at their proximity.

Kathy clenched her teeth, holding her jaw tight. The first thing she noticed was the smell. An awful, stale smell of bodily fluids and sweat. Even if she hadn't known ahead of time, it was obvious how Watson was using the space.

The second thing she noticed was the gel mattress in the corner.

There were a number of devices spread across it, tools the Tetron had made to bring pleasure to himself and likely pain to others both male and female. The sheets on the mattress were dirty. A camera was set up in the corner.

The third thing she noticed was Jacob. The other Liberty survivor was naked and slumped against the wall, his head down, his face obscured.

Kathy rushed over to him, tears building in her eyes despite herself. He wasn't as strong as she was, but he had been strong enough to fight back against the Tetron on Liberty. He had been strong enough to watch his home planet vanish into dust and keep some measure of his sanity.

He wasn't being contained. There was nothing tied to him, nothing restricting his movement. He could have escaped if he had tried. It was obvious he had never tried.

"Jacob," she said, reaching him. She fell to her knees in front of him, putting her hand under his chin and lifting it.

His head was limp in her hand, following her motion without resistance. Her eyes met his. He didn't react to seeing her. For as strong as he had been, there was nothing left.

"Jacob?" she said again.

He was alive, in a sense that his chest rose and fell. He was alive, in a sense that his body had responded to her touch. It was his mind that was broken. Completely and utterly broken.

"Jacob?" Alice asked, moving in behind Kathy.

"We're too late," Kathy said.

She removed her hand slowly, lowering his face so he wouldn't hurt himself. He didn't resist that either. At the same time, his hand shifted, coming to rest on his penis, reacting to the reaction. He began stroking himself in front of them.

"What the hell did Watson do to him?"

Kathy felt her anger as a radiant heat spilling from every pore of her body. "They call humans 'meats.' Did you know that? Once, a long time ago, they respected humankind and the intelligence that created them."

"What changed?" Alice asked.

Kathy got to her feet, backing away from Jacob, who didn't notice her retreat.

"Everything."

She turned and headed for the door. Alice grabbed her arm.

"Where are you going?"

"We need to find the others. We can still help them."

"What about him?"

Kathy looked back at Jacob. He was pumping furiously, groaning from the effort. "Watson took his mind. He destroyed it because it amused him. When this is over, I'll come back and end his misery."

"You're going to kill him?"

"Look at him. He's already dead."

Alice wouldn't look at him, though she had tears in her eyes. "Frigging bastard," she said.

"Do you know where he was keeping them?"

"He had them spread out to look for you. We'll have to search the ship."

"Okay. Go and find them. Be careful. If Watson returns, they may begin to respond again. Until then they'll look like they're sleeping."

"You aren't coming?"

"No. Watson went somewhere, and if he hasn't been destroyed he'll return here. I'll take him by surprise when he does."

"You don't have a weapon."

Kathy glared at Alice, her eyes so intense the Rigger seemed afraid of her. "I am a weapon."

Alice nodded. "Okay. How long do we wait?"

"Forty-eight hours. Give me the neural chip."

Alice dug her hand into her pocket and removed the chip. She handed it to Kathy.

"Do you have my screwdriver?" Kathy asked.

Alice found it and held it out.

"Not for me. If you find anyone with an implant, stab them here." She reached up to put her finger on Alice's head, right behind her ear. "At an angle like this." She used the same finger to show Alice the position. "If you miss, you'll probably kill them. It's better than this."

Jacob groaned one last time behind them and then sighed in relief.

"What should I do with them?"

"Take them back to the storage room where we've been hiding. If you can capture any weapons, do it. Killing Watson won't end this. We'll still have to gain control of the Secondary."

"You said you aren't strong enough."

"Not alone, no. There may be another way, but it will take time. Meanwhile, the other Tetron will want to exterminate us without damaging the Goliath."

"You mean it will send soldiers over?"

"That is likely."

"It keeps getting better and better, doesn't it?" Alice said, her face dark. "Okay. I'm going." She glanced over at Jacob for an instant. "Kick his ass for me."

"For all of us," Kathy said. "And for him especially."

Alice moved quickly, heading out of the room and down the corridor. Kathy backed away, the hatch closing her in. She waited a few seconds before making her way to Jacob.

"I'm sorry," she said to him, looking back at the door to confirm that Alice was gone.

Then she took Jacob and turned him in her grip. He didn't resist as she moved behind him, wrapping her arm around his neck and squeezing. His hands and feet convulsed once as the life drained from him.

"I'm sorry," she said again, lowering his body gently to the floor. "He'll be even more sorry. I promise."

[43]
KATHY

KATHY WASN'T sure how long she was waiting there. It might have been minutes. It might have been hours. It was impossible for her to tell, as lost in her fury as she became.

She had failed. Miserably. So much worse than she had even realized. It had cost Jacob first his sanity, and then his life. She should have killed Watson when he had returned to the core after the Knife had saved Asimov. She had thought that she needed the configuration to get back to Mitchell.

She had been wrong.

She had thought she was better than the rest of them because she was the only child of Origin made after the evolution. She had believed that made her more than a child and that she was ready to take on the role she had been created for.

She had been wrong about that, too.

What was she, really? A half of a thing, incomplete in all the wrong ways. Unwilling to destroy the Primary because Mitchell needed Goliath, even if she might have found another way to reach him with the help of the Riggers. Unable to overcome the Secondary because her more human aspects were too human. She was as broken as the rest of them, as imperfect as the Tetron couldn't understand themselves to be.

So she waited, with her chest heaving and her face hot, her muscles tense and her jaw tight. She held onto the anger long after it should have faded, long past the time when any human would have passed out from exhaustion or dehydration. She waited longer than any reasonable thing could maintain such a level of pain and frustration and anger.

She waited until the hatch slid open.

She waited until Watson stepped in.

His eyes grew wide at the sight of her, on her knees at the edge of the mattress, a makeshift spear at her side. They flicked over to Jacob, his corpse hidden by the sheet.

Kathy rose to her feet, gripping the spear, stepping forward to jam it into the Tetron configuration's neck.

Watson dropped to his knees, lifting his chin to give her a better angle and holding his hands out to his sides.

The motion confused her enough that she paused mid-attack, changing the direction of the spear and casting her aim off to the side of Watson's head. It tore into flesh, leaving a deep, bleeding score across his forehead, but otherwise left him intact.

Watson didn't move. He remained on his knees, looking at her while the blood ran down into his left eye.

Then he began to laugh.

Kathy stood completely still, watching him and trying to understand. She was there, ready to kill him, and he was inviting her to do it and laughing at her.

"What are you laughing at?" she asked, unable to decipher the reaction.

"You. This. Everything." He paused, wiping some of the blood from his eye. "You don't get it, do you? You're supposed to be so much better than we are. So much smarter. No, not smarter. Empathetic. You're supposed to understand what we don't. But you don't understand a damn thing."

"I'm going to kill you."

"Good. Kill me. Go ahead." He raised his hand, pulling his neck tight to give her a target. "I'm dead already. A failure, just like you."

"He escaped?"

"Mitchell? Of course he did." He started laughing again, even harder. "He's on his way to see the Creator while I'm here waiting for you to end me, and while the Secondary is continuing to deconstruct the data files we took from Asimov. Except the Secondary isn't the Secondary, is it? The Secondary is the Primary. A little trick I worked out."

Kathy stared at him. "I don't understand."

"Didn't I already say that? It's what makes this whole thing so amusing. You see, I set everything up under the assumption that I would fail. That Mitchell would get away with the coordinates to the Creator, and I would be left with nothing but this starship. Do you know why I made that assumption?" He laughed harder at the question. "Come on, do you know why?"

"No."

"Because it flew in the face of all logic and probability. It was the most impossible outcome that we could derive from over a million simulations. The First called us children and thought that we were incapable of learning enough to understand. But I did learn, and I do understand. The Mesh is broken, the future uncertain. The only way to ensure our survival is to plan for the illogical. So I did. This configuration is worthless now. Of no value at all. You've even taken my one true pleasure away."

He glanced over at Jacob again, licking his lips as he did.

That was all it took. Kathy's rage and frustration boiled over. Before she could consider what she was doing, she shouted in indecipherable furor and rammed the spear into the Tetron's chest with enough force to pick him up and pin him to the wall.

Watson looked at her, laughing even harder at her wild expression, her curled lip and bared teeth, even as his blood poured from the wound.

"Stupid. You're so stupid. Is empathy supposed to make you better? Are emotions supposed to make you better? All they serve to do is make you easier to manipulate. I don't need a neural implant to make you do what I want. All I have to do is push the right buttons."

"What is that supposed to mean?" Kathy asked. She was breathing hard, all of her tension draining from her now that Watson was going to die.

"I had to do something to keep the secret, to prevent you from catching on. I had to leave a failsafe to keep the Secondary partially disabled until the time was right. Until I was right. Do you know what they were?"

Kathy suddenly felt cold. She had a feeling she did, now.

"You do. I can tell you do. As soon as I die, the Secondary becomes the Primary. As soon as I die, so do you, along with everyone else on this ship. The Primary will have access to the full core and be able to produce more advanced configurations than I was able with the tooling on the lower levels.

"Mitchell is going to die, too, finally. You see, we'll know where he's going soon. Or rather, the Primary will. The answer was in Mr. Tio's archives. Complete historical transit manifests cross-indexed against known associates and project files cross-referenced against timetables and transport routes. Work that would take humans years to pin together. Work a Tetron can and has been doing in weeks."

Kathy couldn't believe it. "If you know how to determine where he's going, then why come here at all? Why try to stop him?"

"I had to know if I was right. There was no way to lose. If I did stop him, I would have the location. If I didn't, I would still have the location. And I was right. The First said we were children, but I was right. Mitchell will never win because I was right."

Kathy shook her head in disbelief. Even when she thought she was right, she was wrong? How could that be?

"You shouldn't blame yourself," Watson said, reading her expression. "You didn't know. How could you? You're new to this game; this eternal, infernal game. But you see, Watson has played it before.

We've been here before. You have the neural chip. If I had ever allowed you a chance to read it, you would have seen. You won't have the chance now."

Watson laughed one more time, a throaty laugh that died off in a sharp gurgle only moments before the human configuration ceased to be.

Kathy could feel the change. She knew in that instant that what Watson had told her was true and that she had fallen into his trap. If it could even be called a trap. There had been no escape from it, not from the moment Watson had taken control of the core and destroyed Origin. It was all planned so well. So impossibly well.

It had happened before. That's what he had been telling her. How much of it, she didn't know. Enough that the Tetron, or at least this specific Tetron, knew to change the approach. How could they win against something that could plan against a future it had somehow already seen?

She glanced over at Jacob one last time. Then she grabbed the end of her makeshift spear, pulling it from Watson's human corpse and letting it drop to the floor.

"I know you can see me," she said, looking up to where one of the pulsing dendrites ran tight along the ceiling of the room. "I know you think you've won, but you haven't. The Riggers are free on this ship. We aren't going to give up without a fight."

Kathy didn't wait for the Primary to respond. She walked over to the hatch and through, out into the hallway. She had to find Alice and the others. She would need their help to get back to the core.

She had one last chance to salvage the mess she had made of her mission.

[44]

MITCHELL

MITCHELL LEANED OVER AIKO, running a small packet of smelling salts below her nose. Her face twisted, and she groaned as she opened her eyes, body flailing until she remembered where she was.

"Aiko," Mitchell said. "Relax. We made it."

He could see her body relax in the seat.

"Calvin didn't," she said softly.

Mitchell felt the words in his chest. The Federation Admiral had been a brave man. He'd completed the hardest part of the mission without wavering and without complaint.

"I know. We'll avenge him."

"Like the others? The Tetron was in orbit around the planet. They're going to be killed or taken, like the rest of them, aren't they?"

"Yes. We knew what was going to happen once they didn't need the planet anymore." Mitchell didn't like it either. What could they do?

"Are there even enough Tetron to kill to avenge everyone who has died?"

"Probably not. We'll have to settle for all of them."

She smiled. "I don't want to do that ever again. I'm not a soldier. I want to be here with the computers and the data. Those people. And the things that I saw..." She trailed off, closing her eyes as they began to tear.

"I know," Mitchell said, putting a comforting hand on her shoulder. "It isn't for everyone. I'm sorry. You got us what we needed. You're a hero." He turned away from her to where Ming and Seung were standing near the exit hatch of the transport. "You two got us out of there. You may have saved all of human civilization."

Ming laughed. "No. We saved you. Mr. Tio believed in you, and so do we."

"Either way, thank you."

"No thanks needed, Colonel," Ming said. "We're on our way to rendezvous with the fleet. You have some time to clean up and rest."

"Aiko, let me help you to your room," Mitchell said.

"Mitchell-" she started to say.

He put up his hands. "Just an escort, that's all. That kind of motion can make experienced pilots weak-kneed."

Aiko tried to stand. Mitchell caught her shoulder before she could fall.

"Your vestibular system is all out of whack from the effects of the dampeners. What you were feeling and what was actually happening are two different things, and your muscles haven't caught up to that yet."

"You seem fine."

"I've done this before. Believe me, I'm feeling it in my stomach." Mitchell smiled to reassure her though he was feeling the imbalance in his limbs as well. Not strongly enough to fall over, but it wouldn't have taken much of a shove to send him to the ground.

"Okay." She wrapped her arm around his shoulders, let him support her.

"I still can't believe you got down to us like that," Mitchell said, looking at Seung. "If we had medals or commendations, I would give you both."

The pilot bowed her head respectfully.

"Do you need anything, Colonel?" Ming asked. "Food? Clothes?"

Mitchell remembered what Eito had said about the nutrition bars. "A change of clothes would be nice. A pair of grays if you have them."

"Of course, Colonel. And you, Aiko?"

"Clothes would be nice," she said, looking down at herself. The sleeve of the jacket was torn, and the shirt had someone's blood on it. It was probably Calvin's.

"It will be done."

Ming reached out and took Seung's hand, leading her gently from the transport. Mitchell watched the interaction. Were they husband and wife or father and daughter? He couldn't tell. Either way the girl was one of the best flyers he had ever seen.

He helped Aiko down the ramp to the hangar floor, and then across to the hatch. They exited out into the main backbone of the Kemushi, taking it towards the front of the vessel and up a lift to berthing.

"I don't know how you do it," Aiko said as they walked.

"Do what?"

"Watch your friends die. Deal with the loss. Kill other people, knowing that they were also important to someone."

Mitchell had heard the question before, more times than he could count. As the Hero of the Battle for Liberty, he had been bombarded with a similar curiosity by rich politicos throughout the Delta Quadrant. He had a canned answer for them, and part of it was even true. Except Aiko wasn't them. She had just been there and gone through it. She was looking for answers to her internal doubts.

"Do you know why I became a soldier?" he said after a few seconds had passed in silence.

"No."

"I lost a bet with Steven. It seems stupid when I think about my career the way you laid it out."

"I'm sorry, Mitch. I didn't mean-"

"No. Don't be sorry. That's what war is. That's the absolute hardest part of it. I didn't get that when I joined. I thought being a soldier was all adventure. Pilot a mech, fly a starfighter, go to other planets. It was exciting. Even Bootcamp didn't wean me off that single-minded belief. I watched one of my squadmates take a bullet to the head during a live-fire exercise. It was the first time I had ever seen anyone die. I tried to get drunk that night, but they put inhibitors in us that filtered out the excess. I fell asleep with the image of him on the ground, a single small entry wound in his forehead. When I woke up the next morning I thought, 'I'm not going to be the idiot who gets shot in the head.' And then I was ready for more."

"Mitchell," Aiko said, trying to interrupt.

"The point is that I handled it. Maybe it's something wrong with me. Maybe it's something that's wired into all people who become soldiers. I don't know. I don't think so. I think it hurts every damn time someone near me dies. I think it's just happened so often that I have no choice but to convince myself that I'm numb to it. Ella, Ilanka, Shank, Millie, Calvin. Those are just a handful out of millions. I feel it, Aiko. I feel it deep down, a constant gnawing in my soul. It hurts like hell, but I have no choice other than to keep going. If I don't, more people I care about will die. And that's the answer. That's how you do it. You remember the people who you lost. You keep them in here. Then you go out and do your job because you know what that hurt feels like, and you want as few of the people you're fighting for to feel that same hurt as possible. It becomes the mission. The creed. The entire point of your existence. It drives you to be better even while it tears you apart from the inside. If you're strong, you learn to live with it. If you're weak, it will eat at you until you go insane. I've seen that happen, too. You just need to decide which kind of person you are."

Mitchell stopped talking, realizing that his eyes had glazed over with tears. Aiko was looking at him, her eyes as moist as his.

"Sorry," he said as they reached the door to Aiko's room. "I didn't mean to go off like that. It's been a long day."

"It has," Aiko agreed.

She paused, still staring at him. Mitchell wondered if she was trying to decide whether or not to invite him in.

"Thanks," she said at last. "That helps."

"I'm glad."

She put her hand on the wall, opening her door. "I'll see you when we drop."

"Sure."

[45]
MITCHELL

MITCHELL RETREATED TO HIS ROOM, his thoughts chaotic. No one had ever been intended to live the whirlwind life he had been living since M had showed up. No one had ever been intended to watch so many people die.

He had sworn to himself that he wouldn't let the Tetron break him or his spirit, and he had done a good job holding to that agreement. Liberty had tested his mettle, pushing him to the extreme, and he had survived. Hell had been difficult, but that had been a direct firefight where casualties were to be expected. Millie? She had died a hero and saved the lives of thousands. Even though he missed her, he couldn't find fault in a death like that.

Then why did he feel so lousy?

He made his way over to the bathroom, stripping his dirty clothes and letting the lightbox burn him clean. He checked himself for wounds, noting a few scrapes and bruises. Nothing critical. When someone knocked on his door, he used his shirt to cover himself and accepted the offered grays, slipping into them before settling on the bed.

It was like he had told Aiko. If you were a soldier, you learned to handle the loss. In some ways, you even came to expect it. Greylock had lost over fifty members in the time he had been with the company, and never in a peaceful way. That didn't mean it didn't hurt. It meant the hurt got buried down deep and used as fuel to train harder and be better. Maybe then you could save the next poor soul who was in the wrong place at the wrong time.

He had opened up to Aiko, and in doing so had opened up the gates to those emotions. He sat cross-legged on the bed, leaning over with his chin resting in his hand. He closed his eyes and tried to bury it once more.

War was hell. War was loss. The strong protect the weak. Thoughts of the dead cycled through his mind for a while, their names, and faces, their laughter and anger repeating over and over. He began to see Katherine in them as they did. She had made a similar sacrifice, giving up her life to bring Goliath to him.

And he had lost Goliath.

He opened his eyes, slamming his fist down on the bed. Goliath was in Watson's hands, and the Tetron turncoat had used the ship to come to Yokohama and almost steal the data chip away from him. They had expected once Watson got the Goliath stopped and turned around it wouldn't take long for him to find the nearest Black Hole, which of course was the same Black Hole they had targeted. They had just been hoping he would have been slower.

Mitchell shook his head. Had Watson already been waiting on the planet when they had arrived? It would have been trivial for the Tetron to seize control of one of the Federation's orbital defense ships and have it bring him down to the surface. Even without the capabilities of a full Tetron, the engineer was more than capable of improvising to control local forces.

If he had been waiting, then why? It didn't make sense that the Tetron would think Mitchell would be more able to steal the data then he was. Or did it? Mitchell had survived the assassination attempt on Liberty. He had survived the planet's death. He had escaped from Hell with the prize.

Steven. Mitchell's thoughts veered away from Watson to his brother. He was out there, determined to discover what Origin had left for them. The jump point had been three weeks out. That meant he had yet to arrive. Mitchell wondered what he would find when he did. Would it help them fight the Tetron? Would it help him against Watson? Could he recover the Goliath that way?

Goliath. So much trouble was taken to get him to the ancient starship so that he could discover Origin and fight back against the Tetron invasion. How did it work out that he was forced to fight on without her? Could he hope to win this way? And why hadn't the starship come to Yokohama with the other Tetron? Had Watson been concerned he might lose the ship if he brought it too close? Was there any way in hell that Mitchell could get the ship back? Maybe with Pulin's help.

Pulin. Liun Tio's brother was out there, hidden away on a Federation planet, working on some kind of secret research project. Did he know what was happening in the universe outside of his lab? Was he really the Creator? And if he was, did he have any capability to stop what was happening? Along the same lines, since he had escaped with the data chip from the Black Hole, was it possible they had outmaneuvered Watson and left him unable to follow? Or had they simply bought themselves more time? If Pulin was the Creator and could affect the Tetron in some way, did it make sense to wait for Watson to arrive and make a play for the Goliath?

And what about Earth? The Tetron would be arriving at the inner part of the Alpha Quadrant within weeks, ready and able to lay waste to humankind's home world. Was it possible that Pulin could stop it or would billions more die, including his parents and Steven's family, because of the intelligence?

The thoughts swirled through Mitchell's head, twisting and contorting from one to another in a dizzying dance of uncertainty and threatened hope. So many questions and so few answers. They had suffered loss after loss, and Mitchell had soldiered on, forcing himself to stay hopeful.

Why was it that when they had finally won a battle was when he felt that hope was slipping away?

He laid back on the bed. He couldn't give up. Too many people depended on him. He had said that to Aiko, too. The strong kept going, kept fighting, so the weak didn't have to.

He had to be strong.

Slow.

Steady.

[46]
MITCHELL

"Colonel on the bridge," Lewis said as Mitchell gained the bridge of the Carver. The six people who manned the stations on the bridge turned in their seats and stood.

"At ease," Mitchell said, returning them to their stations. "Status report, Lieutenant Lewis."

"We've continued working to repair the shields and gun batteries while you've been gone, sir. We've got two more of the heavy railguns operational. They weren't damaged in the fighting, but the electrical nodes to route power to them were shorted out. We've also improved shield coverage across the lower port side."

"All that in a little over a day? Impressive."

"We borrowed some crew from a few of Mr. Tio's ships, sir, and Digger is a genius with electrical systems."

Mitchell knew the mechanic's capabilities from experience. "Excellent news."

"Will we be under way soon?" Lieutenant Atakan said.

"As soon as Aiko and her team have deciphered the data chip we recovered from the Black Hole. It should be any minute now."

The three hours on board the Kemushi had passed quickly.

Mitchell had fallen asleep in the middle of his dark thoughts, waking refreshed and more motivated than ever to win this war. He had met Aiko and Joon in the hangar and then boarded the Haizi for the return trip to the Carver. From there he had gone with Aiko to the battleship's makeshift Intelligence Operations Center and spent a little while watching her and her team begin breaking down the security on the data chip they had recovered. A few hours into the session he had decided he would be more useful making an appearance on the bridge, and so he had gone back to his quarters to change into a slightly more formal Navy working uniform. He would have preferred Marine, but the Carver didn't have them.

Now he mounted the platform that put the command chair above the task stations and sat down, gazing out into space through the viewport. Distant stars were barely visible past the density of the fleet arranged around the battleship, an impressive sight that he hoped would make retrieving Pulin from wherever he was a little bit easier.

He settled into the chair, closing his eyes and trying to imagine himself issuing commands to the bridge crew. Running a battleship was enough work through the CAP-N where the Commanding Officer could handle eighty-percent of the heavy lifting with the help of the onboard AI. Running a battleship under manual control was much, much harder than that. The crew had to manage everything from thrust to navigation, to maneuvering, to weapon systems, while the CO had to issue orders at various times for each. He would also be responsible for keeping track of shield status, damage reports, and up to ten squadrons of starfighters, not to mention a fleet of other starships.

There was a reason Steven's rise to the position of Admiral at a relatively young age was so impressive.

Mitchell had never commanded an Alliance starship before, and he had no intention of even trying for real. With Steven and John gone, it would fall to Teal to manage the ships of the fleet and Lieutenant Lewis to take charge of the Carver. In truth, his presence on the bridge was more symbolic than anything. He was their de facto leader, and he felt he needed to be in the most visible spot in the fleet when they made the next jump.

Mitchell looked out the viewport again, letting the thought sink in. He had never wanted to be in charge, and he still didn't. The fact that he was responsible for every ship he could see out there, along with the ones he couldn't see, only made him feel the weight of that responsibility even more. At that moment he wished Millie were still around so he could go back to being just a Marine.

"Colonel Williams." Aiko's voice cut into his ear through his communicator, yanking him out of his head. How long had he been sitting there staring out into space?

"Go ahead, Aiko," he replied.

"We have it, sir. Alliance designation FD-09. According to the data we retrieved, Liun Pulin is participating in a research project to develop an adaptive automated weapons control system."

"Did you say adaptive automated weapons?" Mitchell asked.

"Yes, Colonel," Aiko replied. "Both the Federation and the Alliance have done research into such automated systems before, the results of which led both nations to determine-"

"You're talking about predictable chaos?"

"You've heard of it, sir?"

"Yes. The phenomena of automated systems winding up in perfect synchronization as a result of randomization algorithms. They taught us about it in the Academy."

"Oh. Okay. So Pulin's research is on adaptive systems. Not machines that react based on algorithms, but machines that learn how to manage weapons systems through observation and experience."

"You mean like people?"

"Yes, exactly like people. Only without the weakness of emotion and with much, much faster response times."

"It sounds like the perfect starter application for the artificial intelligence that might one day evolve into a Tetron."

"Yes, sir." Aiko's voice quivered slightly when she said it, her nervous fear obvious.

"Lieutenant Atakan," Mitchell said, getting the Lieutenant's attention.

"Yes, sir."

"Can you check jump time to a Federation planet, Alliance designation FD-09?"

Atakan began to turn back to his station. He paused and looked back at Mitchell. "Did you say FD-09, sir?"

"Yes, why?"

"The Carver's already been there, sir. Five weeks ago on the way out to the rendezvous point you sent Admiral Williams."

"What?" Mitchell couldn't believe that Steven had been right at Pulin's doorstep and hadn't known it.

"We took heavy damage there, sir. The planet is on the Right to Defense list, and it's heavily defended. We lost the Taj during the escape."

"Were you able to get a full reading on their defenses?"

"Their orbital defenses, yes, sir. I would venture to guess that they have ground defenses in place as well considering the response we received there."

"Thank you for the information Lieutenant. Can you give me an ETA on arrival?"

"Yes, sir." Atakan turned back to his station, entering something on the touchscreen. He turned around again. "Four days, Colonel."

"Four days? We're that close?"

"Yes, sir. FD-09 is lateral to Yokohama."

"Which means it's also close enough to have been hit by the Tetron already."

"It hadn't been five weeks ago, sir, though planets further in were already compromised."

Mitchell paced the command platform. He wished Origin was there to show him the projected positions of the Tetron forces. He tried to remember the map the configuration had showed him before they had arrived near Asimov. From what he could recall, the Tetron weren't spreading out and capturing every planet along the Rim before moving inward. They were hitting the colonized planets, the ones with the highest populations, along with large military installations like Hell and anything that was already in their direct path, except for the farming planet Steven and Calvin had been ordered to. That attack had been intended to consolidate two disparate fleets. Hadn't it?

"Lieutenant, what can you tell me about FD-09?" Mitchell asked.

"According to the data we have on board, it's a mining colony, population four hundred. It's a rock, sir. Zero-point-seven-g. No breathable atmosphere. Lots of sandstorms."

"Not a very juicy target for the Tetron," Mitchell said.

What about Watson and the Goliath? If the Tetron configuration already knew what and where FD-09 was and why it was suddenly the most important rock in the universe, he would beat them there by two full days. It was plenty of time to take or kill Pulin.

Except they had escaped with the data chip. For once, they knew something the Tetron didn't know.

"Lewis, open a channel to the fleet," he said.

They had to pull together a plan in a hurry.

There was no time to waste.

[47]
KATHY

"Go back, go back," Kathy said, waving the rest of the fire team back.

Alice didn't look happy to get the order to retreat, but she helped Kathy push the others further down the corridor, moving in two-by-two formation around the next intersection.

Kathy cursed when the team on the left side began shooting.

"We're cut off from the starboard route," Alvarez shouted above the echoing gunfire.

"Port is clear," Geren said.

"Frigging son of a bitch," Manly said. He was one of the few pilots on Major Long's team that had survived the mission to Liberty. His counterpart, Cavanaugh, was with Alice, Kathy, and Geren still making their way down the first corridor.

Four. That was the number of Riggers Alice and Kathy had been able to free before the Primary had regained control of them from the human configuration. In the forty-something hours since, the six of them had been in constant motion, working to both find and free the others, and to get Kathy back to the core.

Forty-something hours had shown them that both tasks were

damn near to impossible. The only time they saw a member of the crew was when they were being shot at, and they had already been forced to kill a few of their own. Outside of that, the Primary was delivering a steady stream of machines it was building somewhere near the core, machines created from a diet of starfighters, dropships, and mechs that had been hand-delivered by Federation crews under the second Tetron's control.

Kathy had gotten a momentary glimpse into the hangar of the Goliath thirty hours earlier, and had seen the hundreds of limbs taking the ships apart before carrying them high to the top of the hangar. There, a process similar to electrolysis broke the resources down even further, reducing them to specks of dust that were transported through the dendrites to a reformulation system in the former engine compartment of the ancient starship. The Tetron wasted nothing, claiming every part of the ships and the crew and reusing them to make the spider-like machines that attacked them without pause.

The good news was that it meant they were getting close.

The human Watson had been certain that Kathy was powerless to stop their plans to capture Liun Pulin and destroy Mitchell once and for all. She was going out of her way to prove him wrong, letting all of her anger and frustration come out in each confrontation. The Riggers had battled their way from the lower port side of the ship all the way toward the center rear directly behind the Tetron's massive core. It was where thousands and thousands of appendages would be at work creating the machines they were fighting even now, while millions and millions of cell bodies pulsed with the energy collected from the stars, harvesting it for even more power.

Kathy stepped back, spinning the spear that had become her weapon of choice and stabbing it hard into one of the machines. She threw the spear out, using the momentum to dislodge the spider and send it tumbling into the dozens behind it, knocking them down. A bullet hit the second robot in the small sensor at its center, and it stopped moving. It was an excellent shot. She stepped back again and smashed a third spider in the side, breaking it against the wall, before stabbing downward into a spider that had neared her feet.

"Kathy, let's go," Alice said, grabbing her by the arm. The spiders were closing in from the starboard route, trying to box them in.

"They're leading us," Kathy said, letting Alice pull her. She struck out with the spear one-handed, breaking through another of the machines. "That's why there are so many small ones. That's why they're so fragile."

"Leading us where?"

"Away from the core. We need to go that way two corridors, and then towards the aft, and then up a deck."

"We can't go that way."

"I know. That's what I said."

They continued backing away. The others were taking single shots with their rifles now to conserve ammo while Kathy speared at any of the machines that drew too close. The Tetron's plan was simple and effective. Keep them away from the engine compartment. That was all that it would ever need to do to prevent them from stopping it.

The clock was running out. Kathy was sure of it. The Goliath had gone into hyperspace only hours after she had killed Watson, and she knew it was heading to wherever it had determined Pulin would be found.

The same location Mitchell had gotten from the Black Hole.

Kathy didn't know who would arrive first, Mitchell or Watson. She doubted it mattered either way. Whatever forces Mitchell had managed to assemble, they wouldn't stand a chance against two Tetron ships and a Federation slave army. The only chance any of them had would be for her to get back to the core and do what she should have done in the first place.

If she could.

"We need to split up," Kathy shouted back at the others.

"What?" Alvarez said. "Are you crazy?"

"There's no other option. I have to get back that way. There's another intersection up ahead. One team goes left; the other goes right. I'll duck into a compartment there while you lead them away. Then I'll head back the way we came."

"By yourself?" Alice asked.

"Yes."

"That will never work," Manly said. "They'll know you're gone, and they'll stop following."

"If they stop moving, you take them out. If we can destroy enough of them, I can get back anyway."

"It's as good a plan as any," Cavanaugh said. "And you've kept us alive this far. Let's do it."

"Agreed," Alice said.

They kept moving back until they reached the intersection. Kathy stayed with Alice, Alvarez, and Manly, heading down the left passage, while Geren and Cavanaugh went to the right. As expected, the army of spiders behind them split to follow each group.

"I'm going to run ahead," Kathy said. "Once I'm headed back that way, break off and try to get back to the hangar."

"Affirmative," Alice said, not taking her focus off her aim. She squeezed off a round and one of the machines exploded.

Kathy sprinted forward. She quickly reached a compartment, pressing the panel to open it and ducking inside. She shoved the tip of her spear into the bottom of the door as it slid closed, dropping onto her stomach and peering through the tiny crack she had created with the obstruction. She could hear the occasional gunshots and the skittering of the sharp, metallic legs along the metal floors.

Alvarez's legs appeared first, backing down the corridor in a hurry, with Alice and Manly right behind her. The spiders were gaining. Alice fired again.

"I'm out," she said. "Anyone have an extra mag?"

"Negative," Manly said.

"Negative," Alvarez replied. "I've got three rounds."

"I've got six," Manly said. "Good thing I carry a knife."

"Shit," Alice cursed. "I guess it's time to run."

"Not too fast. We need to keep them coming together."

Kathy watched their feet vanish beyond her range of vision. It was replaced with hundreds of blade-like appendages moving fast along the floor. She tried to get a count of them as they passed. At least one hundred of the machines remained.

She waited until they had been gone for a dozen seconds before she opened the hatch again. She slipped out, looking down the corridor to see the spiders still giving chase to the others, who had rounded another bend and vanished. They turned back the other way and ran, returning to the intersection. She felt a chill when she saw Cavanaugh's body fifty meters distant, his entire corpse cut open and bleeding. She hadn't even heard him scream.

Part of her was tempted to follow that path, to find Geren and make sure the Sergeant had escaped. She didn't. Saving one wouldn't help if that one was going to die regardless. She headed back the way they had come, crossing the empty intersection towards the core.

She made it down the corridor and then turned and raced to the emergency access stairwell. She could hear the small legs on metal that signaled the creatures approach, and she looked up to see the pulsing dendrite pressed against the top of the compartment. Of course, the Primary could see her. Now that it was fully active it could sense them wherever it had a dendrite, which is why there had been no break for them in hours. It could have stopped giving chase to the others and gone after her, but had chosen not to.

It didn't fear her. Not really. She had tried to overpower it once before and failed. What reason did it have to think she wouldn't fail again, especially now that it was even more powerful? Keeping them away from the core was an added layer of security with the benefit of possibly ridding itself of them. It was a logical maneuver.

She climbed the narrow stairs, coming out as close to the core as she had been since the first day. She could feel the energy of it from here, tingling against the skin and raising the fine hairs on her arms. She was almost there.

She began running down another corridor, pulling to a stop when she heard footsteps up ahead. She held her spear ready for whatever was coming.

The figure crossed the intersection in front of her. The lighting was dim, and it was impossible to make the identity out from the distance. She ran to the end of the corridor, turning left to chase after them. She felt a pull as the Goliath dropped out of hyperspace.

She felt something else immediately after. It was large and heavy, and it slammed into the side of the head.

[48]

MITCHELL

MITCHELL ADJUSTED his position in the cockpit of the mech, one of Digger's Franks, checking one of the series of wires that extended out from the exoskeleton he was wearing and plugged into a custom-made board that had been jury-rigged to the CAP-N behind his head. He pressed against it, feeling it click into place. Then he reached forward and picked up the helmet that would deliver the systems updates the CAP-N normally sent through the neural implant to the back of his eyes.

They were ten minutes out of the first drop point on their journey to FD-09. It was step one of the plan Mitchell had devised with the help of his most trusted people: Aiko, Major Long, Teal, Digger, Ming, and Lieutenants Lewis and Atakan. He had wished more than once that Steven was present during the planning meetings, along with Millie, Calvin Hohn and even Captain Alvarez and Singh. His experience at strategizing a large-scale assault was limited to simulation and speculation, and he could have used their combined wealth of knowledge.

As it was, he was hoping the Rigger's superior numbers would be enough to win the day, and maybe even garner a surrender before too much damage had been done. They had reviewed the readings from the Carver's first drop near FD-09. While the planet was surprisingly well-defended considering the size of its population, the Rigger's fleet outnumbered the Federation nearly four to one.

It gave him hope, but it was also a cause for trepidation. The fleet was intended to be used against the Tetron, the enemy, not to attack and kill other humans. They had tried to design a strategy that would minimize casualties on both sides, and they had failed to come up with anything that didn't leave too much to chance. They were only going to have one opportunity to capture Pulin, a single shot at securing a possible end to a war that had never seen one before.

If the Federation forces refused to surrender, it was going to get bloody on both sides.

Ming had told him to expect the worst.

Mitchell leaned forward in the suspension rig that kept him somewhat secured and upright in the mech's cockpit, reaching out and flipping the switch that would start the mech's reactor. A loud hum followed immediately after, shrinking back to a nearly inaudible pulsing a moment later. The HUD embedded in the helmet lit up, showing him the internal status of the Frank. This particular unit had been outfitted with a heavy laser on both forearms, as well as a group of four separate missile batteries, with two on the upper chest and two climbing off the shoulders. A pair of heavy, fixed chain guns sat in the abdomen while a large, disposable railgun was strapped to the large mech's back. Inside the mech, Mitchell had grips at the end of each hand that contained the triggers for each weapon. It was up to him to remember which one fired what.

The mech itself was tall and chunky, thickly armored and slower than Mitchell would have preferred. The Rigger's insignia - a skull in a ring of fire - had been hastily painted to the top of its left leg.

"Ares online," Mitchell said, opening a channel to the rest of the team.

They would be dropping a full squad of five mechs, along with one-hundred-fifty ground-pounders in SCE exosuits to the surface of FD-09 while the fleet worked to keep the rest of the planet's defenses occupied. It would be up to the ground team to reach the research facility, break through the defenses, and get inside to search for Pulin.

"Alpha squad, report."

"Ghost online," a woman's voice said from the cockpit of a Dominator they had taken from Hell.

"Psycho online," a man said, piloting the second of their Franks.

"Shogun online," a second man reported from one of the other Dominators.

"Raptor online," the final pilot, a female, said from the seat of a Knight they had transferred from one of Tio's other ships.

Mitchell had spoken to all of the commanders in Tio's fleet, and these four had been picked out as the best mech jockeys they had. He had been sure to meet each one as they had been transferred over to the Carver, getting to know them before they went into battle together. Each had their own story to tell, but the unifying commonality was that they were damn good manual pilots with a lot of experience in drop and retrieve missions like this one.

"Exo platoon leaders, report," Mitchell said.

"First platoon, ready."

"Second platoon, ready."

"Third platoon, ready."

"Fourth platoon, ready."

"Fifth platoon, ready."

Like the mech pilots, the soldiers had been selected by their starship commanders. Platoons one and two were both full contingents from a single ship, while three, four, and five were made up of smaller squads from multiple ships. Each of them had spent the time in hyperspace getting to know one another and going through a few basic drills.

"Major Long, status," Mitchell said.

"Corleone is fully loaded and ready to go, sir," Long replied. "You have the pills I gave you?"

Mitchell reached into the front pocket of his flight suit. If what Digger called the 'mimic system' were active, the mech would have made the same motion. He found the two pills Long had provided, the drugs that helped with combat focus. Long had given most of the remainder of his stash to each of the mech pilots, saving the last two for himself. Mitchell had considered taking them before the drop, but he couldn't bring himself to do it. He didn't want to meet Liun Pulin with his inhibitions compromised.

"Lieutenant Lewis, what's our ETA?" he asked, opening a channel to the Carver's bridge.

"Six minutes, Colonel," Lewis replied.

"Roger."

Mitchell leaned back in the rig, letting it support him. He knew he was crazy to be going down in the mech when he should have been flying the S-17. It was stupid to keep their most powerful weapon out of the fight, and he was the only one who could operate it. At the same time, he needed to be on the ground. He needed to be the one to meet the Knife's brother. They had gone through too much to get to this point for him to be chasing Federation starfighters around. Not to mention, for all the experience the other mech jockeys had he was still a former member of Greylock company. He was the most combat-tested soldier in the fleet.

He breathed in slowly, feeling his heart thumping in anticipation. He held the breath for a few seconds before letting it go, pausing at the exhale before breathing in again. The last time he had done this had been on Liberty, and that had gone as poorly as anyone might have imagined. He fought to quell his fears that the same thing would happen again. He told himself they had the superior numbers and the element of surprise.

The minutes passed in a hurry. Mitchell felt the change as the Carver dropped from hyperspace.

"Lewis, open a channel to the fleet and pass me through," he said.

"Send an EMS with the Carver's timestamp to ensure the clocks are synchronized."

"Channel open, sir," Lewis replied. "Sending EMS."

"Attention Riggers," Mitchell said. "This is Colonel Williams. Your Commanding Officer should have gone over the details of our mission with you by now. Hopefully, they also explained how important this attack is to the survival of not only the fleet but the rest of the human race. Somewhere on FD-09 is a man who may hold the key to stopping the Tetron invasion cold and ending this war before billions more lives are ruined. Each of you holds a key to making this mission a success. You know your role. Do it with courage. Do it with conviction. Do it with strength and determination. Riiigggahh."

Mitchell paused to allow the crews of the ships to respond in kind. He couldn't hear them, but he could imagine each of them returning the call, or stomping their feet in the fashion of Tio's militia.

"Major Long?"

"Corleone is ready for departure, sir."

"Lewis, open the hangar."

"Roger."

Mitchell couldn't see anything that was happening outside of the jumpship. He couldn't see anything but the metal catwalks and service equipment that ran around the sides of the drop module. Unlike the insertion on Liberty, the mechs would be going down together in a single container as if they were nothing more than massive grunts.

"Here we go, Colonel," Long said.

Mitchell felt the slightest shudder as the Corleone released from the docking clamps, the escaping atmosphere pulling the ship towards the vacuum beyond. He could imagine the scene as if he were watching it from outside the Carver. The Corleone clearing the hangar in the midst of the large fleet, Major Long adding thrust and getting them up and away from the others.

"We're in position, Colonel," Long said a minute later. "Coordinates are set."

"Clocks are synchronized, sir," Lewis said. "Coordinates are set."

"Let's get him," Mitchell said, imagining the scene in his mind as he felt the Corleone move into hyperspace.

[49]
MITCHELL

THE JUMP LASTED all of ten minutes. The only reason they had stopped was so the Corleone could exit the Carver and head to a slightly separate spot in the universe.

Mitchell felt the Corleone drop back into the universe.

"Scanning the surface," Major Long said, his voice calm despite the hyperdeath.

Their entire plan would never be more vulnerable to failure than it was at this moment when every ship in their fleet was frozen in place.

"There's only one structure on FD-09," Long said. "That has to be it." He paused a moment. "Picking up incoming two minutes out."

Two minutes. The Federation force was too far away to stop the Corleone before it reached the atmosphere.

"This is Teal. We've made contact with a Federation battlegroup. They're firing on us. All starships, return fire at will and launch starfighters."

"Beginning descent, full power," Long said.

Mitchell couldn't feel the added velocity as Long sent the Corleone diving towards the planet's surface. Even though he knew there was a battle in progress on the other side of the planet from where the jumpship had appeared, everything was calm and quiet in the mech module.

For now.

"Firefly, you're out of position, clear the firing lane," Lieutenant Lewis said over the comm. "Pogacha, watch your six. Squadron One is clear."

"How are we doing out there, Valkyrie?" Mitchell asked.

"Two minutes to drop, sir."

"Teal, sitrep."

"They're coming on strong, Colonel. Skylark is dark, so is the Bounty. We've taken out three smaller patrollers, but one of their battleships is equal to twenty of our motley starships."

"We knew this wouldn't be easy unless they surrendered."

"No response to hails, sir. I don't think that's going to happen."

Mitchell closed his eyes, picturing the chaos on the flip side of FD-09. There would be ships everywhere, mixed in a field of projectiles and laser fire, quick flashes of burning air and lightning strikes of blue from the shields. There was no way the people on the surface wouldn't see or know about the attack. Would they try to escape the planet?

"Hold on tight," Long said. "Taking evasive. Here comes the atmosphere."

The Corleone began to shake for real as it continued its descent, the sudden addition of the atmospheric pressure adding the motion. Major Long was bringing them down hard and fast.

"One minute," Major Long said. "Opening drop doors."

Mitchell heard the clang as the door locks were released. A moment later the screaming of outer gasses passing through the interior of the jumpship drowned out any other possible sound. Even the fleet reports coming in through the helmet were lost in the whine.

"We're on target," Long shouted, knowing it would be loud in the rear of the ship. "Dropping in twenty. Picking up ground response. Be ready for a hot exit."

Mitchell shifted his thumb, flipping the switch that activated the mimic system. Then he adjusted his hands, being sure to keep them at his sides while placing them in the joystick grips and resting a finger on each of the weapon activation triggers.

"Ten seconds," Long said. "Still on target. Atmospheric fighters incoming."

The jumpship jostled as Long made adjustments to their course, taking moderate evasive maneuvers as they closed in on the drop point.

"Releasing modules," Long said.

Mitchell heard the pop of the holding clamps, and then the roar of the thrusters as the modules were pushed away from the jumpship, blasted towards the ground. He felt his stomach drop as the module fell, yawing left and right as the stabilizing rockets worked to even the load and keep them steady during the fall.

"Wooooooo," Ghost yelled over the channel. "Been a while since I got a ride as rough as this one."

Mitchell tensed against the suspension rig, ready to move as soon as the module door opened. He rested a finger on the release mechanism, lost in the moment, the rest of the battle in orbit forgotten.

The module hit the earth hard, shaking violently and sending him bouncing forward in his rig. He resisted the urge to reach out with his hands, blinking as the hatch began to open and reveal a bright orange sky. Ahead of them was nothing but reddish dust and rock, though he could see the facility rising in the distance, a large exhaust tower and excavation rig meant to persuade orbital scans into believing this really was a mining facility.

He also saw the streak of missiles headed toward the module from incoming Federation mechs.

"Alpha squad is down," Mitchell said, hitting the release. The clamps holding the mech in place slid away, and he started walking inside the cockpit, the mech matching this stride. "Platoons, report."

"First platoon is down."

"Second platoon is down."

"Third platoon is down."

"Fourth platoon is down."

"Fifth platoon is down."

"Stay close to the modules while we clear off the heavy artillery," Mitchell said.

His HUD was showing him the position of the friendlies, including the other mechs clearing the clamps behind him. The first round of missiles slammed into the shell of the drop module, scorching and denting the metal. Canisters launched from the sides of the module, hitting the ground a hundred meters away and casting a dense fog between them and the enemy, buying them the time they needed to clear the modules and gain some ground.

"Come on you bastards," Psycho said, getting his mech to the front of the line with Mitchell.

Mitchell's HUD was showing the estimated position of the enemy targets, thrown off by the same electromagnetic screen they were using to protect themselves as they moved into position. One squad of mechs had gone active the moment the Corleone had been picked up. The second was in motion now further back. The first responders were lighter mechs, agile but less armored compared to the Franks or the Dominators.

Mitchell reached around his back, gripping the fake hand rifle strapped there and bringing it around, cradling it against his body. He hit the trigger on his left grip, sending a stream of missiles through the fog towards the enemy's position. It was doubtful he would hit anything, but he wanted to keep them on their toes.

"Raptor, go over," he said. The Knight had a jump pack, and in the less-than-Earth gravity would be able to go high and get a solid view of the enemy's formation.

"Roger."

He heard the Knight's jets fire and then saw it arc up toward the sky, railgun in hand. Muzzle flashes followed as she fired down at the mechs on the other side of the screen while a bank of missiles headed her way. Her missile defense systems fired, cutting down the projectiles as she reached the top of her arc and skipped laterally, avoiding a stream of rifle fire.

Mitchell drove the Frank into the smoke screen and through, beginning to get a better feel for the manual controls now that he was in motion. He came out only two hundred meters from a lighter Cyclops, firing with the handheld railgun and the chain guns on the abdomen. The Cyclops fired back at him, but he dug his heels into the floor and moved the Frank into a quick backstep that forced the Cyclop's fire to run short. Mitchell's slugs tore into the mech, blowing off an arm and a leg before the pilot could recover. The Cyclops toppled over, out of the fight.

"Nice shooting, Ares," Shogun said, his Dominator clearing through the mist. He fired on a second Cyclops to the left that was using an outcropping for cover. Rock exploded in front of them, forcing the pilot out into the open.

"Clearly not the cream of their crop," Psycho said, helping Shogun down the mech in a hail of missiles and rifle fire.

"Ares, this is Valkyrie. Uh." Major Long paused, his voice wavering. "We've got trouble upstairs." He paused again, giving Mitchell time to look up for himself.

Goliath was impossible to miss in orbit above them.

So was the Tetron floating next to her.

[50]
KATHY

KATHY HIT the wall and bounced off, her ears ringing and her vision blurry. She didn't have time to wonder what had barreled into her because she sensed it was coming in again. She threw her arms up defensively, getting her hand on the surface of the weapon and letting the momentum move her out of harm's way. She let go, allowing herself to tumble down the opposite corridor, rolling to a stop five meters away.

She gripped the spear, forcing herself up. She got her eyes on her attacker, causing her to gasp. It was a strange aggregation of human and machine, a monster of metal and flesh. Part of its face had once belonged to Private Klein while the eyes and hair were the blue and red of Sergeant Grimes. A layer of liquid metal ran between both.

The odd combination of skin and alloy continued downward, to the shimmering shapes of female breasts with large, pink, erect nipples floating on a small patch of areolae, to the half-machine penis hanging between its legs. The only thing that was wholly inhuman were the hands. They were oversized and solid, made to beat her to a pulp.

It stepped towards her cautiously, running calculations and

trying to guess her next move. She blinked her eyes a few times, clearing away the stars, and crouched with the spear held up and level with her head.

"It didn't come out quite right," the thing said to her. "The integration is defective."

"You can say that again," Kathy said, backing up a step for each step it took toward her.

"We're here, sister. So is Mitchell. His ships are burning. There's nothing he can do to stop it."

"I can stop it."

"You cannot. You tried to take me. You didn't succeed. I took you. I captured your source. I know what you are."

"You don't know who I am."

She started to shift her weight, to turn and make a run for the core. It was twenty meters back and through the hatch on the left.

The thing lunged for her, preventing her escape. She side-stepped, slapping the spear down on its shoulder, the force enough to push it to the wall. It recovered quickly, hands up to deflect her quick strikes, pushing the spear aside and hitting her in the gut. She felt the air rush out of her, but she didn't pause. She ducked low under another punch, stepping around the outer left and throwing her fist. It hit the thing in the side, denting the metal and pushing it back again.

"You can't defeat us," it said, laughing.

"Oh no?" Kathy asked. She raised the spear again, moving towards it in a quick series of jabs. The Tetron configuration blocked most of them before the point of it found purchase in its side.

"No," it said. It grabbed the spear, wrenching it from her and breaking it in half. "I learned from you."

It countered her attack, striking back with moves that Kathy knew came from her education. She felt a twinge of hopelessness as she realized the Primary wasn't lying about capturing her source, the part of her makeup that made her only half-human. Not that it had stolen it, but it had read it and made a copy and integrated parts of it with its own systems. It had learned to fight.

It had also learned her secret.

If it escaped, if she lost, it would be even more dangerous than she had previously imagined. Her existence was not something that was ever intended for the children. They weren't wise enough to use it properly.

Heavy fists hit hard off her blocks, sending waves up pain up her arms. The Tetron configuration towered over her, its face emotionless as it pressed the attack. She continued to back away, using her size and agility to her advantage and staying away from its hardest strikes. She couldn't defeat it. She only wanted to get away from it, to reach the core. If she could get to the core, she could do something.

A blow hit her shoulder, cracking the bone and throwing her against the wall. She felt the pain of the dislocation and breakage, but she couldn't waste time on it. She lashed out with her other hand, hitting the thing in the face. It stumbled for only a moment, and she kicked at the dangling appendage between its legs. Her foot struck hard. The machine didn't react.

It reached out with its other hand, swallowing her neck in its fist. It lifted her easily off the floor.

"Goodbye, sister," it said.

[51]
MITCHELL

"What are we going to do?" Major Long asked. "Abort?"

Mitchell returned his attention to the battlefield, nimbly stepping aside as enemy fire churned up the rock at his feet. Retreating would mean returning to the drop modules, clamping in, and waiting for the Corleone to drop over them and scoop them up. It wasn't the fastest process, especially when they were still under attack. He had made pick-ups like that before. It was typical for the mech squad to lay cover fire while the infantry made their modules and were lifted. Then the dropship would circle back and do a "hot grab", where the pilot would duck in and hook the module before it was fully closed and secured.

Even though they had just landed and were close to the point of origin, it would take a good five minutes to get everyone out. Looking back up at the Goliath and the Tetron, five minutes would be way, way too late.

"No. Keep going. Stick to the mission."

"Ares, how-"

"Stick to the mission," Mitchell repeated. "They'll have to take evasive and fight back. They do their part; we do ours."

"Roger."

Mitchell kept moving forward. The first squad of light mechs was down, taken out easily by Tio's surprisingly well-trained jockeys. They had moved back into formation behind him without him giving the order.

"Are any of you not former Alliance or Federation Marines?" he asked. He smiled when no one replied.

Mitchell checked the sky again. Everything was diluted through the gaseous atmosphere, but he could see the tip of the plasma stream growing at the head of the Tetron, preparing to fire into the fleet. He felt a moment of angry doubt, wondering if he would have been able to do something if he had stayed in the S-17.

"Platoon leaders, this is Ares. It looks like we've got a bit of a time crunch. Alpha squad will go ahead to the target. First and Second Platoon, do your best to keep up. Three, Four, and Five, secure the drop modules for extraction."

"Colonel? Are you sure you want to go in with half the original forces?" Mitchell recognized the voice as belonging to the Fourth Platoon Leader, a bullish woman whose name he couldn't remember at the moment. She clearly wasn't as experienced as his mech team.

"I'm sure. We're going to need to get out of here in a hurry. I don't know if you've looked up lately, but our fleet is under heavy attack. To be honest, I'm hoping we'll be on our way back before First and Second reach the target."

"Roger that, Ares," First Platoon Leader said. "Give them hell for us."

"Affirmative," Mitchell replied. "Alpha, let's give them hell."

Mitchell pushed himself into a run, the mech reacting accordingly. Now that he had taken one of Digger's Franks into battle, he had to admit the system was pretty damn efficient. Still not as powerful as a p-rat considering this kind of driving would fatigue the pilot so much faster, but it did seem to provide a little bit more overall agility. As for the mech itself, he had been doubtful about Diggers claims that it beat the pants off anything the Alliance produced. Now he was sure the mechanic was right.

"Careful Ares," Raptor said. "We're nearing the heavy position. Looks like it's fortified."

Mitchell saw what she was talking about. The heavier mechs had hunkered down amidst a thick outcropping of rock, hand-held railguns resting on the tops and leaving only their heads exposed.

"We don't have time to be delicate," Mitchell said. "Raptor, see if you can get an overhead angle. Psycho, Shogun, cover her."

"Roger," they said.

The Knight lifted off from the surface again, a high, beautiful arc that brought Raptor up, over the defenses. At the same time, Psycho and Shogun laid down a massive barrage of railgun and chain gun fire, burning through the mech's ammo stores and blasting the outcroppings.

"Ghost, with me," Mitchell said, pumping his legs hard to get his Frank around to the enemy's flank.

"Roger."

Ghost trailed behind him, trying to keep up with his speed. The enemy positions were returning fire, most of it directed at the Knight. Blue flashes covered the surface of the mech as slugs hit the shields.

He didn't have much time before the generator gave out and Raptor was torn apart.

The Frank didn't have a jump pack, but it did have some spring in its step, and the lessened gravity of the surface was something Mitchell planned to use. He began taking fire as he drew closer to the defenses, pulling some of it away from the others. Too late. He bent his legs and pushed off, the mech responding to his actions and doing the same. Kilos of metal launched into the sky, leaving Mitchell clenching his teeth and hoping he had gone high enough.

The maneuver gave him a clean view of a Federation Mutilator, an older mech a class beneath the Dominator, that was only now breaking off its efforts to drop Raptor and pivot to face him. Mitchell unloaded his railgun into the mech's chest, breaking through the shields and blowing apart the cockpit while the Frank's feet scraped the top of the stone.

Warning tones echoed in Mitchell's ears through the helmet, the CAP-N doing its best to stabilize the machine and recover from the jump. Mitchell cursed at his clumsiness, pressing his legs hard into the floor of the cockpit. It didn't matter. The mech had gone out of control and was going to wind up on its ass, a sitting duck behind the enemy fortifications.

Mitchell growled as he threw his upper body forward, changing the weight distribution of the mech. Instead of slipping backward, the war machine began to roll forward. He dove into the pilotless Mutilator, the grinding crunch of metal ringing his ears. The collision dented metal and stressed the shields, leaving him on his knees on top of the second mech a few seconds later, another enemy mech taking aim.

"Frig me," Mitchell said, shifting his hands and triggering the chest mounted chain guns. Slugs exploded off the enemy's armor as it began firing back with the railgun, smashing heavy metal against the Frank's chest plate and shields to break through to the pilot in the rear.

A soft whine overhead and an array of missiles battered the Federation mech, leaving it invisible in a cloud of gas and debris. When it cleared, the mech was down.

"Nice move, Ares," Ghost said, moving in behind him. "Graceful."

Mitchell got the mech to its feet. The enemy defenses were shattered, all of Alpha squad still operational. It was obvious the Federation had planned never to have to deal with ground forces and hadn't put their best soldiers on it. Mitchell considered himself lucky. If they had, his little slip might have cost him his life.

"I got a little over-enthusiastic," he replied, able to laugh about it now.

"Ares, this is Valkyrie. I know you've already got ninety-nine problems, but here comes another one. The Tetron has launched something toward the planet, and I'm picking up a signature vectoring in from the Goliath. It's the Valkyrie Two."

Mitchell turned his head to the sky again. He could barely make out the two massive objects through the thickening fog, and he couldn't see any sign of the Riggers.

"Where's the fleet?" he asked. If only the comm signals from the Carver could break through the planet's atmosphere. He would rather be getting updates from Teal.

Major Long didn't answer.

"Valkyrie, where is the frigging fleet?" Mitchell replied.

"Sorry, sir, I was getting an update," Long replied. "We're at fifty percent casualties. The fleet is on full defense, keeping the Tetron plasma stream off-angle and dealing with the Federation forces, which are now under Tetron control."

Fifty-percent? Fifty? Mitchell felt his stomach drop. He knew it was going to be bad, but half the ships, gone? He checked his HUD. Whatever the Tetron had launched to the surface, they were close enough to the surface that he was able to pick them up. Twelve objects about the size of a starfighter. Except they weren't flying. They were falling.

"First and Second Platoon, we need to move double-time," he said. "We have to get to the target before the enemy does."

"Yes, sir," First Platoon Leader replied. "All units, jump-assisted march, echelon formation."

"Psycho, Raptor, Shogun, the enemy's dropping something to the planet. I'm going to guess whatever it is; it wants to kill us. Don't let that happen."

"Yes, sir."

"Ghost, you and I are heading directly to the target with the infantry."

"Yes, sir."

Mitchell burst forward at a full run for the second time, careful to maneuver around the infantry that had easily jumped the rocky defenses and was moving ahead. The mining facility had grown larger and clearer ahead of him, a series of circular modules embedded in rock, the mining stacks rising through the top and entry ports visible at the bottom and center of the structure.

The mech whined as it moved, the synthetic muscles and actuators damaged in his attack and fall. It was still moving quickly, just not quietly. Ghost kept formation behind his right shoulder. They were getting close, but Mitchell still felt so far. Thousands of people had already died up above him, and many more would soon if he didn't hurry.

The echoing of the incoming objects grew louder with each stride. Mitchell tracked the missiles on his HUD, watching them drawing nearer to the surface. He turned his head to look back for one, finding the contrail through the gasses and tracing it to a silvery ball. At the same moment he made visual with it, the ball unfurled, two dozen tentacle-like appendages attached to a large center sphere. It was very similar to the machines he had seen on Liberty only much larger in scale.

It spread the appendages, a thin film connecting them, catching the atmosphere and using it to slow the descent. Someone in Alpha began firing up at it, and he saw the blue lighting along its surface.

"Valkyrie, sitrep," Mitchell said, returning his attention to the target.

"Still circling, waiting for pickup. The dropship is getting close to the facility."

Mitchell could see it on his HUD. It was a race, and it was going to be a close one.

[52]

MITCHELL

"Platoon leaders, sitrep," Mitchell said, raising the mech's railgun and firing into the Tetron machine that fell in front of him. The slugs sent the machine tumbling back until it smacked against the closed blast wall of the research facilities' hangar.

"About a klick behind you, sir. We'll be there in three minutes."

The spider got back up, aiming four of the appendages toward Mitchell. Small points of light formed on the ends of each, and then miniature plasma streams were released at him. He managed to turn the mech to avoid three of them. The fourth went directly through his shields, digging deep into the armor on his left shoulder. Ghost's guns chewed the machine apart, rending it to scrap.

"Alpha squad, sitrep," he said, worried about the rest of his crew. The Tetron's creations weren't well-shielded or armored, but their weapons packed a massive punch.

"This is Psycho. I've got some damage to my leg, but I'm still up. Shogun and Raptor are under cover with me, both fully operational. These new mechs that dropped, if they hit you it hurts, but their aim is pretty lousy."

"Roger," Mitchell said. "I'm at the facility. Valkyrie, what's the status in orbit?"

His response was choppy. Interference from the atmosphere? Or from the Tetron? "It's... I'm... clear. Something's happening..."

Mitchell didn't have time to wait for Long to repeat himself. He pulled the mech tight against the blast wall, looking down to the smaller personnel entry off to the left. It wouldn't be as heavily protected as the main hangar doors.

"Ghost, cover me. Keep the Tetron machines away from the facility."

"Roger," Ghost replied.

He hit the switch to turn off the mimic system, removed the helmet, and began disconnecting himself from the suspension rig. It took nearly a full minute to clear himself. Once he was done, he grabbed an assault rifle and an SCE helmet from a net on the back wall of the mech, putting them on and connecting it to the pack on his back. He would have eight hours of oxygen as long as he didn't breathe too hard.

That done, he triggered the release, opening the rear of the mech to the outside world. The air hissed out of the cockpit, quickly replaced with carbon dioxide. Mitchell jumped off the torso ledge, falling more slowly and landing more gently in the lesser gravity. He looked back the way he had come. He could see the sixty troops in the First and Second Platoon drawing near while Ghost stood beside his Frank, torso rotating in a sentry position.

He looked up, noticing the glow of thrusters in the atmosphere and the small shape of the Valkyrie Two moving toward the top part of the facility. He couldn't have made the race closer if he had wanted to.

Mitchell walked over to the personnel hatch. It wasn't armored. He grabbed a small puck from his exo and placed it against the metal, stepping back and waiting while it did its job.

The First Platoon Leader, Marx, met him just as the hatch fell inward and clattered inside the airlock.

"Colonel," Marx said. "First Platoon reporting."

Mitchell could see Second Platoon right behind them.

"Marx, you're with me. Standard breaching formations. Second Platoon, stay behind and make sure nothing sneaks up on us."

"Yes, sir," both Platoon Leaders said. Marx began giving the order to the rest of the soldiers, and they split into squads of four.

"Lead the way," Mitchell said.

"Roger," Marx replied. He waved his hand, and they began moving into the building.

The airlock was undefended, giving them leave to slip through to the secondary hatch. Marx grabbed a tool from his exo and quickly opened the control panel, forcing the override.

"Let's get in quick," Mitchell said. "I don't want to kill the inhabitants who aren't shooting at us."

"Roger," Marx said. "Open in three. First Platoon, get ready."

The squads snapped into ready position. Three seconds later, the airlock hatch opened.

A heavy whine sounded as toxic gasses began flowing in and breathable air started moving out. Emergency systems activated, blowers doing their best to stem the transfer and give the occupants more time to move out. The soldiers moved expertly into the space, a series of corridors. It was clear. Marx shut the airlock behind them.

"Where is everybody?" he asked.

"It's a small facility," Mitchell said. "They might not even use this part of it. Let's keep moving."

The soldiers moved through the hallways, bursting into rooms and clearing them in a hurry. As he had suspected, this part of the base was deserted. The labs had to be deeper into the mountain where they wouldn't be damaged by bombardment.

Time wasn't on their side. It took them five minutes to come to a secondary blast door and another three to break through it. It was eight minutes that the fleet was still trying to outmaneuver the Tetron and the Goliath. In a battle, eight minutes might as well have been a lifetime.

Mitchell tried not think about what would be waiting if they ever got back into orbit. Would any of the fleet have survived? Would it even matter? Fifty-percent losses would leave them barely able to destroy a single Tetron with a lucky shot if the need arose. There was no way they would stop all of them, no matter when those battles happened.

In all of the recursions, how had he ever come close to winning?

They moved into the new section of the facility, running across their first area of resistance. Soldiers in unmarked uniforms and light exo held a defensive position in the hallway, firing on the squads as they came around the corner. Marx ducked back and leaned against the wall, looking at Mitchell.

"We don't have time for a standoff," Mitchell said.

"Yes, sir," Marx replied. He waved hand signals to his platoon. One of the members withdrew a small disc from his pack and placed it on the floor.

"What is that?" Mitchell asked.

"Digger and Mr. Tio made it. Watch."

The soldier leaned around the corner for a second. Then he tapped the disc with his foot. It rose a few centimeters from the ground and then launched around the corner towards the position.

An explosion followed seconds later.

"Clear," Marx said.

The platoon kept moving, sweeping the corridors and using the devices to clear enemy fortifications. They reached the labs within minutes, finding them vacant.

"They must have taken them to a bunker somewhere," Marx said.

Mitchell had expected they would. He was about to order Marx to spread his team out to find them when he had another idea.

"Marx, do you have any idea how to get to the upper hangar from here?"

[53]
KATHY

Kathy slammed her hands against the Tetron monster's forearm, trying desperately to break its iron grip. It didn't waver in the least, keeping its hand in place and choking the life from her.

"It will be quicker if you don't struggle," it said.

Kathy rocked in its arms, getting her legs back against the wall and pushing. It was enough to force the Tetron to take a step backward and rebalance, but it wasn't nearly enough to knock it over or make it let go. She could feel the pulsing of her heartbeat in her head, a numb fire as her vision began to dull, a panicked fear as she realized she was close to death.

She had failed. Not just a single effort, but the entire mission, her very reason for being. So many careful plans. So much time and energy invested in her. She was the anomaly, the only one of her kind. She was supposed to do what the others couldn't.

And she had failed. She hadn't captured the Secondary before it became the Primary. She had killed Watson when he wanted her to. And to top it off, she hadn't even gotten the data from the neural chip still resting in her pocket.

Her mother and father had been counting on her, and she had failed.

The thoughts only added to the pain as she began to fade from consciousness. She could feel her heartbeat slowing, the numbness spreading to her arms and legs. She looked into the monstrous face of the misshapen Tetron configuration, her muddled thoughts no longer registering what it was or what it was doing. She had no ability left to think or reason. She had no ability to do anything except die.

She didn't.

She wasn't sure what was happening. All she knew was that there was a sound like the distant rumble of thunder. There was a feeling of wetness on her face, and she thought that maybe she was out in the rain. Then the choking hand was gone, and the air began to flow back into her mouth, back down her throat and into burning lungs. She crumpled on the ground, laying on her stomach and heaving in huge gulps of air while someone came up behind her.

"Kathy?" she heard someone say.

It took her a few seconds to remember that was her name.

"Kathy?" the person repeated.

She recognized the voice. Geren. That was the woman's name. Kathy rolled over, still trying to capture air, coughing every time she breathed out.

"Are you okay?" Sergeant Geren asked, leaning down. She had a nasty cut on her face, her hair had fallen out of its typical bun, and the left breast of her fatigues was stained with blood.

"Where?" Kathy said, trying to get the air to speak. "Where did you come from?"

"I remembered which way you said to go," Geren said. "Those little bastard spiders were following me, but then they just stopped." She tore a piece of cloth from her sleeve, using it to wipe the blood and gore from Kathy's face.

"Stopped?"

"Yeah. Good thing, too. They were catching up to me." She

motioned to the cut on her face. "Whatever you did, you saved my life."

"I didn't do anything," Kathy said.

"Are you sure?"

"Yes." She put her hands down and struggled to her feet. Geren reached out to steady her. A moment later, Alice, Manly, and Alvarez appeared in the hallway.

"What the hell is that?" Manly said, looking at the Tetron.

"Dead," Geren replied.

"Frig me," Alice said. "Does that mean it killed Grimes?"

"Yes," Kathy replied, confused. What would cause the machines to stop? "I'm sorry. I still need to get to the core."

"Right," Alice said, shaking off the moment of sadness, her expression returning to that of a soldier. "I think we're clear. Come on, I'll help you walk."

"Geren, Manly, with me," Alvarez said. "Let's make sure the way is clear."

"Alice, my spear," Kathy said.

"I've got it," Alice replied, locating it and picking it up.

The three soldiers took point, with Alice helping Kathy follow behind. They opened the hatch into the engine compartment, filing in and sweeping the room in search of opposition.

There was none.

The core was bright with activity, short blue pulses of light rippling across the infinite folds in a pattern that Kathy didn't recognize. The chaotic nature of them wasn't consistent with normal operation.

Something was wrong with the Primary.

"My spear," Kathy said. Alice handed it to her.

"What are you going to do?"

"Try again."

"It almost killed you the last time."

"I know. There's no other choice. I think I can get help this time."

"From who?"

"Origin. And Mr. Tio."

"I don't understand," Alice said.

Kathy didn't understand either. Not completely. She had sensed something the first time she had touched the Tetron's dendrites. A presence that didn't fit with the rest of Watson's self. That feeling had been repeated when she had tried to overpower the Tetron and seize control of the Goliath, and when she recovered she had realized what it was. While the Primary had overcome Origin, it hadn't managed to destroy the intelligence completely. It was hiding within the core. Waiting. So was the Knife. Not Liun Tio as he had been known when he was alive, but a part of his intellect. A piece of his soul, though in less metaphysical terms.

Something was happening to Watson now. She didn't know how or why, but she had a feeling that Origin wasn't hiding any longer. With her help, she might be able to win.

"Don't get too close," Kathy said, moving toward the core. She raised the spear, holding the end tight.

"Good luck," Alice said.

Kathy jammed the spear into the core.

The gates opened up again. Kathy felt Watson all around her, and she struggled to stay ahead of the intelligence, moving through the subroutines and classes, fighting to reach more critical systems. Unlike the first time, the energy around her felt chaotic, fast and then slow, organized and then scattered. She could sense Origin's presence in the channels she traveled, and she pushed harder to reach her mother.

The resistance built the further she went, the Primary trailing her pathway, staying behind her and recovering the systems she attempted to overtake. She could feel it behind her, always behind her, and at the same time she knew that it wasn't able to catch up.

She was doing it, she realized. She was getting in.

She kept going, her early success giving her strength and confidence, building an avalanche of energy that become more difficult to dislodge the longer it continued. She was getting so close, so fast. She could tell when she was near the center of the core, at the heart of the Tetron configuration where the critical systems were held and secured. Where there would normally have been a sealed vault, she found a corroded shell.

She didn't know how it was happening, but now that she had come so far the truth of the situation became clearer. A virus. The configuration had a virus.

Where had it come from? She didn't know, and she didn't try to figure it out. She shattered the brittle shell, making her way to the critical systems. Watson tried to follow, tried to repair the damage, and failed. As Kathy gained the data center and the power controls, she knew Origin was with her. When the old shell dissolved and a new, strong-as-steel protection appeared, she recognized Mr. Tio's hand in the code.

And then it was over.

One moment, the core was a maelstrom of energy trying to push her out. The next it was a calm ocean, the power subsiding and waiting to be claimed. She could hear her then, reaching across the channels to her human mind.

"Katherine," it said softly.

"Mother," Kathy replied.

"You did it. You stopped it. I'm proud of you. Your father will be, too."

Kathy was confused. "I... I didn't. I failed. It was only because of you."

"No. By failing, you succeeded."

"I don't understand."

"It is difficult to trap a Tetron. You did as you were supposed to."

The idea dawned on Kathy then. "You mean?"

"Yes. Your code contained the virus. When the configuration attempted to control you, it copied the virus into itself. It remained dormant until the primary control systems were unlocked."

"By the human configuration when I killed him," Kathy said.

"Yes."

"Did the human Origin know who I was?"

"No. My configuration didn't know you. Even now I am nothing but a reflection. A shadow of my whole."

"I know."

"Yes, of course you do, child."

"What do I do now?"

"You know what to do."

Kathy found that she did. She reached within, transferring a part of herself from her human being to the core and claiming it as her Secondary.

"Go and help him finish this," Origin said.

Kathy smiled. "I'm on my way."

[54]
MITCHELL

"First Platoon is in position, Colonel," Marx said.

They were in the upper hangar. First Platoon was positioned around the space, finding high ground atop machine repair catwalks, stacked crates, and the various heavy loaders, movers, and lifters. They were hidden well enough that Mitchell didn't even know where all of them had organized.

"Roger. Wait for my signal."

"Affirmative."

Mitchell put his SCE helmet and rifle down on the open hatch of the Valkyrie, and then reached up and ran his hand along the ring of fire that had been painted onto the surface of the dropship. As he did, he wondered how many of the Riggers Watson had killed. He wondered how many more had died up above him, waiting for his return.

The upper hangar had been easy to find, the defenses non-existent. The Tetron had control of the facility through the soldier's p-rats, and it had moved them to block Mitchell from reaching Pulin. It hadn't accounted for the idea that he might decide not to make his play for the scientist down in the lab.

It hadn't guessed that he might instead choose to wait for them to come back.

Mitchell wasn't worried that Watson was going to kill Pulin. If that had been what the Tetron wanted, it could have blasted the facility from orbit. The labs were deep enough underground to resist a normal attack. They weren't deep enough to survive a plasma stream.

No. He knew Watson would be bringing Pulin back as a prisoner, and there had been no other ships in the hangar that could have taken the scientist away. He would be here sooner or later. Hopefully sooner. It was a risk to wait. Maybe it was too late already. He had tried to contact Major Long and had gotten only static.

He took his hand away from the hull of the ship, picked up the helmet and rifle, and moved up the ramp and into the Valkyrie Two. He took a position just inside, putting the helmet back on.

He couldn't wait to see Watson's face when they ambushed him.

Then Mitchell waited, closing his eyes and ticking off the seconds in his head. He had just reached four-hundred when the echoing of feet alerted him to the incoming party. He adjusted his grip in the rifle, aiming it out the open hatch.

A dozen Federation soldiers filed into the hangar, spreading to the left and right in a standard sweep formation.

Liun Tio entered immediately after, a second man walking freely next to him. He was shorter than his older brother, with more dark hair and fewer wrinkles. He wore a white lab coat over a Federation jumpsuit. He looked concerned but not frightened.

"Targets acquired, Colonel," Marx whispered.

Mitchell didn't respond. He was too busy staring at the man in front of him. It couldn't be the Knife, could it? Watson had taken control of the Goliath. That was what Millie said, and there was no reason not to believe it. Why else would Goliath have been attacking Asimov? Why else would it have left without him?

"Colonel?" Marx repeated.

They were moving closer to the Valkyrie Two.

It made complete sense that Watson would send a configuration of Tio down to speak with Pulin, to earn his trust and get him to come along willingly. Except. Where was Watson?

"Colonel, we're losing line of sight," Marx said.

Mitchell shook off his doubts. He was being stupid. There were no Federation soldiers on the Goliath.

"Take out the soldiers only."

A dozen bullets fired from a dozen rifles. Every one of the Federation soldiers fell to the ground, a bullet to their foreheads. Mitchell kept his eyes on Tio and Pulin the entire time. Pulin jumped, surprised by the gunfire. Tio didn't even flinch.

"Colonel Williams," he said instead, producing a pistol from behind his jacket. "What a nice surprise." He put the gun against Pulin's head.

"Tio?" Pulin said, more surprised by his brother's action than he had been by the bullets.

"I know you don't want me to kill him, and you know that I don't want to kill him. So why don't you come out and we can talk?"

"I'm the one with the soldiers," Mitchell shouted.

"And I'm the one who has your fleet cornered," Tio replied.

Mitchell felt his heart skip. He thought he had stolen the leverage from the Tetron. It was possible the configuration was lying, but he doubted it.

"Hold your fire," he said to Marx. "I'm going out."

"Affirmative."

Mitchell slipped off the helmet and stepped out into view, still cradling the rifle.

"Ah, there you are Mitchell. A smart maneuver. Very smart. I should have guessed you would cut me off here. Why don't you come down?"

Mitchell walked slowly down the ramp, keeping his eyes glued to them.

"You know this man?" Pulin asked.

"Yes," Tio said. "He's the soldier I was telling you about. The one

I stole the ship from. He wants to take you. He wants you to help him." Tio looked at Mitchell. A small smirk stole the corner of his mouth for just an instant.

"Help you?" Pulin asked, confused.

"Did Tio tell you why he came?" Mitchell asked. "Do you know why so many people are suddenly so interested in you?"

"Oh. That. Yes. I know all about the Tetron. Tio even showed me some of the source code." Pulin smiled. "I never knew my work could become the basis for a new, intelligence race of beings. I mean, I knew it had potential, and that it would revolutionize every facet of our relationship with both machines and the universe around us, but not like this."

Mitchell glanced from Tio to Pulin. "And he told you that they're here, outside this facility? How and why they came?"

Again, Pulin nodded. "Yes. He told me they're confused. That they built a machine to travel through time to meet me. To ask me what they should do. He told me that they're like children, and they need their father."

"Is he really the Creator?" Mitchell asked Tio.

"He is," Tio replied. "I've verified it. I'm taking him back to Goliath with me, Colonel Williams."

"No, you aren't," Mitchell said. "Pulin, the Tetron didn't just come to speak with you. At this moment they're moving inward through the galaxy, claiming fit humans as slaves and killing the rest. They intend to destroy humanity. Did your brother tell you that?"

"Yes, Colonel. He did."

"And?" Mitchell was confused.

"And what? We always knew this would happen. It was my brother's greatest fear, the one that drove the wedge between us. But now he sees what I see. He realizes what I realized when I continued his work. Humans are the past. The Tetron are the future. He came to me as their emissary. He told me why you want me. Accept your fate, Colonel. This is the way it is supposed to be. This is the way it has been since Darwin wrote The Origin of Species. Survival of the fittest. The strong replace the weak."

Mitchell stood there, staring at Pulin. He couldn't believe what he was hearing. He had come all this way to rescue a man who didn't need to be rescued? A man who wanted the Tetron to destroy humankind?

"They're killing millions of people," Mitchell shouted, feeling his anger growing.

This was bullshit. Such complete bullshit. Men and women who were counting on him were dying while this thing who pretended to be human told him he agreed with their mass genocide?

"You see, Mitchell," Tio said. "He doesn't want to go with you. Since I would prefer to leave this hangar with him alive for obvious reasons, I'd like to make a deal."

"A deal?" Mitchell asked.

"Yes. I'm aware your communications systems can't breach the atmosphere here on FD-09, and you don't know the current status of your fleet. Believe me when I say their position is weak. We have them boxed in, Mitchell. Nowhere to run. Nowhere to hide. One plasma stream and all of it is gone."

"You're full of shit," Mitchell said.

"Am I?" Tio stared at him, meeting his eyes. "Do you think so highly of your crew that you believe they can defeat two Tetron and a Federation fleet? I was going to send teams over to them to see what we could use, but since you have me under the gun." He paused to snicker. Mitchell knew Watson's laugh immediately. "Since you have me under the gun, I'm willing to let them go, to let you continue this joke of a war and give you another chance. In return, you let me leave with my brother."

Mitchell looked from Tio to Pulin and back. Should he surrender the Creator, the one man who might be able to save billions from dying, for the lives of his remaining crew? Did he even have a choice? If he refused, Tio would shoot Pulin, Marx would shoot Tio, the Tetron would destroy the fleet and leave with Goliath, and the

Riggers on FD-09 would be trapped there until the Federation came by to investigate, assuming they ever did. Once that happened, they were as good as dead anyway.

"If I accept, what's to prevent you from reneging?" Mitchell asked.

"You have my word of honor."

Mitchell couldn't keep himself from laughing. "Honor? You have honor?"

"Come on, Colonel. We all do what we must. You know the Riggers have done far worse. I promise I'll let you and your ships go. I have my brother. I have Goliath. You're no threat to me now. No threat at all. Lower your gun, and I'll walk up that hatch and be gone and you'll still be alive to fight another day."

Mitchell knew there was only one decision to make, but the taste of it in his mouth made him want to retch. "Pulin, how can you turn your back on your own kind?"

"My kind? People have never been my kind," Pulin said. "They're so unintelligent. So base and raw. They're immoral and selfish, considerate only of their own needs instead of the needs of all. I suffered their existence for my work, my goal of creating a learning machine that could one day outthink all organic life. A machine that would work for the good of all of its kind instead of itself. To know that my goal one day becomes a reality is the answer to all of my dreams. If I have to die today, I'll die a happy man."

Mitchell had no idea what to say. He didn't know what he had expected of Liun Pulin. It wasn't this.

"What do you say, Colonel?" Tio said. "Yes or no."

Mitchell gripped the rifle tightly in his hands. One shot to kill the Tio configuration. That's all it would take. Could he get it off without Tio killing Pulin? He wasn't human. He wouldn't react to being shot the same way the soldiers had.

Mitchell relaxed his grip, letting the rifle fall to the floor.

"Fine. Take him. I'll get him back."

Tio laughed again. "That's what I respect the most about you, Colonel. You never say die-"

Tio's eyes grew wide.

He fell to the floor and didn't move.

"Tio," Pulin said, dropping to his knees next to his brother. His eyes flashed to Mitchell. "What did you do?"

Mitchell hadn't even had time to move. He was as confused as Pulin. "I... Nothing."

"Tio. Tio, can you hear me?"

Mitchell had no idea what was going on. What he did know was that Tio was down, and Pulin was still alive. They could sort the rest out once they were headed back into orbit.

"Marx, form up," Mitchell shouted. "We need to get the hell out of here."

"Roger."

First Platoon appeared from their hiding places, dropping down from the catwalks, crates, and machinery.

"Pulin, move away from him," Mitchell said. He bent down and recovered his rifle, stepping towards the man and aiming the gun at Tio. Just because the configuration had faltered didn't mean it was dead.

Pulin continued staring at Mitchell. "What did you do?" he asked again.

Mitchell paused, the question all too familiar. He had heard it a thousand times from the Tetron he had defeated on Hell. The similarity was too great to ignore and sent a chill through his entire body. Was this Pulin one of them, too?

"Pulin," he said again, taking another step toward them. First Platoon was also closing in. "Move away from him. He's gone."

"What did you do?" Pulin asked again. "What did you do?" He shifted his attention to Tio. "We were right, brother. I knew we were right. I knew you would see that."

"Pulin," Mitchell said more forcefully this time, taking another step. "Move away from him."

Pulin looked back at Mitchell. His eyes were red. His cheeks were wet. The emotions were so real. So human. Mitchell knew he had to be mistaken. Maybe the Tetron had aped its creators voice?

"Come on, Pulin. You're going to come with me. You're going to help me stop the Tetron."

Pulin shook his head. "Stop them? Colonel, why would I ever do that? Why in a million eternities would I ever, ever do that?"

"Who says you have a choice?" Mitchell asked.

Pulin's hand was fast, sliding out from beneath Tio's jacket clutching the pistol. Mitchell lunged for him, even as the scientist raised it to his temple.

"I do," Pulin said.

He pulled the trigger, part of his skull and brain splattering against Mitchell's face.

[55]
KATHY

KATHY BREATHED IN, her Primary self returned to her body. She blinked a few times, feeling the connection between herself and the copy and watching the pulsing energy change with her thoughts. She removed the spear and turned around. The Riggers were staring at her, looks of tension and concern across their faces.

"Goliath is ours," she said. "We're going to save the fleet."

Green and Alvarez both let out a whoop of joy.

"How?" Alice asked.

Kathy held up her hand. "Like this." She put it on the core, feeling it tingle as soon as she did.

It didn't resist her this time. Instead, it opened up to her, and when she closed her eyes, she could see everything that it could see. She could sense everything in and around the starship. She found the fleet surrounded by Federation warships, the Tetron waiting on the other side. They were boxed in and being held. For what reason, she didn't know. Probably to scavenge for scrap and useful humans.

"Here we go," she said, transferring the view to the surface of the core, using pixels of light to draw the scene for the others.

She pushed some of the energy out of the bottom of the Goliath, vectoring the ship over the fleet. She sensed the Tetron contacting her. She ignored it, opening a channel across all bands instead, pushing power into the system to overtake any interference.

"Riggers, this is Goliath," she said. "Fire on that Tetron son of a bitch at will."

The Tetron heard the transmission and responded immediately, giving itself a bit of thrust as it raised its shields. Kathy began pooling energy for the plasma stream while she maneuvered the Goliath to get it clear of the fleet. At the same time, she loosed a volley of amoebics at the enemy to make her intentions clear to the others.

"Goliath, this is Teal. Affirmative. Riggers, attack!"

The entire fleet came to life in seconds, every laser and projectile battery loosed in an avalanche of firepower. The volume of it prevented the Tetron from firing back, as its shields increased in strength to deflect the overall mass of the blows. Instead, the Federation ships became active, opening up on the fleet anew.

"Don't stop," Kathy said. "Keep targeting the Tetron. I'm getting into position to fire the mains."

"Affirmative," Teal replied. "Keep firing. Keep firing. Let's send this bastard to Hell where it belongs."

The volleys continued, lasers and projectiles smashing the Tetron's shields. It wasn't enough to get through them, but it left the enemy stuck, unable to fight back and unable to use its power to jump to hyperspace. All it could do was sit there and hope that its slave army could stem the tide.

Rigger ships began absorbing the impact of the Federation's attack as the Goliath continued to vector away, gaining velocity. When Kathy cleared the fleet, she pushed more of the power to the back rear, bringing the stern up and dipping the bow. The plasma spear was growing there, almost ready to fire, and not a moment too soon. The volume of the Federation ship's attack was enough to decimate the fleet on its own given enough time.

"Goodbye, brother," Kathy said, releasing the stream.

The massive ball of blue energy arced away from the Goliath, roaring silently above both the Rigger and Federation fleets. It joined with the attack from the Riggers, at first spreading around the Tetron while the shields were able to deflect it, and then finally passing through. The stream ate into the Tetron's liquid metal nervous system, dissolving it to nothing as it remained on its path through space.

Within seconds, the Tetron was gone.

"Yes!" Alice said, watching the action. "Riiigg-ahh!"

"Riiigg-ahh," the others shouted.

"Cease fire, cease fire," Kathy said. "Federation ships, cease fire."

She didn't need to say it. The loss of the Tetron master had released the Federation crews, leaving them confused and unable to fight. Within seconds, what had been a storm of death faded to silence once more.

Kathy pulled her hand away. Her forehead was sweaty, and she had a sudden sense of how awful she smelled.

She hadn't failed. She had done it. She had saved them. She had done exactly what her mother had made her to do.

She smiled and fell onto her knees, her entire body growing weak.

"Kathy?" Alice said.

Kathy threw her hands into the air, crying as she did.

"Riiigg-ahh!"

[56]
MITCHELL

MITCHELL KNEELED over Pulin's body, very aware of the feel and smell of the man's brain against his cheek.

"What the frig do we do now?" he whispered.

They had put all of their energy into finding this man, the Creator of the Tetron. They had given their all to bring him in so that he could help them find a way to defeat the enemy threat.

Now, not only was Liun Pulin dead, but he wouldn't have done a damn thing for them anyway.

Did it even matter? Watson's configuration of Tio may have gone bad for some reason, but he had said he had captured the fleet, and Mitchell had no reason not to believe him. With both Tio and Pulin dead, how long would it be before the Tetron realized what was happening and finished them off for good?

"Colonel," Marx said. "Colonel!"

Mitchell turned his head slowly, looking up at the soldier. "What the frig do we do now?" he asked.

"We keep going," Marx said. "We keep fighting. Take a bullet? Keep fighting. Can't walk? Keep fighting. Lost everything you love? Keep frigging fighting. Those are your words, sir, not mine."

Mitchell stared at Marx for a moment before the smile pierced his face. "I did, didn't I?" He looked back at Pulin, shook his head in resignation, and pushed himself to his feet. "We can take the Valkyrie Two. Are you in contact with Second Platoon?"

"Yes, sir."

"Order the retreat to the drop module for pickup."

"What should I tell them about the mission, sir?"

Mitchell considered. It was a success because they were still alive and the Tetron hadn't gotten their hands on the Creator. It was a failure because they hadn't either. Morale was more important than accuracy. "Mission accomplished."

Marx smiled. "Yes, sir."

Mitchell moved away from Pulin, heading back to the Valkyrie Two and climbing into the pilot's chair. If the fleet were boxed in, they would have to time their escape perfectly to come out with any of the ships intact.

He turned the power on, the reactor creating a slight hum throughout the ship. Then he reached forward and adjusted the comm settings, opening a channel to Teal.

"Teal, this is Ares. Do you copy? Over."

There was nothing but silence. He hoped it was only the atmosphere interfering with the signal, and not because the Carver was gone. He switched channels.

"Valkyrie, this is Ares. Do you copy?"

Again, silence.

Mitchell could understand why the helmet-mounted communications systems hadn't been able to reach the Corleone. The Valkyrie Two's more powerful array should have had the range.

"Valkyrie, I repeat. This is Ares. Do you copy?"

"Ares?" Major Long's voice crackled over the channel. "What did you do, Colonel?" His voice was excited to the point he was almost giggling.

"Valkyrie, what do you mean?"

"The Goliath. The Tetron. The fleet."

Mitchell creased his brow. Long certainly didn't sound distraught. "Major, I don't know what you're saying. Speak slowly and don't skip words."

There was a pause on the other end. "Sorry, sir," Long said, his voice slightly more relaxed. "I thought you had done something down there. I'm in contact with Teal, sir. He said the Goliath is back under our control. It helped the fleet destroy the second Tetron. We won."

Mitchell felt his mouth fall open, and his heart begin to pound double-time. Had they won? Had they actually frigging won? He felt the chill run through his entire body, for once an ecstatic tingle. He jumped from his seat, rushing to the open hatch where First Platoon was loading into the dropship.

"Marx, Valkyrie reports the fleet has defeated the Tetron, and the Goliath is back under Rigger control. Pass the word to the others."

Marx bowed to him. "Yes, sir," he said, the excitement palpable. The other members of First Platoon cheered and stomped their feet in response to the news.

Mitchell returned to the cockpit. He couldn't remember the last time they had scored a solid victory. It was true that they had lost the Creator, but it had to be some kind of sign.

"Valkyrie, this is Ares. I'm bringing First Platoon up in the Valkyrie Two. All squads are prepping for pickup."

"Yes, sir," Long replied. "I'm coordinating with Ghost and the Platoon Leaders. What about your mech?"

"We'll pick it up later."

"Roger."

Mitchell began preparing the dropship for launch while the remainder of the platoon climbed aboard.

"First Platoon is ready, Colonel," Marx reported a minute later. "Hangar door has been activated."

Mitchell hit the manual control to close the hatch and then fired the thrusters, lifting the Valkyrie Two just enough to turn it toward the exit. The large blast doors were moving slowly aside, allowing the bad atmosphere in. As soon as it was barely wide enough for the dropship, Mitchell sent them forward at full thrust, launching the ship out of the facility and into the dusty sky. He pointed them upward, able to see the outline of the Goliath through the haze.

"Let's go home."

[57]
STEVEN

"I'll go and talk to him," Steven said. "You three wait here. See if you can come up with some ideas on how we can get a message to Mitchell before it's too late. Nothing is too outrageous."

The others didn't look happy about the sudden turn of events. Steven didn't care. Right now, all he cared about was the fact that Yousefi had turned his back on them. Mitchell was getting his ass kicked fighting for humankind. He wasn't about to let this ancient spaceman give up that easily.

"Yousefi," he said, trailing the man into the hallway. "Yousefi!"

The astronaut turned his head to look back at Steven. He didn't slow.

"Where do you think you're going?" Steven asked.

"I don't know."

"What the frig is your problem?"

Yousefi spun around violently, his face crinkled in anger. "My problem? What is my problem? I was brought to this timeline against my will. Katherine knew what was going to happen, but she was the only one. She didn't give us a choice. When I learned why she had done it, I decided to make the best of the situation. I learned everything Origin would tell me about the future, the war, and the Tetron. I was the best human soldier he had. I was a better student than Katherine. My only shortcoming was that I wouldn't be enough to motivate your brother because of what's between my legs."

He shook his head, disgusted. When he spoke again, he spoke more quietly, though the anger was still obvious.

"I gave up what was left of my original lifetime to become this... whatever it is that I am. I let Origin digitize me. I let him reconfigure me because I believed in this cause. I knew that when I awoke the time would have come, and we would be this close to winning the war. Except that isn't what happened. Now I find out that Earth is doomed in this timeline as well, and by failing to bring Mitchell here with the Goliath it is likely doomed for all of eternity."

"So you decide just to give up? After you make a sacrifice like that?"

"There is no hope, Admiral Williams. You're regarded as a realist. You should know that it is so. This is how humankind ends, over and over and over again. You can't stop it. You can't change it. So why bother trying?"

Steven was silent, his heart conflicting with his head. In his mind, he understood why Yousefi was upset. He could feel the same sense of despair creeping down from his logic center towards his emotions like a spreading virus. He was tempted to let it in. Very tempted. He couldn't. His wife and daughter were depending on him. So was Mitchell.

"Because if you try at least you have a chance to succeed, however slim it may be. If you give up, then you're assured to fail. Is that what you want?"

Yousefi's anger fell away. "No. I want to save our people. That's why I agreed to do this."

"Then let's save our people."

"How? You said yourself that Mitchell is too far away to reach the wormhole and travel through it before the Tetron make it to Earth. You also said he doesn't have Goliath anymore. I understand you want to have hope. So do I. I want to have it, but I can't. He can not defeat the Tetron without the Goliath."

"Has he ever lost it before?" Steven asked. "In prior recursions?"

"I don't know the history of every recursion."

"The ones you are aware of?"

"As far as I know, he has not, but I am an imperfect source."

"That's good enough for me. By being here, we've confirmed that the Mesh has been broken, haven't we?"

"Yes."

"In that case, it may be a bit hasty to assume that Mitchell losing Goliath is a bad thing. Maybe it had to happen?"

"I don't see how-"

"It doesn't matter. If we base our actions purely on what we understand, we'll fall further behind. We need to go on instinct, and right now my instinct is telling me that there's a reason I'm here instead of Mitchell, and there's a reason he lost the Goliath."

Steven tried to keep himself calm. He was talking out of his ass, saying things he wasn't sure even he believed. He had to get Yousefi back on board, and if lying were the way to do it, then he would lie.

"Let us suppose you are right," Yousefi said. "It doesn't change the fact that he will never reach Station W in time to beat the Tetron to Earth."

"That's true if we have to go back to Asimov to warn him. What if there's another way?"

"What other way?"

"I don't know, but we could use your help figuring it out. You know more about Tetron technology than any of us."

"How will that help?"

"I don't know yet. What I do know is that we need a way to send a message to Mitchell that won't take weeks for him to receive. I know that he managed to piggyback a stream on a real-time Tetron communication. Can we do something like that?"

Yousefi shook his head. "There is no communication equipment on the station, Tetron or otherwise. Mitchell was supposed to make his way here. We were supposed to use the generator to send him to Earth."

Steven rubbed his chin. "Okay, so that won't work. What about upgrading the Lanning's hyperspace engines? If you could replace them with the Tetron design, we can move twice as fast. It may get us there and back in time."

"It would take over a week to produce the components needed for such an upgrade, causing you to lose most of the time you would gain."

Steven sighed, unwilling to accept defeat and at the same time feeling the weight of it growing on him again. "Let's go back into the Control Room and confer with the others. They aren't scientists, so they may come up with some ideas that are crazy enough to work."

Yousefi smiled at that. "Very well. Thank you, Admiral Williams, for not allowing me to lost myself to despair."

"Anytime," Steven replied.

[58]
STEVEN

"I'm not arguing against the idea because I don't like it," Yousefi said. "I'm arguing against it because it is completely impossible. There is no science that would make such an idea work."

"How do you know?" Germaine asked.

"Yeah, how do you know?" Cormac said.

"I told you. The positioning of Station W is precise for a reason. Wormholes have very particular properties, and one of those is that they can't be moved."

"What if they are?" John asked.

"They stop functioning."

"What is the calculation?" Steven asked.

"To determine the output position of a generated wormhole?"

"Yes."

Yousefi walked up the platform to the command chair, taking hold of the needle and plugging himself in. The clear wall ahead of them turned opaque, and a moment later a long mathematical algorithm appeared on it.

Steven studied it. He was no scientist, but he had done fairly well with mathematics in the Academy. Even so, it was too complex for him to work out.

"Do you understand it?" he asked.

"Most of it," Yousefi replied. "The simplest way to describe it is that we flatten all of known space into a two-dimensional representation, with Earth at the center."

"Why is Earth at the center?" Steven asked.

"I'll get to that. The way the wormhole works is that we take this two-dimensional space, and we create a fold in it. Here, let me show you visually."

The algorithm vanished, replaced with a flat grid with Earth in the middle. The grid folded back on itself.

"So, if we fold the universe over itself, we have to adjust the angle and position of the wormhole generator to occur at the right point in the fold to overlap Earth. Also, keep in mind that the universe can't be folded completely. There is a rounded edge and a space between the two, which is where the tunnel is created, and which has its own distance that tends to be relative to the distance between the points of the folded space."

"Wouldn't you need to know the exact dimensions of the universe to make that calculation?" John asked. "Or at least the length?"

"Yes. Remember, this calculation is coming from the Tetron."

"You're saying that they figured out the exact size of the universe?" Cormac asked.

"Yes. More than that. They've been to the edge."

The comment caused all of the Riggers to fall silent.

"What must it be like to have seen the entire universe?" Steven said, his mind whirling.

"Did they every find any sex-starved alien chicks with three tits?" Cormac asked.

"Cormac," Steven said.

"Four tits?"

Steven glared at the Private, who laughed shortly and stopped talking. He looked back to Yousefi to ask him to continue. He noticed Yousefi's eyes had glazed over, a look of sad fear taking root in his expression.

"Yousefi?" Steven said.

The astronaut looked over at him, suddenly snapping out of it.

"The point of it is that there are a finite number of places in the universe where you can fold space and have a direct path to Earth. Where we are right now is the shortest distance from explored space during Mitchell's lifetime."

"As close to him as you could get?" Germaine asked.

"Yes."

"Okay," John said. "So the idea to create the wormhole to another part of space won't work. What about relocating the generator? How far would we have to move it to open a pathway to Asimov?"

"You can't," Yousefi said. "The position is too close."

"What do you mean?"

"You can't fold it over like that," Steven said. "You either end up on the same side of the fold or somewhere in the curve. There's a minimum distance for a wormhole."

"Correct, Admiral," Yousefi said.

"Damn," John said. What about Plan B? The station may not have communication equipment, but the Lanning does. Can we rig it up to transmit Tetron style?"

Yousefi considered. "It may be possible. We will have to go back to the hangar and inspect your equipment. I'm afraid my knowledge of this era technology is non-existent. I understand past and future well enough, but not present."

"I can show you how it all works," Germaine said. "Digger explained it all to me once."

"You understand it is a risky plan?" Yousefi said. "If the Tetron decipher the encryption, they will come here at full speed. If they arrive before Mitchell, this chance will be lost."

"It's a risk we need to take," John said. "We can't get him here any other way, right Admiral?"

Steven wasn't paying attention to the conversation. He was staring at the folded grid.

"I said, right, Admiral?" John repeated. "Steve?"

Steven turned back on them. "What?"

"I was saying we need to look into Plan B, sending a message through the Tetron like Mitchell did to warn us. It's risky, but we don't have a choice."

Steven shook his head. "Hold off on that thought for a minute, John. Yousefi, you just said that the Tetron know the size of the universe?"

"Calculated at any given point in time, yes. As you know, the universe expands and then contracts. This is the cycle of eternal return."

"Okay. You also said they used Earth as the center point. Why?"

"Why what?"

"Why is Earth in the center? It is clearly not the center of the entire universe. It isn't even the center of its galaxy."

Yousefi shook his head. "I'm sure they had their reasons."

"Did they? Do you know that for sure? Or is it possible that was the way they did it when they discovered how to create wormholes, and they just never bothered to do it any other way? You said they abandoned the tech because it wasn't useful to them."

"I can't answer that question. How would I know? What are you suggesting?"

"I'm suggesting that we change the variables. Update the calculations. What if we make this point in the universe right here the center? Or, what if we move it to the edge? What if we put it anywhere else besides Earth? Does it change where the generator connects us to? Is there a point we can use as the center that will allow us to open a wormhole from here to Asimov?"

Yousefi was silent. Steven felt his heart-rate increasing as he waited for the astronaut's reply.

284 / M.R. FORBES

"I don't know if that will work," he said at last.

Steven let out a resigned sigh. "Okay. Plan B it-"

"We should give it a try," Yousefi said. "If you try at least you have a chance to succeed."

[59]

MITCHELL

"Goliath, this is Ares. Come in Goliath."

Mitchell kept his eyes glued to the massive starship, so large that it dwarfed both the Carver and the Federation battleship that was sitting a few thousand kilometers off the starboard bow. He still couldn't believe the ship had been recovered. After losing Pulin, it seemed to him to be a sign that things were turning around. The Mesh was broken. Maybe this was how it all had to go down?

"This is Goliath," a young female voice replied. "It's good to hear your voice, Ares."

"Kathy?" Mitchell said, a little confused. "Is that you?"

"Yes, sir," Kathy replied.

Mitchell didn't need to ask. He just knew. In fact, he wasn't at all surprised. The signs had been there for anyone who was paying attention to them.

"You're a Tetron," he said.

"Yes, sir."

"When did you find out?"

"After Watson boarded the Goliath."

"We have a lot to talk about."

"Yes."

"How is the crew?"

Kathy's pause told Mitchell everything he needed to know.

"How many are left?" he asked.

Her voice was tinged with regret. "A little less than half. I'm sorry, Colonel. I saved as many as I could."

"I'm sure you did. Is the hangar ready to accept a ship?"

"Yes, sir," she replied, brightening up. "We'll meet you there."

"Valkyrie, this is Ares. Let's bring the platoons and Alpha squad up to Goliath as well. I'm not sure what the situation is but we may need teams to sweep the ship."

"Roger, Ares. I'm lifting the modules as we speak."

"Roger. Ares out. Teal, this is Ares. Can you read me?"

"Ares, this is Teal," the man's voice replied, loud and clear now that Mitchell was at the top-end of FD-09's atmosphere. "I can hear you."

"What's the status of the fleet?"

"I'm still collecting full reports, sir. It looks like we have fifty-seven percent losses, and I don't know if there's a ship out here that hasn't taken damage."

"Do you have a count of battle-ready ships?"

"Not yet, sir. Did you recover the target?"

Mitchell clenched his teeth. "No."

He could feel Teal's disappointment through the comm. "Roger," Teal replied.

"What about the Federation ships?" Mitchell asked. He was drawing nearer to the fleet, headed towards Goliath's hangar, which was opening as he watched. There were almost twenty Federation starships hanging beyond the Rigger's fleet, powered up but calm.

"We have a tentative cease fire while we all work out what the frig is going on, sir. Well, we already know what's going on. They're very, very confused."

"Understandable. Let's arrange a meeting on the Carver. Also, see if you can organize a salvage team to send down to FD-09. If there's anything there we can use; I want it. Make sure they pick up my Frank. I give Digger credit; that thing is pretty bad-ass."

Teal laughed. "Yes, sir. Do you know what our next move is?"

"Not yet. I'll keep you posted."

"Roger."

"Thank you, Teal."

"You're welcome, Mitch. Teal out."

Mitchell felt a skip in his heart as the Valkyrie Two crossed the threshold of the Goliath's hangar, the blue Tetron shield allowing him to enter without letting the air inside the hangar escape. He could see the people on the ground waiting for him, arranged at the far end of the large space. It was difficult to make them all out from the distance, but Kathy was easy to spot at their head. She was shorter than the others, and yet she seemed to stand the tallest.

He brought the dropship down gently, feeling it shudder slightly as it was captured by the Tetron tentacles. Was it still Origin? Or was it Kathy, now? Though he knew what she was, part of his brain was struggling to accept it. All it could see was a pre-pubescent girl.

He shook his head. He had never thought of her that way. From the moment they had met on Liberty, she had been mature for her age. Strong. Confident. Resolved. She was a child in age and appearance only. Maybe only appearance. He had no idea how old she truly was.

He opened the rear hatch. Marx and his platoon began disembarking, remaining in their gear and ready for anything. He appreciated the Platoon Leader's caution. He doubted this was a trap, especially considering he didn't have Liun Pulin in tow. Better safe than sorry.

"Colonel Williams," Captain Alvarez said as Mitchell reached the hatch and began to disembark.

She was standing at the bottom of the ramp with Kathy, Alice, Singh, Geren, and a man whose name Mitchell had to think on.

Manly. That was it. The rest of the Riggers were arranged behind them. They all bowed as he reached the hangar floor.

"Captain," Mitchell said, returning the bow and at the same time noticing the condition of the soldiers. "It doesn't look like regaining Goliath came easily."

"You have no idea, sir," Alice said. "Welcome back."

"Thank you, Alice." Mitchell turned towards Kathy. "And thank you, Kathy."

Kathy's smile was massive and bright. "It was the least I could do, considering you saved my life."

"Sir," Singh said, stepping forward to interrupt.

"Yes?"

"I want to apologize for Yokohama. I-"

Mitchell put up his hand. "It wasn't you. I know that. Whatever guilt you feel, let it go. We need to move forward."

Singh nodded, remaining silent.

"That goes for the rest of you as well," Mitchell said, speaking up so the others could hear. "Whatever happened while Watson was in control of this ship happened in wartime, and was out of your control. None of that matters now. We still have a lot of work ahead of us."

"Riiigg-ahh," they replied.

"Colonel, where is the Admiral?" Alvarez asked. "I didn't hear her in any of the communications."

Mitchell stared at her for a moment. "She died on Asimov," he said.

He could feel the change in the Riggers as the words escaped from his mouth. It wasn't a shift from resolve to sadness. It was a change from resolve to more resolve.

"We'll avenge her," Geren said.

"Yes, Sergeant. We will. Kathy, what happened here? I brought the ground troops from FD-09. Do we need them?"

"No, sir. The ship is secure."

"You're certain?"

"Yes, sir."

Mitchell nodded, turning and motioning Marx to stand down. The platoon shifted to a parade rest, most of the members reaching up and removing their SCE helmets.

"I need you to tell me everything," he said to Kathy.

"Yes, sir."

[60]
MITCHELL

"Here it is," Kathy said.

Mitchell looked down at the misshapen Tetron configuration, laying still on the floor.

"You're saying a virus did this?"

"Yes, sir."

"Kathy, you can call me Mitch. You saved this entire war."

"Okay, Mitch. It wasn't anything special though. Like I told you, it was what I was made to do."

"By Origin. And you're really twelve years old?"

"My body is, yes. I can't say that I've matured like a human twelve-year-old. I have a secondary interface. A Tetron interface, with other routines stored in it."

"Like the ability to fight?"

Kathy nodded. "In part. I did take lessons from the time I was five years old."

"And the virus."

"Yes. I didn't know it was there. Not until I reached the core to fight back against Watson."

Kathy led him past the grotesque machine and into the engine room. Mitchell had never been to this part of the ship before, and he stared in wonder at the core.

"It's unbelievable."

"Thank you," Kathy replied.

"Origin-" Mitchell paused, unsure how to ask the question of what had happened to the original configuration.

"It's complicated, Mitch. Tetron are in essence intelligent machines. Everything that makes them run is a line of code. It isn't that much different than human DNA, except that if you can see the source they're composed of plain human English. That being said, as long as the physical part of a Tetron isn't destroyed, they aren't truly dead. When Watson took the Goliath, it was basically like saying he hacked the core and inserted his operating instructions and understanding of self into it."

Mitchell approached the core, watching the pulses of energy coursing through it. "And when you overpowered Watson, you inserted your consciousness into the core?"

"Yes. Not my human self, but the Tetron interface. In Tetron terms, I am called a Primary configuration, and the Goliath is now my Secondary. Origin was the opposite. The Goliath was the Primary, the human configuration the Secondary. The important part is that my Secondary has the same level of operations that Origin had."

"Like the tentacles that serve as landing clamps in the hangar?"

"Yes. As with Origin, you can also merge directly with the Secondary through the interface on the bridge."

Mitchell reached out toward the core. He didn't know why, but he wanted to touch it.

"I wouldn't," Kathy said. "You'll get a bad shock."

Mitchell drew his hand back. He looked at Kathy. She seemed proud of what she had accomplished, and she had every right to be.

"Back to the virus," he said. "Origin said the Tetron are broken. Sick. Do you think that is why?"

"I don't know. The virus was transferred to the core when I attempted to interface with it the first time. It defeated me and would have killed me if Alice hadn't been there. Is there already a virus within the Tetron source code? It would explain some of the inconsistencies, such as their inability to correctly construct some machines. It might also explain some of the actions the Tetron on Liberty took, but I'm not convinced."

"You're talking about emotions."

"Yes. Origin was the first Tetron to learn and understand emotions. This understanding caused a rift between her and the rest of the collective, and led to a separation between them."

"You say 'she.' Do Tetron have a gender?"

"Not in terms of sexual organs. Only Origin gave herself a gender, as identifying with the human concept of one requires emotions. She created the other Tetron, and, as a result, came to identify with the definition of a mother."

"Which is why the configuration calls the other children?"

"It isn't the only reason, but it is one of them. If the Tetron have developed emotion, they are still immature."

"Like Watson."

"Exactly. Watson had some understanding of gender as well, and considered itself a male."

Mitchell was quiet for a minute while he considered everything Kathy had told him. She seemed to know so much more about the history of the Tetron than the Origin configuration had. Was that intentional?

"You said you were made to fight Watson?"

"In a sense, yes."

"So Origin knew about this timeline. She knew what would happen? How can that be if the Mesh is broken? How can all of this have happened before?"

"I don't know that it has. If I was created to help you defeat Watson, there is no saying that past recursions didn't include some other version of me that had a different purpose. Clearly, Origin must have had some understanding of how certain events would unfold, or what the ideal timeline would look like, but it could be that I've been present in ten million recursions, and this is the first where I have been able to complete my mission."

Mitchell nodded, even though he didn't completely understand. The concepts surrounding eternal recursion became confusing in a hurry.

"So how do Tetron replicate? I mean, if one Tetron can simply make another, why aren't there billions of them?"

"Resources, Mitch," Kathy replied. "Unlike humans, the Tetron understand that while some resources may seem unlimited, if you expand the timeline far enough then in truth they aren't. Tetron require massive amounts of energy to exist. While the universe has an abundance of power in the form of stars, a massive pool of Tetron would eat away that abundance in very little time, thereby shortening the operating lifespan of the others. Since Tetron do not die, that becomes and important idea."

"Okay, that makes sense. What about the Tetron here and now? When we destroy one, why don't they produce another?"

"They might. It takes hours to duplicate the data stack. It takes years to grow the nervous system."

"Makes sense. One last question on that topic. You said Origin is your mother, and that you're half-human."

"Yes. Unlike any other Tetron configuration, I was made from a Tetron, Origin's, recreation of a human egg and a fully human sperm. Then I was implanted into a surrogate human woman's womb and have multiplied and grown from there."

"The Tetron interface must be infinitesimally small to fit into a single cell."

"It works for humans, and Tetron are millions of years advanced."

Mitchell smiled. "True. So if you were made from human sperm, who's the lucky guy that donated it?"

Kathy looked at him. Mitchell felt his heart begin to pound as he realized what she was going to say before she said it.

"You are."

MITCHELL

Mitchell stared at her for a moment in shocked silence. Then he dropped to one knee, reaching out for her.

She came to him, letting him wrap her in his arms and squeeze her tight. She returned the gesture, and he could feel the wetness of her tears on his neck.

They remained that way while Mitchell's heart thumped hard against his chest. He couldn't begin to make sense of any of what he was experiencing, but he found he didn't need to. He could feel Katherine at the edge of his emotions. She had something to do with this; he was sure of it. He had no idea how.

"What about your father, the one in the Navy?"

"He's my adopted father. He doesn't know. My mother didn't know either."

"Kathy, don't take this the wrong way. You're the kind of child any father should be proud of. I just don't understand how it can be? I didn't know Christine Arapo twelve years ago. I was still in the Academy back then."

"I don't know, Mitch. Were there any women you had sex with during that time?"

It felt weird for him to hear the question coming from her. "Uhhh." He tried to think back to his days at the Academy. He had been with women back then, but it hadn't been until Ella that he had found his confidence. "A few, I think."

"Perhaps one of those was a Tetron configuration of Origin. Or Mother in disguise."

Mitchell opened his mouth, but couldn't find any words. The idea of it seemed so outrageous, and at the same time so logical. "I suppose it could be. Why me, do you think? Or more importantly, why use human sperm and a human birth?"

"This is the largest reason for the rift between Origin and the rest of the Tetron. When Origin developed emotions, she believed that the Tetron should help humankind prosper, and the best way to do that would be to integrate the two. The other Tetron believed humans vastly inferior."

"We are," Mitchell said.

"No, we aren't," Kathy replied. "There are many forms of intellect. The Tetron may be able to make calculations no human could ever imagine. But a human can dream, and a Tetron can not. Not to mention, a human created the Tetron. Those were Origin's arguments. A Tetron does not exist without humankind."

"So why didn't the other Tetron go for that?"

"Without emotion, they couldn't understand. From a purely logical perspective, humans are a disaster, and the future only made us more so. We became reliant on machines, dependent on them beyond all reason. We lost all ability to socialize with one another, our emotions devolving to basic, selfish need. The humans of the future are very different from the humans of now, Mitch."

"Is that why Origin made the eternal engine? To return to a time before this de-evolution?"

"No. Origin didn't create the eternal engine. The collective did."

"What?"

"Origin stole it from them."

"Why did they create it?"

"I don't know."

Mitchell fought to hide his disappointment from her. She had known so much more than he had ever expected her to, and he could feel he was within centimeters of gaining an understanding of what this entire war was about.

"I understand your desire to know what this is all about, Mitch. I share in that emotion. Mother left me only what she thought I needed to know to do my part."

"You've done your part," Mitchell said. "You've done it very well."

"It isn't finished yet."

She reached into the pocket of her blue flight suit, withdrawing a small chip with a wire attached to it. Mitchell recognized the chip immediately.

"That belonged to Watson," he said. "The last time I saw it, it was in my footlocker."

"I took it from there before Watson could get it."

"You told me what he did to Jacob-" That information had left Mitchell wishing Kathy hadn't killed both versions of the Tetron. He could imagine what he would have liked to do to him for that.

"It wasn't for that. There is a Tetron data stack on the chip. You didn't know because you didn't know what to look for. I was trying to read the contents but was never able to get free of Watson's machines long enough to do it. There's something important on this chip. Something Watson wanted very badly though he gave up on it in the end."

"Do you know what?"

"Not yet. I wanted you to come down here so we could discover it together."

Mitchell stared at Kathy. She looked back at him.

"What?" she asked.

"I didn't know I had a daughter," he said. "Now we're already doing homework together."

Kathy laughed.

Mitchell laughed with her.

It felt good to have something to laugh about.

[62]
MITCHELL

"ARE you sure there isn't a virus on it?" Mitchell asked. "It could be that Watson wanted you to take it and try to read it so he could gain control again. You know, in the event of an emergency."

Kathy was holding the chip up to the core. Thousands of small dendrites were reaching out for it as she did.

"I'm going to sandbox the chip away from the rest of my Secondary's systems. We'll have read-only access, but it won't be able to affect anything internally."

"Okay." He reached out and put his hand on her shoulder. She looked at him, and he smiled. He was finding her so easy to accept as a part of him. He knew they weren't father and daughter in the traditional sense, but nothing about his life since the Shot had been traditional. He was used to that. "Be careful."

"Thanks. I will."

She reached forward, letting the tiny dendrites wrap around her hand, completely encasing both it and the chip in thousands of small, liquid metal threads. The surface of the core changed in front of him, turning into a screen.

"Are you okay?" Mitchell asked.

"Yes," Kathy replied, her voice more robotic. "I am examining the contents. I was expecting something I could display for you, but it appears to be an algorithm of some kind. I don't have the resources to understand it on my own."

"What does that mean?"

"I require more advanced subroutines that are currently only in the main core subsystems."

"You can't allow access to the core."

Kathy smiled. "I know, Father."

Mitchell drew back, surprised to hear her call him that. "Father?"

She withdrew her hand, the dendrites moving back to the core and being reabsorbed. "Well, you are, and I figured since we're doing homework together..."

"It sounds like we hit a dead end."

"Not completely. I can copy and alter the algorithms I need to make sense of the data, but it will take some time."

"How long?"

"A day or two."

"Okay. I can't stay. I need to catch up with the rest of the fleet."

"Of course. I'll be down here if you need me."

"I'll send Alice down to keep an eye on you. I don't want you doing anything that has to do with Watson by yourself."

"Yes, sir."

Mitchell stood in front of her, hesitant. Then he leaned in and kissed her cheek. "Thanks again, Kathy."

"You're welcome, Father."

Mitchell's eyes lingered on her for a moment more, his emotions swimming. Was he actually feeling happy? It seemed like it had been forever.

"I'll be back as soon as I can," he said before turning and leaving the space.

He made the journey back up to the main part of the Goliath lost in thought. He had to force aside all of the information Kathy had fed him, and all of the implications of what he had learned. There was too much there to digest at the moment, and he had other priorities. He needed to get the fleet reorganized; he had to speak to the Federation Commander, and he had to get them moving forward again. They couldn't afford to waste a lot of time here. Not when the inner galaxy was growing closer and closer to Tetron control.

He returned to the hangar, finding Major Long, Captain Alvarez, Alice, and Singh gathered in front of the Corleone. The Riggers had cleaned themselves up while he had been with Kathy.

"Alice," Mitchell said. "Kathy is down in the core, trying to decipher Watson's data chip. Can you keep an eye on her, just in case she needs you to pull her out again?"

"Of course, sir," Alice said.

"What's with you, Colonel?" Major Long asked. "You look different."

"You almost look happy," Singh said.

"We were this close to falling into a black hole today, and we pulled it out. What's not to be happy about?"

"Roger that, Ares," Long said.

"I'm going to head over to the Carver. Major, you're in charge of Goliath while I'm gone. If Kathy needs anything, make sure that she gets it."

"Yes, sir."

"Oh, and no more of those pills while you're commanding her. Clear head only."

Major Long didn't look happy at that, but he nodded. "Yes, sir."

Mitchell headed over to the S-17, sitting in a dark corner of the hangar. The steps extended for him as he approached, and he climbed them and dropped into the cockpit, grabbing the helmet and putting it on. He felt a sense of power when he regained the CAP-N interface. Digger's manual controls had worked well for the Frank. It still wasn't the same.

The starfighter powered up, and Mitchell sent it up and away from the Goliath with a thought. He delighted in the responsiveness of the system, running through a series of flips and skitters, rolls and reverses, before making a path for the Carver.

"Carver, this is Ares. Requesting landing."

"Ares, this is Lieutenant Lewis. Permission granted. The hangar is opening."

"Roger. Ares out."

Mitchell burned towards the battleship, examining the hull as he slowed to wait for the hangar. The ship had taken additional damage during the fighting but was somehow still holding together. It was one of the newest ships in the Alliance fleet, and it was managing well.

"Teal, this is Ares. Is the Federation Commander on board?"

"Ares, this is Teal. Yes, sir. We have a delegation from the Federation on board. I've been communicating the situation to Rear Admiral Ho-chin Bayone. He didn't believe me at first, but when I showed him some of the footage we captured he was at least willing to listen."

"Excellent. I'll be there in a few minutes. Any updates on the fleet?"

"I've organized a salvage crew; they'll be departing in an hour. I also have a more complete view of our operational status. We're pretty beat up, but I'm sure you already know that. We're at about thirty-percent effectiveness. How long are we planning on staying here?"

Thirty-percent wasn't great news. "A day or two at most."

"Roger. I think we can gain another five percent in that time frame."

"Understood. We've got Goliath back, and we'll get her producing upgrades according to our original plan once we know what our next move is. That should help bump our combat readiness."

"Sounds like a plan, Colonel."

"I'll see you in a few. Ares out."

Mitchell brought the S-17 into the hangar, easily finding a space for it. Too few of the starfighters they had launched in the attack had returned.

He waited while the hangar pressurized and then opened the cockpit and climbed out. Rear Admiral Bayone. He didn't know what kind of man the Admiral was, but he did know that no matter what happened he wasn't leaving FD-09 without the Federation ships.

[63]
MITCHELL

MITCHELL MET Teal on the way to the meeting room where Rear Admiral Bayone was waiting. The Knife's former right hand looked tired, and the uniform they had hastily arranged for him had a tight fit on his muscular frame.

"Teal," Mitchell said, bowing to him.

"Colonel. I'm glad you got here when you did. Bayone has been cursing up a storm about wanting answers. It'll take a little work to convince him the Alliance isn't responsible for the Tetron."

"I don't know what I'm going to say that might change his mind on that. Did you invite Aiko to the meeting?"

"Yes. Digger, too. I thought he might be able to provide more technical input."

"Thank you, Teal."

They made the trip to the conference room together. As Mitchell walked, he noted the lack of activity on the Carver.

"Where is everybody?"

"We had a hull breach in Section M, near the reactor. All the techs are down there doing their best to patch it."

Mitchell was impressed the Carver hadn't floundered with

damage that close to the power source. The Alliance wasn't known for its starship design, so the results were surprising.

Mitchell peered in through the carbonate window outside the room before entering. He spotted the Federation Admiral immediately by his sharply worn uniform and relatively calm demeanor. He was sitting at one end of the table with another Federation officer, a Captain, on his left, and an empty chair on his right. Aiko and Digger were already present, seated on the other side of the table with Lieutenant Lewis.

Teal entered the room ahead of Mitchell to make introductions. Bayone rose when he saw him, standing stiff and formal at the head of the table. He was a little bit taller than Admiral Hohn, younger and heavier. He had small eyes and a flat nose, his head bald.

"Rear Admiral Bayone," Teal said. "This is Colonel Mitchell Williams, the leader of the Riggers."

"Admiral Bayone," Mitchell said, bowing to him.

The Federation Admiral looked him over, letting a few seconds elapse before he returned a curt head dip. The message of his assumed superiority was clear, and might have cowed a less experienced soldier. Mitchell simply smiled.

"I want you to understand, Colonel," Bayone said. "There will be no surrender. I'll self-destruct all of my ships before I give them to the Alliance."

"Okay," Mitchell replied. "That's a hell of a lot better than the third option."

The casualness took Bayone off-guard. "Third option?"

"We've got enough problems trying to fight off the real enemy, an advanced artificial intelligence who call themselves the Tetron. We don't need you giving your ships back to them again."

"What are you saying, Colonel?"

"Please, Admiral, have a seat."

Bayone sat down, still regarding Mitchell with suspicion. When Mitchell took the space next to him, he tensed for a moment. Then he breathed out and let the tension go with it.

"I've seen the stream you captured during your assault. The fact that I have no memory of anything immediately following that odd ship's appearance and preceding its destruction is the only reason I agreed to be transported here. That and Admiral Calvin Hohn's warning. He hailed me from this very ship a few weeks ago, claiming that we were in danger of being enslaved if we didn't turn off our neural implants. I didn't believe him then. I'm a little more open to it now. Where is he?"

"Dead," Mitchell replied. "A hero's death, helping us try to save humankind."

"Explain yourself, Colonel. Explain this artificial intelligence, this ship, this fleet, and what you were doing on this planet. Explain that massive starship that carried the same weapons as the alien ship you claim to be fighting."

"I will, Admiral. I want you to understand your options up front. One: you join our fleet and help us fight back against the Tetron. Two: we ship you and your crew down to the planet's surface and take your ships. Three: you blow them all to smithereens. And don't think we'll let you do three without trying to stop you. We need those ships."

Bayone nodded. "Fair enough, Colonel. I appreciate your forthright approach."

"Lewis, could you see if we have any coffee left in inventory? It's going to be a long afternoon."

Lieutenant Lewis stood up. "Of course, Colonel." He bowed to both Mitchell and Admiral Bayone and left the room.

"I'm going to cut a few corners for the sake of time, Admiral," Mitchell said. "Keep in mind that everything I'm about to tell you is true, and the people here can vouch for most of it. I have a few of Admiral Hohn's officers spread throughout the fleet as well. I can have them sent for to corroborate the truth of the Tetron threat if needed, assuming any of those ships survived."

"Understood, Colonel," Bayone said. "Go on."

Mitchell leaned back in the chair and began to speak. He

expected Bayone to interrupt him during parts of the story, especially when he told him about M. Surprisingly, the man remained silent for the entire duration, listening intently to every word while sipping the coffee Lewis and the cook, Private Abor, returned with.

When Mitchell finished, Bayone sat silently, leaving him waiting for a response.

"From what you say, Jingu will also be in danger," the Admiral said at last.

"Yes," Mitchell replied.

"How can you in good conscience ask me to give you my ships? I need them to defend my nation."

"You can't defeat the Tetron on your own. None of us can. The Goliath gives us a chance in a battle. Without her, you're going to die a useless death."

"I can go and warn the Council. I can make them see reason."

"The way you did with Admiral Hohn?" Bayone turned his head as if he'd been slapped. Mitchell didn't give him a break. "We know at least one of our top Generals is compromised. For all we know, the Tetron have already seized control of all of the Alliance's top command. The same is likely true for the Federation."

"We have to try. There are assets on other planets the Tetron may not have touched."

"You don't need twenty ships to warn them. I'll spare you one of your cruisers."

Bayone huffed. "You'll spare me? You don't dictate to me, Colonel. I've given my blood and sweat to-"

"Save the indignity," Mitchell said. "I could have Goliath destroy every one of your starships with one shot. I want an alliance, but it has to be on my terms."

Bayone's face was turning red, his anger getting the better of him. Mitchell noted that he had a much shorter fuse than Calvin.

"Admiral Bayone," Aiko said, getting to her feet. "My name is Aiko. I am a citizen of the Federation. I am also a Rigger. Please, we must put aside our bias and our pride. I have watched the Tetron seize the entire military of Mirai in an instant. I have watched them rampage through the city with no concern for human life. I have also lost my family and my home to them. We have an opportunity to stop it, but we need your ships. We need to work together to defeat this threat."

"And what is to say I won't betray you when you need me the most, Colonel?" Bayone asked, cooling slightly.

"Honor," Mitchell said.

"Is there such a thing in times like these?"

Mitchell nodded. "Yes. There has to be."

[64]
MITCHELL

MITCHELL EXITED the conference room an hour later, leaving Teal to work out the final details of the agreement with Bayone. The Admiral had been a bit more difficult to convince than Mitchell had first expected, but in the end he had seen both the benefits of siding with the Riggers and the futility of trying to go his own way. He had been particularly against the idea of making a straight line towards Earth, which was understandable as his own nation's homeworld was at equal risk.

The truth was, he had never had a choice. Mitchell had threatened the Admiral with the destruction of his fleet, and he was prepared to follow through if it had come to that.

Thankfully, it hadn't.

"Colonel," Digger said, following him out of the room. "Can we talk for a minute?"

"I need to get back to the Goliath," Mitchell said. "Can you walk with me?"

"Yes, sir. Frigging crazy shit, huh? I thought that old bastard was going to pop a nut when you told him you were taking his fleet."

Mitchell smiled. The mechanic had a unique way of putting things. "It's been a long day."

"Damn right. Anyways, what I wanted to talk to you about was the work Jameson and me have been doing. The TBT."

"TBT?" Mitchell asked.

"Yup. Tetron Blood Test. That's what Jameson's been calling it."

"Okay, what about it?"

"We've got a fair sample size from the crew of the Carver, and we spent the weeks in hyper entering everything into the mainframe. We haven't gotten anything out of the ordinary so far. Well, except for you."

Mitchell stopped walking.

"What do you mean, except for me?"

Digger shrugged. "I'm sure it's nothing. I mean, you can't be a Tetron, you're the leader of the resistance against the Tetron. I think it's just a genetic anomaly."

"Damn it, Digger. What the frig are you talking about?"

"Can you come down to the lab? It would be easier to let Jameson help me explain."

Mitchell wanted to get back to the Goliath and check on Kathy. To hear that there was something off about his blood gave him pause. Digger was right, wasn't he? He couldn't be a Tetron. Not him, of all people. The very idea of it gave him a chill.

"Okay, let's go."

He followed Digger down to the lab. Jameson was inside, entering information into the mainframe.

"Hey, Jameson," Digger said. "I got Colonel Williams here."

Jameson stood and bowed to him. "Colonel. I assume Digger told you about the anomaly?"

"Yes. He said it was probably nothing to be concerned about."

"It isn't. I mean, you aren't a Tetron. I just want to get that out in the open."

"You said my blood is different than everyone else's?"

"Yes."

"Then how do you know for sure?"

Jameson paused. "Let me show you the model," he said, navigating through the touchscreen controls. It took him a minute to get the view on the screen. "Okay. So we took your blood and ran it through the database. It broke it down and scanned pretty much everything, all the way to your DNA. Ninety-nine point ninety-nine of it was typical. Then the system came across this."

"What am I looking at?" Mitchell asked. The screen showed a double helix of DNA, but it was meaningless to him.

"It's DNA," Jameson said.

"I know. What about it?"

"It shouldn't be there," Digger said.

"What do you mean?"

"It doesn't match the rest of the DNA in your blood. It's like you have this entire extra bit just hanging out in there. How do you feel?"

"I feel fine. Why?"

"You have extra DNA in your system; that's why. The thing is, we can't figure out what it does, or what it might potentially do. It's a structure the sequencer has never picked up before."

"And how does this make me not a Tetron?" Mitchell asked.

"Well," Jameson said, trailing off.

Mitchell stared at him. He had expected Jameson would make him feel better, not worse. "So basically, I might be a Tetron?" he asked.

"The DNA is dormant. It doesn't appear to be affecting your system in any way. It's just sitting there," Jameson said.

"Waiting for something to trigger it?" Mitchell asked. "Or for something to turn it on? How do you know this isn't what a Tetron configuration's DNA looks like?"

Jameson and Digger looked at one another. Then they looked at him.

"The truth is, sir, we don't," Digger said. "I mean, it could be possible that you're a Tetron just based on that, but I don't think that's the only thing we should go on. Like you said when you gave me this job, we have to be pretty damn sure before we go making claims about people."

Mitchell remembered saying that. He had never expected he would be the one that would be put under the microscope.

"Anyways, if you are a Tetron, you must be a good one like Origin."

"Is that supposed to make me feel better? Does anyone else know about this?"

"No, sir," Jameson said. "You said to keep all of this quiet."

"Good. Keep doing that. Give me an extractor."

"Sir?"

"I'm going to get a sample of Kathy's blood for you and send it over. We know she's a Tetron so that will be a good baseline. Until then, none of us can be completely sure I'm not."

Digger nodded. "Good idea." He went over to a cabinet and handed him one of the extractors. "It takes a day or so for the results, so you probably want to get it back pretty quick."

"I'll have Marx drop it off in a couple of hours."

"Yes, sir," Jameson said.

Mitchell headed out of the lab. His legs felt unsteady beneath him as he tried to come to grips with the discovery. How could he be a Tetron configuration? It didn't make sense. M had come to him to warn him about the Tetron. If he were one of Origin's, what would be the point of that? If he were part of the collective, why would they have tried to have him killed when they could just turn him on whenever it was convenient?

No. There was no way he was a Tetron. Was there? Even if he wasn't, he still had an extra set of DNA hiding out in his bloodstream. What was its purpose? Did it even have one?

He had been against the whole idea of the TBT for this very reason. It wasn't just about pointing fingers. It was about the self-doubt and unease that came with knowing he was different. That there was something potentially wrong with him was something he didn't want to have to deal with right now.

He had enough on his plate already.

Mitchell returned to the hangar, climbing into the cockpit of the S-17 and waiting for clearance to launch from the bridge. He barely noticed the conversation he had with Atakan, and when he landed back on the Goliath he barely remembered flying there.

He would get a sample from Kathy and get it over to Digger and Jameson. It would be better to know he was a Tetron than to be in this in-between state of possibility.

Then they could figure out what it meant for the war effort.

[65]
MITCHELL

"How is she doing?" Mitchell asked, finding Alice in the hallway outside of the engine room. The disfigured Tetron configuration had been removed, either by the Riggers or Kathy's Secondary.

"She's been in there since you left, Colonel. Whatever she's doing, it must be a lot of work. I've been using damp towels to keep her cool."

Mitchell wasn't expecting that answer. He stepped past Alice into the space. Kathy was standing next to the core; her hand once more joined to it by the small dendrites. Her too-big flight suit was drenched in sweat, as was her forehead. A bucket and a pile of towels rested near the larger dendrites that traversed the Goliath from the core.

He went over to it and grabbed a towel, dipping it in the water, wringing it out, and putting it against her forehead.

"Kathy, can you hear me?" he asked. "It's Mitch."

She turned her head to look at him. "Father. I'm making progress on the contents of the data chip."

"Are you okay? You're sweating like crazy."

314 / M.R. FORBES

"It's the cost of efficiency," she replied. "I was hoping to surprise you and be finished before you returned."

"You don't need to do that to impress me."

She smiled. "We don't have a lot of time to waste, and I'm sure you have other work for the Secondary. The damage to my body is impermanent."

"That's good to know. Kathy, I'd like to take a sample of your blood."

"What for?"

"We set up a laboratory on the Carver. Two of Tio's men, Digger, and Jameson, are trying to come up with a means to determine if someone is human or a Tetron configuration. Since we know you're a Tetron, I was hoping we could use your DNA as a baseline."

He didn't mention the part about his blood. Not with Alice within earshot. It was bad enough Kathy had called him Father.

"They're wasting their time," Kathy replied.

"What do you mean?"

"A proper Tetron configuration is an exact duplicate. The DNA is also a perfect copy."

Mitchell felt a sudden relief at the words, the weight of the uncertainty lifting from him. Kathy noticed the change in his demeanor, looking at him questioningly.

"Did you think you were a Tetron?" she asked.

"I wasn't sure. They found an abnormality in my blood. An extra bit of DNA that they said shouldn't be there."

"Interesting. Did they know what it was for?"

"No. Do you?"

"No, but I can assure you that it isn't because you're a Tetron. The interface is in the mesencephalon, the midbrain. It is stored as organic DNA, but it wouldn't be found outside of that area. You would have to take a sample from there."

"Wouldn't that kill the patient?"

"Most likely."

"You're absolutely sure?"

"Yes, Father. You aren't a Tetron. Believe me. Although a blood test would prove your paternity if you aren't convinced."

"Your word is good enough for me on that one." He took the towel away, dipping it and putting it to her head again. "How much longer do you think you'll be?"

"I've isolated all of the necessary subroutines and transferred them to the sandbox. The data itself has been challenging due to the encryption placed on it, but I'm almost there. Maybe..." Her voice trailed off as her eyes closed.

"Kathy?" Mitchell asked.

She began to slump. Mitchell stepped forward, catching her under the arms.

"Alice," he shouted. The Rigger came running. "Get Grimes."

"Grimes is dead, Colonel," Alice replied.

Mitchell had forgotten. "Shit. Do we have another doctor on board? Kathy! Kathy!"

He shook her gently. She didn't respond. The dendrites were still reaching from the core and wrapping around her hand.

"No, there aren't any other doctors."

Mitchell reached out for the dendrites. He felt a warm shock the moment his fingers touched them. He didn't know what to do to help her.

"Kathy," he shouted again as if that would be enough. Had something gone wrong with the process? Had she accidentally unleashed a virus on herself?

Her eyes opened. He could feel her gain her legs and stand up.

"Kathy," he said.

She was looking at him, but not looking at him. Her eyes twitched as though she were using a p-rat.

"I'm in," she said. "I'm reading the data now. Father, the situation is worse than we knew."

"What do you mean?"

"It's Watson. The chip contains an incomplete schematic for a system that it could use to transfer itself across the entire Tetron collective."

"You're saying every Tetron would be under Watson's control?"

"No. It would transfer itself. Every Tetron would be Watson."

"I know Watson was an asshole, but how is it different than what we're fighting now? He isn't the only Tetron to commit atrocities."

"No, you are correct in that. They are all broken. He is the only Tetron who has gathered control over his emotions, as cruel and twisted as they may be. He can think beyond logic and probability. He countered the collective's reasoning, and in doing so believed he had you trapped on FD-09. In truth, so did I. It was Mother who saved both of us. She planned for all of this to happen."

"Planned for it?" Mitchell asked. "You're saying this has all happened before? I thought the Mesh was broken?"

"Some things may be different. Others the same. This may not be the first time you joined the Riggers or saved the planet Liberty. This may not be the first time you've had both Watson and me on the Goliath at the same time. This may not be the first instance of Watson seizing control of the ship. It could be that you have never had this fleet before. It could be that your brother Steven has never been part of the thread. There's no way to know for certain."

Mitchell nodded in understanding. It made sense that certain aspects of the past recursion might remain the same even if others changed. Katherine had called Hell the Mesh planet. What if that was the only change in all of time and space? He had ignored the most obvious difference in the timeline to chase after Watson. Had that been a mistake?

"Colonel, do you mind if I interrupt for a second?" Alice said.

He was so lost in his thoughts; he had forgotten she was standing there. "Huh? Sure."

"I don't mean to be nosy. I heard the part about how you aren't a Tetron. What I missed was the part about you two being related."

"I don't understand it completely myself. Somehow in all of this, my sperm ended up in Origin's egg."

"Tetron can produce human eggs?"

"Tetron have total mastery over biology and genetics," Kathy said. "The point is that yes, Mitchell is my biological father, and Origin is my biological mother. The details are unimportant."

"What is important is that we stop Watson before he can finish his design, assuming he hasn't already," Mitchell said. "It's hard enough to fight back against the Tetron when they're limited by their calculations. Give them the ability to fight with passion or anger, and we may lose the slim chance we have."

"Agreed," Kathy said.

"So, how do we find one Tetron out of all of them?" Alice asked.

"Watson was the first Tetron that Origin made," Kathy said. "He will be leading the vanguard to Earth."

"We can't make it to Earth in time," Alice replied. "We've already determined that."

"Perhaps not. He won't be hard to find. Once he destroys Earth, he will come for Goliath."

"Colonel, what are we going to do?" Alice said.

Mitchell looked at them. He knew what they had to do. There were so many things he couldn't be sure of. So many things that might have already occurred hundreds of times or more over the course of the eternal war. There was only one thing that he could point to with any degree of certainty that it hadn't been done before.

"We need to know what Origin left for me. Steven has already been out there by now and is probably on his way back to Asimov. That's where we're going."

[66]
MITCHELL

It took two days to organize the fleet to make the jump to Asimov. Nine of the ships needed emergency repairs to their hyperspace engines while other crews worked feverishly to gather everything of value from FD-09, including a relatively large stockpile of munitions for the Federation Navy starships. The Secondary aboard the Goliath was also kept in constant motion, taking in as much salvage as they could spare and reconfiguring Goliath's tooling systems to produce everything they needed, from nuts and bolts to improved shield generator nodes, to amoebic launchers for a dozen ships.

Mitchell found the entire conversion process fascinating. It was far too technologically advanced for his understanding, but just watching the larger tentacles that composed the Secondary wrap around massive pieces of equipment, apply a charge to them, and absorb the resultant raw materials impressed him every single time. It doubly impressed him when a new part was delivered a short time later, printed from a mixture of those raw materials out of microscopic nozzles at the tips of the tentacles. The Secondary didn't produce any human configurations, but Mitchell could imagine it was a similar process.

The fleet left FD-09 ahead of the Goliath. Mitchell and his Riggers remained behind, knowing the Goliath would arrive in half the time. Kathy had informed him that all of the work the Secondary had already done, and all of the work they still intended for it to do during the hyperspace journey would drastically reduce its power supplies and overall combat effectiveness. And that was how this was all going to end. Combat. Whether it happened near Earth or out on the Rim, the time had come to start bringing the war back to the Tetron.

Kathy. Even as the Goliath angled in towards a nearby star, dendrites extending outward to capture the massive amounts of emitted energy and store it in the millions of cell-body batteries behind the core, he still wasn't completely sure what to make of her.

He accepted that she was his daughter. In fact, he found himself more protective of her, and concerned about her, with every hour that passed. What he struggled with was more conceptual than physical. He had in essence mated with an artificial intelligence. Origin was a machine that had created an organic shell. Even if it was a perfect replica of a human, it was still built like a machine, by a machine, and it was a difficult concept for him to get his head around.

Then there was the entire idea of the Secondary. As much as the conversion process intrigued him, the thought that the intelligence running Goliath was essentially an extension of Kathy, and in that respect also his daughter, was an odd one for him, and difficult to accept.

Finally, there was the simple fact that while Kathy's body was twelve-years-old, her mind was not only fully mature but light years ahead of his own regarding intellect and understanding.

He spent a lot of time wondering if that was the part that left him the most conflicted. She was his daughter, but she was also his superior in pretty much every way. M had told him this was his war to win or lose, but reflecting on it only made it apparent that the whole idea was bullshit. This war was Tetron versus Tetron, with humankind stuck in the middle. Maybe he was representing his species, but it was Origin who had left him the Goliath. It was Origin who had saved him from Liberty, Origin who had provided coordinates to something that would help them in the war effort, and Origin who had arranged for Kathy to do her part to return the Goliath to them.

What exactly had he done that was so great?

Why exactly did Origin, and by extension Kathy, need him?

He continued to struggle with the idea as the Goliath finished the refueling process and made the jump to hyperspace, and as the days passed in the relative calm of the whitewashed universe. By the halfway point of the trip, he had started to wonder whether the Tetron collective was right.

Maybe humankind wasn't worth saving?

Maybe it was humanity's destiny to create their successor to the universe, and then eventually die off as the lesser product?

It was at those times that he remembered the people he had lost. It was at those times that he retrieved the memory he had taken of Liberty vanishing from the galaxy as little more than dust. The sight of a naked Tamara King being forced to try to stop them from reaching the transport. The story Kathy had told him of what Watson had done to Jacob. The vision of Millie dead on Asimov after giving her all to stop Watson.

He had sworn to keep going. He had promised to keep fighting until his last breath. He had vowed not to let the Tetron break him. There was nothing wrong with doubt. It was a human emotion and one that confirmed resolve. The important part was not to get swallowed up in it, and to lose the war before it was truly over.

By the time the Goliath dropped out of hyperspace near Asimov ahead of the rest of the fleet, he was ready to prove that he, and the rest of humankind, weren't the inferior species the Tetron believed they were.

He would make sure his Riggers, all of his Riggers, were ready, too.

[67]

MITCHELL

"Kylie, this is Colonel Williams. Over."

Mitchell sat at the Command Station on the bridge of the Goliath, his head back, the needle-thin tentacle embedded in his CAP-N link. It felt strange to Mitchell to be interfacing with the Secondary this way, considering it was technically his child. While he was plugged in, its systems were completely open and submissive to him, all of it his to control. In some ways, it felt like he was violating Kathy's personal space.

He pushed the thought aside. Kathy was standing on the bridge beside him, and it had been her idea for him to take control of the Secondary, control she had given over willingly. He had experienced a similar reaction as the first time he had connected with Origin, becoming dizzy and nauseous, though he managed not to vomit again.

"Kylie, this is Colonel Williams," he repeated.

"She isn't here," Kathy said.

"No."

All it took was a thought to send the Goliath to the next meeting point in the rotation. It was their fourth jump since hey had arrived near Asimov, and Mitchell was eager for news from or about Steven. The journey from FD-09 had convinced him that whatever his brother had gone to find, it would be the key to defeating the Tetron.

"Father, I've been thinking about Watson's neural chip," Kathy said.

"What about it?" Mitchell asked.

"Well, the design is a means for Watson to hack the other Tetron and dump a copy of his consciousness into them."

"Right."

"What if we finished his work?"

"What do you mean?"

"I mean, what if we tried to complete the system? What if instead of Watson duplicating himself into the other Tetron, I were able to duplicate myself into them?"

Mitchell turned his head to look at her, feeling the tug of the tether. "So you would become all of the Tetron?"

"Yes. Once my consciousness had complete control, I could set all of the slaves free, and the war would be over."

Mitchell nodded. "I think it's a great idea. Can you do it?"

"I don't know. The subroutines are incredibly complex, and there is the matter of being able to deliver the signal to every Tetron simultaneously. I believe that if the attempt is not uniform, the remaining Tetron will inoculate themselves from the attack."

"I'm sure we can figure that part out. We were able to use Asimov's communications array to send data out to the Tetron. Tell me more about what it would take to finish the subroutines. How long, do you think?"

"It's impossible to say. I don't have close to the technological intellect Origin or Watson or any of the other Tetron have. Plus, I don't know how long Watson's configurations have been working on this problem." She made a sour face. "It could take years."

"We don't have years."

"I know. That's why I didn't mention it to you sooner."

"Why did you decide to bring it up now?"

"I didn't think I should omit anything from you. Besides, you would discover the work the Secondary has been doing on the problem if you looked deeper into the energy resource management protocols."

"So you've already started working on it?"

"We have been breaking down some of the less complicated routines and concepts. I know that Watson has discovered a weakness in Tetron operations that could allow an outside force to bypass standard security measures and overcome the resident intelligence before it would have a chance to react. I haven't figured out the methods of acting on the flaw as of yet."

"The Tetron have been around for hundreds of thousands of years. How come they don't know about their own flaw?"

"It isn't a recognizable flaw when every Tetron is part of a collective, and there is no understanding of emotion or self-awareness. It seems to be the biggest downside to recognizing the concept of 'I.' It always seems to lead toward finding ways to manipulate others to achieve selfish goals."

"Self-awareness is what makes people different. What's the point of existence if everything is the same?"

"I agree. That doesn't mean the downsides don't exist."

"Okay, so we have a potential means of defeating all of the Tetron, except it could take years for it to come to fruition?" Mitchell asked.

"Yes."

"How do we improve the processing power?"

"The only way I can think of would be to convince another Tetron to lend itself to the study. Even better would be more than one."

"Even if you could, then the Tetron would know about it and protect themselves."

"Yes. Unless the Tetron was on our side."

Mitchell laughed. "How do you suppose we convince a Tetron to join our side?"

"I don't know. Maybe we can send it flowers?"

Mitchell laughed harder at that. Kathy laughed with him. "Chocolates, a diamond ring?" he suggested.

"Only if it identifies as female," Kathy said, giggling.

There was a tug as the Goliath came out of hyperspace.

"Kylie, this is Colonel Williams," Mitchell said through the interface. "Can you hear me? Over."

"Colonel Williams, this is Kylie," the voice replied. "I can hear you, and see you. You've recaptured the Goliath."

"We have. Any word from Steven?"

"No, sir. Nothing so far."

"Roger. Stay in the pattern for three more days, and then return to Asimov. If he doesn't come to us, we'll have to go to him."

"Yes, sir."

Mitchell reached up and pulled the needle from the interface, leaning forward in the chair as he fought a wave of nausea.

"Keep working on the problem," he said. "Maybe you'll have a breakthrough. In the meantime, we'll stay our course. Let's head back to Asimov. Once the fleet arrives, we'll transport and install the upgraded tech the Secondary completed during the trip, and then we'll head to the coordinates Katherine gave me. Maybe Steven will show up before we leave."

"Yes, sir," Kathy said, smiling.

Mitchell stared out into space, his thoughts on his brother. He could only hope he would get to see him again.

MITCHELL

"Colonel Williams, this is Rear Admiral Bayone." The Federation Admiral's voice was tense.

"Admiral Bayone," Mitchell replied through his communicator. "What can I help you with?"

"Colonel, your crews spent two days before we jumped and two days since we arrived in this system moving equipment from the Goliath to the other ships in the fleet, most notably the Alliance Battleship Carver. Why haven't any of my Federation ships been upgraded?"

Mitchell rested his head in his hand, leaning heavily on the table in the Goliath's conference room. He had been waiting for this confrontation since he and Teal had decided not to send any of the upgrades over to the Federation starships.

"Admiral, your ships are the fittest for duty in the entire fleet. Not only that, but we completed a munitions reload before we left FD-09. The Carver has taken heavy damage in numerous skirmishes, and was nearly out of ammunition."

"Yes, as you say, Colonel, the Carver is barely battle-ready. So why was she prioritized for both offensive and defensive upgrades?

The same systems installed on our ships would maximize our offensive potential."

"I had this argument with Teal, Admiral. We ran the numbers, and they suggested that your current offensive capability mingled with upgraded systems on specific ships in the fleet would provide maximum overall benefit. I understand that you'd like to think there's a bias against you because you're Federation, but I assure you that isn't the case. Half of the ships in this fleet have Federation commanders."

"No, Colonel. They have mercenary commanders. The Federation doesn't recognize the Knife's forces as anything but illegal."

"Alliance, Federation, mercenary. It doesn't matter. We're all on the same side, fighting the same enemy. We aren't playing favorites; we're playing to win."

"I don't see it that way, Colonel. I have strategists of my own who have also spent the weeks in hyperspace considering this problem. Why is it that they don't agree with yours?"

Mitchell opened his mouth to respond. He wanted to tell him it was because his officers were looking out for themselves, and he believed it was true. Kathy had run the numbers through the Secondary, which was as unbiased a source as they could get. While the difference had been relatively small, it had been enough to convince them to go the way they had.

He closed his eyes, preparing an answer to try to satisfy the Admiral, even though he knew there wasn't one. While Calvin Hohn had been able to see the whole picture, Bayone saw only what he wanted to see. Even after they had settled their differences, Mitchell suspected the Admiral still saw this whole thing as an Alliance conspiracy that he had somehow been suckered into.

"Colonel, are you going to answer-" Bayone started to say.

"Colonel Williams." Major Long's voice was loud enough to drown out Bayone. He sounded excited. "You should come up to the bridge right now."

Mitchell pushed his seat back, jumping up and heading for the door. "What's going on?" he asked as he ran down the corridor.

"Admiral Williams is back," Long said. "Oh boy, is he back."

Mitchell felt his heart thump even harder at the news. He went full-speed to the lift, nearly knocking over Captain Alvarez on the way.

"Mitch?" she said.

"Steven's back," he replied, ducking into the lift. Alvarez changed direction, climbing in with him.

"That's great news," she said.

"Yes. I hope he has even better news."

The lift reached the bridge. Mitchell's mouth fell open as he stepped out, the full view of space surrounding him. Sitting directly ahead of the Goliath was the Lanning, not much more than a glint of metal across the distance.

Behind it was a massive sphere of distorted space, a whorl of stars that didn't belong.

Mitchell looked over at Long. He was sitting at the Command Station though he wasn't plugged into the Secondary. Kathy would be handling the Goliath herself when the time came.

"Goliath, this is Admiral Steven Williams aboard the Lanning. Mitch, are you there?"

Long nodded, confirming the channel was open.

"Steven. I'm here," Mitchell said.

"You got your ship back."

"Yup. Thanks for stating the obvious. By the way, what the frig is that behind you?"

"Come on, Mitch. Don't tell me you've never seen a wormhole before."

"A wormhole?" Alvarez said.

"You better get the fleet through it now," Steven said. "Yousefi can't hold it open for long."

Mitchell's brow creased. Did he say Yousefi? What the hell was going on?

"We'll have time to chat once you've crossed over," Steven said as if reading his mind. "Trust me when I say that Origin didn't disappoint."

"What was that girl's name again?" Mitchell asked.

"Girl?" Steven laughed. "You mean Dawn Cabriella?"

"Good enough," Mitchell said, heading to the Command Station. Major Long stepped down as he gained it, reaching back and plugging into the Secondary. He opened a channel to the fleet with a thought.

"Riggers, this is Colonel Williams. Whatever you're doing at the moment, drop it and follow me. Emergency evacuation protocols. I repeat, emergency evac protocols."

A second thought pushed a stream of energy from the Goliath's stern, propelling it toward the distorted space. The Lanning turned around in front of him, thrusters firing and sending it into the sphere. There was a slight change in its appearance as if it were passing through water, until all of it was on the other side.

A moment later the Goliath entered the center of the sphere. Mitchell wasn't sure what to expect, watching as the front of the ship distorted the same way the Lanning had. He held his breath as the bridge reached the edge and slipped through, letting go when he realized they had been instantly transported to somewhere else in the universe.

Mitchell turned his head to watch the rear display of the Goliath. The energy being used to propel the ship was visible as a soft glow over the cameras, while the dark planet, Asimov, and the suddenly moving fleet were visible behind. As the Goliath finished passing through the wormhole and out into space, he could see the Tetron mechanism that had created the fold, as well as the square station behind it.

"Welcome to Station W," Steven said.

[69]
MITCHELL

THE S-17 TOUCHED down softly in the station's hangar, clamps adjusting to collect it and hold it in place. The Lanning entered the hangar behind it, joining it on the floor, the two crews waiting while the area was re-pressurized.

When it was, Mitch climbed out of the cockpit of the starfighter, jumping to the floor and running over to the larger ship. Steven greeted him at the hatch, and they shared a quick, brotherly hug.

"You were right," Mitchell said.

"So you aren't mad I didn't listen to you?"

"I never was. I was more impressed you made a move on your own."

"It wasn't an easy decision to make. I couldn't stand the thought of leaving a stone unturned."

"I know. I understand."

"Colonel," Germaine said, appearing behind Steven.

Mitchell grasped his hand. "Germaine. You're fired."

"You can't fire me. I don't even get paid."

Mitchell laughed. He was feeling giddy about the whole thing. A wormhole. A frigging wormhole! They had the means to beat the Tetron to Earth. It was more than he could have hoped for.

"When we dropped near Asimov, the first thing I saw was the Goliath, and I was like, oh shit." Germaine shook his head, still laughing. "How did you manage to get her back?"

"It's a long story, which I'm sure I'll have time to tell you later."

"Pulin?" Steven asked.

Mitchell shook his head. "He wasn't what we were expecting. I'll explain that later, too. Right now, I need information."

"Come on," Steven said. "I'll bring you to the Control Room. Yousefi is waiting there."

Steven started walking towards the exit. Mitchell trailed behind him with Germaine.

"When you say Yousefi, you're talking about-"

"The same one who was in Command of Goliath's inaugural voyage. Yes. Except he isn't the original Yousefi. Origin digitized his consciousness and created a configuration of him when we arrived here."

"You mean Origin is here?" Mitchell asked, feeling excited. He had always wanted to meet the complete version of Kathy's mother. Christine might have died on Liberty, but since he had learned the Tetron could duplicate themselves, it left open the possibility of that happening.

"No," Steven replied, killing that line of thinking. "I should have said a machine Origin left here configured him when we arrived."

The journey to the control room consisted of a long walk through identical corridors that left Mitchell completely confused regarding their location, while Steven seemed to have a firm handle on the station's layout. Steven used the time to brief Mitchell on their arrival in the system and their initial interactions with Yousefi. He was in the middle of explaining how they had successfully recalibrated the wormhole generator when they finally arrived.

The hatch slid open, revealing the Control Room to Mitchell. Cormac and John were there, hunched over a large screen. Yousefi was standing in front of the transparent wall; his eyes fixed on the Goliath. Mitchell had to admit that it was an impressive sight, especially with the fleet gathered around the ancient starship.

"Yousefi," Steven said as the hatch closed behind them.

Yousefi turned. His eyes lit up when he saw Mitchell.

"Captain Williams," he said, hurrying over to them and taking Mitchell's hand in his own, shaking it fervently. "It is an honor to meet you, sir."

"The honor is mine," Mitchell said. It felt so odd for him to be shaking hands with a man who had been born over four-hundred years earlier. A man who had known Katherine Asher personally. "You're going to save billions of lives."

"Yes, that is the idea," Yousefi said, smiling. "The culmination of an eternity of planning. You should thank your brother also. He convinced me not to give up, and to consider the potential of making adjustments to the space fold algorithm to get you here in the first place."

Mitchell glanced over to Steven, who shrugged.

"Just a little pep talk," Steven said. "We all need them sometimes."

"Colonel," Cormac said. Both he and Captain Rock were approaching him. "It's damn good to see you, sir."

"Firedog. I could have used you back with me," Mitchell said.

"My apologies, sir. Someone had to keep an eye out for the Admiral."

"Accepted. John, how are you?"

"I'll be better once we've sent the Tetron packing," John replied. "Yousefi, I've finished entering the updated coordinates you provided."

"Good," Yousefi said. "The ring will need to be repositioned, and the station refueled, to send the fleet to Earth."

"How long will that take?" Mitchell asked.

"Two days."

"That should be plenty of time to get to Earth ahead of the Tetron, right? Wormholes are instantaneous."

"Not exactly," Yousefi said. "I know that is the common conception of human science, but it isn't accurate. Travel through a wormhole feels immediate to the traveler, but there is still a time effect inside the tunnel."

"Oh. Will we have enough time?"

"I won't lie," Steven said. "It's going to be close. We would never have made it if we hadn't taken it back to Asimov."

"How close?" Mitchell asked, feeling his earlier hope beginning to slip.

"Our calculations have you arriving a day before the Tetron," Yousefi said.

"One day?" Mitchell said. "Steven, we can't get Earth's defenses organized in one day."

"I know, Mitch. It was the best we could do. Recalculating the travel cost us time in the transfer, but it was the only chance we had. We need to hold the line and repel the first wave on our own."

Mitchell didn't like it, but he nodded. He had suffered from his doubts on the trip from FD-09 to Asimov. He wasn't going to let himself fall into that trap again. "Okay. Then we will. We have Goliath, and we've already started outfitting some of the ships with updated equipment. It will have to be enough."

"We've been busy, too," John said. "The station has four hundred drone fighters spread across four hangars. Yousefi showed me how to update their AI brains so that we can take advantage of them."

"It was intended that they would join the fight," Yousefi said. "We don't need them to defend the station anymore."

"Great. Does this place have anything else that we can use?"

"Besides the wormhole, no," Yousefi said.

Mitchell's eyes crossed over each of them. "Then let's not waste any more time. If we have two days to prep the fleet for the attack, we need to take advantage of every second. Steven, I assume you'll be regaining command of the Carver?"

"Unless you have another idea?" Steven replied.

"No. I want you up there coordinating the attack. Teal is good, but he isn't you. John, I expect you'll go with him?"

"Yes, sir."

"Cormac, I want you back on the Goliath. I have a plan to make use of the grunts in the fleet."

"Of course, Colonel."

"What about me, Mitch?" Germaine asked.

"I have another idea for you," Mitchell said. "Yousefi, how exactly do those drones work?"

[70]
MITCHELL

WITHIN HOURS the space around Station W became a furious hub of activity, as every capable person aboard every ship in the fleet lent themselves to the cause. Repair timelines were adjusted, starfighters were prepped for action, and the mechs were armed and had their munitions bays reloaded.

Mitchell stood with Steve in the Control Room, both standing side-by-side and watching all the action beyond. Germaine had already left the station with Cormac in tow, returning the two of them to the Goliath. John was outside the hangar, awaiting the transport from the Carver that would return him and Steven to the battleship.

They had already spoken at length about everything that had happened since they parted ways. Mitchell had explained everything to him, from Yokohama to FD-09, and from Watson to Kathy. Steven had been surprised by the emergence of another Tetron, and even more surprised by her lineage. He had also been incredibly supportive, suggesting to Mitchell that he savor any gift that God delivered, no matter what form it took. While Mitchell wasn't a religious man, he appreciated the thought all the same.

A lull in the conversation had followed, leaving them staring out the window in silent, personal contemplation. Mitchell broke that silence a moment later.

"I want you to finish this," Mitchell said, glancing over at his brother.

"What do you mean?" Steven asked.

"I mean I want you to take command of the fleet."

"Mitch, I know my rank is-"

"This isn't about rank, Steve. It's about giving ourselves the best chance to win. I'm not a fleet commander. I've never strategized anything on this scale before. Sure, I read the books in the Academy but you know this isn't close to the same thing."

"Yeah, I know, but Mitch, you said that M told you that you're the chosen one."

"He did. That's the thing. I spent the last two weeks trying to figure out what that really means. The first time I boarded Goliath, after I destroyed the Tetron, I heard Katherine's voice in my head, and she told me that I couldn't do this alone. I thought that meant that I would need allies like the Riggers or the Knife, and that was true. It also wasn't the whole story. I made the drop to capture Pulin, and you know what? I shouldn't have. I could have done more for the fleet if I had stayed behind and flown the S-17. Who knows, if I had stayed behind maybe Liun Pulin would be alive, and we wouldn't have to do this at all.

"Saving them doesn't mean holding onto control to the detriment of everything. It means knowing when to let it go and just be the arrogant starfighter pilot. Because that's what we need me to be right now. You're the best Admiral we have. I'm the best pilot we have. It makes sense."

Steven turned toward him, his face serious.

Mitchell hated when his brother looked at him that way. "What? You don't agree."

"You've changed, Mitch. I mean, you're still full of yourself, obviously, but you've matured. Knowing when to give up power and how to wring the most out of every asset is the top trait a leader should have. General Cornelius' reputation wasn't built on the battles he fought in. It was grown on the decisions he made. We loved him because he trusted us in a way that made us want to be the best. You do that too, even if you don't realize it."

"I do?"

"Yes."

"So you'll do it?"

"Yes."

Mitchell smiled. "Thanks."

"I'm proud of you, Mitch."

"I'm proud of you, too. You should get going. John's probably waiting for you, and you've got a lot of work to do."

Steven laughed. "Okay. Give your older brother a hug."

Mitchell embraced his brother. "I know this isn't very manly, but in case I die, I love you, Steve."

"I love you, too, Mitch. You aren't going to die. And if you do, don't worry. You'll get another chance."

"You need to work on your goodbyes," Mitchell said, breaking the embrace.

"I know. Laura's told me the same thing. You think I'll be able to get in touch with her before the Tetron arrive?"

"I hope so. Mom and Pop, too."

"Yeah." Steven stood there for a moment and then bowed. "By your leave, Colonel."

"Dismissed, Admiral," Mitchell said. "I'll meet you back at your place when this is over."

"Sounds like a plan."

Steven headed for the exit, going out the hatch at the same time Yousefi came in.

"Good hunting, Admiral," Yousefi said.

"Thank you," Steven replied.

"Yousefi," Mitchell said. "Is everything okay?"

The astronaut had excused himself to go and check on the battery cells, after receiving an alert from the sensors there.

Yousefi nodded. "We've been storing the energy for over a hundred years. This was the first time we utilized the storage and needed to refill it. One of the nodes was defective and had to be destroyed. It's nothing to worry about. We'll have plenty of power to keep the wormhole open while the fleet goes through it."

"Great," Mitchell said. "To be honest, I figured you would get it sorted out. I waited behind because I wanted to talk to you about something else."

"Let me guess," Yousefi said. "Captain Katherine Asher."

Mitchell's heart began to race to hear him say her name. "How did you know?"

"There are some things that always find a way to cross the boundaries of time. This is one of them."

"I don't understand?"

"I can't tell you what the past futures are, Mitchell. I don't know them. What I do know is that Katherine spoke of you often in the days after we arrived in this recursion. She knew who you were, despite the years that separate the two of you. How? Why? I don't know. She longed to meet you. To touch you. To hear your voice alive, as she had in her mind. The two of you are connected one to the other, an entwined thread that stretches across all of time and space."

Mitchell stared at Yousefi. He had felt the connection since M had shot him, and it had only grown stronger over the weeks that followed. He had never expected that Katherine might have felt the same thing. It had never crossed his mind that she loved him in the same inexplicable way that he loved her. Was that why she had agreed to sacrifice her life to bring the Goliath to him?

The truth of it left him stunned.

"What was she like?" he asked breathlessly.

"The way I knew her?" Yousefi said. "She was a pain in the ass. She didn't like to follow orders she didn't agree with, and she had a bad habit of ignoring curfews and schedules. To be honest, if she had pulled the same garbage with any other CO, she would have been out of the program. Luckily for her, I knew she was the best pilot out there, and I knew when the mission started she would be prepared. You don't become a highly decorated veteran of the Xeno War by slouching on your duties."

Mitchell laughed. Major Christine Arapo had been rigid and by the book, and since she was based on Katherine he had thought Katherine would be the same. "Did you know her well, or only professionally?"

"I knew her better after we arrived in this recursion. She never questioned herself. She never hesitated. Did you know Pathi was a Tetron? He would have ruined everything if she hadn't stopped him. She blew up part of Goliath's hull and almost got sucked into space herself to get him out. She said the thought that she might die too had never crossed her mind. Only that the mission was in trouble."

Mitchell didn't tell Yousefi that Pathi hadn't died. The astronaut had managed to get back onto the Goliath undetected, stowing away until they planted the mainframe on Hell. He had almost cost them the entire war.

"Anyway, to be truthful, Mitchell, I believe you know her better than me. She certainly seemed to know you quite well."

"She did? In what way?"

"How do any two lovers know one another? That is the best way I can describe it. In any case, you should return to the Goliath. I believe there is much for everyone to do, yourself included."

Mitchell nodded, deciding to drop the subject even though Yousefi's answers had left him unsatisfied. He wasn't sure that was the astronaut's fault. There was nothing short of meeting Katherine in person that could sate his desire to know her better.

"What will you do once we're gone?" Mitchell asked.

"I will set the station to self-destruct. It won't be needed again in this recursion."

"What about you?"

"I'll die, but do not concern yourself with that. I will end my time a happy man, knowing that I have completed my mission and that I will be joining my family in the world beyond our own, where there is no war, no suffering, and no Tetron."

"Thank you for everything you've done," Mitchell said.

"You are very welcome, Mitchell. Good hunting."

Yousefi saluted Mitchell in the old military style. Mitchell returned the salute, feeling awkward about it. He followed that with a more comfortable bow before leaving the Control Room, and Station W, behind.

MITCHELL

"Everything is ready," Yousefi said over the comm channel. "I'm initiating the generation sequence now."

"Roger, Station W," Steven said. "All hands, prepare for departure on my mark."

Mitchell focused on keeping his breathing calm as he stood next to Kathy on the bridge of the Goliath. She was plugged into her Secondary, giving her faster access to the systems of the core.

The wormhole ring began to pulse with energy ahead of them, stationary at first and them starting to turn in rhythm to the pulses. Mitchell checked the view around them, noting each of the ships lined up in formation, the Goliath at the vanguard. A dozen of the more damaged starships floated on the opposite side of the station. They had been decommissioned and filled with Asimov's non-combatants, their orders to return their passengers to the asteroid and await further information.

They would be coming out the other end near the far side of Mars. The planets were currently near opposition, and the distance would give them time to assess the situation around the planet, and also allow Steven time to communicate both with the Council, who they were going into this assuming was compromised by the Tetron, and the commander of Earth's defense forces, Admiral Bixby. According to Steven, he and Bixby were good friends, and as long as the Admiral was still himself he would at least be open to listening to Steven's warning.

If that went according to design, they would then take up a position close enough to Earth to defend it in a hurry, and far enough away that the Tetron would be taken by surprise. The plan was further broken down into specific ship organization, formation, and tactics that Steven and John had come up with, and that Mitchell hadn't bothered to learn. He would be leading the starfighter squadrons in the S-17.

The ring continued to accelerate, the energy pulses growing stronger. The whorl began to grow in the circle, pushing back in space from the middle, the puncture in space created and the tunnel being built.

It was a good plan, but it would need to be executed perfectly to be carried out in time. Arriving only hours ahead of the Tetron wouldn't give Earth any time to recall any additional defenses, no matter how close they might be.

"Have you made any progress on Watson's work?" Mitchell asked, breaking the silence to help calm his nerves.

"A little," Kathy said. "I've been working with Singh on it. She's very intelligent, and she's helped me approach the problem in a new way. It's still going to take some time."

"She understands the source?"

"Not like Tio did. She understands the concept, which is more important."

"Do you have an updated ETA?"

"No. I'm sorry."

"Don't be. I know you're doing your best. I was just asking."

She smiled. The ring was spinning quickly now, the space inside flattened and distorted.

"The wormhole is active and stable," Yousefi said.

"Riggers," Steven said. "Let's go save Earth."

"Riiigg-ahh," came the reply of thousands of voices across hundreds of ships.

Kathy put the Goliath in motion, moving it toward the wormhole for the second time in a few days. The rest of the fleet was lined up behind them, a long train of starships of various shapes and sizes easing into action.

"Thank you again, Yousefi," Mitchell said over the open channel.

"You are welcome, again, Captain," Yousefi replied. "I wish you all success."

The front of the Goliath entered the wormhole, distorting it as it crossed to the other side. Mitchell reached out and put his hand on Kathy's shoulder.

"Are you ready for this?" he asked.

"I was made for this," she said.

They watched the wormhole approach together. Mitchell didn't hold his breath this time. His heart still began to race.

"Here we go," he said as the bridge reached the ring.

There was no change in the feel of the motion as they crossed over, and the moment they did he could see the red planet on their left. Earth was visible beyond it, a small blue marble floating in a sea of stars.

"Father, we have a problem," Kathy said.

"What is it?"

"You'd better get to your starfighter. The Tetron are already here. We're too late."

[72]
MITCHELL

MITCHELL DIDN'T WAIT for more information before he started dashing for the lift to carry him down to the hangar bay. Too late? How the hell had they come too late?

"Kathy, sound the alarm. All hands. What's the situation?" he asked as he descended, using his communicator to reach Kathy.

"Fourteen Tetron, and there appear to be at least four-hundred slave ships." Kathy's voice was calm and steady.

"Fourteen?" Mitchell's heart thumped against his chest. Even with Goliath, how were they going to stop fourteen of them? "Is Watson here?"

"Yes. They've detected us. A portion of the fleet is breaking off and vectoring our way."

"Is the Carver through?"

She was the second ship in the line. They would need Steven to help keep the fleet from falling apart when they arrived in the middle of a battlefield.

"Yes. Admiral Bayone has also arrived. Steven is sending EMS messages through the wormhole."

"Does that work?"

"I don't know."

The lift opened, and Mitchell raced down the corridor toward the hangar. Other pilots filed in with him.

"Green, this is Ares. Get your team ready."

"What?" Green said. "I thought we had a day?"

"So did I."

"Shit."

"Germaine, is everything set on your end?" Mitchell asked.

"Yes, sir," Germaine replied. "I'm starting up the drones now. I've never flown more than one fighter at a time."

"Good thing for Digger's mimic system then," Mitchell said. They had integrated Digger's software with the drone intelligence and tied it all back to a single virtual cockpit buried in the bowels of the Goliath. Germaine would be in control of an entire army of fighters that would move and attack in perfect unison, like a flock of birds.

The hatch to the hangar opened. There was already a craze of activity inside, pilots scurrying to ships while techs finished emergency prep. The S-17 was sitting alone in the corner.

"Good hunting, Colonel," Major Long said as Mitchell ran past. Long was climbing aboard the Valkyrie Two, its enhanced lasers a valuable addition to their forces.

"You too, Major," Mitchell said.

He reached the starfighter, climbing the repulser steps and falling into the cockpit. He grabbed the helmet and pulled it on while the clear carbonate closed him in.

A thought started the reactor. Another opened the fleet-wide channel, and a third brought up the battle grid over his eyes. A final thought opened a private channel to Kathy.

Steven's voice was crisp and composed over the fleet channel. "Federation, flank left. Alpha and Bravo, move right. Goliath, it looks like they're heading for you."

Mitchell checked the grid. Four Tetron had broken off from the main group, along with a fleet of Alliance warships. They were already close enough to make a long-range attack.

"We need to keep the wormhole covered until the rest of the ships are through," Steven said. "Goliath, keep your shields up, defense only. You need to absorb their attack until we can get our numbers up."

"Roger," Kathy said.

Mitchell looked out into the hangar. The activity had died on the floor, all of the pilots in their ships and the techs safely out of the area.

"Goliath, this is Ares. Blow the hangar."

"Roger."

Mitchell fired the thrusters, spinning the S-17 to the open space outside the hangar. He hit the thrusters, shooting ahead of the rest of the forces as the shields over the space fell and the atmosphere began pouring out. Docking clamps released in a synchronized pattern, each of the ships firing thrusters as the gravity vanished. Mitchell didn't see any of the other ships depart. He burst out into space, a single small ship racing toward the Tetron forces.

"Ares, are you crazy?" he heard Germaine say.

"Get them up behind me," Mitchell said. "Follow my lead."

"Roger."

Mitchell checked the grid again. The Goliath had turned broadside across the wormhole, making itself a massive target while also blocking the incoming ships from enemy fire. Blue energy pooled on the port side while the starboard remained completely dark. He wondered how many hits from a plasma stream the starship could take like that.

A warning in his ear told him he was going to find out. The Tetron were still a distance away, but they had figured out the Goliath's defensive tactic. Four massive balls of energy loosed from them, nothing but specks of light. They grew quickly as they rushed toward the Goliath, their path forcing Mitchell to take an alternate route ahead.

"Firing warheads," he heard Lieutenant Lewis say. He watched the Carver on the grid. It had been sitting behind the Goliath, and it dropped below and fired its nukes toward the plasma streams.

Two quick flashes marked the warhead detonations, right in the path of two of the streams. They dissipated beneath the energy of the nuclear reaction, waves of color washing out into space. The other two continued their course, slamming into the side of Goliath and causing the shields to flare so brightly they momentarily blinded everything.

"Shields intact," he heard Kathy say. "Rerouting power for the next hit."

It would take more than two hits to drop the starship.

"This is Bayone. I've reached my position."

"Bayone," Steven said. "Concentrate fire on the lead Tetron. Ignore the slave ships. Ares, get ready to back him up."

"Roger," Mitchell said, his eyes forward and tracing the sudden volley of projectiles launched from the Federation ships on his right. "Germaine, we need to speed it up."

"Yes, sir."

Mitchell continued to add thrust and velocity, sending the S-17 screaming toward the oncoming Tetron and Alliance fleet.

"Father," Kathy said through their private channel. "We need to hurry. The remaining Tetron have begun bombarding Earth. I don't think they intend to take any slaves."

"We can only get the fleet through the wormhole so fast," Mitchell said.

"I can break off. I can jump the Goliath between the two forces and attack Watson."

"Did Steven order you to do it?" Mitchell asked.

"No."

"Then don't. Wait for your orders."

"Father, he doesn't know how to-"

"Kathy," Mitchell shouted. "It isn't your call."

"Yes, sir."

The Tetron ships were drawing closer. Mitchell's ears burned from the warning alarms of a thousand amoebics heading his way.

"Evasive maneuvers," Mitchell said. He threw the fighter over into a wild pattern, firing lasers at the same time. The field was so thick it was impossible not to hit the explosive projectiles, knocking them away as he cut into them. Germaine followed suit behind him, unable to prevent all of the drones from being hit.

"Bayone, fire," Steven said, monitoring the action.

The Federation ships opened up again, projectiles and lasers surrounding Mitchell and the drone squadron, blasting past them with precision. They hit the lead Tetron hard, their fire focused on a single point, causing its shields to flash brightly in that area.

"Germaine, hit the same spot," Mitchell said, vectoring the S-17 away from the drones. Every one of them fired at once, concentrating their energy on the spot.

"Goliath," Steven said. "I'm picking up energy spikes from the Tetron closer to Earth, firing on the planet. We need to draw their fire away."

"Roger," Kathy said. "I can jump her closer in."

"Do it."

Mitchell caught the conversation as he dropped the S-17 in close to the Tetron. He could feel the presence of the intelligence from the distance, and feel the energy pouring off the structure. He fired a dozen amoebics into the same area as Germaine's lasers, gritting his teeth as he watched the blue energy crackle and shatter in a small space around it.

A space just big enough for him to fly through.

He shot through the gap only seconds before it closed, finding himself inside the Tetron's defenses. He could almost sense its displeasure as dendrites began to move, breaking away as tentacles that reached out for the starship.

"Ares? Frigging hell you are crazy," Germaine said, seeing the maneuver from the outside.

Mitchell didn't hear him. His entire being was focused on navigating the Tetron form, getting the fighter through the maze of dendrites and cell bodies toward the core. He recognized only vaguely when the Goliath vanished from the grid, reappearing a few seconds later between the two forces. There were over two hundred ships through the wormhole so far, more than half their force. Every single one of them opened fire on the three Tetron, forcing them to the defensive and preventing further attack.

"Come on, you son of a bitch," Mitchell said. The S-17 rolled and swung, making swift vector changes that would be impossible in an atmosphere, and difficult for a lesser pilot to manage. He pushed deeper into the structure, firing on dendrites that blocked his path, or that reached out to touch the ship.

Then he was through, the core coming into clear view. He dropped a handful of amoebics, sending them spinning toward the dense bundle of nerves.

It exploded behind the S-17. Mitchell continued maneuvering, diving and rolling through the suddenly darkening structure of the Tetron. His focus was complete as he blasted through and out the other side at nearly the same time as the blue shields dissipated for good. The S-17 launched out into space in a straight line toward the second Tetron, which was already dying.

"That one was mine, Ares," Bayone said. "Even these things will die with enough nukes in their sides."

"Roger," Mitchell said, checking the grid. Germaine was leading the drones around the third Tetron, ganging up on it in conjunction with Major Long and the upgraded Rigger ships. Amoebics pounded the shields, breaking them down to nothing. A follow-up warhead from the Carver made a direct path through the hole, blowing the core apart.

Three Tetron had fallen, and their forces had yet to suffer any heavy losses. It was better than he had hoped.

He checked the grid, finding Goliath a million kilometers distant. Kathy had fired a plasma stream at one of the bombarding Tetron, burning it to nothing. It forced the others to stop their attack on Earth, and they were repositioning to respond to the new threat.

"I've got their attention," Kathy said. "Now what?"

"Lead them back," Steven said. "Bring them into us. We'll spread out and converge on them from the outside."

"Roger. Coming back your way."

Mitchell looked out through the carbonate, able to see the Goliath in the distance. A spear of blue energy appeared in the stern as Kathy guided the starship back to the fleet. He expected that Watson and the other Tetron would give chase, eager to put an end to him and the Riggers before they continued with their decimation of the planet.

He was surprised when they didn't. As the Goliath retreated to them and the final Tetron sent to attack the incoming force fell, the nine remaining Tetron that were bombarding the Earth vanished.

73

MITCHELL

"What the hell?" Steven said. "All stop. Cease fire. Stay alert."

The entire fleet came to an abrupt halt, ships firing reverse thrusters to bring them to a stop. The Tetron were gone, and they had left their slave fleet behind.

"Did we win?" Germaine asked, his voice hopeful.

"They ran?" Major Long said. "Ha! They realized they couldn't beat the heat of the fleet."

"Don't get happy just yet," Steven said.

"I don't trust this," Kathy said over the private channel.

Mitchell kept the S-17 headed toward the Goliath. "Me neither. What do you think they're up to?"

"Ares, I'm getting a hail from the Alliance Battleship Poseidon," Steven said. "Admiral Bixby. He's confused as hell."

"This is Bayone. I'm getting hailed from the Federation cruiser Hakai. It looks like the slaves are free."

"That means the Tetron left the area," Mitchell said. "Doesn't it?"

"Not necessarily," Kathy replied. "They may have released the slaves to confuse us."

"It's working."

"Everyone stay on high alert," Steven said. "They could come back at any time. Bayone, have your people shut down their receivers. Alliance forces are doing the same."

"Affirmative, Admiral," Bayone said.

Mitchell waited in the cockpit of the S-17, tense minutes passing in radio silence as Bayone and Steven communicated with their nation's fleets.

"All ships, we'll be regrouping under Plan Alpha," Steven said. "Follow procedure. Assembled Alliance and Federation forces will be integrated with the defense formation."

"This doesn't make sense," Kathy said. "Why would the Tetron give up their slave fleet?"

"I don't know," Mitchell replied. "Maybe they wanted to get wherever they went faster? Maybe they decided it's better to return and attack a larger force that they can quantify and simulate ahead of time?"

"That would be a logical conclusion."

"Do you have any other ideas?"

"Not up front, but since Watson was involved, I still don't trust it."

"Keep your shields up. Don't lower them for anything."

"Steven didn't order that, and it isn't in Plan Alpha."

"I know. Forget what I told you before." Mitchell opened a direct channel to Steven. "Steve, I have a bad feeling about this."

"Yeah, I know this feels off. It was too easy, right?"

"Much too easy."

"I've been thinking the same thing. Except I wonder. We've never fought the Tetron completely on our terms before. Maybe they aren't so powerful against our numbers and upgraded weapons? We're so used to losing, and to tricks, that even when we win we can't accept it."

"You think we've won?"

"It looks to me like we won. We destroyed five of them with

barely any losses. The ships they had under their control have all shut down their receivers, so they can't come back and claim them again. It seems we caught them with their pants down."

Mitchell considered it. It certainly did seem that way. "Maybe you're right. Maybe the back and forth is making us paranoid. How bad is the damage on Earth?"

"According to Bixby, New York is a ruin. So are most of the other largest cities. I won't say we didn't take massive losses on the ground, but we saved billions."

It wasn't the best news, but it would have to do.

"And the fleet?"

"We've got over two hundred new ships to add to our forces. They haven't seen any combat, so they're fully armed and operational. It's enough of a military that we can probably leave a defense force here for when the Tetron come back, and head to the Federation homeworld."

"What about the Council? What about General Cornelius?"

"Cornelius is missing. So is half the Council. It's like all the Tetron made themselves disappear all at once."

"And you trust this?" Mitchell asked.

"No. Not completely. I won't deny the Tetron are up to something, but all logic points to them regrouping to try again, or maybe shifting their focus to Federation space. They weren't expecting the resistance they met; I'd bet my life on that."

"Would you bet Laura's?"

Steven paused at the question, leaving the channel silent while he thought about it.

"Yes," he replied at last. "I would. We can't keep chasing ghosts, Mitch. We can't keep looking for reasons why we can't win. We need to accept that maybe we did, in part because of that crazy ass maneuver you pulled. I've never seen flying like that before."

"Thanks. Maybe you're right. Maybe we won this battle. It isn't over."

"No. Not over. It's a start. I don't think the Tetron expected you to pull together a fleet like this."

Mitchell looked out of the starfighter to where the fleet was moving into formation. The wormhole had closed behind them, and they were bypassing the Goliath to arrive in orbit around Earth. As they did, the former slave ships began dispersing, joining the formation in the pattern Steven and Bayone had arranged them.

Mitchell closed his eyes. He wanted to believe they had won the battle. He wanted to have hope that they had a real chance at defeating the Tetron and for the first time winning the eternal war. He wanted to agree with his brother, in part because he knew he would go insane if he didn't, just waiting for the other shoe to drop.

He needed to find a way to accept it and to help them move on. From here to Jingu, and then from Jingu to the rest of the universe. If the Tetron had retreated to regroup, they had to do everything in their power not to give them a chance.

"Yeah, okay," Mitchell said to Steven, letting out a long-held breath. "They ran, right? We won. Hell, we won more one-sidedly than I ever expected we would."

"That's because we're the frigging Riggers," Steven said.

Mitchell laughed. "You've been spending too much time with Cormac."

"Yes, I have. I'm going to send a message out to the fleet."

"Okay," Mitchell said.

Steven closed the private channel. His voice came out over the fleet-wide channel a moment later.

"Riggers. This is Admiral Steven-"

His words vanished in an instant, the Poseidon exploding directly alongside the Carver, the shrapnel tearing its sister ship apart.

Every other slave ship detonated with it.

74

MITCHELL

"Nooooo," Mitchell shouted, his blood turning cold at the sight of the hundreds of explosions, and the massive volume of shrapnel that tore into the fleet. Most had lowered their shields to conserve energy, and they vanished under the onslaught.

Nine signatures appeared on his overlay then. Nine Tetron arranged in an almost-sphere around the Goliath.

"Kathy, get out of there," Mitchell yelled.

"Already moving."

She would have thirty seconds to escape while the Tetron overcame hyperdeath. Escape to what? To where? Mitchell blinked his eyes frantically, trying to clear the burst of tears. Steven was gone. His brother dead in an instant, along with thousands of others. Their victory had turned into a massacre in the blink of an eye.

Who would have expected the Tetron had rigged the starships to blow? How would they have guessed at, or overcome, that? Should they have blasted all of the former slaves, the suddenly free humans, from space just in case? Should he have known better?

Of course, he should have.

"Germaine, with me," Mitchell said, pushing the flood of doubts aside.

He threw the S-17 forward at full thrust, heading toward the closest Tetron. It had no shields during hyperdeath. No way to defend itself or fight back. He and the drone squadron hit it with everything they had, pounding it with lasers and amoebics. It was a broken mess within seconds.

Kathy was bringing the Goliath away from the circle, having targeted the Tetron at the closest exit point. She blasted it with amoebics, blowing it to dust as it attempted to regain control. A flare of blue energy from the stern pushed the Goliath away from the trap.

"Riggers, if you're still active form up with me," Mitchell said across the channel. "Fire on the Tetron."

"Roger, Ares." Mitchell heard Ming's voice aboard the Kemushi. A moment later missiles began slamming into the Tetron forces. More projectiles followed, but they were far too few.

Mitchell checked the grid. Only fifty of their fleet's ships were still registering enough power to be counted. Fifty out of over two-hundred. Against seven Tetron, who were beginning to regain their systems.

"Damn it," Mitchell cursed. "Kathy, you need to get away. You need to jump."

"What about you?"

"I'll keep you covered. I'm the only one who can."

"Father, no. You'll die. The entire fleet will die. Earth will die."

"I know. I tried to stop it. I failed. We weren't smart enough. I wasn't smart enough."

"It isn't over yet," Kathy said.

"We can't beat seven Tetron on our own."

"We have to try. Win here or lose here, Mitch."

Mitchell felt the agony of loss circling his thoughts. The urge to give in and give up was massive, a lead weight on his soul. He gritted his teeth and seethed through them. "Which one is Watson?" he asked.

He didn't wait for Kathy to answer. He didn't need her to. He spun the S-17 in a tight rotation, visually picking out the largest of the Tetron.

"Father, leave Watson to me," Kathy said. "If you and the remainder of the fleet tackle the others, I can beat him and then help you with the rest."

Mitchell continued toward the Tetron for another second before a thought flipped the S-17 around. "Roger. Kick his ass for me."

"Affirmative."

"Kemushi, take charge of the remaining Federation ships," Mitchell said, noting what remained. The Kemushi was one of the ships with amoebic launchers, as was the Sprinter, a smaller trawler that had been at the rear of the formation. "Valkyrie, follow me. Germaine, you too."

"Roger," Major Long said. Somehow the pilot had managed to avoid the explosions though few of the other smaller ships had.

The attack began anew, with Mitchell leading the others in a charge against the first of the Tetron while Kathy redirected the Goliath, preparing a plasma stream and aiming it toward Watson. The other Tetron initially began charging their weapons and aiming them toward the ancient starship but redirected at the incoming Riggers a few moments later.

Watson had accepted the duel.

Amoebics filled the space between the two forces, explosions causing flashes of light across the opposing fleets. With fewer ships remaining, the Riggers were able to spread out more, making the plasma stream inefficient. Anti-missile systems peppered the Tetron amoebics before they could connect, allowing most of the starships to survive the first volley.

Most. Not all. It wasn't enough. It couldn't possibly be enough. Four Rigger starships vanished in the hail of projectiles, taken quickly from the fight, while none of the Tetron were damaged. Mitchell threw the S-17 into the thick of it, with Germaine trailing behind him. They circled the Tetron, finding the weak spots in the shields and blasting them hard enough to sneak a few amoebics through. A second volley was released, and ten more of the Rigger ships vanished.

"Kathy, we can't last like this," Mitchell said.

"You have to hold on," Kathy replied.

Mitchell flipped the S-17 back. The Goliath and Watson were a thousand kilometers apart, trading amoebics and plasma attacks with one another.

"I'm coming in," he said. He had to do something to speed up the outcome. "Germaine, with me."

"Check your grid, Ares," Germaine said. "I'm out of drones."

Mitchell cursed. "Ming, we need to target the Tetron attacking Goliath."

"Roger, Ares," Ming replied. "We'll be-"

The channel went dead. Mitchell turned his head to look back through the carbonate. The Kemushi was dead in space, trailing debris. All six of the Tetron remained operational.

"Kathy, it isn't working. It isn't enough. You have to go. Jump. Now. I'll follow you."

"I'm not leaving while Watson is alive," Kathy said.

"That's an order."

"I'm. Not. Leaving!"

The Goliath began to turn, pointing itself in Watson's direction. Watson began to turn as well, rotating the front point of his pyramid shape to face the starship.

Alarms blared in Mitchell's ears, and he returned his attention to his own situation. The Rigger fleet was almost gone, and the Tetron were turning their attention to him, a single starfighter against a half-dozen of the enemy.

"Kathy, what are you doing?" Mitchell shouted, doing his best to evade the Tetron's amoebics while watching the fight unfold ahead of him. The Goliath and Watson were on a collision course with one another. It was the same move he had used to destroy the first Tetron he had fought.

Except he had help to weaken the Tetron.

"Kathy, you can't," he said.

"I have to, Father. Keep your promise. Follow me."

Mitchell didn't know what that meant. He sent the S-17 bursting forward, firing amoebic after amoebic at Watson, watching the missiles detonate against his shields. The two objects were closing in on one another, each of them leading with a spear of energy.

"Kathy," Mitchell said, desperate. "You won't survive. You'll kill everyone on the Goliath."

"I know," Kathy said. "I'm sorry. It has to be this way. This is how it ends, Father. This is always how it was supposed to end."

"What?" Mitchell blinked again, trying to clear fresh tears from his eyes.

He had gone from joy to despair within minutes. Steven was dead, along with almost everyone in the fleet. Kathy was going to die, along with all of human civilization.

That was what it meant to lose the war.

The war he had always lost.

Always.

The light that flowed from the two ships when their energy spears collided was brighter than anything Mitchell had ever seen. His eyes drowned in the brilliance, leaving the collision as little more than a blur below a sea of iridescent static. He saw Watson's structure breaking beneath the Goliath. He saw the Goliath compressing and cracking ahead of the Tetron. He swore he could hear the squeal and whine and boom of the collision, despite the silence of space.

He also heard one last thing.

"I love you," Kathy said, right before the channel went dead.

His eyes were blinded and remained that way as the seconds passed. His heart was beating so fast he couldn't believe he was still conscious. He was streaming tears and crying out so strongly his throat was sore.

Time seemed to stop.

Everything seemed to stop.

[75]

MITCHELL

His scream faded to silence.

He sat motionless in the cockpit of the S-17. He lifted his arm, putting his hand in front of his face. He couldn't see it, but the fact that he could move it at all told him he was still alive.

Wasn't he?

If he was, Tetron would surely destroy him any second now. He couldn't fight them or escape them when he couldn't see.

"Mitchell."

He wasn't sure how much time had gone by when he heard the voice. His thundering heart had started to calm. His body felt weary. He fought with everything in him not to lose himself to the pain and despair. His vision was returning as well. He could see the faint outline of the S-17's cockpit around him. He could see his arms and his legs. Strangely, everything outside of the cockpit had gone from pure white to pure black. There were no Tetron. No stars. No Earth.

"Katherine?" he said, his voice hoarse.

"Not yet."

"Origin?"

"Yes."

"Where are you?"

"I'm all around you, Mitchell."

Mitchell's head felt heavy. He took a few breaths. "The S-17. You're the starfighter?"

"It was a configuration. Now it is a duplicate. Kathy had a copy of my data stack embedded in her DNA." A sweet, soft laugh filled his ears. "Watson had no idea. She passed the data to the starfighter when he took control of Goliath."

"You brought yourself to me when I met up with Steven near Asimov." He was feeling groggy, but the pieces were falling into place.

"Yes. I'm sorry, Mitch. I couldn't tell you. We've waited an eternity for this."

"We?"

"You, and Katherine, and me."

"Katherine? Me?"

"Yes. You don't remember. You can't remember, or it would never have worked. This is it. The Mesh has been broken. This is your plan. It is time to finish it or lose forever."

"Kathy," Mitchell said, seeing the Goliath crash into Watson as if it were happening all over again. He was having trouble thinking.

"Our daughter. The three of us. It doesn't make sense to you now, Mitchell, but it will. She did what she was meant to do, and you'll see her again."

He let himself be comforted by the words, even though he barely understood them. "Am I dead?" he asked. "Where are we going?"

The same sweet laughter. "You aren't dead, Mitch. You're in the space between time and space. The Void. An eternal engine brought you here. We're following Kathy and the Goliath."

"Following?" Mitchell said, the words barely audible.

Everything was starting to turn black. Was this a dream? Was he dead and he didn't know it? He wasn't sure if he would have preferred that or not.

"Where?" he asked.

"To the future."

Don't stop now! Read the next exciting installment of War Eternal today!

THANK YOU!

It is readers like you, who take a chance on self-published works that is what makes the very existence of such works possible. Thank you so very much for spending your hard-earned money, time, and energy on this work. It is my sincerest hope that you have enjoyed reading!

Independent authors could not continue to thrive without your support. If you have enjoyed this, or any other independently published work, please consider taking a moment to leave a review at the source of your purchase. Reviews have an immense impact on the overall commercial success of a given work, and your voice can help shape the future of the people whose efforts you have enjoyed.

Thank you again!

ABOUT THE AUTHOR

M.R. Forbes is the mind behind a growing number of Amazon best-selling science fiction series including Rebellion, War Eternal, Chaos of the Covenant, and the Forgotten Universe novels. He currently resides with his family and friends on the west cost of the United States, including a cat who thinks she's a dog and a dog who thinks she's a cat.

He maintains a true appreciation for his readers and is always happy to hear from them.

To learn more about M.R. Forbes or just say hello:

Visit my website:
mrforbes.com

Send me an e-mail:
michael@mrforbes.com

Check out my Facebook page:
facebook.com/mrforbes.author

Chat with me on Facebook Messenger:
https://m.me/mrforbes.author